Also By

NON FICTION

Exploring Other Worlds: Margaret Fox,
Elisha Kent Kane, and the Antebellum Culture of Curiosity

Freshwater Passages:
The Trade and Travels of Peter Pond

The Auglaize Conspiracy

A Novel of Early America

David Chapin

ISBN: 979-8-9924269-0-8 (e-book)

979-8-9924269-1-5 (paperback)

979-8-9924269-2-2 (hardcover)

Cover image: "A View of Detroit, July 25th, 1794," by E.H.

Courtesy of the Burton Historical Collection, Detroit Public Library.

Cover design by Alissa Yarbrough.

 Created with Vellum

The Auglaize Conspiracy

Detroit in the British Era

"The country called Detroit, is that washed by the strait which forms the communication between the Lakes St. Clair and Erie. The improvements on the eastern banks of this strait, extended north and south, about nine miles; and those on the western banks, about seven. In purity and wholesomeness of air, and richness of soil, it may be said to equal, if not excel any, even the best parts of America. Every European grain flourishes here in the utmost perfection; and hemp and flax, in particular, might be raised to the greatest advantage. The woods are every where filled with vines of spontaneous growth; and their grape yields a juice equal in flavour to the most excellent burgundy. The country around it appears like one great park stocked with buffaloes, deer, pheasants, wild turkies, and partridges. Domestic animals and fowls are here in the utmost perfection. Aquatic birds of every species are in the greatest plenty, and of the highest flavour; and the rivers afford an astonishing variety of the most delicious fish. The soil and climate are so favourable to vegetation, that every vegetable is to be procured with the smallest trouble. In short, a man that can shoot and fish, and understands the art of making wine, may enjoy every luxury of the most sumptuous table, at the sole expence of his own labour."

-Thomas Mante, *History of the Late War in America*, (1772).

Prologue

Ben Stone: The Maumee River, spring, 1766.

The light of the Worm Moon filtered through bare branches onto Ben Stone's campsite. Spring was awakening the dormant trees. Their sap was beginning to run and their buds were ready to emerge, but a whiff of winter still lingered in the night-time air. It gave the trader a slight chill, which his campfire, burned down now to a few smoldering embers, did little to assuage. Out of the shadows came sounds of life reemerging. Peeping frogs joined a chorus of insects to keep up a pervasive hum. Beyond that, quiet reigned along the Maumee River. All seemed peaceful.

Yet Ben could not sleep.

By any reasonable measure, he should be content. He and his men had acquired a full cargo of deerskins and furs at the Miami villages at the headwaters of the river. The Miami had a great demand for the wool blankets, copper pots, powder, shot, sewing needles, tobacco, and rum that he had brought up from New York, and their winter hunts had yielded enough skins and furs to fill his canoes in return. Business had been good, and it was time to go home. He planned to stop in the morning at the Ottawa villages near Roche de Bout, then he would go back to Detroit, then east to Albany. That was his plan at least, but it depended on much

1

that was out of his control. The winds on Lake Erie seldom cooperated with a trader's timetable, and his canoemen did not always cover as much distance as he hoped.

His men slept now, recouping from another long day of river travel. Three snored heartily beneath a canvas tarp strung between trees while the others bedded down in a small tent nearby. They were *Canadiens*, of course, as the French-speaking inhabitants of Detroit were called. They spoke their native language, as well as enough of the local Algonquian languages to be understood throughout the region. That made them invaluable as guides and interpreters to English-speaking traders like Ben. They liked nothing more than to joke and sing while paddling the canoes, and at night around the campfire, they had no end of stories to tell about the Upper Country, most of which were of dubious veracity. Ben liked them. He appreciated their knowledge and the hard work they did. But he had not forgotten that a few years past they had been sworn enemies.

There was rustling in the bushes, and for a moment, Ben imagined a wolf or bear stalking him, but he reassured himself that it was more likely some harmless little critter. Maybe a grouse or a squirrel was disrupting last autumn's leaves, looking for a meal. Out on the river, he heard the splash of a fish rising to the surface. Or was it a beaver slapping its tail to warn his friends that humans were nearby?

This country along the Maumee River amazed him. In many ways, it resembled the woods around his New Jersey home—but wilder. The forest could seem endless, with stands of oak, ash, maple, and hickory joined occasionally by chestnut, sycamore, elm, and cottonwood. The woods sometimes opened onto grassy meadows or closed into thick swamps that made travel impossible. Rivers carved highways through this wilderness, leading to vast lakes whose waters might reach the horizon. Every day, this wild land showed Ben something new and wonderful.

But it was not wilderness that brought him here. He came for trade. Ben thought fondly—and a little greedily—of the packs of prime furs stored for the night under his canoes. Once he got them back to Albany, he would sell them at a nice profit. Enough, he hoped, to pay off his creditors and buy a new cargo without taking on more debt. A few more journeys like this one, and he would have enough saved to buy a farm back home. The backcountry trader's life could be profitable if its many risks were avoided, but it was not how he wanted to spend the rest of his days.

He imagined having a wife someday soon, and a nice farmhouse surrounded by tidy fields somewhere in the British colonies, maybe in New Jersey or the new lands being opened up in western New York or Pennsylvania. He could settle down, clear land, raise a family, and grow old without the risks of wilderness travel.

He was thankful that the Upper Country was at peace for now, but memories remained. Images of war. Thoughts of less settled times. Six years had passed since Canada and the *pays d'en haut* had fallen to the British, but many Natives still missed *Onontio*, as they styled the French Governor of New France, and many of the *Canadiens* who remained did not hide their dislike of British authority. There were scars everywhere, scars that would only heal with the passage of time.

Ben had gotten along well with the people he traded with at Kekionga and the other Native villages. At least he thought he had. But, like his French crew, they were old enemies. Maybe that was why he was on edge—old fears were slow to die.

He hoped his unease would subside when he arrived back among the British soldiers at Fort Detroit. He refused to let a little fear outshine his ambitions. His canoemen had proven themselves trustworthy, and his Miami and Ottawa trading partners had done nothing to cause concern. Lingering memories of war might rob him of a little sleep, but he would not let fear take charge. So he stayed up.

Listening.

Thinking.

An owl screeched in the distance. He let his mind drift. He thought of home. He thought of the farm he would buy and the woman with whom he would grow old. He threw another stick of dry oak onto the smoldering fire. He drank from his tin cup of watered-down rum and imagined that the whole world slept, except for him. Solitude prevailed. An uneasy peace.

Then the rustling in the brush resumed, and there was a sudden pounding of feet. Someone by the canoes shouted. A blur in the darkness. Then Ben felt something strike him hard in the center of his chest. There was no pain, only a feeling that something was terribly wrong. He could not stand up. He could not lift his arms. A shadowy figure reared up before him. A face from his past. Another blow struck his back, then he felt a third dull impact in his side. His world faded, leaving the light of the Worm Moon to reflect off of sightless eyes.

There was another screech from the owl, but this time, Ben Stone could not hear it.

Chapter 1

Marguerite Boyer: Detroit, Spring 1766

In a small wooden building on the outskirts of Detroit, that served as both a home and a shop, Marguerite Boyer and her mother were preparing packs to send into the backcountry. The two women were surrounded by trade goods. They filled the shelves that lined the walls, as well as three large tables in the center of the room: woolen blankets in red or blue, copper pots, beads, knives, scissors, looking glasses, and other assorted items frequently in demand by Native people of the *pays d'en haut*.

"Margot, *s'il te plaît*," Sally Boyer called to her daughter, "would you reach up to the top shelf there and get me a dozen short needles?"

"*Oui, Maman*," Marguerite replied. She had been getting things off the top shelf for her diminutive mother for many years, indeed since she was twelve years old and first surpassed *Maman* in height. Sometimes when she worked with her in their shop, she felt like a convenient substitute for a stepladder.

"I'm putting together a couple of packs to supplement what Mr. Kennedy brought up from New York," Sally continued. "He has an adequate selection of dry goods and rum but lacks some of the smaller items that they will want in Kekionga."

"Have you decided to send Joseph with us, *Maman*?" Marguerite reached up to tamp down some stray black hair that had escaped the confines of her braid.

"Oh, yes. Didn't I tell you? I think you could use the extra help in case Mr. Kennedy is difficult." Joseph Papan was an older canoeman whom Sally often hired to manage the younger paddlers. "Do you still plan to leave first thing in the morning, my dear?"

"If the weather holds." Marguerite looked out into the yard where a young boy, perhaps eight years old, played with a toy horse next to several large birchbark canoes tied down to a scaffold. "Are you sure you can handle Daniel on your own? He has been finding new ways to get into mischief lately."

"Oh, don't you worry about young Daniel, my dear. We will have a grand time while you are gone. I've promised to take him fishing."

"He will enjoy that." Marguerite looked forward to her upcoming journey, though she knew she would miss her son. She had been cooped up in Detroit for weeks now and longed for a chance to get out into the backcountry.

"What do you know of Mr. Kennedy, *Maman*?"

"*Pas beaucoup.* Just that he's a big, scary-looking fellow supplied by Mr. Campbell. He is American, I think, and has not been around long. At least that's what Mr. Jacobs said when he referred him. He has some ugly scars and a fat face, but besides that, he seems civilized enough." Sally Boyer's expression betrayed her disapproval more than her words. Marguerite's mother knew how to work with British traders, but that did not mean she liked them.

Marguerite, on the other hand, was growing accustomed to the British and found that some of them could be likable enough, even if many were haughty. For several years now her mother had supplied canoemen, canoes, guides, and interpreters for English-speaking traders coming up from New York and Montreal who wanted to venture into the backcountry. Marguerite was her most accomplished interpreter. While French was her primary language, she also spoke several varieties of Algonquian and Iroquois. Since the end of the war, as English, Scottish, and American traders followed British soldiers to Detroit, she had picked up their language as well. She knew other people could not absorb languages as she did, but she never understood their difficulty.

"I hope he is not a fool." She brushed at an unknown substance that stained the front of her light blue calico shirt.

"Maybe. Maybe not," said Sally. "But you've dealt with fools before, Margot. And trust me, my dear, you will again."

C'est vrai, thought Marguerite. *Maman* would surely prove right about that. Sally Boyer did not see into the future, but she knew people. And she had encountered plenty of fools in her day. She and her family had grown accustomed to navigating a business landscape where being a fool could have fatal consequences. The traders who came up from the British colonies were bold and ambitious men, but they seldom understood local conditions. They had different—often arrogant—ways, which could lead to violent altercations.

Sally's business was to fill the gaps in British knowledge of the *pays d'en haut,* or what English speakers called the Upper Country. Few were better connected than her in this world except perhaps her late husband, Gabriel. He had been *métis*, like her, the offspring of several generations of Frenchmen settling down with local Native women. Between the two of them, they had kin in the Wyandot, Ottawa, Miami, Ojibwa, and Potawatomi villages, not to mention the French communities. Of course their children did as well.

Since the end of the wars, Marguerite and her brothers, under their mother's guidance, had taken advantage of their family connections to become some of the most sought-after guides and interpreters in the region. They made transactions in the Native villages go smoothly. At least they did when the men who hired them were wise enough to follow their advice.

"This one seemed to accept my suggested route well enough," Sally continued. "You'll head south to the Maumee River and stop first at the Ottawa villages, but don't dally there. Trade a little to lighten up your load, then go up to the Miami towns. There will be more demand for goods there and a better supply of deerskins."

"Yes, *Maman*. Has Mr. Kennedy agreed to your limit on rum?" Some traders came up from New York with their bateaux loaded with kegs of rum and little else, but the Boyers refused to work with that sort. Such traders wreaked havoc in the back-country and left their customers with nothing but resentment and aching heads. The Boyers supplied a limited amount of rum, but most of their cargos were made up of useful items.

"*Ah, oui,*" Sally replied. "He didn't seem to have a problem with it. But you will need to make room in the canoes for his friend. Mr. Kennedy travels with a strange little companion, Jabez Cole. I'm not entirely clear what his role is, but Kennedy insists on bringing him along."

"Very well. That should not be a problem."

THE REMAINDER OF THE DAY, Marguerite set about her preparations. She had provisions packed. She visited her canoemen and confirmed they would show up in the morning. She had two canoes brought down to the wharf, close to where Mr. Kennedy's cargo was stored. She wanted to have everything ready to go in the morning. Her mother had secured the necessary passes earlier that day.

Yes, thought Marguerite, a trip into the backcountry was what she needed. She had not left Detroit since winter ended. She loved her family, but weeks cooped up inside the store with *Maman* and Daniel could get tedious. Not to mention that the smells of the town became oppressive as the weather warmed. She longed to return to the woods, to breathe its fresh air once more, and to visit with friends and relations in the Native villages.

Backcountry travel represented freedom to Marguerite, but it also grounded her. The work was hard, but nothing else made her feel so connected with her world. In town she often felt shut off, isolated within the confines of the shop, tending to the needs of her son and her mother. But in the backcountry, she felt like she was part of something larger. She felt a connection with the water she drank and on which her canoes glided, as well as the wind that caressed her cheeks and the sunlight that told her when to wake and when to sleep. She felt thankful for the land that offered up its bounty for her sustenance.

But most of all, she felt her kinship with the wider community that peopled the backcountry—who had been here since before the British took over. The *pays d'en haut* was her world, and its people were her people. Despite all the changes that continued to come, as long as she still had the ability to roam this country, she would have a home.

Sometimes, she felt guilty when she left Daniel with her mother for weeks on end. Maybe it would be better to stay with him all the time. But she would not be herself if she never traveled. One day, Daniel would be old enough to come with her. Then she could share with him all the wonders of their world.

Chapter 2

Marguerite Boyer: The Maumee River

By the time they got to Kekionga—more than two weeks after leaving Detroit—Marguerite felt that she had expelled some of the cobwebs that had invaded her mind over the winter. She was feeling healthier and stronger, and trade had been good. Miami families were returning to the village from their winter camps, bringing with them furs and skins of the animals they had hunted over the colder months. They were eager to trade them for items out of Mr. Kennedy's cargo.

Marguerite was satisfied to find that Mr. Kennedy was a tolerable business partner, if not always the best companion. He was a beefy man with brown hair, sunburned skin, and a long, angry scar running down the left side of his face. His one great drawback was his garrulousness. He lacked the filters that most men and women employ to keep random thoughts and impulses from spilling unbidden and unwelcome into the world, so he was happiest when he was allowed to hold forth with a running monolog. Little of what he said was of any interest to Marguerite, but it did not matter, for she did not listen most of the time, and she never had the opportunity to respond.

Kennedy's principal audience was his friend Jabez Cole. Cole was a short, quiet young man from one of the British colonies. He had dark stringy hair that came down past the frayed collar of his dirty brown jacket. His tan tricorn hat, which he seldom removed, was stained with a ring of sweat. He had been brought along at Kennedy's insistence but did not always fit in with the rest of the group.

"He is my assistant, my right-hand man, and he is quite the woodsman," Kennedy told Marguerite in justification of Cole's presence, though she hadn't asked. "He can hunt and track and could probably survive in the woods even if he were dropped off blindfolded in the middle of nowhere. And don't worry, I'll see to him out of my own share of the profits."

She could see that they enjoyed doing things together—especially hunting. While traveling up the river, whenever they had the chance, the two of them would venture off into the forest on short expeditions. One time, when the river travel had been slow, they had departed on one of their hunts for two nights, meeting the canoes upstream. Marguerite had warned him that two traders traveling alone might run into trouble, but Kennedy seemed unconcerned, and he was confident that Cole's skills as a woodsman would prevent them from getting lost.

Despite some social deficiencies, Kennedy was not a bad man or a bad business partner. He rarely questioned her advice when it came to trade with Native hunters. He did not object when she offered small gifts out of their cargo to sweeten a negotiation. He was smart enough to see that Miami and Ottawa villagers preferred to trade with a person they knew, and as a result, they lined up to trade with her. Too many British traders tried to bully Native customers into bad deals, or got them drunk in order to cheat them, but Kennedy did not try anything like that. He was content to trade fairly, which Marguerite had told him was the most profitable course in the long run for anyone who wanted to remain in the Upper Country for more than a single voyage.

The packs they would take back to Detroit held prime deerskins, joined by an assortment of buffalo, muskrat, fox, and beaver furs. They had even traded for a few high-quality bear and wolf pelts. These furs and skins would demand excellent prices down in New York. Kennedy seemed pleased, and *Maman* was sure to be pleased as well, for when they got back to Detroit, everyone's share of the profits would be substantial.

As their trading concluded at Kekionga, their days became less busy, and Marguerite and the canoemen took the opportunity to pay some social calls. Kennedy and Cole went off to hunt again, with the permission of the local leaders. Kennedy wanted to see a live buffalo, though he knew it was unlikely. They were within the winter range of those great beasts, but now that the weather was warming, most would be out on the grasslands to the west. It was no surprise when the two men returned empty-handed after two nights away. Kennedy would have to make do with the buffalo pelts hunters had procured over the winter.

Their journey had been a success so far, and Marguerite saw no reason why the trip home should not go smoothly as well. But she knew not to let down her guard, for dangers were always lurking. Perhaps a late spring snowstorm would hit, forcing them to hunker down, or a sudden squall of wind might catch them unaware on Lake Erie. Or maybe one of their canoes would overturn in swift water because the canoemen became complacent. There would be something. She knew it.

There always was.

ALL WAS STILL GOING SMOOTHLY when they arrived for the night at a campsite called Auglaize, a few dozen miles downstream from Kekionga. The canoes pulled in to shore and Marguerite and the men got out to stretch their legs. They began to unload the canoes so that they could set up camp for the night. Joseph Papan was carrying a pack up to the clearing when he stopped short and cried out. Marguerite and the others quickly followed him, and what she saw filled her with horror. Skins, furs, and torn canvas were scattered around the riverside clearing, along with an assortment of trade goods. Packs were ripped apart as if by wild animals. Over by the remains of a cooking fire, lay a body—or, more accurately, most of a body—chest down, naked, and discolored. It no longer had a head. The flesh nearest the ground looked bruised and purplish, while the upper side was unnaturally pale. She noted a slight whiff of death, but it was still faint. It could not have been very long since this broken thing had been a living man.

Marguerite lit her pipe to mask any unpleasant odors. The taste of tobacco smoke streamed across her tongue as she puffed. She forced herself to take in her surroundings despite a strong impulse to turn away. Unwelcome images burned into her mind, and a variety of emotions competed for dominance. She quickly tamped down her fear, and then a flash of anger came and went. Soon she was left with only disgust and disappointment.

"*Merde*. I thought we were done with this sort of thing, Joseph." She sighed.

"*Moi aussi*, Margot." Joseph Papan, looked flustered by the situation. "Perhaps you should go back to the canoes and let me handle this." The scene seemed to trigger an instinct in the older man to protect her.

Sam Kennedy called out from a cluster of debris across the clearing, "There's more here." His voice trembled. He was looking at several more bodies near what was left of a canvas shelter and a birchbark canoe that had been crushed in several places. Marguerite and Joseph went over and made a reluctant examination. Unlike the first victim, these men had not been stripped naked, but like the first body, their heads were gone, leaving only dark stains where blood had soaked into their shirts and into the soil. What remained of their necks looked as if the flesh had been nibbled at by passing scavengers.

Marguerite had seen death before. Perhaps more than most

women her age. She had been little more than a child when she helped *Maman* prepare *Papa* for burial. That seemed so strange and unnatural to her then. She remembered that the corpse looked like Gabriel Boyer had in life, yet everything important was gone. His smile, the love in his eyes when he looked at her, all gone. The thought that a few simple knife strokes could remove the vital essence of a person had bothered her then, but in the years that followed, she'd seen the inevitable transformation in multiple ways.

During the war with the British, men she had known since birth went east to Niagara, Montreal, and Lake Champlain and never returned, Daniel's father among them. News of those deaths sometimes came with stories, but they always left a dull sense of absence, as if the men had not really been killed but simply vanished from her world. Then, during the Natives' uprising, the violence and death had been more immediate—not far from her own doorstep sometimes. But that had all ended years before—she hoped for good.

But she had never seen anything like this.

Joseph again urged her to go back to the canoe and let him and the men deal with the scene, but Marguerite refused. She appreciated that her foreman was protective, but she was determined to confront adversity, not hide from it. *Maman* had not raised her to be fragile. Besides, she knew from experience that women were far better than men at coping with bodies after death. Men could be so squeamish.

"Joseph, you recognize them by their clothes and equipment, don't you?" she said.

"*Oui*, Margot. That's Baptiste Beaulieu and his brother Pierre over there, and this is Lucien Tremblay, Barthelemy Bruno, and Pero."

"I didn't know Pero, but I grew up with the others," she said.

"They were good men," said Papan. "Pero was alright, if you looked past the scars."

14

She turned to Sam Kennedy and addressed him in his own language. "Mr. Kennedy, that body over there is surely Ben Stone and these others his canoemen. Men from Detroit. They left the Miami villages not long before we did."

"I'd gathered that. Who else could it be? We need to get out of here before the savages come back."

"These men are friends and relations, Mr. Kennedy. We can't just leave them for the scavengers." Shifting to the French of the *pays d'en haut,* she turned back to Joseph. "Get all the men together and start them digging. Use what tools you can find. We'll want to have them in the ground before the day gets any hotter."

"We don't have time," urged Kennedy. "Let's get out of here. The fiends who did this could still be around. Let Captain Turnbull send a detachment of soldiers to deal with the bodies and punish the perpetrators."

She spat onto the ground. "You are welcome to leave if you wish, Mr. Kennedy, but nobody is going with you until these men are properly put to rest. Besides, any perpetrators, whoever they are, are as likely to be downstream of us as anywhere." She strode away, confident that the men would ignore the pleas of the trader and do as she asked. As long as *Maman* paid their wages, they did as Marguerite told them.

She felt a bit sorry for Kennedy. She had not seen him so flustered before. He kept up a constant monologue about Indian massacres and mutilation as he paced around the clearing, but he argued no further. At some point, he had gotten his fowling piece from the canoe, which he loaded and kept in his grasp, eying the surrounding woods. This was an unfamiliar country for him, full of threats he did not understand. Marguerite was sympathetic to the trader's fears. Indeed, she shared some of them, though she dared not show it.

She saw Kennedy's friend Cole looking around the scene, bending down to coldly examine the bodies. Even when things were going well, Cole had made her uneasy. The little man was so quiet as to be practically mute. He murmured to Kennedy sometimes in hushed tones, but, since their journey began, he rarely spoke with anyone else. Now Cole rolled the bodies over, looked under their clothes, apparently examined their wounds. Her first impulse was to stop him, to tell him not to disrespect the dead, but then she realized that he was right to take a closer look.

"Ben took some sort of spear to his chest," she heard him mumble to no one in particular. "For starters."

She watched his further examinations. Two of the men had no visible injuries besides the glaring absence of heads. Another had a broken arrow shaft protruding from his back and a gaping abdominal wound, while the last two had deep gashes on hands and forearms from some sort of blade and what appeared to be stab wounds to their guts, as if they had struggled with their assailant before being stabbed. Ben Stone had been mutilated worse than the others. A deep puncture in his chest certainly looked like it would have killed him, but his body had sustained a half dozen other fatal wounds, as if killing him just once was not enough.

"It must have been those Potawatomi we heard about in the Miami villages," announced Kennedy. "Full of resentment against British traders they said. I just hope we can make our way downriver without encountering them ourselves. God willing, Pontiac and his Ottawa weren't involved."

Cole looked up at his friend but said nothing. He continued wandering around the area looking at the ground.

Marguerite shook her head. "This isn't right..."

"Good God, that goes without saying," exclaimed Kennedy. "These men have been massacred. We've become too complacent, come to forget the savagery of the fiendish hellhounds. Poor Stone. Jabez and I knew him, you know. We served with Ben back in the war, and we'd just seen him again."

She ignored Kennedy's rambling as she tried to make sense of this scene. Of course murder wasn't right, but there was something else—something off. Why would an entire trader's party be wiped out like this? It did not look like their goods had been plundered. This looked like a pointless act of rage. The Potawatomi resented British traders in their country, even if they also craved the goods they offered, so yes, Ben Stone might be a target of their wrath, but the presence of the Detroit canoemen should have protected him. Frenchmen from Detroit usually got along well with the Natives of these parts. She even thought that a couple of the dead canoemen had kin in the Potawatomi village. It did not make sense for any of the local tribes to do this thing now, not unless they wanted a war with both the French and the British, and she had heard no rumors of that. The people they had talked with in the Ottawa villages on their way upriver had not seemed riled up about anything, and the Miami in their village above had seemed eager for peaceful trade, even if they were not entirely reconciled to the ways of the British interlopers.

Kennedy's conclusion that the Potawatomi were responsible was based on ignorance, but when his feverish mutterings began to irritate her, she reminded herself that he was still a stranger in the *pays d'en haut*. Of course he would point to the local tribes when he knew so little about them. Everyone was a stranger to him, and it is natural to fear a stranger. She reminded herself that up until now they had worked well together. But this massacre changed everything. Who could have done such a thing? There was nothing about it that made sense to her. There had been too much fear and violence in the *pays d'en haut* in her lifetime. She longed for a lasting peace. The future she envisioned had no room for war. She wanted to travel the backcountry in safety. Without fear. She wanted to trade and see new parts of the world. She wanted to raise Daniel in a land free of violence. There was no profit in killing. No future in revenge.

Apparently not everyone had yet learned these simple facts.

Chapter 3

Marguerite Boyer

For a week, a northeast wind funneled into Maumee Bay, keeping Marguerite's party idle at the mouth of the river waiting to cross the broad expanse of Lake Erie on their way back to Detroit. The delay was tiresome, as the men were on edge from what they had seen. If Stone and his party could be killed so inexplicably, how could anyone in the backcountry feel safe? Was another Native uprising beginning? No one knew. She instructed the men to keep a watch at night, but who or what were they watching for? There had been war and murder in these parts for much of her life, but the strangeness of the killings at Auglaize, the missing heads, the unanswered questions, had everyone spooked.

Marguerite tried to calm the men, but Kennedy's agitation threatened to become contagious. Ever since Auglaize, Kennedy had remained up in arms against the St. Joseph Potawatomi, whom he loudly blamed for the atrocities. Not that he had ever met anyone from St. Joseph. When she questioned him about why he blamed them, he hardly heard her. Instead he talked of an expedition that must certainly be launched against them by the army. He was convinced the country would once again explode into war like it had during Pontiac's uprising.

With each diatribe, the canoemen became more nervous. They had no wish to take part in another British war. Nor did Marguerite understand Kennedy's fixation on the Potawatomi. Admittedly, they were the most disgruntled nation south of Detroit, but she saw no evidence they killed Stone and his men. Would they take men's heads like that? Maybe, but she had never known them to do such things. She had never known any of the local tribes to decapitate their victims. There were stories of such practices from long ago, perhaps, but not in recent years. Yes, traders were sometimes killed and robbed in the backcountry, but at Auglaize, there had been no sign of plunder, only the aftermath of brutal and inexplicable violence.

The murders triggered fears in some of her canoemen. Few of them minded that Mr. Stone had been killed. To them, he was just another British interloper who had probably brought it on himself, but the killings of five local men was a whole other matter. Those men were *Canadien* canoemen like themselves.

Was it possible that the Natives felt betrayed by their erstwhile French friends and now chose to punish them alongside the British?

That had not been the case during Pontiac's siege, when the French-speaking population of the Upper Country had largely kept to the sidelines, but had things changed? Were they no longer safe in the backcountry where they earned their livelihood? The men understood theft and drunken outbursts. They knew war and violence. But such brutality, without any explanation, fed their worst fears.

Some of the more imaginative men began to talk about the murders as the work of supernatural forces. With no apparent killer or motive, they looked to the creatures of their imaginations, rooted in both their Catholic upbringings and local beliefs. Surely the heads had been taken for some demonic purpose, they murmured among themselves. There were evil things in the forest that made use of such trophies, they whispered: Demons. *Rougarou. Mishipeshu. Windigo.*

"My *pépère* used to tell me about *rougarou*," she heard one of the men tell the others. "Where he was born in France, folks knew all about them. He always said that some men turn into beasts when the moon is full."

"But around here, we have *windigos* not *rougarou*," insisted another. "Once a man tastes human flesh, his heart turns to ice, and he can never stop the hunger."

"But *windigos* only make themselves known in winter," said the first man. "And they consume flesh. More like a *rougarou* to rip off heads and carry them away."

"Or *Mishipeshu* came out of the river to attack them," said a third. "The Great Lynx gets hungry."

"*Mishipeshu* only lives in deep lakes, not on the shallow river," said the first man. "It was clearly a *rougarou*."

"Or the Devil himself," offered Joseph Papan. "Either the Devil or some demon doing Satan's work."

This last comment quieted the men as it sank in. Like the men, Marguerite believed in many sorts of supernatural beings, but she knew that humans were the most likely monsters in this case. She did not understand why men become monsters, but she had known since she was a girl that they often do.

In time, the weather cooperated, allowing them to return to Detroit. Seen from a canoe on the river, Detroit had a humble appearance. It was a vital British military outpost overseeing a vast region, but it was little more than a village surrounded by a stockade made of logs set on end. The riverfront was a jumble of falling-down sheds, warehouses, makeshift docks, and an assortment of boats. From the wharf, a pathway led up a steep embankment to the gates.

After setting the men to unload, Kennedy announced that he was going to see the commander to report what they had found.

"I'd like to go with you," said Marguerite. She did not trust Kennedy to give an accurate account of the situation to British authorities.

"No need, Marguerite. I'm sure the commander would prefer to hear this from me."

"I will come." She gave him no opportunity to object. She had found in her dealings with Englishmen that it was best to simply state intentions rather than enter into a discussion. You could seldom convince one of anything, but most grudgingly accepted an unavoidable reality.

Kennedy's scar flushed a deeper red for a moment. "As you please, *Mam'zelle*." He turned to Cole, "Jabez, see to our things while I'm gone. And if you see Mr. Jacobs, tell him I need to speak with him."

"Of course," said Cole. More words than she had heard the strange little man utter all day.

Sam Kennedy strode into Captain Turnbull's office, ignoring Patterson, the captain's secretary in the waiting room, and proceeding into the inner office. "There has been a massacre, Captain, a bloody Indian massacre on the river."

Marguerite trailed behind him. She saw the captain with his two sergeants: the older one, Ramsay, and the younger, Graham. They all looked up and stood as they entered. Annoyance showed on the captain's face, but he spoke with courtesy.

"Please come in, Mr. Kennedy. And Miss Boyer, glad to see you back from your voyage. Let me offer you a chair." The room was sparsely furnished with a single desk and several wooden chairs. The captain spoke with an accent from the northern reaches of England. He was a tall man, about thirty-five years old, with the weathered appearance of a soldier who had spent most of his life outside. Marguerite considered him a measured and fair commander of his small garrison.

"Sergeant Ramsay," Turnbull said, "would you ask Patterson to bring tea for our guests?"

"Yes, sir," said Ramsay. With a disapproving glare at the unwelcome arrivals, he left the office.

"Sergeant Graham, why don't you stay."

"Aye, sir," Graham replied in the Scottish accent so common in the British Army. The sergeant had been stationed in or around Detroit since the war ended. He was tall and Marguerite thought quite handsome, despite some disfigurement she assumed was the result of wartime misfortune.

One of Graham's eyes was covered with a patch, he walked with a slight limp, and the deerskin gloves he wore did not disguise the fact that he was missing several fingers. But the mutilations did not detract from an otherwise pleasing appearance. His uncovered eye was hazel green, and he had thick brown hair worn long. She had spoken with him several times in the past couple of years and always found him charming, and the way he smiled at her sometimes made her feel that he might be interested in becoming better acquainted.

"Please Mr. Kennedy," said Turnbull as he sat back down behind his desk, "start from the beginning. Who has been massacred and where?"

Marguerite sat down in a plain wooden chair, but Kennedy remained standing. Sergeant Graham took out a pad and pencil to take notes.

"Well, sir," began Kennedy, "looks like the New York trader Ben Stone and his crew have been murdered, but we cannot be certain as the bodies were missing their heads, but it certainly looked like Ben's outfit. They left the Miami villages a few days ahead of us on their way back here. We found them at the campsite at the mouth of the Auglaize. Six men sent home to their maker, their bodies mutilated by the Potawatomi." Kennedy paced as he spoke, though the small room left him only enough room for a couple of steps in each direction.

"Why do you say the Potawatomi were the culprits, Mr. Kennedy?" Turnbull asked. "Did you see them?"

"No, not directly, but it had to have been them, sir. We heard they were on the warpath when we were in the Miami villages."

Marguerite's face must have betrayed her displeasure, for Turnbull turned to her. "You disagree, Miss Boyer?" British officers had a habit of calling her "Miss" or "Mademoiselle." They seemed unaware that she had a child and knew only that she lived with her mother. She did not mind.

"Yes," she answered.

"Why is that, Marguerite?" asked Sergeant Graham.

"I'm not sure," she answered, suddenly self-conscious.

"You know these parts better than any of us, Miss Boyer. You must have a reason for your opinion," Turnbull pressed.

She did not like to be put on the spot this way, but she appreciated that the captain and his sergeant remained calm despite Kennedy's agitation. She gathered her thoughts and began to speak softly. "The Potawatomi, Captain, they have their usual gripes about the British, and there was a party that visited Kekionga shortly before we were there, talking loudly against the way things are now. Especially against the British being here without having been invited. But they weren't a proper war party. They offered no war belts. I heard they were going southwest, toward the Wabash and Illinois country, and on to the Mississippi. They had heard rumors of a new French army that might be gathering soon to retake Fort Chartres, and they wanted to join it."

"Will those rumors never die?" sighed Turnbull. He stood and walked over to the room's single window. Sunlight shone on his face as he looked out. "There is no chance of a French army returning to these parts. I assure you. At least not anytime soon."

"You know best, sir," she deferred. "In any case, the Potawatomi party would not have been near Auglaize when this business happened. Like I said, their plan was to go the other way. Now they might have changed their plans, but I don't think so."

"It could have been another group of Indians then, the Ottawa or the Shawnee, maybe Mingo," insisted Kennedy. "This was certainly the work of savages."

"That does seem likely." Turnbull turned away from the window to address his sergeant. "Did you hear any rumblings when you were last at Pontiac's village, Graham?"

Graham shook his head. "No, sir. Though I don't imagine Pontiac would have confided any violent intentions to me despite the rapport we've managed to establish."

"If it was not Potawatomi, then who?" Turnbull asked her. "The Shawnee, perhaps? Or could it have been Pontiac and his gang?"

"I haven't heard any word of Shawnee war parties coming north," she replied, "and we thought best to slip by the Ottawa villages quietly after dark in case there was a war we didn't know about. It seemed quiet. There are plenty of folks who might be traveling along that stretch of river between the Ottawa and Miami villages, but I doubt any other nation would attack a party so near *Roche de Bout* without Pontiac giving the nod. He still has great influence over his neighbors when it comes to making war." She paused, fearing what she wanted to say next would be dismissed out of hand. "And, sir, don't assume it was Indians. It could have been anyone."

"Graham, thoughts?" Turnbull looked again to his sergeant.

"I think Marguerite's instincts are on target, sir, as usual." Graham smiled at her. She thought for a moment he winked as well, but with the eye patch it was not easy to tell. "Like I said, I saw no sign of Pontiac preparing for war during my recent visit. But the fact remains that the men are dead, and they were killed in Indian country. Stands to reason it was either Indians or renegade Frenchmen. There are still plenty of *Canadiens* in the backcountry who I'd judge capable of murder."

"It must have been Indians," said Kennedy. "Who else? It is not like the French renegades to murder a whole party like this."

"No?" questioned Turnbull. "We've seen disgruntled *Canadiens* murder British traders before, Mr. Kennedy."

"But not local canoemen," said Kennedy.

"They were *Canadiens*?" said Turnbull.

"Yes, sir. Ben Stone engaged men from Detroit to man his canoes. Some of the *Canadiens* in the backcountry are brutes, but if you ask me, they would not kill their own kind this way."

"Nor would the Potawatomi, Ottawa—or any of the other Nations—kill local men without cause," Marguerite did not want them blamed for these killings unless there was better evidence. "It did not even look like anything was plundered."

"Unless they were in liquor, sir," observed Sergeant Graham. "We all know Indians and Frenchmen alike can be pretty free with violence after some strong irrigation. And the Natives don't hold themselves responsible for what they do when they're in their cups."

She remained silent. She knew Graham was right. Rum caused even the best people to commit horrible atrocities. In the back of her mind, she suspected that alcohol would be the true demon behind these deaths. It usually was.

"Who were the canoemen?" asked Graham.

"There was Lucien Tremblay, Barthelemy Bruno, Baptiste and Pierre Beaulieu, and Pero," she told him. "They all grew up here, except Pero who came up from Quebec."

Graham wrote the names in his notebook.

"Pero," repeated Captain Turnbull. "Is that the one with the revolting burns all over his face who only grunts?"

"By all accounts he was a good paddler," said Marguerite. "But he was badly injured during the war."

"I remember him. God awful to look at," said Turnbull. "The reward for doing his duty, I suppose."

"These murders were certainly the work of savages," Kennedy insisted. "And I have some small experience in the matter during the war." He reached up and touched his scar. " Potawatomi,

Ottawa, Miami, Shawnee, Delaware, what goddamn difference does it make?"

"You've made yourself clear on that point," said Turnbull, scowling.

"And I sure don't trust that fiend Pontiac," Kennedy continued.

"Nor do I, Mr. Kennedy," snapped the captain. "But he is no fool. And if he wanted to resume fighting, he would have killed you as well. This is a nasty business. I expect the culprits will soon come to light."

Patterson arrived with a tray of tea, which he set on Turnbull's desk. The captain resumed his seat and poured for his guests. "Had you planned on heading back to the Maumee villages soon, Mr. Kennedy?"

"No, Captain, I have some business in Michilimackinac, then back to New York."

"How about you and your brothers, Miss Boyer?" He handed Marguerite a cup. She brought it to her lips, but it was still too hot to drink.

"I don't know yet. My mother will tell me her plans when I see her. There is still trade to be had out that way, so I expect so. At least after this business is sorted out. The game has been plentiful this past winter, and there were several families who had yet to get in from their winter camps when we were there. Assuming that the backcountry remains safe, I'd expect to make another journey to Kekionga soon."

"We will wait and see what further news arrives," said Turnbull. "I may need to restrict travel until we know more. There are too many inexperienced traders peddling rum in the Indian villages as it is."

"Sir, I could take a trip south with a few men to see what can be found out," offered Graham. "I feel pretty comfortable among the Ottawa these days, and I've made a few friends among them who would tell me what they know. I'd wager this is all the result of some argument that got out of hand after a drink too many."

"Just so, Sergeant. I may indeed need to send you, but let us sit tight for a day or two and see what news comes to us."

Marguerite was concerned about trade closing down but relieved that the captain sounded calm. There was no talk from him of war or hasty retribution, only a desire to discover the truth. While Kennedy had reacted to the violence with fear, Turnbull just sounded weary. It also helped to have Sergeant Graham's quiet competence in the room to drown out Kennedy's hysteria.

Turnbull turned back to Kennedy. "I do hope you gave the poor souls a decent burial when you found them?"

Kennedy glanced at Marguerite then quickly looked away. "Yes, sir. Our canoemen knew most of those killed, so we saw to them, though we never found their heads. The killers must have taken them as trophies. We couldn't bring Stone's packs out, as we had a full load already, but we had the men cache them properly, so the weather and critters don't get to them."

"And whose concern are those packs now?" asked Turnbull.

"Stone was supplied by Daniel Campbell, out of Schenectady," Marguerite said. "Amos Jacobs is his agent here. He will want to fetch everything to settle his accounts."

"Well, I suppose I will need to deal with that," sighed Captain Turnbull with little sign of enthusiasm. "As if there wasn't too much on my plate as it is."

Chapter 4

The Dreamer

The Dreamer sniffed at the moist earth, looking for beetles. The large ones were the best—the brown shiny ones he found when he broke open chunks of rotting wood. Their grasping legs were sharp on his tongue when he first put them in his mouth, but when he bit down, they cracked, and their fine juices filled his mouth like honey. The fat white wood grubs were good too—juicy but not crunchy. He liked the crunch.

The Dreamer sometimes imagined he had always been here in this forest, beneath these trees, as he had no specific memory of being anywhere else. The eyes of his companions were lined up, looking at him. Not that they had eyes any longer, but if they had eyes, they would be there in those empty sockets looking at him. A dozen, in pairs of two. After dark, the mouths spoke. They told him he was not a man but an ethereal thing.

"A Manitou?" he asked.

"Hardly. Maybe a demon," they told him. "Or a ghost."

He did not want to be a demon, but perhaps he could be a ghost.

He had a dream once. Or was this all dreams? He was running through the forest dressed in his underclothes. Something had frightened him. Blood. Pain. He ran and ran. Branches whipping at him, scratching him. Going somewhere. His bare feet were cut raw. His body was torn. He had to find someone. He had to tell someone.

Then he found his companions. He came upon them in the forest after wandering—how long? Or had they summoned him? He hardly remembered. They kept him safe. He woke with them there. They told him he would be alright if he abandoned his former life. He belonged with them. He should not stand on his feet anymore. Standing was for men, and he was a part of the forest. The earth was soft and damp and held treasures he could eat. It smelled fresh—like life. There was nothing to be frightened of. He was safe as long as he stayed with his companions.

Then, the buzzards and crows came to visit. They spoke with his companions in their animal language. The great birds picked at their flesh and ate their eyes. At first, the Dreamer thought that this would hurt them, but his companions told him that the birds were friends. They no longer needed eyes to see. They did not need flesh to feel. Nor did he. Flesh was for human beings. Flesh was for the living. They would all sink into the dirt and become part of the dream world.

It was all for the best.

Chapter 5

Marguerite Boyer

The summons came two days later. Marguerite was playing a game with Daniel that involved a toy canoe plummeting over an imaginary waterfall when a soldier arrived to announce that Marguerite and her mother would be required at the commandant's office first thing the following morning.

"What is this about?" asked Sally.

"It's not my business to know," answered the messenger, "but if I were one to overhear, I'd say it has something to do with the murders down on the Maumee River. The captain wants the business settled."

"How is that our concern?" asked Marguerite.

"I'm just the messenger, ma'am. Eight o'clock in the commandant's office."

"Very well." Marguerite was not really puzzled when she thought about it. She was one of those who found the bodies, after all, and her mother's business was deeply affected by the temporary closure of trade on the Maumee River. Of course the captain would want to talk with them again.

In the morning, they arrived at the captain's office only to be redirected to the officer's dining room down the hall. Sally and

Marguerite entered to see Captain Turnbull at the head of the table, with his second in command, Lieutenant Christie, next to him. His two sergeants, Graham and Ramsay, were there, as well as a tall, young-looking, officer Marguerite did not know.

The largest dog Marguerite had ever seen lay on the floor in the corner. As she entered the room, the beast leaped up and rushed towards her. It had long legs and a square head, and its back was as tall as a man's waist. It was mostly black with some white markings on its paws and chest. Marguerite was relieved to see that the young officer had it on a leash and pulled him up short.

"Brutus, down," scolded the officer. "Sorry, ma'am. Brutus will do you no harm, but sometimes he gets excited to meet new people." The dog looked at Marguerite with a sort of longing, letting its long pink tongue hang down out of a huge black face, then he returned to his corner to lie down. But still, his eyes were on Marguerite.

"No harm done, sir," she said. She usually loved dogs, but the size of this one made her apprehensive.

Sam Kennedy and the clerk Amos Jacobs were at the table. Jacobs was the local agent for Daniel Campbell, a Schenectady merchant who supplied fur traders on credit. He had outfitted Ben Stone's venture, so his firm could only be made whole if the skins and furs left at Auglaize got down to the markets in New York. Turnbull's secretary, Patterson, was serving tea and biscuits.

"Madam Boyer, Marguerite. I'm glad you are here," said the captain. "Please take a seat. Patterson, offer them some tea, please."

The secretary served them as they found two empty chairs near the foot of the table.

"I believe everyone here is acquainted," began Turnbull, "except Ensign Philbrook here, who just arrived in Detroit recently. Introduce yourself, Ensign, if you don't mind."

The young man with the dog cleared his throat. "How do you do? I'm Ensign Phineas Philbrook. I'm pleased to make everyone's acquaintance." He smiled at Marguerite. She noted that his accent

31

was American—New England, she thought. He was a nice-enough looking man—tall and slim, with dark brown hair worn long and tied with a black ribbon in back, but she thought that he looked more like a shopkeeper than a soldier. His features were a bit too rounded to be called truly handsome.

"Ensign, you've already met Lieutenant Christie and the sergeants," continued the captain. "Let me introduce Mr. Amos Jacobs who is here because responsibility for Ben Stone's cargo falls to him. Next to him is Sam Kennedy, the trader who discovered the murders, along with Miss Marguerite Boyer, a local interpreter and guide. I wanted them here to repeat their account of finding the horrid scene. Finally, let me introduce Madame Sally Boyer, Marguerite's mother. She supplies canoes, canoemen, interpreters, and guides for traders going into the backcountry."

The ensign nodded to everyone around the table and smiled affably. His dog had settled back down, but it continued to look at Marguerite as if she fascinated him. She wondered if perhaps she had spilled something on her clothes which might make her smell interesting to a dog.

"I've been mulling over this business of those men killed at Auglaize," Turnbull resumed. "You are all aware that I've suspended all new trade along the Maumee River, but I've waited a few days to act further in the hope that more information would come our way through natural channels, but the time has come to take active measures. Mr. Jacobs has been nagging me to let him send someone down to fetch the furs and skins left at Auglaize, but I've been holding off just in case the situation is unsafe. But so far, there has been no word of further violence, so it is time for us to retrieve the packs and find out who was responsible for the deaths."

Marguerite eyed Mr. Jacobs. He had been in Detroit for more than a year, but she had never been interested in getting to know him. There was something about him that she found off-putting.

Perhaps it was the fact that he always smelled like he had been drinking.

"Now Lieutenant Christie has something to add," continued Turnbull. He turned to his lieutenant, who cleared his throat.

Marguerite did not like Christie. He spoke in what she understood to be an upper-class English accent that to her ear exuded contempt and an air of superiority.

"There is an unrelated issue we need to address with Pontiac down in his village," said Christie. "As most of you know, the murderer Alexis Cuillerier escaped from our gaol several weeks ago. The man has always been friendly with Pontiac and the Ottawa, so it seems likely that he fled to their village on the Maumee. The Ottawa may be harboring him, or they may know where he has gone."

Turnbull resumed. "All this leads me to conclude that I must send an official party up the Maumee River to find answers—one that includes an officer. Ensign Philbrook will be in command, tasked with interviewing Pontiac about both Cuillerier and the Auglaize murders. We hope he will share some useful information. After seeing the Ottawa chief, Philbrook will travel up to Auglaize to examine the scene of the massacre. I do not want traders to roam freely in that area just yet, but Mr. Jacobs will be allowed to accompany Ensign Philbrook with a bateau and crew as far as Auglaize to fetch Mr. Stone's cargo. After investigating at Auglaize, if Mr. Philbrook feels that our questions have been answered to his satisfaction, the whole party will return here together, but if further investigation is needed, Jacobs will return with his bateau crew while the rest will travel up the Maumee to Kekionga where Philbrook will interview Pacanne and the other chiefs of the Miami Nation."

"One question, if you don't mind, sir," interjected Ensign Philbrook. "This fellow Cuillerier is a murderer, you say. Who did he murder, and is there any chance he had something to do with the murders at Auglaize?"

"A good question, Ensign," said Lieutenant Christie. "I suppose it is possible that Cuillerier had something to do with Auglaize, but the murder we want him for happened years ago during Pontiac's uprising. Alexis Cuillerier was a local Detroit man who thought it in his interest to throw in his lot with Pontiac and his gang when they rebelled. Then he murdered a little American girl at Pontiac's bidding."

"Murdered a child?" said Philbrook. "Barbaric." Marguerite noted that his face was paler than it had been a moment before.

"You will soon learn that the Frenchmen around here are hardly civilized," said Christie with an expression of contempt that was not lost on Marguerite. "Some have more in common with the savages than with us." Christie looked over at Marguerite and her mother, seemingly oblivious to the idea that his words might bring offense. "The Ottawa took Betty Fisher at the outbreak of hostilities after slaughtering most of her family. It was a young family that had just moved up from Pennsylvania. Simple farm folk. A lovely little child, I've heard. They dragged her off to their village on the Maumee River as a captive. After a few weeks she got sick with the flux, Pontiac grew irritated with the urchin's whimpering and filth, and ordered the scoundrel Cuillerier to drown her in the river. He held her head under the water till she stopped her struggles."

"Horrible," said Philbrook, shaking his head.

"I wish we could punish Pontiac himself for such atrocities, but it would not be diplomatic to try," said Turnbull. "Cuillerier, on the other hand, became a subject of King George in sixty-three, so we can hang him if we please."

"Have not the tribes submitted?" Philbrook asked. "Can you not demonstrate the king's sovereignty over these regions and all its people by arresting who you will?"

The captain laughed and shook his head. "No, Ensign, we cannot. British sovereignty in these parts is a tricky matter. The local Frenchmen, or *Canadiens* as they are called, are now British subjects, 'new subjects' we call them, with all the privileges and duties that entails. That was all part of the Paris treaty. The Indians, however, are still Indians, and they largely do as they please."

"The Natives are not considered subjects of the king?" asked Philbrook.

"We treat them as foreign nations," said Turnbull, "so everything is a negotiation. We like to think we took this whole land from the French, so that it now belongs to King George, but the local Nations say it never belonged to the French. They say the French were simply their guests. What is more, they deny that they ever surrendered to us. Rather, as they see it, they've merely stopped fighting for now. If we tried to arrest Pontiac for ordering that poor child's death, or if we demand submission from the tribes, the whole goddamn backcountry would explode again. For now, it is enough to demonstrate our right to administer justice among the *Canadiens.*"

"Two undermanned companies of British soldiers can hardly be expected to rule by force over thousands of acres of wilderness filled with wild beasts and savages," added Christie. "No, everything beyond our little stockade here is contested ground, even if our betters in London consider the war won and the land conquered for our king."

The ensign nodded in understanding. Marguerite, meanwhile, sipped her tea and began to wonder what all this had to do with her and her mother. She had known Alexis Cuillerier. He was a weak man, who had done something terrible, but she was not sorry that he had run off.

"Let me return to the matter at hand," said Turnbull. "As I said, Philbrook, you will command, and since you are new to this country, I'll be sending Sergeant Graham with you to assist. You will find that Sergeant Graham is more familiar with the local tribes than just about anyone in the British Army." Turnbull turned to the sergeant. "Sergeant, pick four good men to join you, men who can handle themselves in the bush and can paddle a canoe."

"Sir." Graham nodded his head.

Finally, the captain turned to Sally.

"Now Madame Boyer, could you supply us with two canoes, four skilled canoemen, and your daughter as interpreter? We will reimburse you at your normal rate, of course."

"You want my canoemen and your soldiers to paddle together?" asked Sally.

"Just so," said Turnbull.

"Joseph Papan is available to guide," she said, "but he must have final authority over my canoes and canoemen. I will not subject him, or the men who work for me, to military discipline or the orders of inexperienced soldiers."

Turnbull looked over to Sergeant Graham, who subtly nodded in ascent.

"Yes, yes, just so, Papan will have the final word over your canoes and all canoe travel. I could not ask for better. And Marguerite?"

"What Margot does is up to her."

Turnbull turned to her. "Miss Boyer? Your services will be invaluable, both as an interpreter and as a witness who discovered the bodies."

Marguerite hesitated. She glanced at the ensign who was to be nominally in charge and saw a greenhorn American with no knowledge of this land. Could she consent to the leadership of such a man? British officers were known to be haughty and stubborn, sometimes foolish. But then she looked to Sergeant Graham, and considered that it was quite likely him who would be the true leader. Graham was a competent man. Turnbull had surely decided to send the ensign so he could learn a thing or two from him. And Papan would be there. Between Graham, Papan, and her, she thought, they should be able to guide the ensign in the right direction. He looked like a man who might be easy to control.

"I'll go," she said, hoping she would not come to regret the decision.

"Excellent," said Turnbull before turning his attention to Philbrook. "Ensign, I asked Sam Kennedy here so that you could speak with him before you leave. You will be able to interview Miss Boyer and Mr. Jacobs during your journey, but pick Kennedy's brain before you leave so you have his impression of how the scene looked when it was discovered. Lieutenant Christie and I have other business to attend to now. I trust you can handle things from here."

"Yes, sir," said the ensign. Sam Kennedy immediately began to harangue Philbrook with his theories about the Potawatomi as Turnbull and Christie left. Marguerite had no interest in hearing more of Kennedy's thoughts, so she excused herself.

THE NEXT MORNING, at the appointed time, they came together at Detroit's main wharf. It was a cold day, with clouds that looked like they might begin to drop rain at any moment. The wind was calm, so there was no reason not to proceed as planned. Joseph Papan had arrived first with two birchbark canoes belonging to Marguerite's mother and the men he and Sally had chosen to paddle them. The canoes were close to twenty-five feet long and constructed of cedar and the bark of white birch trees. The bark was stitched together with twine and sealed with black pitch. Four men would paddle each one, and they could hold over a ton of cargo each.

Next to them floated a solitary bateau, belonging to Amos Jacobs's employers, looking sturdy yet inelegant next to the slimmer canoes. Jacobs had hired four American bateaumen to help him row or sail the craft as needed.

Papan was busy arranging paddlers and provisions that had come down to the wharf in a donkey cart. He had brought three other canoemen with him, all of whom were named Bourassa. They were cousins rather than brothers. Jean was the oldest at close to thirty, while his cousins, Vince and Luc-Marie, were both nearer to twenty. When Sergeant Graham got there, Papan instructed the four soldiers with him on their roles in the canoes. Graham himself would ride as a passenger, as would Philbrook and Marguerite.

Marguerite was conferring with Joseph about the canoes when the ensign arrived. She was amused to see that he had his enormous dog with him, which she pointed out to Joseph.

"*Mon Dieu,*" Papan exclaimed when he lay eyes on the beast. "That creature is the size of a moose calf in June. Mons. Philbrook asked me if he could bring a dog in the canoe. I told him that taking one along was *pas de problème,* but I did not realize..."

As the ensign approached, Papan exclaimed, "That dog is very large, *très grand!*"

"This is Brutus," said Philbrook. "He is a great Danish dog. At least that is what the man in London I bought him from called him. He has ridden in bateaux before but not canoes. I can leave him behind if your canoes cannot handle him."

Marguerite knew that Papan was a proud man, and he seemed to take this as a challenge not to go back on his word. She was not surprised to hear him say, "*Non, non*. It is fine. But he is very large. He must sit still." As Papan spoke, the dog lunged toward Marguerite as if he wanted to play. With some difficulty the ensign held it back by the leash.

"No worries," Philbrook said. "Brutus just wants to say hello. He seems to like you, but he greets new people a bit too enthusiastically sometimes." Marguerite hoped that she could avoid any more enthusiastic greetings. She reflected that the beast might send them all into the river before this journey was over. The dog then saw Captain Turnbull approaching and jumped up to greet him.

"Brutus, down," Philbrook cried, but the captain already had the dog's paws in his hands and was holding him like a dance partner, their eyes level.

"A magnificent beast," Turnbull exclaimed. "Are you taking Brutus with you? Nothing like having a good dog along on a journey." He let go of the dog's paws and let him drop back down to all fours.

"Have you ever seen such a dog, Miss Boyer?" the captain asked her. "I bet you haven't. The dogs around here are all mongrel creatures, but in Britain, we have noble breeds like this." She admitted that she had never seen such a large dog before.

"I came down to see you off and give a few final words of advice," the captain told Philbrook as he looked over the canoes. "I don't expect you will have any troubles. Everything points to the murders being an isolated incident. If you are lucky, the perpetrators will be identified and they will confess without too much discussion, and they may even submit to you."

"I hope so, sir." A light rain had begun to fall, but not enough to penetrate the officers' tricorn hats or woolen coats. Marguerite wrapped her shawl around her head and shoulders so that the drizzle would not bother her.

"Don't let Pontiac or any of his people intimidate you, Ensign," the captain continued. "They will try. Pontiac especially. The man is a bully, though a chastened one these days. They will be looking for any sign of weakness to exploit, so don't give them the satisfaction. Same goes for Pacanne and the Miami. Back in sixty-four, up at Kekionga they stripped poor Captain Morris and tied him by the neck to a post, where he expected to be tortured to a slow and painful death, but he met these threats with manly fortitude, so Pacanne gave him his freedom. Indians are like that. They reward bravery and despise cowardice."

"Yes, sir. I will keep that in mind."

The ensign put on a brave face, but Marguerite observed that he looked worried. But the captain was right. If the murders were part of a general uprising, they would have seen signs of it by now. She was confident that the backcountry was safe, as long as they did nothing foolish to provoke the people who lived there.

Chapter 6

Phineas Philbrook

When it was time to set off, Philbrook carefully stepped into the canoe under the charge of Joseph Papan, while the interpreter and Sergeant Graham got into the other one. Brutus followed him enthusiastically, stepping first on one gunwale and then the opposite one, setting the canoe lurching from side to side. After much shouting and some panic, Philbrook was able to convince the dog to sit calmly on the packs, but he could see that the canoemen were nervous about his dog. Perhaps he should have left him in the officers' kennel, but he hated the thought of leaving Brutus behind. If he was going to stay in the Upper Country long, he would need him to learn all the local ways.

His orderly, Billy Smyth, followed into the canoe. Smyth was a small, wiry soldier, with the body of someone who had been underfed as a young child. When Philbrook had first arrived at Detroit, Smyth had been on the wharf helping to move army provisions that were stacked nearby. He directed the new ensign to the captain's office and saw to his baggage. From this starting point the soldier established himself as his orderly—or personal servant

—a role that came with several perks. He soon became indispensable to Philbrook.

Mr. Papan shouted out instructions to the men. He took the stern position in one canoe, and he placed the *Canadiens* in the bow and stern of both canoes. Then he directed the soldiers, including Smyth, to the middle positions. He explained this to Philbrook. The man in the bow was called the *avant* while the man in back was the *gouvernail* or steersman. These roles required the skills possessed by the *Canadiens*. The middle positions, occupied by the soldiers, were called *milieux* and required less skill. They would simply paddle as instructed. These men had been chosen by Sergeant Graham—John Young, Thomas Bellows, and Simon Grant.

Papan wielded his paddle to send the craft gliding out onto the river, and the others joined in. Rowing was an act of brute strength, Philbrook mused, while paddling, as Papan and his *Canadiens* did it, took grace and skill. Papan set the pace and coordinated his strokes with those of the other paddlers, sometimes yelling out a brief command or lightly mocking the soldiers' lack of skill. The soldiers took this in stride and seemed intent on matching the strokes of the *Canadiens* as best they could. The *Canadiens* seemed at home in the canoes, and a casual observer might think that they put less effort into their paddling, but Philbrook suspected that they just made it look that way.

It was a calm day with very little wind, despite the gentle rain, so Jacobs's bateau could not set its sail. With four men rowing, his boat was no match for the canoes, so Papan slowed the canoes to make sure all three craft stayed together. Jacobs sat at the bateau's tiller, and Philbrook noted that he had his flask with him and was frequently bringing it to his lips.

Every hour or so Papan would call for a break, and all the paddlers would put down their paddles. Most took the opportunity to pull out their pipes for a five minutes smoke-break before paddling resumed. This cycle of long stretches of paddling interrupted by short breaks lasted throughout the day.

The first night of their journey, they camped on a point where the Detroit River enters Lake Erie. An expanse of water stretched away to the east as far as the eye could see. After several hours sitting in the canoe, Philbrook was eager to get out to stretch his legs. He hoped to spend the rest of the day getting to know the people with him. He had concluded that learning everything he could about the Upper Country and its people was the best path to discovering what happened to Ben Stone and his crew. After their campsite had been established, he approached Jacobs, who sat near the fire with his back against a pack watching some of the men cooking fish that they had caught during the day.

"What can you three tell me about Mr. Stone?" Philbrook asked, taking a seat on the ground next to Jacobs. "I feel that it would help me to know something about the man who was killed. Did you know him?"

"Yes, I knew him," said Jacobs. "Knew him pretty well in fact. We were in the war together. Didn't Kennedy tell you that?" Jacobs sipped at the cup in his hand. "We had some adventures."

"The ensign doesn't need to hear all your old war stories, Jacobs," interrupted Sergeant Graham who stood nearby. "Can't have anything to do with the present issue."

Philbrook saw that Graham had little regard and even less patience for Amos Jacobs.

"I wasn't planning on sharing my life story." Jacobs looked up at the sergeant with a strange expression. "But the ensign asked, didn't he?"

"Indeed, I'd like to hear what I can of Mr. Stone's background," Philbrook said.

"Like I said," resumed Jacobs, "I first met Ben Stone back in the war. I signed up with a friend of mine to spend a summer with the New Jersey provincials marching against the French. Ben was in our company. As it happens, so were Sam Kennedy and his assistant, Jabez Cole. Kennedy was the sergeant."

"You joined the provincials. What year, and where were you sent?' asked Philbrook.

"'Fifty-seven. Fort William Henry. It did not go that well, so I never enlisted again."

"I've heard about the fall of that fort," said Philbrook. "You are fortunate you made it back home."

"I made it back eventually," said Jacobs. "But, like the good sergeant says, that is a story for another day."

"Did you like Stone?"

"Yeah, he was tolerable. Smart. He didn't like being told what to do, so he butted heads with Kennedy pretty often."

"Strange that you, Stone, Cole, and Kennedy all ended up out here after serving together," said Philbrook.

"You'll find, sir," said Sergeant Graham, "that most of the British traders and boatmen coming into this country served in the war, either as American provincials or British regulars. The men who made up the companies that took Niagara and Montreal got a taste for Canada and the Upper Country. And they heard about the opportunities offered by the Indian trade."

"You don't have to tell me," said Philbrook. "I was a provincial myself. I joined a New Hampshire provincial regiment for the last two summers of fighting. I was with General Prideaux and Sir William Johnson at Niagara in fifty-nine and with Amherst the next year, when we took Montreal."

"Really, sir," said Graham. "You were a provincial before you received your commission in the regulars? I'd no idea."

"No reason why you should, Sergeant." Philbrook recalled his two summers in the New Hampshire provincials. When they were over, he thought he'd had his fill of army life. But after a few years as a clerk for his uncle's shipping business in London, he began to miss the wilderness and the life of a soldier.

"But getting back to Stone," Philbrook resumed. "What was he like, Mr. Jacobs?"

"He was solid and willing to work hard. He spoke French pretty well, so when he showed up in Detroit, it was easy to set him up with a good crew. He had ambitions. He wanted to make a fortune as quickly as possible then retire back east, like a lot of the Americans who come here."

"Did he get along with his men?"

"Yes, I think so."

"Mr. Kennedy said neither he nor Mr. Cole maintained any contact with Ben Stone after their wartime service—that he was surprised when he showed up in Detroit." Philbrook had spoken with Sam Kennedy back in Detroit, and had heard from him about his shared background with Stone and Jacobs, but he wanted to know if Jacobs remembered things the same way.

"That sounds about right. Those two were not friends. Kennedy was kind of a bully when we were in the war. He thought his rank as sergeant made him better than the rest of us. Ordered us around. Ben resented it more than most." Philbrook noted that Jacobs was frequently sipping his drink. He could smell the rum. He was no stranger to heavy drinkers, but Jacobs's fondness for rum seemed extreme. The soldiers and canoemen each got a limited ration each day, but Jacobs was not bound by any rules— to his own detriment it seemed.

"How about you? Did you keep in touch?"

"I'd see him now and then. Maybe have a drink. He is from a town neighboring mine in New Jersey, so when I was back home, I'd run into him now and again. He knew I was out here when he decided to try his hand at the Indian trade, so he wrote me for advice, and I wrote back that if he supplied through Daniel Campbell's firm, we'd give him a good deal."

"That was nice of you," said Philbrook. "Do you have any theory about what happened? Was he a violent sort? Do you think he might have cheated someone or started a fight?"

"I can't say. He was inexperienced, so maybe he offended some of the Indians. But he wasn't foolish. I think it more likely he was in the wrong place at the wrong time when some young warriors decided to blow off some steam."

Philbrook was starting to get a picture of Ben Stone, and he was learning more every minute about this world he had recently entered, but he was a long way from knowing what happened at Auglaize. He resolved to keep asking questions until a fuller picture emerged.

In the morning, the sun broke the horizon at an early hour. It was a setting up to be a clear late spring day to leave the river behind and embark on the lake.

"*Mam'selle* Boyer." Philbrook approached Marguerite while they broke camp. "I'd like to talk with you about what you found at Auglaize. I was hoping that you could ride in the same canoe as me today."

"Please call me Marguerite, Ensign."

"Very well... Marguerite."

They sat shoulder-to-shoulder in the middle of the canoe, on top of a couple of packs. Brutus lay at their feet. Philbrook had noticed that his dog had an unusual attraction to the interpreter. He hoped she did not mind. Marguerite reached out and let the dog lick her hand, then Brutus rested his chin on her moccasin and stared up at her as they spoke.

"I see he likes you," said Philbrook.

"I'm glad," she said. "I would hate to make an enemy of such a formidable beast."

"Tell me about the times you encountered Stone on your last voyage, Marguerite. Anything unusual happen that you remember?"

"I met him briefly in Detroit before we commenced our

voyages. His party left several days before us, so as we ascended the river we could see where they had camped, but they were always ahead of us until we got to Kekionga."

"That's the Miami Indian village?"

"Yes. Stone was finishing up his trading when we got there." Marguerite lit her little clay pipe as they talked. Philbrook did not smoke, but he enjoyed the smell of the tobacco. "We spent one night camped near each other outside Le Gris's village."

"Le Gris's village? Is that the same as Kekionga?"

"It's on the other side of the river, and traders usually set up there rather than in Kekionga proper. Le Gris's people are a separate band of Miami from Pacanne's band at Kekionga."

"So you saw Stone and his crew there, and then they left in the morning?"

"That's right. Stone had traded away the cargo he'd brought with him and had a full load of skins and furs. He would not have wasted any time getting back to Detroit and then down to New York to sell them. Time is money in this business, and getting furs down to New York earlier in the season can be profitable." As the interpreter spoke, Philbrook reached over the canoe gunwale and trailed his fingertips in the water as they cruised along, creating little wakes behind them.

"Time is of the essence, as they say, in every business," said Philbrook. "Did you notice if anything was wrong? Did Stone mention any altercations or conflicts? Had he upset the local people on his way up the river?" He wanted to know if Stone's trip into the backcountry was unusual in any way.

"No, not that I heard, but I didn't talk to him long. I just asked him how his business had gone, and he said it had gone well. He talked with Sam Kennedy longer. Stone had more in common with Kennedy than he had with me."

"Because they were both American traders and knew one another from the war?"

"Yes, but I'll admit that I was not really listening. Kennedy rambles on so."

"When I spoke with him back in Detroit, Mr. Kennedy told me that the Potawatomi at St. Joseph are the most likely culprit in this business. Do you agree? I've heard the Potawatomi are the least content among the local nations since the peace."

"Sam Kennedy doesn't know anything. He just pretends he does." Philbrook noticed her irritation. "He is a nice enough man much of the time, but don't take him to be any sort of expert on this country."

"That is what Captain Turnbull told me as well," said Philbrook, "and he also told me that you are something of an expert on the Upper Country, and I should listen to your council." Philbrook was not normally someone who liked to flatter, but he wanted to be on the interpreter's good side. The captain had indeed told him that he thought Kennedy was a fool, while Marguerite was quite sensible.

She had been looking out at the lake as they cruised along, but now she turned to look him in the face. "It is not unusual for folks to get killed in these parts," she said. "The French and British governments may have finally made their peace, and Pontiac and the other chiefs may have put away their war belts for now, but there are plenty of people around here who have not come around yet. There are lingering resentments. The French and Natives resent the British for taking over their country. The Natives resent the French for surrendering to the British and abandoning their local allies. The war left plenty of deaths that have yet to be resolved."

"Death can be resolved?" Philbrook asked, glad that she was making an effort to explain this world to him. "Death has a certain finality to it, does it not, even in these parts?"

"You have to understand how Natives look at justice, Ensign, because it is different among them than with your people." He saw that she was intent to make her point clearly. "I'm not saying these murders were done by Ottawas or Miamis, but if they were, you need to try to understand it in their terms. When someone is killed among them, the death causes an imbalance that has to be set right. It might be put right with gifts offered by the killer's relatives to the relatives of the one killed. They call this covering the graves of the dead. But if not, it might have to be set straight with a revenge killing or by taking captives to replace the dead. Gifts are usually preferred since revenge can go on forever."

"So you are saying that Stone may have harmed some group of Indians in some way in the past?"

"Or some other British trader or soldier did. Indians do not always take their revenge on the same individual as hurt them. They can put it off for years, then take it out on a relative or someone else from their enemy's people."

"Like Montagues and Capulets," he said. "A universal story I think."

"I'm not acquainted with them. Are those tribes where you live?"

"They're rival families from an old English story." Philbrook was a great admirer of Shakespeare, but he often forgot that not everyone was familiar with the Bard. "So you are saying that Stone could have stumbled into a feud that somebody else began?"

"It's possible. Most controversies come to an end with a series of gift exchanges that cover all previous slights, but the British are often selfish. That opens them up to violent retribution when the local nations feel slighted or when their world is out of balance."

"Captain Turnbull thinks that the men at the Ottawa and Miami Villages will have a good idea who did the killing."

"They should," she agreed, "but only if the perpetrators came from among them. Be aware, Ensign that when folks get murdered around here, it's either liquor or revenge that is the cause most of the time, sometimes both, and the act is seldom kept secret. I'm not convinced that the Natives had anything to do with these killings, but I do know that if they are responsible, they will not hide it."

"No?"

"No. And don't forget, sir, that most of the men killed were *Canadiens*. A couple of them had a Native *grand-mère* or two, as I do. Ben Stone wasn't necessarily the only target."

"You and Mr. Kennedy both have said that Stone was stripped naked—while the others were not—and that he had received more wounds than the others," said Philbrook. "That seems to suggest he was the victim that mattered most to the killers, that their hatred was directed towards him."

"That may be true, Ensign, but the *Canadiens* were killed as well. I think you need to ask why. If the perpetrators were Native, and they acted out of revenge, that would mean they wanted revenge on everyone killed, not just Stone."

Philbrook realized she was right. Stone was from the English colonies, as he was, and he was the leader. Perhaps that was why he focused on him. But he knew he must follow the interpreter's advice.

"Perhaps the murderers did not want to leave any witnesses," he said.

"If that was the case, Ensign, then the murderers were not Natives looking for revenge. Among them, revenge is supposed to be witnessed. That's the point."

"Yes, of course. Thank you, Marguerite. I'll keep that in mind."

Philbrook realized that he had much to learn from this woman. She was not the sort he was used to interacting with, but he found her interesting. She was not pretty in the conventional sense, but she had a certain appeal. He sensed that she was skeptical of him, but he did not mind. If he was in her position, he would be skeptical of a newcomer as well.

THE SECOND NIGHT, they camped at a clearing on a large island not far from Maumee Bay. Cornmeal and salt pork were the standard fare, and Graham saw to the distribution of a well-measured ration of rum to the soldiers. Some of Jacobs's bateaumen went out to hunt, but returned empty-handed before dark. Papan and the canoemen were playing a card game. Philbrook joined Graham for a cup of tea by the campfire where dinner was prepared. He had a favorable impression of the sergeant, but had yet had the chance to have a real conversation with him.

"The captain says you know this river, that you've spent a good deal of time with the Natives and understand their language," Philbrook said.

"Yes, sir. I've been posted in the Upper Country for several years now, and it was my misfortune to get captured a couple of times. I was held for almost a year up north of here by Ojibwa. That was during the war. It gave me the opportunity to learn a bit of their language and make some friends among them."

"But my understanding is that we will be going through Ottawa and Miami territory rather than that of the Ojibwa."

"That's right, sir. The Ojibwa, Ottawa, and Potawatomie are related. They speak variants of the same language—Anishinaabe, they call it. Once you learn one, it's pretty easy to pick up the others. The Miami tongue is a little different but similar enough to make yourself understood if you know one of the others. I'm not fluent like Marguerite, but I can get by if I keep it simple."

"I see," said Philbrook. "How else do the different tribes differ?"

"The easiest way to put it is that they are more like each other than they are like us. Here, let me show you." Graham went over to a group of trees and found himself a stick, about two feet long. "This is Lake Erie," he said, drawing an oblong circle in the dirt at his feet. "And this is the Detroit River and the fort." His stick traced out a river flowing into the upper left part of the lake from the north. "And we are down here." He drew the Maumee River going into the lower left end of the lake from the south.

"The Ojibwa are up here." He pointed his stick to the area above Lake Erie and Detroit. "They are a large group whose territory extends well north beyond Lakes Huron and Superior which are up here." He pointed. "They aren't as settled as the folks down here and don't do as much planting. They are mostly hunters, and they harvest maple sugar and wild rice, moving around within an established range. The soil is too rocky for the kind of farming the Miami do."

He pointed to the Detroit River and then to the area below Lake Erie. "Here soils get better. It's less rocky and agriculture is possible—corn and beans mostly—so the Ottawa and Miami are farmers, or at least the women are. The men are still primarily hunters."

"I see. So you've been to Kekionga before?"

"Indeed. I was stationed at Fort Miami in sixty-three."

"Fort Miami?"

"It's abandoned now, sir. Never was much. It was a French outpost before the British took over, right next to the village of Kekionga. You'll see what's left of it when we get up the river." Graham pointed to the upper part of the Maumee.

"It was abandoned after the Indian uprising?"

"Aye, sir," said Graham. "Or during, more like it. When we took over from the French in sixty and sixty-one, we put soldiers into all their old forts. Some were little more than stockades manned by a dozen men. These smaller ones were overrun when the tribes rebelled in sixty-three. After the uprising, General Gage decided not to reestablish them."

"Yes, I'd heard that. And you were there back then?"

"Aye, sir. I was at Fort Miami at the wrong time. That's the other time I got taken captive."

"I've never heard an account of those days from someone who had been there," Philbrook said.

"What's there to say? The Indians rose up and killed a lot of British soldiers and traders. Kept it up for months before it fizzled out. There were some warning signs. In March, one of my friends from Kekionga told me they had gotten a war belt, meaning that some of the other tribes wanted to make war on us and were looking for allies. The belt originated with the Seneca, I think. They live over here." He pointed south and east of Lake Erie. "I informed Ensign Holmes, who spoke to the Miami leaders about it, but they promised to not go through with anything."

"Ensign Holmes spoke their language too?"

"No, not more than a word or two. I was usually his interpreter."

"I see. This was in sixty-three?"

"Yes, sir. So anyway, some weeks went by and things seemed to be settled. We never let more than two of them inside the fort at any one time, so we thought ourselves secure. My Miami friends seemed contented."

"How many of you were there?" asked the ensign.

"Eleven men, plus myself and Ensign Holmes, so we were very much outnumbered. We locked our gate at night, and we were better armed than the warriors in the village. Anyway, toward the end of May, Holmes's girl came to the fort saying that a relative of hers was sick and desired the ensign come bleed her."

"His girl? Holmes had a mistress among the Miami?"

"Aye, sir. She was a handsome lass, though as he learned too late, she was not entirely devoted to his happiness. She led him to a wigwam near the post, where some young Miami men shot him dead. I was foolish enough to go out to see what the shots were all about and was immediately surrounded and bound. After that the jig was up. The men didn't know what to do. How could they? So, when a couple of French traders who lived nearby told them that the best course was to surrender and beg for mercy, they complied."

"They did not put up a fight?"

"No, sir. And I don't blame them. You'll see the remains of the fort when we get up that way. They would not have held it for more than a day or two, especially without an officer to lead them, and if they'd killed any of the villagers, that would only have assured retaliation. Supplies and ammunition were limited, and it was damned clear that no bloody reinforcements would come. We never should have been there in the first place. When the French built their outposts, they brought presents to make sure they'd be well received—so they'd be treated as guests not conquerors—but the British gave the Miami nothing, so they were never welcome. I managed to make some friends among them, but they still saw us as interlopers, which, if you do not mind me saying, sir, we are."

"And you and the men were held captive for the remainder of the conflict?"

"No, sir. Just a few weeks. A Miami war party went down the river to join Pontiac's siege at Detroit, and they took most of us along. I think the only reason they didn't kill us all was because enough of them seemed to like me and some of the other soldiers, even if they hated the British in general. Indians don't always take war personally. I got exchanged shortly after we got to Detroit."

"You mentioned French traders just now. Where did they stand in all this? Surely they didn't side with the Indians?"

"Not really. But they didn't side with us either. Most tried to keep aloof from the whole bloody affair. They could be helpful at times. They tried to mediate. They often gave good advice and prevented more killing. There were exceptions of course."

"Like Alexis Cuillerier?"

"That's right." Philbrook saw an unguarded reaction momentarily pass across Graham's face at the mention of Cuillerier's name.

"Did you know him?" Philbrook asked.

"Yes, Ensign. He was a worthless man. His family is prominent in Detroit. He was related to the old French commandant."

"Really? And Sergeant, I understand you were sent to Pontiac's village to look for him after he escaped."

"Aye, sir. But we've seen the last of him, I'm certain." Graham scowled as if recalling an unpleasant smell. "He is sure to have gone south to the Wabash River. I expect he's found himself a new home in the Illinois Country where the British won't follow—at least for now."

"And how would he have gotten there, Sergeant?"

"He'd go up the Maumee River—the way we are going now, sir." He traced his stick along the Maumee River to its source then planted the tip of his stick. "Kekionga," he said. Then he dragged the stick further down. "And this is the Wabash River. That's why the Miami villages are where they are. They control the portage route between the Maumee and the Wabash Rivers. The Maumee flows north to Lake Erie, while the Wabash flows south to the Ohio River. That makes where we're heading the major thoroughfare between Lake Erie and the Mississippi River."

"Fascinating," said the ensign. "Thank you, Sergeant."

The Mississippi River. Not long ago such a destination was far beyond reach for a young man from New Hampshire. Philbrook longed to see it someday. To explore and to discover new lands had always been a dream of his. One of his motives for seeking out his current placement was a desire to see the western lands. He yearned to follow in the footsteps of great explorers like La Salle and Hennepin, perhaps to become one himself.

Chapter 7

Marguerite Boyer

M arguerite soon discovered that Ensign Philbrook had a penchant for drawing. He would pull out his sketchpad while riding in the canoe whenever he was not talking with her or Sergeant Graham. Everyday sights seemed to fascinate him, prompting him to make pictures of them. Animals mostly. He frequently asked her the local names of various plants and animals. When she told him, he would nod politely and write down her answers in his sketchpad. It was as if they did not have these creatures where he came from.

One evening, a few days into the journey, the ensign showed her some of his recent drawings. She thought them quite good. She imagined they might be well received in a European drawing room, though she knew little of such things. One in particular caught her attention, since it caught the essence of a bird of prey in flight.

"We call it a fish hawk at home," Philbrook told her, "though it is also known as an osprey."

"We call it *le balbuzard pêcheur.*"

"Indeed?"

"And my Anishinaabeg cousins call them *Biijigigwaneg.*

"Excellent! I'm afraid you will have to help me spell the latter."

As she did, he enthusiastically wrote both names under his drawing.

Marguerite was relieved that Philbrook did not seem arrogant, as so many British officers were, and he generally let Joseph and the canoemen do their jobs without interference. In her experience British officers were often much taken with themselves and haughty with local people. Some felt the need to lecture others about everything or insisted on giving orders when none were needed. Lieutenant Christie, the second in command in Detroit, was that sort. No locals liked to work with him. But Ensign Philbrook was content to observe as Graham managed the soldiers, Papan took charge of the canoes, and Jacobs oversaw his bateau. Everyone worked well without interference and without Philbrook pretending to have knowledge he did not have.

Indeed, she was impressed that he seemed eager to learn. As the days went by, she found Philbrook was not too proud to ask questions when he did not know something. At first, this heartened her, but in time, the questions became tedious. She began to wish that there were not so many things that he did not know. And that ridiculous giant of a dog! What was he thinking bringing it in the canoe? The beast belonged in a stable.

At least the weather was cooperating. They had either calm conditions or a gentle north wind aiding their passage across Lake Erie, so they entered the mouth of Maumee Bay in the southwest corner of the lake after only three days. The mouth of the Maumee River, where it entered Lake Erie, was broad, with an easy current, flowing past banks of mud and broken rock.

As the canoes and bateau ascended, the river narrowed, and the banks on either side rose steeply in some places. Long sections of weak current were interrupted by shallow swifts that could be easily paddled or poled up by the canoemen, especially if they had the soldiers get out of the way. Sometimes, Marguerite rode in in a canoe with Graham, and other times, when he had questions for her, she rode with Philbrook. Sometimes Philbrook and Graham rode together and she had the chance to touch base with the canoemen. They were all good men she had known her whole life. At times, when she needed to stretch her back, she grabbed a paddle and joined in for a spell.

The journey up the Maumee was met with no serious obstacles until they arrived at a place called *Roche de Bout,* near the Ottawa villages. Here, the river fell over a limestone shelf, and an island with steep sides rose more than thirty feet out of the water. The outcrop was said to resemble a buffalo, giving the place its name. It was one of the more distinctive landmarks along this stretch of river. The force of the water around the island is not that strong, but it was too rapid to paddle up, so Joseph and the Bourassas poled the canoes. Two men stood in each canoe, each with a pole. They planted one end on the rocky river bottom and pushed the canoes upstream, taking turns pushing and resetting their poles. The soldiers were left out of this work, as they simply did not have the skills for it. Where poling was not possible, the men picked a side channel to pull the canoes up with ropes or by wading in knee-deep water. Jacobs's bateau was brought up with more difficulty, with several bateaumen and soldiers in the cold water to their waists pulling against the current.

The rapids marked the beginning of the Ottawa settlements. They began to see fields, where women planted the three sisters: corn, beans, and squash. They saw several cabins and lodges belonging to Ottawa families. A few hunting parties passed by, shouting out a greeting and moving on. A little farther up the river lay the central village where they hoped to find the Ottawa war chief.

"Have you met Pontiac, Marguerite?" Philbrook asked as they approached the main village.

"Of course. I've known him since I was a girl. He used to live just outside of Detroit." She recalled the strong, playful man who sometimes joined briefly in their childhood games. He was a kind man then, at least to children, though he could be quick to anger.

She realized it would be difficult to explain such a unique man to an outsider. As a child she had been surrounded by people of many different nations. Only as an adult did she become aware that this was not the experience of everyone.

"Is he as fierce as they say?" asked Philbrook.

She thought about how best to describe Pontiac. It was often quite difficult to explain Indians to Englishmen. "He can be. A war chief must be fierce when the situation calls for it. But he can be gentle as well, especially with children. I have observed that Indians are more indulgent with their children than the English or the French."

"I'm not sure Betty Fisher's parents would agree," he said crisply, "were they still living."

No, she thought. That was war, and war changes everyone. She knew the sad story bothered Philbrook, and she remembered the little girl, though the Fishers had not been in Detroit very long. There had been no shortage of atrocities during the wars, but this one had been exceptional. It had surprised her when she heard about it, but then she had always had difficulty understanding violence. Such behavior seemed so pointless, and wars always made things worse.

There was a large collection of canoes—some crafted of birch bark and others dugout—along the shore as they approached the main village. The air smelled of fish and smoke, and Marguerite saw some women putting a catch out to dry on racks not far away.

"I hope to make our time here brief," Philbrook told her as they got out on shore. "I will need you to interpret for me."

"Naturally."

"You know the way around the village?"

"Of course."

"I can lead the way if you'd like, sir," interrupted Sergeant Graham with a smile.

"Thank you, Sergeant," said the ensign, "but I'd rather you stayed here to keep an eye on the men and our things. Marguerite can show me the way. We brought her along to be our interpreter after all."

"Yes, sir." Marguerite noted Philbrook's polite yet unmistakable assertion of authority and Graham's easy deference. It was the first time she realized that the young ensign might have some backbone after all.

"Some of the canoemen would like to visit some friends and relations here," she told him. "If that is alright with you. It occurred to me that the local people might share what they know of the killings more easily with familiar faces than with a British officer."

"An excellent thought, Marguerite. Sergeant Graham and his soldiers can keep watch on our boats while the canoemen visit whom they will. Tell them to find out whatever they can. And Graham, ask Jacobs and his men to stay with their bateau. No need for them to wander off."

"Aye, sir."

Philbrook was glancing around the village rapidly and seemed not to know what to do with his hands. He was tapping his toe and repeatedly adjusting his attire. She knew the scene was strange to him, but she was confident that they were safe there. As they pulled up, one look at the village had assured her that the Ottawa were not preparing for war.

Philbrook gave some additional instructions to Graham, then she led him up the embankment toward the central group of lodges. He had donned his full uniform that morning and looked every bit the British officer. He had instructed Billy Smyth, his orderly, to brush his red coat, shine his black boots, and polish his buttons, buckles, and gorget the night before so that he would look his best. A saber now hung loosely at his hip, though she had not previously noticed him wearing it, and she noted that he had tied back his long brown hair with a fresh black ribbon. Did the ensign have a streak of vanity, she wondered?

There were people around the village going about their business. They pretended not to notice the British officer, though Marguerite knew that they all were paying close attention to his every move. It would be considered impolite to stare or appear too curious, though, of course, they were.

Pontiac's village was a collection of bark wigwams and lodges of various sizes along with some log cabins. It was surrounded by stump-filled fields of corn, beans, squash, and other crops which looked to be thriving. The fields were tended by women, for the Ottawa considered the task of coaxing sustenance from the soil to be a feminine pursuit. It was early in the growing season, but the land was already green with young crops that would feed families later in the summer and throughout the next winter. There were few domesticated animals other than dogs and a few horses, but the people here did not need cows, pigs, or chickens. Ottawa men hunted the forests and fished surrounding rivers and lakes to get all the meat they needed. The result of recent hunts could be seen in skins and furs stretched out to cure in preparation for the next traders to come through.

A young man she knew approached out of a nearby lodge. "This is Pontiac's nephew," she told Philbrook quietly.

He came directly in front of the ensign, thrust out his chest, and spoke, looking not at all pleased to see him.

"He says that British soldiers have not been invited into his village," Marguerite explained.

"Tell him I come to deliver a message to his uncle from Captain Turnbull. The soldiers are merely an escort."

The nephew spoke again, ignoring Marguerite, who passed his word on. "He says to tell him the message, and he will tell Pontiac."

"My message is for a chief's ears," Philbrook said. She saw that he now appeared calmer than he had a moment before. He stood straight and looked Pontiac's nephew in the eye as he spoke. She recognized his type; Philbrook was one of those whose fears were all in the anticipation of an event rather than the event itself. Now that he had something to do, he was focused on the task.

"Fine. Then come." Pontiac's nephew turned and walked back to the bark-covered lodge. They followed.

The interior of the lodge was dark in contrast to the sunshine outside. As their eyes adjusted, they saw smoke hovering over an imposing man sitting near a fire wrapped in a wool blanket and flanked by several younger men and a few older women. Pontiac looked at Marguerite and gave a slight nod of recognition then directed Philbrook and her to sit on the ground nearby. Marguerite remained silent as the two men sized one another up. One was a strong leader sitting in his own village, surrounded by his people, and the other was a young neophyte with little understanding of the world he had just entered. She realized now why Philbrook had taken such care with his uniform today. It was not mere vanity. Rather, he understood the power that lay behind that red coat and those shining silver buttons. Philbrook represented an empire, and he wanted to remind Pontiac of that power.

Pontiac offered Philbrook his pipe, which he took, smoked, and handed back. He looked nonchalant, as if smoking with the most notorious Indian war chief alive was something quite ordinary to him.

"I am Ensign Phineas Philbrook," he spoke in English but slowly enough for Marguerite to repeat his words in Anishinaabe, "and I am here representing Captain Turnbull and King George III. The captain desires your presence in Detroit this summer to speak on the matter of Betty Fisher's cruel murder. He has heard your request, recently delivered by Sergeant Graham, concerning Mr. Cuillerier. He understands your wish for him to be pardoned, but he asks me to remind you that the British and the French are now one people and they must all follow the same laws. When Cuillerier is apprehended he will be treated like any other British subject. He will not be pardoned for the brutal murder of the girl." Pontiac frowned, but Philbrook continued. "The captain looks forward to hearing from you in person about this incident."

He paused here for a moment as Marguerite caught up, then

resumed, "The captain also asks that you turn Mr. Cuillerier over to me—if he has returned to your village—so that I might take him to face justice."

"Your Sergeant Graham already told me these things," replied Pontiac. "Why do the English waste my time with tedious repetition? I told him I know nothing of this Frenchman's whereabouts. Maybe he went up north or maybe down south. Send the captain my regards, Ensign Philbrook. Tell him he will see me in Detroit shortly, but until then, he should stop sending English soldiers to my village."

Philbrook resumed, unperturbed by this rebuke, speaking less formally now. Marguerite sought to interpret without letting her own thoughts influence the words. The best interpreters, she knew, were those who blended into the background.

"The business of Alexis Cuillerier is not the only reason for my visit. I would also like to ask you about some recent murders a short way south of here. The trader Ben Stone and his men were killed at Auglaize. Has anyone in your village heard anything about this?"

Pontiac paused for a few moments before speaking. He looked back and forth between Philbrook and Marguerite, but as he began to speak, he looked directly at the ensign. "Such things are none of my concern. We have promised peace to our English brothers, and peace we have—for now. It is not my business to keep traders from harm, as if they were little children in my care. They are a violent people with a taste for liquor. Such men die easily. I expect the men were killed by one of their own because of their own foolishness, but the culprit has not made himself known to me."

"Thank you." Philbrook nodded. "The captain has also instructed me to inform you that traders will not be allowed to return to this river until he knows who perpetrated this heinous crime. Moreover my party will be traveling through Ottawa territory to visit the site of the murders at the Auglaize. If we need to, we plan to go up as far as the Miami villages in search of answers.

You can be assured that ours is a peaceful journey for the sole purpose of seeking the truth about these deaths." Marguerite noted that the ensign stated this as a fact rather than a request, and she wondered how Pontiac would react.

"The Miami will not like seeing uninvited soldiers in their communities, but I cannot speak for them," Pontiac said. "As we are now at peace you are welcome to proceed through Ottawa lands." Pontiac gave his consent where none had been asked and handed back the pipe.

Philbrook turned to Marguerite. "Please go ask Sergeant Graham to have two of the soldiers bring up the gifts we brought."

She went down to the boats, leaving the two men to sit silently and smoke together. She reflected that the young ensign had done well. He showed the necessary respect to the older man, but he did it with confidence and was not overly deferential. He never displayed fear, even though Pontiac still had the power to intimidate.

Five years earlier, the Ottawa chief would never have consented so easily to a British officer traveling through his lands, especially not a novice like Philbrook. Pontiac's best days were past, she realized, and he knew it.

Chapter 8

Marguerite Boyer

"I found our meeting with Pontiac to be a disappointment," Philbrook told her when they were back in the canoe heading up the river. "The man did not live up to the grand accounts I heard over the past four years."

"What sort of accounts?" she asked. Marguerite did not know that Pontiac was known beyond her own region.

"He became quite famous across the English-speaking world for leading his rebellion. He's likely the most well-known Indian there is. Didn't you know? As far away as London's Covent Garden, I heard romantic tales of Chief Pontiac. Major Rogers even wrote a play about him."

"A play? Imagine that. I recall Major Rogers from when he first came to Detroit with his British troops and again during the Native uprising," she said. She remembered a rough-looking man in a dirty uniform. He had not seemed very educated to her, but his soldiers held him in awe as a warrior. "I did not know he wrote plays."

"He writes all sorts of things—or he has his secretary write them for him. Rogers depicted Pontiac as proud and noble. A great leader. But that man I just met seemed more arrogant than proud, and he gave off the impression of being sadly beaten."

"In truth, he is not the man he used to be," she said. "He has lost the support of many of his people. He is a man—perhaps like your Major Rogers—who thrives best during wartime."

"I have little sympathy. And I kept thinking of that little girl, Betty Fisher." Philbrook scowled every time he mentioned the murder. Marguerite concluded that the ensign had a soft spot for the weak and defenseless—a noble characteristic, perhaps.

The canoes continued up the river for several hours to the scene of the massacre. By late afternoon they were at the junction of the Auglaize and Maumee rivers. Here, two rivers of almost equal size came together. Both were brown, sluggish streams, maybe one hundred feet wide at the junction. Buzzards flew up into the trees and perched there to watch the newcomers, and a collection of crows sat in the treetops making their usual noises.

The canoemen brought the craft in toward a well-used landing on the north shore. They had been talking on and off since leaving Pontiac's village, and Marguerite noted that the ensign was focusing on the task ahead of him now. She had expected he would hang back and let Sergeant Graham take charge when they got to the murder scene, but instead, he took on a commanding tone that she had not previously seen.

"Sergeant Graham," Philbrook ordered as soon as everyone was on land and the canoes had been unloaded and taken out of the river, "have the men survey the campsite and take note of everything significant they see. Write down what you find then report back to me." He turned to Amos Jacobs. "Mr. Jacobs, you and your men can begin to collect what is left of Mr. Stone's cargo. I will want to inspect everything. Report anything unusual or unexpected." He turned back to Marguerite. "Marguerite, please walk with me and describe how the scene looked when you were last here."

"As you wish, sir." She was vaguely amused at his newfound

aura of command. They walked slowly up to the central area of the campsite. "Well, *monsieur*, when we got here the bodies were yet fresh. I think they had been dead a day, maybe two. The one we took to be Stone was over here by what remains of the fire, while five more were over there and there." She pointed around the site. The ground was bloodstained in each location, and the air still smelled heavy and stale. "Like I've said, Stone was stripped naked and had suffered a number of wounds, but the others were attired for sleep."

"And their heads were... absent?" Philbrook looked around as if imagining the scene as it was.

"Yes."

"You never found them?"

"No, but we did not look for long. Mr. Kennedy was impatient for us to be on our way."

"I imagine he was flustered at your discovery."

"Yes, Ensign. Quite flustered. We all were, but Kennedy the most." She was surprise and impressed that Philbrook had figured this out after meeting only briefly with Kennedy back in Detroit.

"Could you tell me again how they had been killed?" he asked.

"Brutally," she answered. "One had an arrow in his back. Others had some cuts and gashes on their bodies, like they'd been attacked with blades of some sort. Stone had a gaping wound in his chest, likely from a spear thrust, as well as several other wounds that might have killed him."

"Interesting. Any sign of them being shot with a gun?"

"Not that I saw." Unpleasant memories were coming back. Marguerite pulled out her pipe, hoping that a smoke might comfort her. She filled it from her pouch and lit it with a flint and steel and a bit of char cloth from her kit.

"Mr. Jacobs gave me this list of names," Philbrook said, drawing a notebook out of his waistcoat pocket. "The men he put together for Mr. Stone's voyage—there are six besides Stone. I'd like to establish if they are indeed the ones whose bodies you discovered. Were any of the canoemen with us now here when you discovered the scene?"

"Just Joseph. The others had no desire to return here so soon after what they saw." She took a deep draw on her pipe then blew out a thick cloud of smoke.

"*Monsieur* Papan," Philbrook called over to where the foreman was tending to the canoes with the Bourassas, "could you please join us when you are done with what you are doing?"

While they waited, they took the opportunity to look around. Brutus was running around smelling everything with his massive nose. The dog seemed to find this place exciting. Marguerite thought she could still smell death hanging in the air. She wanted to leave, but she knew they had to stay to let the ensign investigate, no matter how unpleasant that might be. They looked around the fire where Stone had met his end. Near a small pile of wood sat a pot, sitting upright over the remains of a fire, filled to the brim with rainwater and coffee grounds. A tin cup, of the sort called a pannikin lay on its side near a sticky dark patch of dirt crawling with ants. Stone's blood was a boon to the local insect population it seemed.

They wandered over to the remains of a tent nearby. It was torn apart and partially collapsed—its surface covered in recently-fallen pine needles. Bloodstained wool blankets lay inside.

"I'm trying to imagine the scene when these men were killed," said Philbrook. "I'm picturing nighttime while the men slept. Presumably, some group of people came out of the woods, or landed in boats, crept up, and surprised them out of their slumbers."

"Yes, it certainly happened at night. That is how the men were dressed, all except Mr. Stone. Some were killed outright, I think," said Marguerite. "I think others put up a brief fight. I assume they were roused out of sleep."

"Yes, and the heads were hacked off after death, I presume," said Philbrook. "But for what purpose?"

"I really do not know," said Marguerite. "It is not a practice I've ever heard of before."

"Ensign?" Joseph Papan approached.

"Did you know the men found here?" Philbrook asked the guide in French.

Papan looked down at the torn canvas. His face was ashen, and he crossed himself. "*Oui, je l'ai fait*. Baptiste and Pierre Beaulieu. This is their tent, sewn by their *mère*. And I recognized their clothes when we found them."

"Just the two of them?"

"*Oui*, Monsieur."

"What can you tell me about them?"

"They were good boys, strong canoemen. Their father was a friend of mine."

Philbrook made a mark in his notebook. They walked over to a small clearing where more ripped canvas was strewn around.

"And what did you find here?"

"Lucien Tremblay, my sister's boy. And his friend Barthelemy Bruno. Those two always worked together. Did everything together ever since they were little ones. Pero was here as well."

"Pero?"

"That's is what he was called. I never learned his proper name. Moved up from Quebec not long ago."

"And you are certain the bodies you buried were theirs, even in the condition you found them?"

"*Oui,* Ensign. It was them."

"Anything remarkable about them?"

"Lucien, my nephew, was a smart lad. I figured he would do well in life. Barthelemy was a bit wild but well-meaning. The war with the British was a little harder on him than the others."

"He was a soldier?"

"Oh, yes. We all went down to fight when the governor asked for recruits."

"In the *Canadien* militia?"

"*Oui.* I'm not sure about Pero. He certainly fought, for he bore the scars, but I did not know him then."

"What sort of scars?" asked Philbrook.

"Awful ones," said Papan. "Pero was badly burned, so much that he was hard to look at. The story I heard was that he was manning some artillery in the defense of Quebec when one overheated and exploded in his face. He lost his tongue and had burns all over his face. He couldn't speak in anything more than grunts. But he was a strong paddler. The boys all got used to him after a while."

"And he arrived in Detroit after the war?"

"*C'est vrai.*"

"*Merci, Monsieur* Papan." Philbrook made marks next to their names in his notebook. "Mr. Jacobs has assured me that he hired six men to accompany. One appears to be unaccounted for. Louis Ouellette—what do you know of him?"

"I was reminded back in Detroit that Louis was with this party, but we saw no sign of him. Maybe he got away," Papan offered.

Marguerite realized that she too had forgotten about Louis Ouellette in the excitement of finding the murdered men. He was a nice young man, she remembered, younger than the other paddlers.

"Perhaps he is the one responsible for all this," Philbrook suggested. "He could have killed his companions as they slept, then made off into the forest." He wrote a question mark next to Ouellette's name in his notebook. Marguerite thought this unlikely, but refrained from speaking while the ensign was questioning Joseph.

"Tell me about Ouellette," said Philbrook.

"The Bourassa boys would know more," said Papan, "but from what I could tell, he was a hard-working lad. He was *métis*. His mother is a Menomonie from La Baye and his father was a French soldier who died in the war. He came to Detroit about a year ago and began working for the traders. He worked some with

70

Marguerite's brothers, Antoine and Marceau. They liked him well enough, though they said he was a little strange."

"Strange? In what way?" asked Philbrook.

"Well, I can't remember whether it was Antoine or Marceau who told me Louis used to walk and talk in his sleep. One time, when they were camped up near Saginaw Bay, he got up and walked into the woods in the middle of the night. The boys found him at dawn curled up, sleeping under a tree about a hundred yards from the camp. He couldn't remember how he got there."

"A somnambulist then?"

"*C'est vrai*," said Papan. "And Antoine said when Louis talked in his sleep it was always mumbled in Menomonie, his mother's tongue. They couldn't understand more than a word here or there."

"Marguerite?" Philbrook looked to her.

"Yes, Antoine told me that about the sleepwalking as well. I knew Louis a little. He was a nice gentle boy, or perhaps a man, but he seemed boyish to me."

"Did either of you notice earlier that Louis was not here?"

"*Non, Monsieur*," said Papan. "I mean, I saw he was not here, but did not recall that he should have been until later."

"With all the horror of finding the scene, I forgot about Louis too," Marguerite said.

"Tell me, *Monsieur* Papan, do you think Louis was the kind of person who could have done all this, maybe if he was in drink?"

Papan looked up, surprised. "I've seen plenty of drunken brawls in my time, *Monsieur*, some fatal, but I've never seen a drunk who could kill six men on his own and walk away with their heads. I don't see how anyone would be capable of all this, sir. Except maybe in wartime."

Philbrook shook his head. "No, neither do I. It seems like too much violence for one man alone."

"I can't see Louis doing such a thing either. He did not seem like a violent man," Marguerite added.

Sergeant Graham approached and announced that he and his men had collected several personal items belonging to the deceased, found among the bedrolls. He put these in the care of Jacobs, so that they could be returned to Detroit in his batteau and given to the families. He had prepared a list: Besides clothes and the blankets, all of the men had carried knives, while some had strings of rosary beads. Most had clay pipes and pouches of tobacco. There was a small French Bible that Papan said had belonged to Lucien Tremblay, who, unlike the others, was a proficient reader.

"His mother had hoped he might go down to Quebec and study for the priesthood, but he liked girls too much," explained Papan.

There were a few coins, which Philbrook wrapped to be distributed among the victims' families. They also gathered up Stone's belongings. As he had no local relations, the ensign instructed that they be packed and given to Jacobs, who would send them down to Albany, where his suppliers would know where to send them.

"And, sir, Smyth found this near the edge of the woods." Graham held up a tomahawk with a forged metal head and what looked like dried blood on it, mounted on a hand-carved wooden handle decorated with strips of deerskin and feathers.

"Interesting. And what does this tell you, Sergeant Graham?" asked Philbrook.

"I suppose it means that Indians did this, but I'm not sure that was ever in doubt." Marguerite thought this a rather hasty conclusion, but she refrained from speaking up.

"It certainly looks that way, Sergeant," said Philbrook. "*Monsieur* Papan, what can you tell me about a tomahawk like this? The different tribes decorate their tomahawks in unique ways do they not?"

"*C'est ça,*" answered Papan, "that one looks Ojibwa to me."

"The heads are forged by French and British blacksmiths," Marguerite added. "Some are made in the east and carried up, while others are crafted in Niagara and Detroit. Natives carve the handles and decorate them how they like. I think that one could have belonged to any of the local people. Or it could even have belonged to one of the men killed. Tomahawks are not confined to Indians around here, as they are handy tools in the forest."

"Interesting." Philbrook nodded to Marguerite, then turned back to Graham. "Sergeant, if you could have a man clean that off and put it with my personal things." He then called to Jacobs who was examining a pile of packs, "Have you gathered everything you need?"

"Almost," answered Jacobs. "Whoever did this ripped some of the packs apart, but it does not look like anyone took much of anything. We've repacked it all well enough to get back down the river. I expect this haul will cover Ben's debts and then some."

"As you've probably guessed, I will be going the rest of the way up the river to talk with the people at Kekionga. I'm going to write a quick note to Captain Turnbull to send back with you. Then, when you are ready, you might as well head off. But keep an eye out. There could be a hostile party out there. You told me that Louis Ouellette was with this group, but his body was not found here. Whether he is alive or dead remains unknown."

Marguerite thought she saw a look of fear pass in Jacobs's eyes before he composed himself. She knew he did not spend much time outside of Detroit's gates and seldom interacted with Natives on their own land. His group would be a small one heading back, so perhaps his fear was justified. There was a murderer out there, after all.

Chapter 9

Marguerite Boyer

They camped several miles upriver that evening, not wanting to spend the night at Auglaize so soon after the horror that had occurred there. After supper, Marguerite took a seat by her dying fire to enjoy her pipe. Philbrook approached with his gigantic dog. She was getting used to the dog now, since the beast seemed to like her. At least she assumed that his habit of gently licking and chewing on her as he looked up with his big brown doe eyes was a sign of affection. The dog was ridiculous, of course, but she was open to making friends. If only there were a bit less saliva.

The ensign sat down next to her, and Brutus settled nearby. As usual, he began with a question. The man was a veritable fountain of questions. But his tone was more relaxed than earlier in the day at Auglaize. "Tell me, Marguerite, what do you think of this business? Does any of it make sense to you? The missing canoeman, Louis. It all has me puzzled."

Marguerite thought quietly for a time, and Philbrook began to show discomfort at the silence before she finally answered, "I did not know Louis well since he was brought up elsewhere. We never went on any trading voyages together. But, from what I heard, he was a pleasant young man. Friendly. Gentle. Not long ago my brother engaged him for a trip to La Baye. Marceau said he would hire him again, since he had a strong rhythmic paddle stroke and a nice singing voice. The other men all liked working with him."

"Sometimes good people do bad things," said Philbrook.

She nodded and thought fleetingly of her father. Most of the time he had been a very gentle man, but then sometimes not. "Men have moments of anger that make them do awful things," she told him after a long pause, "but those poor men back at the site—that was not the result of a momentary lapse of control or a drunken fight. I think they were killed deliberately, with forethought and cunning."

"Why?" asked Philbrook. This was not a challenge. She could tell by the way he looked at her that the ensign was genuinely interested in hearing her opinion.

"For one thing, the attackers killed six men but don't appear to have suffered any injury in return. We saw no sign of anyone fighting back. They were taken by surprise, and that takes planning. And there must be a reason for the heads being taken. I don't know what it is, but the killers had a reason."

"You may prove right. But it is certainly possible that Louis became angry with his companions for some reason. Everyone loses their temper sometimes. If he was stealthy, he could have killed them each in turn as they slept. Some of the wounds that you described suggest the men tried to defend themselves—the slash marks on their arms." He touched one of his forearms. "A few were awake at the end at least, but perhaps they were groggy and confused from being suddenly woken."

Marguerite shook her head. The ensign had put no conviction into his words. It was almost as if he were inviting her to contradict him so he could rule out the possibility. "I doubt anyone could have done that alone, Ensign, and angry men are seldom stealthy. No, I think the whole thing was planned and committed by several people." Brutus had been inching closer to her as they spoke, and now he began to wrap his wet mouth around her foot.

"Brutus, stop chewing on Marguerite!" said Philbrook. "I'm afraid my dog has taken to you. He means no harm." Brutus ignored him and continued to seek her attention. Philbrook continued. "Your observations are quite correct. I share your doubts, and I'm almost ready to rule out anyone acting alone. But we might also consider that Louis is a somnambulist—a sleepwalker."

She moved her foot away from the dog, but he followed after it. "Yes, I'd heard that, but what does that matter?"

"Perhaps the sleepwalking is a sign that there was something wrong with his mind. The nighttime affected him in unusual ways. Consider the people we call *lunatics*, from the Latin 'moonstruck.' It occurred to me that if these men were killed two nights prior to your arrival on the scene, that was the night of the full moon, right?"

"Yes?"

"Perhaps Louis's personality is adversely affected by the phases of the moon." Philbrook gestured to the sky. A quarter moon was up already, though the sun had not set.

She looked at Philbrook wide-eyed. "Is that what you are going to report to Captain Turnbull, that you think Louis killed those men because of the moon?"

"The theory of a lunar influence on human behavior is not without its supporters, Marguerite." He smiled, looking a bit sheepish, suggesting that he was not entirely serious. "Shakespeare wrote, *'She comes more near the Earth than she was wont. And makes men mad.'*"

"If you say so." She did not know if the ensign expected her to laugh.

"But no, I doubt that the moon was the cause of these murders. I have a habit of running improbable ideas through my mind as a sort of intellectual exercise. Then sometimes I speak the theory aloud to help me to evaluate its worth. Perhaps I can set the role of the moon aside. In truth, I think it most likely that Louis was a victim. He may have been killed and his body disposed of somehow, or perhaps he ran off and hid when the attack began. Or maybe he ran off injured and died in the forest somewhere. There are many possibilities, some more plausible than others, but as yet, I hesitate to dismiss any. Even improbable ones such as the role of the moon."

She nodded but said nothing. The ensign was a strange one, but some of the canoemen had already spoken of the full moon that night, though they had not quoted Shakespeare. An English taste she supposed. No, the men had made reference to tales they had learned in their youth of beasts that come out when the moon is full.

"I give my imagination free rein sometimes," he said, "but, in the end, I think it better to try to follow the teachings of the new European philosophers in our approach and stick closely to reason and evidence."

"I don't know much about philosophers, Ensign."

"I can find myself torn between my imagination and demonstrable facts. Reason and fancy. One needs to speculate sometimes to connect discreet facts, yet at the same time our imaginations can swiftly lead us astray. It can expose us to our own deep prejudices and assumptions."

She thought of Sam Kennedy and his conviction that the Potawatomie were responsible for the murders. "True," she said. Her pipe had gone out, so she reached for a smoldering branch from the dying fire to relight it.

"I like to think of the imagination as the glue that holds evidence together. We need to keep on collecting facts about these killings, then summon up the right adhesive that binds them together." Philbrook looked down for a moment, then he resumed on a different track. "Joseph Papan and you have both mentioned your brothers. They are guides and interpreters, too?"

"Yes. I suppose you could say it is the family business." She was surprised at his interest in her family.

"Trade is the business of my family as well, though ours is mostly by sea," he said. "I take it your mother is in charge."

"Yes, me and my brothers all work at *Maman's* direction."

"And your father?"

"He died several years ago." She took a long draw from her pipe and continued. "He was a trader too."

"I'm sorry."

The sun was slowly approaching the horizon, and the temperature was dropping, so Marguerite pulled her blanket around herself.

"I still see kin from my father's side. His father was French, but his mother's people were Seneca and Delaware. *Maman* and *Papa* both have family ties all over, so my brothers and I have cousins in most communities around here. It gives us an advantage."

"Interesting. It is not so different with my family. We are from Portsmouth, a seacoast town in the colony of New Hampshire. When my father wants British dry goods, he writes to my uncle, who now lives in London. And we have cousins living in the West Indies with whom we often trade lumber and livestock in exchange for molasses and rum."

"But you chose not to become a merchant yourself?"

"I have clerked for my father and for my uncle and will probably venture into the family trade again when my time in the army is done. If you don't mind me asking, is the business good for your family and the other *Canadien* traders since the fighting ended?"

"Thanks to my mother, it is for us. She has a better head for accounts than Father did or most of the other local traders do." She brought her pipe to her lips.

"She is supplied from Montreal still?"

"A little, but that's not where our main profits lie. She is too smart to try to compete with British merchants. They have sources of capital that are closed to us. Instead, she works with traders who bring their own cargos to Detroit, providing local knowledge, guides, interpreters, canoes. My father never would have done that. He hated the British too much to work with them. But my mother understands that the British have all the connections among the bigger firms in New York and Montreal, while we know people in the villages. My brothers and I do most of the guiding and interpreting. We hire the canoemen and direct trading."

"Your mother sounds like a smart merchant. I would like to become better acquainted with her when we return."

Marguerite was surprised. Everyone in Detroit got to know her mother eventually, but she had not expected Ensign Philbrook to take much interest. But perhaps she should have guessed, for the one thing about him that was most striking was his unbridled curiosity about everything.

"I will introduce you again when we get back, Ensign." She thought for a moment, then asked, "What made you leave your family business and enter the army? Most men I know proceed the other way around—leave the army to embark in trade."

He looked down and did not respond right away. She feared that she had asked too personal of a question. "I had some personal difficulties in London, where I recently clerked for my uncle, so it was a good time to seek a change in scenery. I considered going to sea, perhaps as supercargo on one of his vessels, but then this opportunity arose through his connections in London. I always wanted to see the Upper Country ever since the war ended, and this seemed the best way to do it."

Philbrook looked unhappy as he said this. She thought to ask why but decided against venturing into what seemed a sensitive area.

"And what do you think of the *pays d'en haut* so far, *Monsieur*?"

"This voyage is a wonder to me." His face lit up in a way she had not seen before. "I love its wildness. It is nature at its most beautiful and elemental. I know it has only been a few days, but each day I've experienced fresh sights and smells to feed my soul and make me excited to be alive again. Though the brutality that brought about our present task is distressing."

"Yes, it is."

"Ever since I was a child," Philbrook continued, "I've read anything I could find about the interior parts of this continent. The early journeys across the Appalachians and to the Great Lakes fascinated me. When I served in the provincial army—and came as far as Niagara—I began to daydream of venturing farther west. Exploring. There are those who think there is a river or a strait not too far west of here that leads to the South Sea."

"The Straits of Anian?"

"You've heard of it?" Philbrook looked excited.

"Yes, of course I've heard talk. Everyone has heard talk, but nothing ever comes of it. I think the Western Sea is farther away than your philosophers believe."

"There was much discussion of it and other theories of the Northwest Passage in London and at home in Portsmouth. There are those who hope to find an easier pathway to the Orient. Trade with those far-off lands can be profitable, but it remains quite expensive and risky to outfit ships to venture around the southern reaches of Africa or South America. A more direct route to the riches of China could make many fortunes."

The story was familiar to her. It had led to too much wasted effort and needless suffering. It was unfortunate that so many who came to her part of the world were driven to discover somewhere else, but she was not about to tell Philbrook that.

Instead, she asked, "And you hope to make your fortune?"

"I long to explore and make discoveries. And if a fortune comes from them, all the better. I have a curious mind, so show me a puzzle, and I cannot help but look for an answer. To travel across this land observing nature and making discoveries is a dream of mine."

"I hope you get what you want, Ensign. But before you

discover the South Sea, it seems that you will first have to discover who killed Ben Stone and his men."

"Yes indeed. One step at a time."

LATER, as she lay under her wool blanket, she thought again of her family. She was struck by the ensign comparing his family to hers. It had not occurred to her that her mother, brothers, and she had much of anything in common with the flock of men who came to the *pays d'en haut* from away. Detroit was her home, but she knew it was not like other towns. People came and went in a way that was different from other places.

When she was a girl and the French soldiers held the fort, life was stable. Or at least it seemed that way to her. Their *Canadien* neighbors were settled in, and the surrounding Native villages had put down roots. But still restless people moved on, looking for furs, or looking for faster routes to get somewhere else. Indians from the north and the west came in summertime, along with the French traders up from Montreal. French soldiers and officers served out a few years at the fort before departing. Detroit had always been a place where more people were just passing through than actually lived there as she did.

The war brought changes.

The French soldiers left. The Ottawa and Miami villages moved further away. Men and boys who went east to fight never came back. Then the British arrived. First Major Rogers and his men, followed by a succession of haughty officers and sickly soldiers. The year of Pontiac's siege further traumatized a community already wounded by a war that had previously been waged only to the east. The Boyer family persevered through this time, thanks to her mother.

They persevered because they never stood still. Detroit was the family's home, but, in many ways, it was only one small room in a much larger mansion, for the Boyers were at home as far east as Niagara and as far north as Sault St. Marie. They were at home at La Baye, Kekionga, Sandusky, and St. Joseph. At least they were if one considered home the place where everyone knew you and you had kin.

Marguerite had never thought of someone like Ensign Philbrook as having kin. The British were people from away, rootless people from England, Scotland, Ireland, and the English-speaking colonies, without homes, who came to take hers. Perhaps that was something that she simply assumed but did not really know, just as she assumed what Philbrook was like based on his Britishness and his inexperience. She resolved then to try to know him better.

Chapter 10

The Dreamer

Their flesh was almost gone now. Only bone, hair, and gristle remained, so they spoke to the Dreamer less often than they had. He was not really sure how the voices entered his head at this point. At first, they had spoken to him when he was awake, and he had heard with his ears, but now it seemed as if their conversation was inside his mind. But they were real. He knew they were real.

The buzzards did not visit anymore, but the mice and other little creatures came to gnaw. The ants came in a thin line that stretched off into leaves. They took turns crawling into the eye sockets and the mouths. He tried to catch the mice, but they were too quick for him, so he ate some of the ants. They were hard to swallow, for they clung unpleasantly to his throat on the way down.

The Dreamer raised his head from the moist earth and pushed himself onto his hands and knees. He was weak now, very weak, and he had not seen a juicy, crunchy beetle in a long time. His companions told him he did not need his body anymore. No need to feed it, for he was not a man anymore. Soon, he would be a specter like them. His body could sink into the earth and his soul would journey to the spirit world.

But his flesh objected. Physical weakness sent thoughts into his mind. Unwelcome desires. Sometimes, he thought about gnawing on one of the stinking skulls as the mice did. There was skin and brain and perhaps a little meat left over. Something to subdue the stomach's cravings at least. But those were bad thoughts. He shouldn't entertain such notions.

He felt a new presence. He sensed that he was no longer alone in the physical world. He looked up and saw the turtle about ten feet away. A large snapping turtle with a dark green shell as long as his forearm stared at him. Its rough skin and shell were glistening wet, as if it had just emerged from the river. Its legs were extended, and it had long claws that scratched at the earth in four directions. Its leathery neck was stretched out toward him, and its eyes had a look of curiosity.

The Dreamer thought that he might like to eat it.

"*Posoh*, child," said the turtle. "You would like to eat me?"

The turtle could speak. Why had he not expected that?

"Yes," he replied. He had trouble meeting the turtle's eye as he admitted this.

"Maybe later," said the turtle, "but we should talk first. We should get to know one another. I want to be sure you are not going to choose the Windigo path afterward. I don't keep company with that sort."

The man thought a moment. He was indeed a man, not just a dreamer. He had forgotten that. His companions had told him that he had become a ghost, an ethereal wisp, but now he was doubting them. Or was the turtle a dream—maybe a vision?

"Your companions are dead," said the turtle. "Bad men killed them as they slept. They know that you are still alive, and the knowledge makes them jealous. They feed lies into your thoughts and dreams. If you keep listening to them, you may succumb to the Windigo way. From that there is no coming back."

"Who are you? Why do you speak to me?"

"You can call me Makinag," said the turtle. "Think of me as your guardian."

The Dreamer thought a minute. "I did not think I could have a guardian." He remembered some fragments of a past. "My father was a Christian and did not hold to such beliefs. When I grew up, I never fasted or sought a vision as my mother's people did. Father forbade it."

"Not all visions are planned or sought, child," said Makinag. "You are fasting and experiencing a vision now. Experiencing me. You have needed a proper vision since you became a man, but you were not aware of it. At least not in your waking mind. You wandered and searched for me as you slept, but you were too blind to find me or even to know what you searched for."

"How did I come to be here, Makinag?"

"What do you remember?"

"I remember being here. Talking and dreaming with my friends."

"Then I will tell you the rest." The turtle scratched its blunt nose with its left foreclaw. "One night, while your dream mind searched for me in the forest, men came to kill your companions. When you awoke in the forest, you tried to return to your camp but found a scene of violence. Do you remember that?"

"No, Makinag."

The turtle continued anyway, "You ran away, but the spirits of your companions called you to this place. You wandered for hours until you came to this grove where the bad men had disposed of the heads of their victims. Now their spirits want to keep you here with them. You remind them of life. They are not really your friends anymore, for the dead cannot truly befriend the living."

"They are my companions, my friends," insisted the Dreamer.

"As you wish, but the dead can be jealous of life. They enjoy seeing your body weaken, as it makes you more like them. Now you are so feeble and hungry that you think of chewing on your friends' bones. That would turn your heart to ice."

"I do not remember that. Why do I remember nothing of who I am?"

The turtle clawed the earth. "You will remember in time. Your soul was injured. But first you must leave this place of dreams and death and return to the world of men. You must begin to take care of your body so you can heal your spirit. Do you think you can manage that?"

The Dreamer tried to lift himself, but his efforts were labored. His body hurt. "I feel weak," he said. "Where am I?"

"You are not far from the river, and there will be hunters passing soon. You must slice my flesh with your knife. First, drink my blood, then as the strength returns to your body, you must eat my flesh a little bit at a time."

The Dreamer's mouth watered at the thought. "I have always liked turtle meat," he said not sure if that was a polite thing to say.

"Thank you," said Makinag.

"Thank you," said the Dreamer.

Chapter 11

Marguerite Boyer

Upstream from the Auglaize junction, the Maumee River began to meander. The canoes were constantly forced to turn. One minute, they would point north, then east for a time, and then south a few minutes later, even though, at the end of the day, the river led them west. Frequently, an *avant* paddler in the bow of the lead canoe had to shout back directions to avoid rocks or sunken branches in their path. Trees overhung the water, and fallen ones sometimes blocked off the channel and had to be cut out with an ax. Marguerite always liked this stretch of river. It made her imagine a long-ago flood—perhaps the flood the Catholic priests spoke of when the wise man Noah built a boat for all the animals.

Or perhaps it was the flood from Anishinaabe stories when Muskrat had to swim down to the bottom of the ocean for mud to rebuild the world on Turtle's back.

Signs of past floodwaters were all around. The current ran through a valley between steep ridges that were often set two or three hundred yards back from the present-day river channel but parallel to it, as if raging waters had once carved out the valley. Sometimes, the river would run close to the ridge on one side, creating a steep embankment directly next to the water, but when that happened, the opposite bank would be flat floodplain.

Evidence of habitation and agriculture could be seen all along the fertile bottomland. They passed gardens of corn, beans, and squash. They saw bark lodges, wooden racks for smoking and drying fish and meats, and other signs of the communities that called the river home. A few people, seeing the canoes, came down to the water's edge looking to trade, but when they found soldiers on army business, they went back to what they had been doing.

In the evening, when the day's travel was done, Marguerite was enjoying tea and a smoke with the Bourassa cousins—Jean, Vince, and Luc-Marie—when Philbrook approached. They sat by the remains of the cooking fire, which they kept alive with scraps of wood. The smoke helped to keep at bay the mosquitos that became more active in the evening.

"*Bonsoir*," Philbrook said.

The men looked up with surprise at the ensign's approach, for he had not spoken more than a few words to them since their journey began, but Marguerite was becoming used to the ensign's ways.

"*Monsieur*?" replied Jean. The others nodded an acknowledgement.

"Mind if I sit with you a bit? I wanted to ask your opinion on some things." The ensign spoke to them in simple French. Marguerite was glad that she did not have to interpret. The ensign's French was tolerable and served well when he kept his sentences short, but he was hardly fluent.

"Of course, Ensign," offered Jean. "Please join us."

Philbrook sat down cross-legged on the ground.

"Monsieur Papan tells me that you three know Louis Ouellette," he began, "that you have worked with him in the past?"

"*Oui, monsieur.*"

"What is he like?"

"Well," replied Jean, "he is no murderer, if that's what you're

getting at. Louis doesn't have a mean or violent bone in his body."
Vince and Luc-Marie nodded in agreement.

"He's a gentle lad," added Vince. "He's very friendly. Seems to like everyone. Everyone likes him back."

"How well did you really know him, though?" Philbrook asked. "I thought he had just moved from La Baye."

"Oh, we know him well enough. He came to Detroit more than a year back," said Jean.

"Closer to two," corrected Vince.

"And we all have taken voyages with him," said Luc-Marie. "When you head out to trade in the backcountry villages, you spend all your time with the other fellows. We paddle together during to the day, eat together, sleep together. A few weeks of that, and you know a man better than you want to."

"Not unlike comrades during wartime, I suppose," Philbrook said. "Did any of you know him to sleepwalk at night?"

The men laughed. "That was no big deal," said Vince. "We used to joke about it when I worked with him. Every so often, we would wake up and Louis would be sleeping in the wrong place. One morning, we found Louis in Marceau Boyer's tent, nestled between Marceau and his girl. Marceau was the boss, you see. Must have crawled in there without waking anyone—not even himself. Ha. Marceau threw him out on his arse but with a laugh. Other times, we'd find him under a tree or snuggled next to a rock a short distance from the camp, sound asleep."

"Louis told us he had been doing it for years," added Jean. "He would mumble in his sleep too, but lots of folks do that."

"You wouldn't call him strange?"

"Not really," said Luc-Marie. "Colorful, maybe, but you need to be colorful to be a *voyageur*." The cousins all laughed.

Philbrook laughed with them. Marguerite reflected that the ensign was doing an excellent job putting the men at ease.

He paused for a moment, then asked, "Did any of you know

Mr. Stone at all? Anything you could tell me about what kind of employer he was?"

"He was *Anglais*," observed Vince.

"The ensign knows that, *imbécile*," chided Jean.

"None of us ever worked with him," added Luc-Marie. "And most of the *Anglais* don't take the time to get to know local men. They come and go too quickly. And they see us merely as laborers, not so much as people." The others nodded in agreement.

"I see," said Philbrook. "And I did not get the chance to ask you before, back in Pontiac's village, did you get the sense the people there knew anything of these killings?"

"Nothing," said Jean. "I'm sure the Ottawa there had nothing to do with it. They wouldn't hide it from us if they did. If someone among them had taken revenge for something, they would have boasted about it."

"Good to know," said Philbrook. "What about Alexis Cuillerier? Did you hear anything about him in the village?"

"*Non, monsieur*," said Jean, "nothing at all."

He looked Philbrook in the eye for just a moment before dropping his gaze. The other two both looked up at the treetop as if they saw something interesting up above. Marguerite saw that Jean and his cousins were hiding something but wasn't sure that the ensign could tell. Should she say something? No. She was disgusted by what Cuillerier had done, but it was just as well that he had run off. What the ensign did not know would not hurt him, and no purpose was served by Alexis Cuillerier rotting in a British gaol. His disappearance was best for all.

THEY TRAVELED upstream on a diminishing river for another day. It had been a good-sized river where it flowed into Lake Erie—large enough for any sort of small boat, but with every mile they traveled, the volume of water decreased until it was hardly navigable. As it was springtime, there was still enough water even in these upper reaches for the canoes, but Marguerite knew from experience that by mid-July, it would dry up, making boat travel more difficult. Even now a larger bateau would have trouble negotiating the turns.

"The canoe or bateau is best in the spring when we have cargo to move," she told Philbrook, "but later in the summer it is much faster to travel on foot or horseback. Trails follow the river and others lead anywhere one might want to go. Much of the land around here is swampy, but there are dry routes to follow if you know the way."

Soon, they came upon a cabin built on a dry bluff along the western riverbank. She caught the pungent odor of fish and saw wooden racks along shore with salted fillets laid out to dry.

"That's Cheney's place," she told Philbrook. "The British authorities don't like him living out here, but each time they make him leave, he just comes back again."

Fishing nets hung out to dry nearby, and an assortment of small boats and a few winter sleds were scattered about the clearing. Three dogs spotted their approach and let loose a cavalcade of barking, prompting a short man with a thick dark beard to come down to the river's edge.

"*Salut* Joseph, Marguerite, Vince." He nodded to the rest, giving a hostile look at Philbrook and the soldiers. After a pause, he decided to address Sergeant Graham. "What brings you up the river, Sergeant? Not going to run me off again I hope." He laughed at the idea.

"Don't worry, Alexis, we're on our way up to Kekionga," said Graham. "We're looking into something more important than a bunch of squatters. There were some killings at Auglaize." The paddlers pointed their canoes toward shore.

Philbrook cleared his throat. "Monsieur Cheney, I'm Ensign Philbrook. I don't suppose you've heard anything about men getting killed downstream from here a few of weeks back? The trader Ben Stone and his boatmen?"

"Killed, you say? That's the first I've heard of it," said Cheney. Marguerite was not convinced he was telling the truth.

"How many of you live here?" asked Philbrook, looking around at the humble settlement.

"Three men with families, Ensign. Minding our own business. None of us have been downriver in a month or more."

"Do you mind if we come up and talk a bit?"

Marguerite saw that Cheney was taken aback by the ensign's polite tone. "Not anything I can do about it," he said, eying Graham and the soldiers. "Suit yourself."

Philbrook climbed out of the canoe and up the riverbank, preceded by Brutus who went to greet the local dogs. The three of them eyed the giant beast with some awe before assuming submissive postures. The men and soldiers got out as well, tying off the canoes to a couple of trees.

"Pleased to meet you, Monsieur Cheney," Philbrook said politely, extending a hand to the suspicious-looking Frenchman. Cheney shook it after a moment's consideration.

"Do you know a boatman named Louis Ouellette?"

"Louis? Stone had a canoeman named Louis," said Cheney. "They stopped by on their way downriver. Gabbed about the weather for ten minutes or so, then they were on their way. Shame they were all killed."

"Not quite all," said Marguerite. "Louis is missing. You haven't seen him since then, have you, Alexis?"

"*Non,* Marguerite. There's been some Native hunters passing through, but besides that we've not had much excitement around here lately. You and Joseph were the last traders we've seen on the river. That was just a couple of days after Stone's group, right?"

"Would you mind showing me around your place a bit?" Philbrook asked.

"You ask politely, Ensign, but you know damned well you've

got a bunch of soldiers with guns behind you. It's not like I can say no, is it?" Cheney spat.

"I assure you, I do not intend to shoot anyone," Philbrook said.

Sergeant Graham came up brusquely with the soldier Thomas Bellows behind him. "But I might," he said with a grin. "Show some bloody respect to the officer, Cheney, before I teach you some manners. Bellows, Young, Smyth, search the buildings."

Cheney stepped back, losing his confrontational manner. Pointedly ignoring the sergeant, he turned back to Philbrook. "Yes, of course, *monsieur*, look around all you wish. We've nothing to hide." The other two men with Cheney glared at the soldiers. They were joined by several women, and a collection of unwashed children of various ages. "Can I offer you a drink, Ensign? Got a fine shrub mixed up."

"Perhaps some tea, Mr. Cheney?"

"Hmm. No tea around here, Ensign. I've got small beer."

"Small beer would be very refreshing, thank you."

"This is my brother, Rene, my cousin, Samuel, and the rest." He pointed to the assembled family. "Marguerite can vouch for us, we are simple people, trying to get by in the wilderness. We don't look for trouble."

"That's true," said Marguerite.

"Come on up to the house." Cheney led the way to a small, run-down log cabin, that most people might hesitate to describe as a house. "Get us a pitcher, Mags," he ordered one of the women as they approached. Mags ducked into the doorway and disappeared into the darkness within. "Let's sit out here where we got some light." Cheney sat on a stool next to an extinguished campfire and indicated similar seats for Philbrook and Marguerite. The women dispersed while the children stood at a safe distance and watched the visitors with their mouths agape. Graham and the soldiers, meanwhile, were looking into the outbuildings with an authoritarian efficiency.

Mags came out with a jug and several mismatched clay cups

and began to pour beer for her guests. "So that crew all got murdered, eh?" said Cheney. "I hadn't heard the Ottawa were riled up again. Is that who you think did it?"

"We don't know, *Monsieur* Cheney," Philbrook said. "Pontiac says not."

"Ha! I guess he would," said Cheney.

"You haven't heard anything?" asked Marguerite. "You're so close here to where it happened."

"No, Marguerite." Cheney shook his head. "We don't know anything about it."

Emerging from a shed, John Young called out. "Over here, Sergeant." Cheney shifted in his seat and pushed back his hair with his fingers.

"What do you think he has found, *monsieur*?" Philbrook asked. Marguerite noticed Cheney's discomfort.

Cheney shrugged.

"Ensign Philbrook, sir," Graham called over, "here's something you might want to see." Graham and Private Young were dragging out two packs. They were wrapped in canvas tied with hemp cord. "There's a couple more in there too, sir. Note the mark." Graham pointed to the initials BS on one.

"Can you explain to us how you came into possession of these, *Monsieur* Cheney?" Philbrook asked, dropping the friendlier tone of a moment before. "'BS' is Ben Stone's mark. Let's look inside, Sergeant." Graham took his knife and cut open a pack. It was full of woolen blankets tightly pressed together. He tried another and found it full of furs similarly packed.

"There's also a couple of kegs of rum in there with the same mark," said Graham.

"I came by these through fair trading," insisted Cheney. "A Frenchman can still trade in these parts, can't he? I often buy rum and blankets from the traders when they come through. I store it, then I sell the stuff to the Natives in the wintertime for higher prices when the traders aren't around."

Philbrook looked to Marguerite and Papan for confirmation. "What do you think?" he asked them. "Does that seem normal?"

Marguerite sensed that Cheney was lying. She shook her head. "There is some truth to what he said, but this is more rum and blankets than I think Cheney could afford. And it doesn't explain the furs. Folks around here should be selling furs, not buying." She felt some discomfort casting doubt on Cheney's words, for surviving in the backcountry as they did was not easy, but lives had been lost.

"What say you, *Monsieur* Cheney?" Philbrook pressed.

"Marguerite is right that I would not usually buy furs from a Detroit trader," said Cheney, glaring at her as if she had betrayed him, "but when Stone and his folks came through, they were just about out of provisions. I guess Stone had misjudged their supplies of food. They were having no luck hunting and risked getting hungry. I was able to take this pack off his hands in exchange for some green venison and enough corn to get them back to Detroit."

Papan laughed. "You're a shrewd trader, Alexis Cheney, but not that shrewd."

Philbrook looked questioningly at Marguerite, and she explained, "A whole pack of furs is too much to get for a few days' worth of provisions, no matter how in need Stone was. Besides, we'd seen Stone several days before and he wasn't that desperate."

"Just because I made a good deal doesn't make me guilty of anything," insisted Cheney. "I think they discovered that some of their provisions were unexpectedly spoiled. Anyway, furs change hands around here. So I traded with Stone. What of it? That's what traders do. No one can prove otherwise."

"Look here, sir," interrupted Graham. He bent over one of the packs. "If I'm not mistaken, this is blood." Marguerite saw a dark stain soaked into the canvas. Cheney began to back off, but Private Young leveled his musket. Meanwhile Bellows and Smyth had come over, carrying their muskets, surrounding the nervous *Canadiens*.

"I had a bloody nose," said Rene Cheney. The look in his eye told Marguerite that he did not expect to be believed.

"It's true," said their cousin Samuel.

Panic flared in Samuel Cheney's eyes, and without any other warning, he bolted towards the woods, but Graham tripped him up with a well-placed boot, sending him sprawling. The sergeant hauled him up with his arm pinned behind his back. "Well, it looks like we may have our culprits, sir."

Within minutes, the soldiers had bound the three Cheney men's arms behind their backs and sat them all down by the dead fire. The women protested, and the children watched with their mouths hanging open.

"I think you have some explaining to do, *Monsieur* Cheney," Philbrook said.

Marguerite relayed his words, for the Cheneys, in their distress, were having trouble with his French, adding, "Some of those boys were your relations, Alexis. What is this about? How could you do such a thing for a couple of packs?"

Cheney shook his head and pleaded. "We hurt no one, Marguerite, you must believe me. You must convince these Englishmen." He looked over to Papan as if he might be an ally. "You have to believe I'd never hurt those boys, Joseph," he pleaded. "British traders can be damned for all I care, but I'd never do such a thing to our own people."

"Then what happened?" Philbrook pressed.

"I found them," said Rene Cheney. "None of us hurt a soul, but I admit it. I came upon them."

"When?"

"The morning after they passed by. I went downriver with my wife in our canoe doing some fishing. We found them. All dead. Butchered. There was nothing we could do to help them, and I figured they didn't need the packs anymore. I threw as many as I could fit into my small canoe and brought them back here. The way I figure it, they were up for grabs, having been abandoned by their former owner." Marguerite thought she saw shame in his eyes. He had rationalized what he had done, but inside, she realized, he knew that stealing from murdered men was wrong.

"That is not the way things work, *monsieur*," Philbrook said. "Those packs do not belong to you. They must go toward paying Ben Stone's creditors."

Rene Cheney shrugged. "Maybe. I don't know British ways. The things looked abandoned to me. I didn't see any creditors laying claim."

"Listen carefully, you men," Philbrook said. "As far as I'm concerned you may or may not be guilty of murder. I don't know for sure. What I do know is that you are guilty of theft and of lying to a British officer, which are serious crimes." Marguerite sensed he was improvising, but realized that his severity was appropriate. "At the very least you will receive time in the stocks, as well as a few dozen lashes apiece, that is, if you do not hang for murder. Now tell me, if you did not kill those men, who did?"

"None of us have any idea," pleaded Alexis Cheney. "Rene came back and told us what he'd found. We all piled into a couple of canoes and went to look, but we left the rest of the packs and saw no sign of any perpetrator. Believe me, we cared nothing for Mr. Stone, but his men were friends of ours. We've spent most every hour since then wondering who or what might have done it."

"Why didn't you report the murders to the authorities?" Philbrook asked. "You could have been truthful with me from the start."

"Detroit's a long way off, Ensign," said Mags. She had quietly been watching the men's lies unravel, but now Marguerite saw that she was fed up, both with the men and Philbrook. "It's several days travel each way, and we needed to get our gardens planted. Do you think it is easy living out here, that we can just pick up and go to Detroit any time we want?" Mags's hands were at her hips and she stood with her feet planted firmly. This was a woman who had put up with enough. "The men shouldn't have lied to you. They should be ashamed of themselves for that, but we figured some traders would find the scene and report it, and we were right. Marguerite and Joseph came through soon after we got back, and we trusted them to report the incident. We never expected the army would care much about a parcel of dead traders, anyway. We never asked to be involved in this business." She glared at Philbrook for a moment then spat and turned and went into the cabin, ushering the children in behind her.

After hearing more of the Cheneys' protestations of innocence, Philbrook conferred with Marguerite and Graham. "Do you believe them?"

Graham shrugged. "These renegades generally just want to be left alone. They would know that killing a bunch of men a few miles from their place would bring trouble down on their heads."

"They are not bad men, Ensign," said Marguerite truthfully. "Don't let their obvious dislike of you and the British make you see them that way. They have families and want to live how they wish."

"But the evidence against them is damning," Philbrook pointed out. "And their behavior was unseemly, to say the least. They stole from murder victims."

"Sir, I've had some interaction with this bunch in the past few years," said Graham. "They're rascals alright. They don't like authority, especially British authority, and they'll pilfer or cheat anyone who gives them half a chance. Dead or alive. But what happened down at Auglaize seems a bit beyond their scope. I hate to say it, but I believe them. I still think this looks like the work of Indians or our missing canoeman."

"I agree about the Cheneys," said Marguerite. "Their explanation seems in keeping with what I know of them. They are thieves and cheats, if given the opportunity, but not murderers."

"Sergeant," Philbrook asked, "if we wanted to take them into custody, what would that entail?"

"Well, sir, I imagine that they would run off given half a chance. I think we'd have to give up going to the Miami villages."

"And miss meeting with Pacanne," said Philbrook.

"And you'd be leaving their wives and children behind to fend for themselves during the spring planting," added Marguerite.

"Yes, arrest seems to pose problems," Philbrook said. "I'm not sure I want to end our search for Louis Ouellette just yet. Not on suspicion alone. And I'd still like to visit the Miami. We might learn some things there. Sergeant, have the men load the stolen packs into our canoes while I talk to the Cheneys."

Marguerite interpreted as Philbrook told the nervous *Canadiens* that he would be reporting their thefts to Captain Turnbull. "I'm disappointed that you did not see fit to tell me the truth when I first asked," he lectured. "If you had reported these vile murders when you first discovered them, you would have saved us all a great deal of trouble. I hope what you finally revealed turns out to be the truth. If I find out you have continued to lie, make no mistake, I will be back."

"Yes, sir," said Alexis Cheney. "But, sir, if you could enquire of the captain as to the rights of salvage, I'd appreciate it. Living out here, well, if I find something in the woods, and nobody's about to claim it, seems like I should be able to keep it from going to waste."

"*Monsieur*, I think you are pressing your luck. Thank you for your time. If you hear anything helpful, please send word to Detroit." Philbrook called over to Billy Smyth to untie the men.

"I'll do that, sir," said Alexis Cheney.

As they pulled away, Philbrook asked Marguerite, "How do men with families survive out here? I didn't see much more than a garden and small field at the cabins."

"You can survive pretty well hunting, fishing, and planting a garden if you live simply, but Cheney and his relations do their share of trading, too. And Rene Cheney works as an interpreter sometimes when he needs cash."

"They said they had been run off in the past. Is that true?"

"Yes, Ensign."

"Why?" asked Philbrook.

"I believe the British think French folks like them rile up the Indians," said Marguerite. "It upsets the British sense of order."

"Do they?" asked Philbrook. "Do they rile up the Indians, that is?"

Marguerite shook her head. "Not so much. When the Indians want to get riled up, they can do it on their own well enough. They've got plenty of reasons without Cheney's input."

Chapter 12

Phineas Philbrook

Ensign Philbrook's legs were stiff from sitting for hours in the canoe when they arrived at their camping place on a level bottomland that stretched for several miles along the riverbank. A few hours of sunlight remained, so he decided to get his blood moving by taking a walk with Brutus. He told the others he planned to hunt, but he really just wanted to walk and think, maybe draw. There was so much he had learned and so much he had to reflect on.

"Let me send Billy with you, sir," suggested Graham. "It's not always safe to wander alone in these forests. Besides, he's very good at finding game."

"No, I think not, Sergeant. I won't go far, and I'll have Brutus with me."

He knew the sergeant was right, but he wanted time alone and was willing to take the risk. It could be tiring playing the officer in front of the men all the time. He craved solitude and quiet reflection to organize his thoughts and employ his imagination. His father had often accused him of being a daydreamer, as if it were a bad quality, a sign of laziness, but Philbrook found daydreams to be an essential part of thinking and learning.

He followed the riverbank upstream. There was a path parallel to the water, though he wasn't sure if it was made by human feet or by the paws of animals. As long as he kept the river to his right, he reasoned, he needn't worry about getting lost. Brutus, too, was happy to be out of the canoe. He ran about with his nose close to the ground investigating his new surroundings. A pair of chipmunks scolded him from the branches of an oak tree. He barked at them once, then paid them no more mind. Philbrook carried his fowling piece, so he kept a half-hearted eye out for birds. He had been trying to train Brutus to retrieve game, but he was too easily distracted. The dog flushed out some turkeys, but Philbrook refrained from firing. Maybe on the way back.

He thought of the Cheneys, trying to think up a situation in which they would be driven to kill. Living on the river, they surely saw travelers on a regular basis. Why follow this group to slaughter them? An argument, perhaps? Philbrook had trouble imagining a disagreement that could lead to such craven brutality. There would have to have been alcohol involved or something that inflamed the passions. He pictured a drinking party devolving into an altercation, but no, that did not fit the evidence he had.

All the men besides Stone looked to have been killed as they slept by someone who approached with stealth. Drunks were seldom good at stealth. Perhaps disagreement earlier at the Cheney place? Maybe the Cheneys followed them, waiting for an opportunity. But no. Passions would have cooled in that time. Philbrook had no trouble imagining the Cheneys as opportunistic thieves but not as remorseless killers who stalked their victims and made off with their heads. The story they told seemed more plausible than any alternative that he could conger in his mind.

Brutus caught a new scent. Philbrook could see him getting excited as he huffed air through his nostrils. The dog circled, then turned toward a patch of thick underbrush, perhaps following the trail of a dear. His hair stood up along his back as he pawed at a spot on the ground. Philbrook noticed a dark pile of bear droppings in his path, thick with half-digested berries.

"Brutus, come," he commanded, but the dog ignored him.

Brutus had never seen a black bear before. Would he know enough to stay out of reach of its claws? Probably not, for he had never encountered an animal capable of besting him. Indeed, he had never met a wild creature who did not run from him.

"Brutus, stay," he called, but again he was ignored.

The bear would run away, of course. At least he thought it should. Bears were only aggressive when cornered or surprised. He followed Brutus into the thicker brush, making ample noise to scare away any unseen creature. He heard Brutus growling ahead. He got past a wall of brush and saw the dog approaching an opening at the base of a large tree.

"Brutus, no. Come here, Brutus."

As Brutus plunged forward to gratify his curiosity about this wonderful new scent, Philbrook heard a growl coming from within the den and saw a shining black nose, brown snout, and face of thick black fur emerge, followed by the body of the largest bear he had ever seen. It moved with surprising rapidity for something of its bulk, pulling itself forward with strong shoulders and going straight for the dog who had invaded its home. Behind her stumbled two small cubs, excited and curious to see the action.

Brutus stopped in his tracks, backed off, and then quickly circled, barking at his new foe. The bear stopped and stood up on her hind legs, sniffing at the air and evaluating the intruders. Philbrook froze. He knew he had gotten too close. He had his fowling piece in hand but knew that its pellets could accomplish little but to further anger this beast. Brutus was quick on his feet and kept circling just out of range of his adversary, sniffing excitedly. The dog was fast when he wanted to be, but Philbrook doubted his own ability to get out of the way should the bear turn toward him. She dropped back down on all fours and swung her head back and forth, sniffing at the dog, evaluating its capabilities. Her hackles were up, as were Brutus's.

One of the cubs saw Philbrook and began to walk toward him. The other cub followed her brother. He took a quiet step back, but this only served to draw the mother bear's attention. She turned and approached Philbrook, growling, swinging her head low to the ground. Brutus, now on her opposite side, nipped at her back legs, causing her to turn as he jumped away. He could see no way of getting out of this situation. The mother was protecting her cubs, who continued to advance toward him. She was wary of Brutus, for she surely had never seen anything like him, but her caution would wear off in time.

The bear turned back to Philbrook, put her head down, and charged. He stepped back, leveled his shotgun and fired desperately to no effect. He took another frantic step back before falling as she bore down on him. He had just enough time to roll himself into a ball and cover his head with his arms before the animal was on top of him. Brutus barked and growled, gallantly coming to his defense, then a deep primal growl sounded near his ear, accompanied by hot fetid breath. A great weight crushed down on him. Philbrook stupidly recalled Sergeant Graham's advice to bring Billy Smyth along with his musket. Then, a hard blow hit him in the shoulder, and he heard the fabric of his jacket ripping. Brutus's barking was now constant. The men in their camp would hear and know something was wrong, but by the time they got there, it would be too late.

Then, there was another cry. The whoops of men. The weight of the bear eased off, and he peered up between his arms and saw that the shafts of several arrows now protruded from her muscular shoulders. She swatted at the annoyance, then stepped away and stood, looking for the cause of this interruption. Brutus jumped over and took up a protective station above Philbrook, showing his teeth to the beast with a continuous growl. Three men came into view, dressed in breechcloths and deerskin leggings but bare and tattooed above the waist. All were brandishing long spears, having set aside their bows. Arrows could wound, but the larger blade of a spear could kill more efficiently.

"Ha!" one shouted, jabbing the tip of his spear at the bear. The others circled and did the same. The bear roared in anger and fear at this new assault. She swatted at the spears in turn, but, as she turned, she opened herself up to attack from behind.

The hunters did not hurry to strike a death blow but jabbed repeatedly from every direction, inflicting small wounds when the opportunity came, drawing blood, and wearing her down. She roared and growled and slapped at the offending spears, constantly forced to turn from one adversary to another. Philbrook saw she was tiring.

Brutus barked, but Philbrook clung to his collar now and kept him out of the fray. He watched the hunt with fascination mixing with relief. He checked his body for wounds and found his uniform badly ripped and his shoulder battered, but otherwise he was unharmed. The battle was winding down, finally ending as the youngest-looking hunter jabbed his spear deftly into the exhausted bear's throat, hitting the vital artery. He twisted the shaft as blood spurted, and she collapsed as all her life bled out.

The three hunters let out a whoop then relaxed to congratulate one another. Philbrook stood and brushed himself off, trying to think of the Native words of greeting that Marguerite had tried to teach him. "*Ahneen*,' he tried tentatively.

"*Ahya*," said the young man who had delivered the death blow. Then, much to Philbrook's surprise, continued in excellent French, "That is the largest dog I have ever seen, *mon ami*. Until we saw you, we thought it was two bears fighting." He laughed, looking to his companions for affirmation as he repeated his observation in his own language. The hunter looked to be about sixteen years old, handsome and fully grown, but with a youthful appearance. In the Native fashion he had shaved most of the hair from his head, except for a small patch on top, and he sported tattoos above and behind his ears, one of which displayed a silver ring.

"This is Brutus. He is a Danish dog, not used to bears. And I am Ensign Phineas Philbrook."

"*Bonjour* Ensign," the youth smiled. "Surely you are not traveling alone?"

Philbrook was beginning to explain his presence when he heard the others crashing toward them through the forest. Sergeant Graham was in the lead with Marguerite not far behind. Behind them were the soldiers and canoemen all well-armed. The hunters reached for their weapons.

"They are with me," Philbrook hastened to reassure them. "They must have heard Brutus and come to rescue me."

"Of course," said the young hunter. "My friends and I, and the whole country for miles around, heard your Brutus." He repeated this in his own language to his two companions, who laughed and nodded.

Graham and Marguerite stopped short when they saw the hunters and the slain bear, momentarily puzzled.

"Mihkosita?" said Marguerite, with a broad smile, when she recognized the youth. "This is a surprise."

Philbrook thought he saw the young man blush when Marguerite spoke, but he quickly composed himself. "Margot. It is good to see you again."

"Yes, and it is good to see you, Mihkosita," said Marguerite. "You remember Sergeant Graham, I expect?"

"Yes, of course." The young hunter looked around at the others, who were all trying to catch their breath. He acknowledged them as old acquaintances. "Sergeant, Joseph, Vince."

The other two hunters seemed uninteresting in these greetings and instead set about butchering the bear. As they began their work, Philbrook heard them give the beast thanks for providing them sustenance. One of them lit his pipe and blew smoke into her nostrils. After they skinned the carcass, they removed the skin and usable parts from the skull and left it in the crook of a nearby tree.

"We are headed to Kekionga to parley," Marguerite told Mihkosita. "A trader and his party were killed downriver from here, and Ensign Philbrook is looking into it."

"Is that so? Welcome back to Miami country, Margot, Joseph. It seems like you just left. I hope your journey down to Detroit was successful." Turning back to Philbrook, he said, "You are welcome as a friend of Marguerite's. You are a lucky man to have such friends and even luckier not to be food for Mother *Mahkwa* right now." He turned and translated for his two companions, who laughed again.

Philbrook nodded.

"But this great dog of yours, he did find the old mother and draw her out of her den so we could take her, and you distracted her long enough so that we could encircle her. We will share her meat with you both."

"Thank you for coming up when you did, Mihkosita," Philbrook said. "Your timing was most fortunate."

Mihkosita looked away, dismissing the compliment. "I will start a fire. We will eat our fill now, then return with the rest to our village."

The three hunters, who were from the Miami village upriver, generously shared their kill with everyone. The feast filled their bellies, leaving them an ample supply of meat to take home. Philbrook had never eaten bear meat before. He found it pleasantly greasy and filling, and Brutus was ecstatic over the portion shared with him. After they ate, Mihkosita and his two friends chased down the two cubs, who had refused to leave the area. Mihkosita said he thought they were too young to survive on their own, so they would take them back to the village alive. "Do you want to buy one, Margot? I bet your mother could find a buyer for a live cub in Detroit."

"No, Mihkosita. She might, but we have no room for a cub in our canoes right now. Unless you can teach it to paddle."

"I will try. Ha. But for now, we must be going." Mihkosita smiled at Marguerite. "I will tell the elders in the village to expect you. Tomorrow?"

"Thank you," Philbrook said. "Yes, we should be there tomorrow. I look forward to the visit."

"We will see you in the afternoon at the divide, Mihkosita," added Marguerite.

The boy smiled. "I hope you can stay a while this time, Margot. Mother would love to talk with you and learn all the latest gossip from Detroit."

"I will be sure to call on her."

The hunters disappeared up the trail, hauling pounds of meat wrapped in the skin of the great mother bear, with the two cubs trailing behind with ropes around their necks.

"What a remarkable encounter," said Philbrook as they left. "You seem to know everyone in these forests, Marguerite."

"Most. Mihkosita's mother is Mohican. She lived near Detroit as a girl. Her people were refugees from the Iroquois wars. She and my mother were childhood friends, so I always make a point to visit with her when I come this way."

"You've known Mihkosita for a long time?"

"Oh, yes. Since he was a baby. And his mother never stops bragging about him. Mima loves two things: boasting about her children and gossip. When I visit her at Kekionga, I always get an earful about Mihkosita's latest exploits and how he will grow up one day to be a great chief, then she grills me about all the latest from Detroit."

"Well, perhaps a gossip is just what we need if no answers are forthcoming from the elders," Philbrook said, picking at the torn fabric of his uniform.

Chapter 13

Marguerite Boyer

They came to the junction of two small muddy rivers, where the canoes could go no further. It was an overcast day with the occasional period of light drizzle. There was a village and the half-burned remains of a small stockade off to the right, while between the streams, there was a well-used landing with several dugout canoes pulled up on shore.

"That is Le Gris's village, clustered around the old fort," Marguerite told Philbrook. "It might be best if your men set up camp nearby. It's where most of the traders stay when they come through."

Mihkosita was there to greet them.

"*Salut,* Marguerite," he said with a smile as they pulled their canoes up, and he nodded to the other *Canadiens*. "And welcome, Ensign Philbrook. I've come to take you into the village. It is not far. A group of our chiefs and elders is expecting you."

Philbrook climbed the embankment and shook hands with Mihkosita then turned to the others. "Papan, you and the canoemen should go across the way with the gear while I go up to Kekionga with Mihkosita and Marguerite. Sergeant Graham, direct the men where to set up to keep out of the rain. We may want to stay a few days."

"I'll take care of everything, sir."

"Very good, Sergeant. And Smyth, please look after Brutus while I'm gone. Keep him from following us."

"My pleasure, sir. Brutus, come over here." The dog obeyed immediately, and the ensign's orderly gave him a cracker out of his pocket.

"Let us be off then. Marguerite? Mihkosita, please lead the way."

Marguerite accompanied Philbrook and Mihkosita along a muddy trail. They had not gone far when bark-covered wigwams and log cabins came into view. The smell of smoke was in the air. As in the Ottawa village, there were no stone chimneys like one would see gracing a New England roof. Rather, each structure had a hole at the top to let out smoke. Outside, some women were tending to fires under wooden frames, smoking fish and meat. A number of children could be seen playing a game that Marguerite remembered playing as a child, though she could no longer remember all the rules. They followed their escort toward a lodge that was a bit larger than the rest.

"Some of our leaders will meet you here," said Mihkosita.

"They are welcoming you as a guest," Marguerite informed Philbrook in a low voice. "Don't push too hard with questions right away, or you will be considered rude. They will want to talk a little and get to know you before they trust you."

"I will rely on you to guide me," Philbrook said. Marguerite was surprised to realize that he really meant it.

"Most of the people here understand a little French and some English," she continued, "some of the younger folks, like Mihkosita, speak one or the other well. But they will not readily understand your accent, nor you theirs. I get the feeling that the locals know something. I saw a look in Mihkosita's eyes when I told him the purpose of our visit. He knows more than he lets on.

But that does not mean they will tell you anything. People around here can be very tight-lipped with strangers."

At the lodge, Mihkosita looked like he wanted to follow them in but reluctantly remained outside after taking them to the entrance. Philbrook and Marguerite stooped to enter the lodge, through an opening that could be covered with a deerskin. Within, there were several older men and women and a few younger men assembled around a smoky fire. Philbrook presented them with a twist of tobacco and shook hands all around. Marguerite nodded to the ones she knew in the group. After a pipe went around, they sat, and a young man spoke first.

"This is Pacanne," Marguerite told him. "He asks if you saw many deer or other game on your journey up the river and if you had luck hunting."

The Miami leader was not much older than Mihkosita. Marguerite had explained to Philbrook earlier that Pacanne's position came from heredity, not experience. His head was mostly plucked bald except for a long strip of hair down the back to which a single feather was attached. He had a ring in his nose and an ornament of shells dangling from one pierced ear.

"We saw several deer coming down to the water to drink," he told Pacanne, "but only when the Frenchmen with us paused their constant singing."

Several of the elders smiled in amusement. The noisy habits of *Canadien* canoemen were something they knew a great deal about.

"I was impressed by the quantity of geese and ducks," Philbrook continued. "And we ate several fine turkeys. I found the birds in these parts have a richer flavor than the ones where I live."

The elders nodded. They had no trouble believing that the game of their own land was far superior to that found elsewhere.

"You are welcome to enjoy the bounty of our lands as you pass through, Ensign," said Pacanne.

"We know that the French and the British have used up all the best game in their own countries. That is why they come to us seeking peltry," added one of the older men.

"Would you like to see my pictures?" Philbrook asked. "I drew some of the animals we saw on our journey here." Marguerite was surprised that he had some of his drawings and pictures with him. He must have planned ahead to show them off. The others looked confused, so Philbrook reached into his bag and slid out his sketchpad. He opened it to reveal several loose sheets of paper inside. On top was a pencil drawing of a mink they had seen several days earlier. He had gone over the initial drawing later in pastels, adding life and color.

"You must be careful not to touch the surface, or the colors will smudge," he instructed the gathering as he passed a sheet to the man beside him.

They looked with interest as they gently handed the paper around. The next drawing showed a turkey hen with three small chicks stumbling behind her. After that came a painted turtle depicted climbing the muddy river bank near their last camping place. The elders murmured approvingly and spoke to each other in their own language.

"I doubt they have ever seen such fine pictures before," Marguerite told him. She was impressed with him for his ability to win over the approval of the Miami leaders in such a unique manner. The chiefs and elders looked for several minutes. Their favorite seemed to be a watercolor of a sandhill crane that he had finished just the night before. Pacanne nodded approvingly when the image came to him and said something to the ensign.

"Pacanne is the leader of the Crane People, the most prominent of the local clans," Marguerite explained. "He says that the crane is an old ally of the Miami. There is a famous tale of sandhill cranes helping Miami war parties in a long-ago battle."

"Indeed," Philbrook said. "I would be curious to hear it sometime."

They passed the papers back, and Philbrook put them away, except the one of the crane. He handed it back to Pacanne.

"Please tell him it is a gift, Marguerite."

Pacanne looked pleased. For several minutes more they made small talk, but Marguerite thought that Philbrook had won many of them over. They saw the ensign now as something more than a mere soldier. For the next few minutes, they continued to discuss the attributes of the country's animals, including fish, focusing particularly on which were the best to eat at which time of year and what was the best way to catch them. At one point, Philbrook asked about the varieties of corn and squash grown locally and was answered by the older women present. The men, Marguerite knew, had no interest in horticulture.

In time, Philbrook broached the subject of the murders. "You may have heard," he began, "that six British subjects, including the American trader Ben Stone, were murdered recently at Auglaize. They were here last month. I am looking for any information I might find about who did this."

No one responded. Rather, they waited, expressionless, for him to continue.

"We found a tomahawk at the scene, which I would like to show you to see if any of you recognize it." He reached into his bag, produced the weapon, and handed it gently to the man to his left. "Please take a close look and tell me anything you might know about who it might have belonged to."

The elders passed the tomahawk around. Pacanne responded first. "This hatchet does not come from this village. If it did, I would recognize it. I think more likely it comes from the north. The Cree and northern Anishinaabeg decorate their axes in this manner."

The Miami leaders continued to smoke but did not offer anything more, so Philbrook continued. "It seems that a Frenchmen named Louis Ouellette was present when the murders happened, but he is unaccounted for. I would like to find him—if he remains alive—so that I might speak with him."

None of the men replied, but Marguerite could tell by the way some glanced at the others that this subject was not unfamiliar.

"My task is to discover who was responsible for these vile murders," Philbrook continued. "And if the perpetrator is a British subject, he must face justice in the British manner. Captain Turnbull is particularly concerned that the guilty party be identified so that no false suspicions are directed toward the Miami people. A return of war because of such an unfortunate incident would be most unwelcome."

One of the oldest men present spoke up. He was a short, wiry man, who looked dried out, like a human raisin.

"This man of whom you speak, is he really a Frenchman, or is he one of our brothers of the Menominee Nation?" His voice was high and soft—somehow musical. He was speaking in his own language, but Marguerite interpreted so the words seemed to come directly from his mouth.

"This is Koohsia, a renowned healer among these people," she told Philbrook.

Like the other elders, he had no hair on his chin or on his wrinkled, leathery face, and the long gray hair on his head was confined to the crown and back. He had several intricate tattoos in geometric patterns on his body and several dark lines above his right ear. He seemed fond of jewelry; a medallion hung around his neck, and ornaments hung from both ears. Marguerite had encountered Koohsia from time to time in recent years, and she guessed his age at somewhere upward of seventy years old.

She turned to Koohsia and explained, "Ouellette's father was a French soldier and his mother a Menomonie, but he came to Detroit and chose to live among his father's people. In his youth he and his mother lived among the soldiers in the French fort at La Baye. He has many relatives among the Menomonie, but he never lived as one of them."

Philbrook added, "There are, of course, many *Canadiens* with Native blood, but those who live as Frenchmen in Detroit must be subject to British laws."

Koohsia nodded as if he were considering the issue, "There is a man here, who is maybe the one you seek, but he has thrown off the French ways. He is in my care and under my protection."

"Might we speak with him?" Marguerite asked.

The old man did not answer right away. Instead he looked around at the others, as if inviting them to add something. His face bore no outward expression, but his dark eyes somehow sparkled with an inner fire. The others, even Pacanne, seemed to be deferring to Koohsia on the matter. Eventually, he spoke, "The man I speak of is undergoing spiritual trials, so his mind is much in another world. A party of our hunters found him downriver from here, starving and close to death. He had been going through physical and spiritual ordeals, torn between a path of light and life or maybe one of darkness and death."

"Has he mentioned the deaths of his companions?" Philbrook asked. "We need to know if he witnessed these murders—or committed them."

"I am helping him to overcome the bad spirits that torment him," explained Koohsia. "Some take the form of his dead companions. I do not know if he killed these men. I think maybe not, but something caused him to take refuge in a dream world for a time." Koohsia looked at Philbrook and Marguerite as if what he had said was perfectly simple.

"During the war, I remember men who seemed lost to themselves for a time after a rough battle," said Philbrook. "Is that what you mean?"

"Maybe. You can try to speak with him if that is important for you," he said. "Maybe he will respond. Maybe not. I cannot control such things. Come."

With that, Koohsia sprang up on spindly legs and left the lodge. Marguerite and Philbrook nodded politely to the others then followed. Mihkosita was waiting outside and eagerly fell in behind them as they came out and proceeded down a forest path after the old man. The rain had stopped, but the ground was still wet and the leaves were dripping.

"When our hunters first brought him to me, he did not speak at all," said Koohsia as they walked down a damp forest trail. "I took him into my care and did what I could to free him from the bad spirits that oppress him. I have had some success, but the poor man still suffers. He seemed maybe to appreciate my help, but he would not talk with me directly. Only when he was sleeping did I hear his voice. I recognized the Menomonie tongue, though I could only understand some of his mumbling dream speech. It was always with someone he called Makinag."

"And who is Makinag?" Philbrook asked.

"I believe Makinag is his guardian spirit," said Koohsia. He smiled, showing a mouth that still housed all but one of his adult teeth.

"You might think of him as a great turtle spirit," said Marguerite. "The name Makinag comes from the word for turtle in several local dialects. Most Native boys seek a guardian spirit through a vision when they approach manhood."

Koohsia continued, "Makinag, if this is truly his guardian, may be helping him to recover from his ordeal. Sometimes, the dream state is the best for this. He still does not talk with me, or respond to me directly in any way, but I take him down to a part of the river where there are many turtles, and he sometimes speaks to them."

Louis Ouellette must have lost his mind, thought Marguerite. She wondered if it was a temporary state or if he was gone forever.

"I cannot hear what Makinag says to him," said Koohsia, "but I hear what he says to the turtles. He seeks guidance, and I think maybe Makinag gives him helpful advice. Yesterday, I tried something new. I began to speak to the turtles, too. I told them things that I wanted the young man to understand in his dream world. I think maybe they interpreted for me, just like this pretty woman interprets for you." The shaman gave her a sly smile, and his eyes sparkled for a moment. Over the years she had become accustomed to the way aged Native men sometimes flirted.

"We are heading down to the spot now. I left him earlier with one of my apprentices to watch over him, as I still do not trust him alone."

They came to a place where a creek spread out, flooding a large area. Several ancient trees grew up out of a murky swamp; their gnarled roots were covered by moss and formed islands in the shallow water. The habitat was ideal for a variety of turtles. Several painted turtles basked on logs and roots. Spotted turtles and box turtles sat at the water's edge, and one large snapping turtle in the shallows poked the angular tip of his nose above the surface. Philbrook was looking about the area, his eyes glazed over with the look Marguerite had come to understand was his reaction to seeing something new and interesting in the natural world.

"The turtle is an important friend to our people and most of our brother tribes," explained the shaman. "The French priests come to us with other stories, but the Miami people know that when Sky Woman recreated land after the Great Flood, she chose the back of a great turtle as the foundation of our world." Koohsia walked quietly over to a small painted turtle that stared up at him. "See the roundness of his shell? It reminds us of our Great Island World; his legs extend to the four cardinal directions. Nature is full of such signs if one learns how to see them."

There seemed to be a great variety of plant and animal life here. Under a large oak tree, where the ground was still dry, sat two men, one of whom Marguerite recognized as Louis Ouellette. He was a small man with soft dark hair and dark eyes dressed in a dirty, faded blue linen shirt that came down to his knees over leggings. He looked underfed and had several weeks' growth of wispy dark hair on his chin and cheeks. He stared blankly at a snapping turtle, which seemed to look back at him. She pointed him out to Philbrook.

"*Monsieur* Ouellette, *je suis* Ensign Philbrook," he announced, approaching the man. "I would like to talk to you about what happened to Ben Stone and his men." Ouellette did not respond, but Philbrook continued anyway, "My understanding is that you were a part of Mr. Stone's party, that you were there when the murders happened?"

Still no response. Ouellette continued to gaze at the turtle as if Philbrook was not there.

Koohsia gestured to his assistant that he could go, then he sat down next to Ouellette. Looking out at the snapping turtle in the water, he began to speak. "Makinag, this British officer is called Ensign Philbrook, and the nice young woman with him is his interpreter, Marguerite. They have come to talk with this man, who they say is a called Louis Ouellette. Maybe you could tell Louis that they wish to speak with him." Koohsia gestured to Marguerite and Philbrook to remain silent.

After a few moments, Louis said something to the turtles in Menomonie.

"He says he doesn't want to speak with any Englishman," explained Marguerite.

Koohsia seemed to notice Philbrook's impatience. He addressed the turtle. "Makinag, it is maybe time for Louis to return from his dream world to the world of people. He must face the truth and the fear, not sit down here with the turtles forever."

Ouellette said nothing. Nor did the turtle.

Philbrook leaned toward Marguerite. "I thought you said Makinag was a spirit. That looks to me like an ordinary snapping turtle—as real as you or me."

Marguerite thought a moment about how to best explain it. "When the priests pray to Jesus, they kneel before Christ on a cross, but the figure on the cross is not God or Jesus. In a similar way Ouellette's guardian spirit exists for him in all turtles."

"I think the Reverend at my church in Portsmouth would refer to that as idolatry," said Philbrook, "but I see what you mean."

Koohsia turned to Philbrook and spoke slowly in a stilted but understandable mixture of French and English. "Sit here with me, young man." Philbrook sat, and they looked out into the swamp. "Many years ago, when I was just becoming a man, my family lived near the British traders at a place called Pickawillany, to the south, so I picked up a little of your language then, but I know more of the Frenchmen's words. I think maybe we can do without your interpreter when we must."

Marguerite sat next to them. She saw that Koohsia wanted to address Philbrook directly in order to establish a connection. She decided to listen quietly.

"You do not believe in guardian spirits, I see," continued Koohsia. "Maybe it is not the English way. But you like to observe the creatures of the forest. I could tell by your pictures and by the way you spoke of the animals earlier. You know how to listen to and observe them. You learn from the animals even if they do not speak to you the way they speak to the Miami people."

"I have always enjoyed studying plants and animals and the rest of creation," Philbrook admitted. "Each creature has its own characteristics, its own way of surviving that I find fascinating."

"Yes." Koohsia nodded. "All creatures have qualities that set them apart, that help them to survive. These qualities can sometimes serve to teach us how best to behave if we listen to what they have to tell us. The mouse is cautious, the wolf wise, the bear curious. The turtle too is unique, is it not?"

"There are many different varieties, but they all remind me of old men as they ramble slowly about," Philbrook said. "They are a long-lived species, slow, one might say plodding, defensive. Their shell is a unique feature in the animal kingdom."

"And since they move slowly, they have to be patient."

"Yes, Koohsia. And I see your meaning. Perhaps I need to show patience. But not all lessons can be learned from the animal world. I do not have the option of slowing down or withdrawing into my shell with killers running free. Captain Turnbull expects me to find answers soon."

"No, you cannot hide in your shell, Ensign Philbrook, but you can have patience in your hunt. For the turtle can be a great hunter, too. Its patience does not always lack speed. Have you ever seen a snapping turtle when it catches a frog or fish? It does not give chase. Those other creatures swim much faster, you see. Rather, it watches and waits. In the end, when the opportunity presents itself, a single thrust of the neck and a snap of the jaw does the job." Koohsia smiled and looked at the ensign with eyes that seemed to see into his every thought.

Chapter 14

Marguerite Boyer

Marguerite found Mima, Mihkosita's mother, later that day in one of the gardens on the outskirts of the village, pulling weeds. Surrounding her were mounds of soil holding a variety of young green plants just taking root. Marguerite noticed the usual beans, corn, and squash, as well as a few plants she did not immediately recognize. The clouds had broken up, and the sun now appeared on and off.

"Greetings, Mima."

The older woman looked up from her work. "Margot, dearest. It is good to see you back again so soon. How are your mother and your brothers? Did you see them when you were in Detroit?" Mima was just a few years younger than Marguerite's mother and still hale enough to spend the day at work with her crops, as she probably would be until the very day she died. Mihkosita was her youngest child and the only son still living in her lodge.

"I saw *Maman*. Marceau and Antoine were still up on Lake Huron. She sends a present for you." Marguerite showed Mima a set of brass earrings left over from last month's trade goods.

"Oh, how lovely. You are always so generous to me, Margot.

And how is your mother? Still ruling over everyone around her, I expect."

"She is well."

"I remember when we were girls, Sally was always in charge, always organizing all the boys and girls in some game. I hear she has begun to train the British to follow her instructions now."

"Not quite, but she and I work with the British traders."

"I have heard you are with the British soldiers who have come looking for a murderer?" Mima continued to work with her hoe as she spoke.

"You seem to hear everything, Mima. You remember the other trader from New York? Mr. Stone? The one who was here last month just before me? He and his crew never made it back. They got killed, all except one who made his way back here."

"Oh dear, yes, I heard that Koohsia was caring for a crazy young man who was maybe touched by demons. Some of the people wanted to knock him on the head, just to be rid of him, but Koohsia convinced them not to. You know, it was Mihkosita and some friends who found the awful man when they were hunting downriver." Mima paused for a breath. "Mihkosita has become a very good hunter, much like his father was. Do you know he killed a bear just yesterday? A great, fierce giant mother bear that he killed all by himself. There were many bellies full of meat in the village last night, thanks to him. A woman could do worse than to get him for a husband. Such a good provider."

"Let him be a boy for a little while longer, Mima," Marguerite said. She was used to Mima boasting about her children and exaggerating their accomplishments. Her older boys were close to Marguerite's age, and before they found wives, Mima was always trying to impress her with their virtues.

"I know. None of the girls in this village would do for him anyway," she said, giving the earth a few extra chops to emphasize her point.

"I did not know that it was Mihkosita who found him,"

Marguerite said, trying to bring the subject back to Ouellette. "He is not crazy. At least, Koohsia does not think so. He is just a little confused. His name is Louis. He is from La Baye. I saw him earlier today, but he would not talk with us."

"Do you think he murdered those men?" asked Mima. "I heard they were eaten. Imagine, eating human flesh at this time of year, when food is so plentiful in the forest." Mima reflected for a moment. "Not that any time of year would excuse such behavior."

"They were not eaten, Mima. I was there when the bodies were found. They were mutilated, but there was no sign of cannibalism."

"Too bad," said Mima absently. "I think they should get rid of him anyway if he has lost his senses. Take him back out into the forest and leave him to fend for himself. Such a man only puts the rest of us in danger. Are our men supposed to hunt for this crazy stranger from La Baye? Should we feed him from our gardens? Guard him all the time so he does not bite our children? I hope your soldiers take him away, or he will bring bad luck to this village."

"Do you think he killed his companions?" Marguerite asked.

"Who else?" Mima paused her work and leaned on her hoe. "Mihkosita said he had fresh blood on him when they found him. Koohsia is an old fool to think that he can help a man like that. Ever since his last wife died, Koohsia has been getting softer in the head with each passing moon. If you ask me, anyone who can no longer contribute should not get to eat. When I was a girl, the elders would never put up with having a useless, crazy person in the village."

"But what if he is an innocent victim?" she asked. "What if he ran into the woods to escape violent men, and that is why he almost starved?"

"There's plenty to eat in the forest." she shrugged. Marguerite knew Mima had little sympathy for weakness of any sort. "I suppose it may have been Pontiac's dog, Cuillerier," she offered. "I heard he was at Pontiac's village last month." She resumed her work.

"Alexis Cuillerier was at the Ottawa villages?" Marguerite was not surprised. It made sense for the Frenchman to flee up the Maumee after he broke out of his confinement in Detroit. "Did he come through here too? How do you know he was at Pontiac's village?"

"I went down to visit my oldest son, Noko, the one who married an Ottawa girl. He told me Cuillerier passed through with horses heading upriver. I suppose he must have come through here, too, but I didn't see him. Folks said he was bound for the Illinois country where the British will never find him."

Marguerite thought about the possibility that Alexis Cuillerier was the killer they were seeking. He was a known murderer, and now it seems he was in the area when Stone and his men were killed. But drowning a sick little girl was a far cry from taking on six grown men who could fight back. What would his reason have been? Everyone assumed he only killed Betty Fisher because he was afraid of Pontiac, not because he took pleasure in such brutality. And some of Stone's men had been his friends. No, it did not make sense to her, but she decided she would mention it to Ensign Philbrook anyway.

THAT EVENING at their encampment she told Philbrook about her discoveries.

"I'm glad you found out that Cuillerier passed through Pontiac's village," he said. "Captain Turnbull will appreciate knowing, but I'm not sure it helps us. I'm not authorized to chase him into the Illinois country, even if he was involved. Ouellette is still our best lead. Whether he did it or not, he's sure to know who did. At least he will if his memory returns."

"How do you want to proceed then?" she asked.

"A good question. I was thinking about what Mima told you about not wanting Ouellette to remain in the village. Do you think that view is widespread?"

"Probably," she said. "It would be different if he had family here. Koohsia wants to help him, but I bet many in the village are nervous about a stranger who is not right in the head and cannot take care of himself. I think most would prefer we took him away."

"Let's be patient for now," said Philbrook. "I stayed and talked with Koohsia for a while after you left. With some help from young Mihkosita, we were able to get past our language difficulties. I like the old man, and I think he may be our best way to get some answers out of Ouellette."

Marguerite nodded in assent. The ensign was not dumb, she realized. She was impressed by how quickly he had adapted to Miami ways, especially the peculiarities of the shaman Koohsia. A typical British officer would try to bully or cajole the Miami into compliance with his wishes, but Philbrook seemed to be choosing a wiser path. He was willing to learn.

Chapter 15

The Dreamer

"Louis," said the turtle.

"Yes, Makinag?"

"Louis Ouellette. That is what they say your name is."

"I suppose."

"It suits you."

"If you insist."

"Having your name back is good. It will lead you on the path back to your waking life."

The Dreamer was ambivalent. He was not sure that he really wanted to be Louis Ouellette—to be out there in the world. He'd rather be left alone.

"The old man, Koohsia, thinks you need to get back to your waking life now, to face whatever scares you."

"Why do you listen to the old man, Makinag?

"Because he is wise, Louis."

"Don't call me that."

"It is your name, Louis."

The Dreamer picked up a pebble and threw it at the turtle. It bounced off its rough shell, and the animal slipped beneath the murky water.

126

THAT NIGHT, he dreamed he was in a canoe, paddling up a river with a swift current. He looked in front of him and saw Baptiste. Then he looked behind, expecting to see Pero, but it was not Pero, it was Alexis Cuillerier. Beside them was another canoe with Pierre, Barthelemy, Lucien, and Mr. Stone.

They paddled very hard, but the current was strong and it pushed them back at the same rate they moved forward. When they paddled harder, the current became stronger, and when they eased off, the current declined. No progress was possible, but at least they did not fall back.

"I thought you left us," said Pierre, looking over at him with disapproval.

"He did leave us," said Baptiste. "He hid in the woods like a coward while we were murdered."

"Why did you abandon us, Louis?" asked Lucien. "Why did you run away?"

Louis was afraid. Why did they blame him?

"I did not abandon you. Believe me," he said, not really believing himself.

Yes, he did find them. He was there, but there was nothing he could have done. They were already dead. He did not run away. He remembered bits and pieces now.

"I was sleepwalking, like I do sometimes. I woke up in the woods. I came back, but the thing was done. You were all gone already. I swear. There was nothing I could do. You were already dead."

"You ran away and hid, Louis."

"Coward."

Chapter 16

Phineas Philbrook

That evening, Philbrook relaxed, closed his eyes, and tried to picture the night the men were killed. He released his mind to allow his imagination to take over and go wherever it might lead. He pictured Louis Ouellette slowly and quietly rising from his blanket, tomahawk in hand. Ben Stone was sitting by the campfire, the only other one awake. He imagined a spear in Ouellette's other hand, not bothering just yet to conger up just where it came from. Ouellette snuck up behind Stone, circled, hidden by the shadows cast by the flames.

With a sudden move, he jumped forward and thrust the spear into the unsuspecting trader's chest. It was a swift and efficient death blow. Returning to his tomahawk, Ouellette approached the other sleeping figures. He slammed the hatchet down on the head of one victim and then another...

No, Philbrook thought, his skeptical mind taking back over from his imagination. This scenario was revealed to be foolish every time he considered it. Where had the spear come from? Would a trading party have a spear with them? What about the arrows and the knife wounds? Why would one man wield multiple weapons? How would he carry them all?

Several weapons meant several attackers. If Ouellette was involved, he did not work alone. It was time to set aside that possibility for good.

He relaxed his mind again, allowing his thoughts to once again drift in their own currents. This time, he imagined Ouellette rising from his blanket and going to the edge of the forest to meet accomplices carrying spears, bows, and tomahawks. But who were they? Where did they come from? No, he thought, such a scene seemed doubtful. If strangers came out of the forest to kill Stone and the others, they did not need Ouellette there to meet them. And why would they plan a meeting that was sure to leave Ouellette as the obvious suspect? It was easier to imagine the young canoeman fleeing when enemies appeared. There was no better reason why Louis would end up alone and in such a fractured state of mind.

"YOU THINK that Louis is a victim in all this, don't you, Koohsia?" Philbrook asked the old man the next day as they walked with Mihkosita down to the swamplands where the turtles lived. The trail was muddy from more rain showers overnight, but a bright sun was quickly drying the forest, drawing mist off the leaves.

"I think so, yes," answered Koohsia.

"But who else could have killed those men?" asked Mihkosita. "And why does Louis not speak to us?" Philbrook was not sure why the young man was with them, but he seemed to have decided that it was his job to escort him around the village.

"Have you ever killed a person, Mihkosita?" asked Koohsia.

"No." The boy looked at the ground at his feet.

"Have you, Ensign?"

"I shot my musket at the enemy during the war," Philbrook said, "but I do not know if I ever hit anyone. I hope not."

"Killing another human being is a terrible thing. Many people will do it if they think it is necessary and just, as in war, but few kill without upsetting their spiritual balance. The richer a soul, the more deeply it can be injured by violence in the physical world."

"And Ouellette?" Philbrook asked.

"His spirit is attuned to other men and women. That is his nature. Louis feels what others around him feel. He experiences their joys and pain as if they were his own. I do not think he would be able to kill easily. Even in a war, I think his inner self would stop him."

Philbrook was not sure he understood Koohsia. The shaman's idea of a soul differed from what he had learned in his Portsmouth church, but some of what he said rang true. He recalled men during battle who could not bring themselves to kill. Many fired their weapons over advancing enemies' heads, not from an inability to aim properly but because of an innate wish to not hurt anyone. It was not just Quakers but also men who outwardly professed the justice of the war but could not bring themselves to kill when the moment arrived. Other soldiers, he remembered, could kill men as easily as a farmer chopped the head off a chicken. But those were not the men he most enjoyed being around.

"I think Louis's spirit revolted against the physical world because of the violence he saw and felt," continued the shaman. "He is not only incapable of committing murder; he is also incapable of witnessing such an act without damage. A dream world is a safer place for him to be, at least until his energy rejuvenates."

"The brutality was too much for him?" Philbrook asked.

"Yes," said Koohsia.

"But how do you know this? Did he speak to you? Did he tell you what he saw?"

"Makinag told me."

"Makinag the turtle spirit?" Philbrook was dumbfounded.

"Yes." Koohsia looked at him knowingly. "He came to me in a dream."

The ensign opened his mouth to object to what he saw as foolishness but held back. Catering to the Koohsia's beliefs in dreams seemed the wisest course at present. He needed the shaman's good will to accomplish his goals.

"I know your people do not believe in dreams as mine do," resumed Koohsia. "But dreams have a truth of their own, but that truth only makes itself known when we listen carefully."

"I do not think dreams are real, Koohsia," Philbrook said. "They come from the imagination."

"And the imagination is not real to you?" asked Koohsia.

Philbrook realized that he used his imagination all the time in order to make sense of the world. Just last night he had called upon his imagination to try to picture the scene of the murders. He could not think how to answer Koohsia, so he remained silent.

He could smell the moist air of the swamp ahead. Koohsia told them that Louis had been down here since early in the morning—conferring with the turtles he supposed. He decided to bring up an idea he had been considering since learning from Marguerite that many of the Miami people would prefer that the disturbed young man leave their village.

"Koohsia, I think we agree that Ouellette needs to face his memories of that night. That he needs to come back to the real world."

"Yes, Ensign, if indeed our world is real."

"To be sure." Philbrook chose not to address that particular point. "I wonder, maybe we could take Ouellette back to Auglaize to see if he will face his memories there, where it all happened."

Koohsia shook his head. "I cannot allow soldiers to take him away. Not yet. Louis needs my attention still."

"But I was thinking that you should come too. Ouellette can remain in your care. He will talk to you before he ever talks with me after all." Philbrook paused a moment to let the idea sink in, then played his best card. "Besides, it is to our advantage—both of us. Many of the people in your village do not want Louis here.

There are those who would like to be rid of him, one way or another. Such people will not remain patient forever."

Koohsia looked a bit surprised that the ensign was aware of this, but he smiled and did not argue. "And what if he still does not speak when we get there, Ensign?"

"He has to speak eventually," Philbrook said, "no matter what we do. And he must return to his own people someday, too. You said he could not stay much longer in the dream world he has conjured up. Returning him to the scene of his shock is the best way to bring him back to reality—back to his own life."

"Perhaps. But his dreams and visions help him now in a way that what you call reality cannot."

"Have you seen men behave like Ouellette before, Koohsia? Retreating from their true lives in this way?"

"Maybe not just the same, Ensign. Every soul has its own path, which it follows in its own way. But this land has seen much brutality in recent years, and it has left many wounds. Wander around this village and you will see scars on peoples' bodies, but for every scar that you see on their flesh there are ten more hiding in their souls. A land does not come through years of warfare without spiritual injury. The same is true among the *Canadiens* and maybe even among your people. Some scars bleed under the surface. Look at your Sergeant Graham. Do you think the scars on his hands and face are the only ones?"

"I can't say," Philbrook said.

"No, you cannot say. If you had said you could, I would have thought you a liar. We can seldom see beyond what others choose to show us. Warriors are often proud of their physical scars, but they hide the spiritual ones with great care. This way, they fester and never heal."

Philbrook thought of his own wartime experiences. He always felt lucky that he came through two summers in the provincial army with no more than superficial bruises and blisters that faded in a few weeks. But he never told anyone about the nightmares he had endured back home. He never mentioned all the times he woke up in the dark with his heart racing and a sense of panic overwhelming him.

"Among my people," continued Koohsia, "we do our best to purify ourselves after warfare. We recognize that war is not our true nature. Its influences need to be purged through the proper ceremonies when warriors return to their home villages. Many of my people answered the French call and went to fight the British, and still more joined Pontiac and the other war chiefs in their quest to expel the interlopers. They came home with wounds that I have sought to heal. That is maybe my purpose to be on this earth. I know that the scars will never go away, but I think that maybe I can help the wounds start to close."

"I understand," Philbrook said.

"Do not forget that Louis is going through a healing process. We must help him. We must give his dreams time to take him where he needs to go."

"How do you propose we do that?"

"It will be a long path, but we can start with a sweat."

Philbrook had heard of the Native habit of building lodges to make themselves sweat, but he had never participated in the practice. Koohsia took him to a small round hut, around six feet in diameter, made of willow boughs bent into overlapping arches and covered in skins. Outside of it, coals smoldered within a fire circle.

"I began to heat the stones this morning. I will prepare the lodge," said Koohsia. "Mihkosita, maybe you can fetch Louis and show Ensign Philbrook how to get ready.

The shaman went to build up the fire and prepare the hut. Mihkosita returned shortly with Louis and they both began to disrobe. "The fewer things on your skin the better, Ensign. Your skin will need to breathe. I realize your people do not bathe often, but I think you will like this. A good sweat helps free the spirit. We should rinse ourselves first."

Philbrook began to remove his own clothing, down to his

linen drawers. He was eager to learn about this Native practice, which he knew resembled a similar practice common in the Ancient World. Mihkosita led him and Louis to a clear pool in the stream that eventually flowed into the turtle swamp. It appeared to be a place where men and women often came to bathe. The men sank into the cool water. They were soon joined by Koohsia, stripped down now to a linen cloth around his waist.

"The stones will be ready soon," said Koohsia. "I have had a few good sweats with Louis these past days. The heat has a way of renewing the soul and sharpening the mind. The sweat pours out of us, taking with it the poisons we need to let go of. This is a solemn thing, Ensign, so please keep quiet and follow my lead."

Koohsia dunked himself entirely under the surface then climbed out of the pool. The others followed his lead. He swung open the deerskin covering the hut's door and beckoned for them to enter. It was dark inside. As they sat, Koohsia brought several hot rocks from the fire outside and placed them in the middle of the floor, using a piece of a wool blanket to prevent his hands from burning. He went out and returned with a wooden bowl of water and a cedar bough. Once he closed the door, the darkness was almost complete. The only light was that which shone in slivers through small gaps in the walls and roof.

Philbrook heard the hiss of water hitting the hot stones. Steam filled the hut as his eyes began to adjust. Koohsia began to sing. He picked up a wide flat drum which he spun and beat upon gently with the heel of his hand as he sang. Mihkosita sometimes joined in to sing or hum along. Philbrook felt sweat flow from his pores, starting at his scalp and working down his body. He sucked the humid air into his lungs but still felt out of breath.

The darkness and unfamiliar song transported him to a state of mind resembling a dream. He felt faint, so he closed his eyes and focused on his breathing. He could smell the closeness of the other men's bodies but tried not to think about the strangeness of his surroundings.

Each time the moisture in the air began to dissipate, he heard the hiss of more water flicked onto the stones. He sunk into near delirium, his mind running through all of his thoughts and ideas about the murders and his recent experiences. He imagined that the men killed—and the murderers too—were floating around inside this small hut, mocking him and challenging him to see the truth. He did not know how much time had passed when he felt Koohsia's hand gently touch his shoulder.

"Come, Ensign."

Philbrook followed him out the door, blinded by the light outside. The fresh, sweet air rushed into his lungs. Then his knees almost buckled as he stood erect. Koohsia and the others ran to the pool and jumped into the center of it. He followed, unsteady on his feet. Then he plunged. Every inch of his skin exploded to life as he submerged. His body and mind felt weak, yet reborn. He heard the laughter before realizing that it was his own.

SEVERAL DAYS LATER, Philbrook rode in the first of three canoes descending the river. In the canoe behind him, Koohsia, Mihkosita, and Marguerite paddled together, joined by Louis. Theirs was not a birch bark canoe like the ones that came from Detroit and further north, but a canoe hollowed out from a single tree trunk in the Miami manner. Koohsia sat in the stern wielding a long red and black painted paddle. He was a wiry old man, but his lean muscles had great strength. In front was Mihkosita, who had chosen to accompany them. He said he wanted to look after Koohsia, but Philbrook suspected that it was Marguerite he most wanted to look after. Directly behind him sat Marguerite and behind her was Louis. The troubled man seemed happy to be paddling. He even hummed to himself and looked around, though he still did not speak.

When Philbrook had first told Graham of his arrangement

with Koohsia, the sergeant had looked worried, which made him question his alliance. "If we have the man now, sir, shouldn't we head back to Detroit immediately? A few days in shackles will loosen his tongue."

"Perhaps, Sergeant, perhaps. But we must be diplomatic, and the murder scene is on our way back. I believe Ouellette was a witness to the crime, not the perpetrator. If so, his memories are what we need most. Koohsia wants the same thing we do, so I trust him?"

"Aye, sir. I suppose you catch more flies with honey than with vinegar, as my mother used to say. Wise move, perhaps. I don't know this young lad, Mihkosita, but I remember Koohsia from my time in the garrison here. He's as trustworthy a fellow as any of the Miami. I've heard he was quite a warrior in his younger days, before turning more to the healer role."

"I like the old man."

"But don't forget he's an Indian, sir. Peace is always an uneasy state of affairs in the Upper Country. If the fate of Ensign Holmes taught me anything, it is that you can't fully trust these people even when they purport to be your friends. We need to be wary."

The image of Ensign Holmes trusting his Miami mistress while walking straight into a trap gave Philbrook pause, but not enough to change his mind.

"Yes, we certainly must stay alert. I am well aware that we are a small party. If the Natives around here wished, I expect they could overwhelm us at any time of their choosing."

"You are bloody right about that, sir. And you never know what will set them off. I'd like to post a guard at night. I have no wish to have my throat cut in my sleep without the chance to at least put up a fight."

"Such an event would distress me as well, Sergeant. By all means, post a guard, but instruct the men to show every civility to our new friends."

"Aye, sir." He smiled. "Civility it is."

Chapter 17

Louis Ouellette

Louis liked the canoe. It felt soothing to use his muscles to wield a paddle again, even though he had lost much strength in the past weeks. He felt his unused shoulders and back stretching out and his blood pulsing once more. He was beginning to enjoy his own physicality again, to enjoy being alive. His body was remembering how to move. There were new faces around him.

Smiling canoemen approached, slapped him firmly on the shoulder, and greeted him as if they knew him. Louis did not respond, but he liked it. He was comfortable with these men. At night he slept between Koohsia and Mihkosita, with a tether tied between them, so he had no way to make off without waking the others. He dreamed, sometimes of home, sometimes of his dead companions, but he never woke in a strange place as he used to.

During the days, Koohsia spoke to him as they paddled. Koohsia spoke of Makinag as if he was a common friend of theirs, but he was not sure that Koohsia really knew Makinag. He thought maybe the old man was humoring him. Koohsia told him that he must face his fears, that he must once again take an active part in the world of men. So did Makinag. Louis knew they might be right. But not yet.

Louis saw the British officer riding in the canoe just ahead. He did not know what to think of him, but he decided it was best to avoid him. He seemed courteous enough, but he asked questions that he had no desire to answer or even think about. The ensign wanted Louis to recall things he had no desire to remember. And he was British. His father always told him that the British were greedy.

His father.

Yes, he remembered his father now. When had those memories started to return? Charles Ouellette, the small French corporal. Everyone loved Charles Ouellette, from the officers in the French fort to the Menomonie elders in their village, to women everywhere. He slipped between languages and cultures with ease and could ingratiate himself with anyone—skills his son had inherited in part. But it was his father who had forbidden him to seek a guardian spirit as his mother's people did.

"Christ is the only guide you need, *mon fils*," he told Louis. "Forget the demons your mother's people speak of." He had obeyed his father but never really believed it. It seemed wrong not to seek a vision with his Menomonie cousins.

Charles Ouellette loved everyone. That is why people loved him back. Except the British, thought Louis, looking in the direction of the ensign and soldiers in the nearby canoes. His father told him that British traders were all notorious cheats and that British settlers lusted after land. "They will not be happy until they have all of it, Louis, and every Indian and every Frenchman is gone." Perhaps it was best that Charles Ouellette did not live to see the British victory. He was sent down to Niagara in fifty-nine to help defend the fort, and word came back that a musket ball had taken him away.

Louis began to cry.

Chapter 18

Marguerite Boyer

As they paddled downriver in the canoe, Marguerite could hear Louis quietly sobbing behind her. She had noticed him coming back to himself over the past several days in Kekionga. Having the other canoemen around seemed to help him. Even though he never acknowledged them, she saw a glint of recognition in his eyes when they were near.

Jean and Vince said they had been on a voyage to Lake Huron with Louis the previous fall, and the three Bourassa cousins said they had spent some time with him in Detroit over the winter. Luc-Marie even mentioned that he thought his sister, Anne, had a favorable eye for Louis. Marguerite was not surprised that a young woman would show interest. She remembered seeing Louis around Detroit back before this all started. He had been a smiling young man then, fun and happy in a way that the man she saw now was not.

Philbrook had taken out his sketchpad and was drawing a red-tailed hawk that was following them down the river. It flew from tree to tree along the riverbank but always kept pace with the canoes. His head would tilt back and his mouth would open as he looked up at the hawk, and then it would tilt forward and his nose would point down at his sketch as he drew. He looked rather fool-ish, but Marguerite had become accustomed to how the ensign's sketchpad would suck him in when he observed some creature that interested him.

Despite her initial misgivings, Philbrook was growing on her. His strange ways still sometimes rankled, but there was no denying that he was intelligent and capable. The strangeness, she realized, was not just from his origins in the British colonies. His own people likely saw him as a bit odd as well. He often seemed deep in thought with a faraway look, like he lived simultaneously in this world and some other of his own making.

Koohsia, too, had always been an eccentric. Perhaps that is why the two men got along. Typically, a stranger would not be able to appreciate a man like Koohsia, whose attention so often was taken up by matters beyond the scope of ordinary life, but Philbrook seemed to sense what was important to people even when he did not understand their language or traditions. This quality earned him respect. At the start of the journey, no one took much stock in the greenhorn ensign's ability or authority, but as the journey continued, his influence grew.

Philbrook's questions, which she had at first taken as a sign of his ignorance, now seemed a sign of respect. He wanted to under-stand unfamiliar people and things correctly, as the people who lived here understood them. The typical British officer demanded respect but gave it only to superiors. They understood obedience as respect when, in fact, it was only subjugation.

Philbrook, on the other hand, gained authority by attending to those around him. When he made a decision, it seemed to grow not from consensus exactly but from an appreciation for conflicting viewpoints. Koohsia trusted him because the ensign listened. The same was true of Sergeant Graham. Philbrook listened and learned from him, yet still managed to establish authority. It helped that both Koohsia and Graham had good natured-ways about them.

Marguerite wondered if it had been the same with her. His constant questions had irritated her, but they also made her feel a part of something. When she saw him make good decisions based on what she had told him, she became invested in his mission. At this point, she was just as eager to follow Philbrook to the conclusion of this mystery as anyone.

～

THEY ARRIVED BACK at the mouth of the Auglaize River on a warm afternoon with more than a hint of summer in the air. The sun gave more warmth than it did a few weeks before, and she could smell the richness of life around her. Even the late-blooming trees were now lush and green, and yellow pollen from the pine trees coated the surface of eddies in the river.

No one seemed to mind making an early camp. After unloading the canoes and setting up, Mihkosita left with the Bourassa cousins to try their luck hunting while the soldiers went down to the riverbank to fish with a hook and line. Sergeant Graham sat in a patch of sun and watched the soldiers fishing, smoking his pipe, and sharpening the long knife he carried in his belt. Joseph saw to repairing some wear on the canoes.

Marguerite and Koohsia joined Philbrook as he tried to jog Louis's memory.

"You have been here before, Louis?" Philbrook asked.

Louis stared down at the ground and ignored the question.

"Do you remember being here with Mr. Stone?"

Louis did not respond.

Koohsia spoke up. "Marguerite, could you tell me what this place looked like when you first arrived here and found the bodies?" He addressed her, but she could tell that Louis was his intended audience.

She looked around. "There were things scattered all over," she said. "Some trade goods, but mostly furs, provisions, personal belongings. Stone was by the fire, or I should say his body was. Baptiste and Pierre were over there." She pointed to where the tent had been. "And Pero, Barthelemy, and Lucien's remains were over there."

"And their heads were gone?" asked Koohsia.

"Yes," she said, briefly remembering the terrible sight.

"Did you look for them, the heads, that is?" Philbrook asked her.

"A little," she replied, "but we did not know where to start. Kennedy was in a hurry to get away, so we buried the men without them."

"My men scoured the area within a quarter mile when we got here on our way up," said Philbrook, "but they were unable to find any trace. Whoever killed them must have taken the heads away with them."

"Maybe," said Koohsia. "To do so could be a way to disrespect them. Some say that the souls of the dead cannot be content with their heads parted from their physical bodies. I don't know this for a fact, but some say it is true. It would be good to reunite them either way. We wouldn't want them wandering the afterlife headless."

Louis looked intently at Koohsia as he spoke. Marguerite saw his mind was processing something.

"And how are we to accomplish this reunion?" asked Philbrook.

Louis stood and looked down at the others, then off into the woods. He circled the clearing, then examined the whole area like a blind man whose vision had just been restored. He went over to where some of the bodies had been found. He stood there for several minutes seemingly in deep thought. Koohsia gestured to Philbrook and Marguerite to be patient as Louis walked over to the middle of the clearing. He looked south as if seeing something there, then he closed his eyes tight and did not open them again for over a minute.

Finally, he opened his eyes and looked at the others.

"Come," he said.

He headed into the woods to the northwest, not fast, but at an easy trot with the rest following along behind him. They must have gone almost a mile, angling away from the river, when he stopped and knelt by a large rotting log and began to sob.

The air smelled of death.

Nearby, they all saw the cause; six human skulls lay on the ground. The flesh was mostly rotted away, and scavengers had been at work. Their eye sockets were vacant, and their faces were unrecognizable—more bone than anything else, but there were patches of skin and gristle here and there. Hair lay about the skulls much as it must have appeared in life.

Marguerite looked away. There was nothing in these gruesome relics that recalled to her the men she had known.

Koohsia knelt next to Louis and put his hands on his shoulder. "We can bury them now with their bodies, and they can go to the spirit world and be happy. They will not talk to you anymore."

Koohsia removed the blanket from his shoulders and spread it out on the ground, then he gently gathered up the skulls and wrapped them within. "Marguerite, you will please lead us back to the graves. Louis, you may carry the bundle."

"Koohsia," asked Philbrook as they walked back, "why would someone take their victims' heads into the woods like this?"

"I do not know. It is not a practice among my people or neighboring nations to remove heads. Is it a habit among your people? I heard a story once about an English king who liked to chop off heads so much that he did it to some of his wives."

"That was a long time ago," began Philbrook. Marguerite thought he was going to say more, but instead he just kept walking.

At the campsite, Marguerite showed them the common grave they had dug weeks before. Philbrook summoned Graham and the soldiers to dig. Koohsia began some kind of ceremony. Louis's eyes followed every movement. Marguerite did not understand the significance of much of Koohsia's performance, but she had seen similar ceremonies in Native communities. The dead and the living needed to be put right.

"That's far enough," she told the soldiers when their efforts came close to the depth of the bodies. She did not want to unearth anyone, only add their heads to the common grave.

"Quite right," said Koohsia. "No need to disturb them further."

He lowered the skulls down with great care, asking Louis to help him. He pulled out a pouch of tobacco, sprinkled some of it into the grave before filling his pipe. He smoked, passed the pipe around, then took a small flask out of his bag and took a swig. He poured a little rum into the grave and handed the flask to Louis, who took a sip, poured some in the grave, and passed it on to Marguerite. The flask went around everyone. Even the three solders put down their tools to join in. Billy Smyth had a look of disapproval on his face every time he saw the rum splashed into the grave, but he remained respectfully silent.

"These were good men," said Koohsia when the flask had finished its rounds. "I hope they can now move on to the spirit world—or wherever it is that four Frenchmen and an Englishman might choose to go. I hope this tobacco and rum will ease them on their pathway. Louis has done his duty for his friends, so they will no longer bother him in his dreams." Joseph and Marguerite crossed themselves, and Joseph led them in reciting the Lord's Prayer.

"*Au revoir*, Baptiste," said Louis, speaking in a clear voice to Marguerite's surprise. "I will miss you, Pierre. I thank you for your friendship. You too, Pero. Lucien and Barthelemy, I will miss your singing. Mr. Stone, you were the first Englishman I ever knew. You were a fair employer and I wish you well on your journey." He threw his pouch of tobacco into the grave, then grasped a shovel and began to fill the hole back in.

Soon after, Mihkosita and the canoemen returned with a deer they had killed. Marguerite joined them in butchering the carcass as Philbrook sat nearby writing in his journal. Brutus kept watch on the meat.

"Someone was through here on horseback a few weeks back," Mihkosita told her as they worked.

"Why do you say that?"

"About a half mile from here, we came across the main trail from Detroit to Kekionga. I saw prints of horses that had gone through and some sign that they had been tied for a few hours, several weeks ago."

"Lots of folks travel around these parts," she said.

"Yes, but the spot where these horses were tied caught my eye. It looks like the riders walked down here to the river."

Overhearing, Philbrook took his nose out of his journal and looked over. "How many?" he asked.

"Four horses, I think, and I saw old tracks of four, maybe five, men on foot. One was wearing boots, the rest moccasins. But I can't be sure they were together or if all the tracks were made at the same time."

"And they came directly here from where they left their mounts? To this spot?" asked Philbrook.

"Well, I can't say they came all the way. Once I got closer to the camp there were so many tracks overlaying the older ones that I couldn't follow any particular trail any longer."

Philbrook scowled. Marguerite recognized the expression as the one he often displayed when he was thinking. "Several weeks old, you say? That might put the riders here around the time of the murders," he said. "Show me the spot, Mihkosita, if you don't mind."

She and Mihkosita washed the blood from their hands, leaving the rest of the job of cleaning the deer to the Bourassas. The three of them set off into the woods, joined by Brutus. This was land that had never been cleared, so the forest was open, and the canopy of branches above filtered the sunlight and prevented the growth of underbrush. The walking was easy. After half an hour they came to a trail. It was not very wide but looked like it had seen many feet and hooves over the years, compacting the soil, so that not even weeds could sprout.

Just off the path the trunk of an old oak tree showed signs of a rope rubbing the bark smooth where it was tied. There were hoof prints and horse manure on the ground beneath. "I see what you mean, Mihkosita," said Philbrook. "Maybe some folks stopped here to go down to the river for water."

"Except there are closer sources of sweeter water. There is a fresh spring near the trail not far from here. It's much better than the muddy river." Mihkosita knelt and examined the ground a short distance away. "See, one pair of boots and the rest moccasins. Leading toward the clearing. It's as if they tied their horses here so that they could approach with stealth."

Philbrook examined the tracks, though Marguerite could see that they did not tell him a story the way they told one to Mihkosita. There was a clear imprint of a boot of an average size for a man and another smooth-soled moccasin print.

"But who?" asked Philbrook.

"Most travelers around here would be in moccasins," said Marguerite. Not many wear boots like you and whoever made this track, except army officers and some British traders." A strange thought came to her as she said this, but she quickly dismissed it.

"What is it, Marguerite?"

"Oh, nothing, I'm sure. Just a fleeting thought." She looked away. She did not want to distract Philbrook with her random ideas.

Mihkosita resumed. "I can see no sign of any larger party."

"So, we have evidence of four or five men on horseback but no war party," said Philbrook.

"That is my observation."

Marguerite thought this interesting, but was not sure if it helped. People were always moving about in the backcountry, for all sort of reasons. Not many men wore boots in the backcountry, but doing so did not make one a murderer. She hoped Philbrook had the sense to put the information in perspective.

Chapter 19

Phineas Philbrook

S o far, Philbrook was satisfied with his decision to bring Louis back to Auglaize and the scene of the murders. They had discovered the missing heads, and they were triggering new memories in the young canoeman every day. Philbrook had decided to stay here for a few days to see if they could discover more, but with each passing day, the pressure to continue back to Detroit increased.

If it were not for the unpleasant aspect of their investigation, Philbrook would be enjoying himself. The sky had been blue for several days, and the temperature pleasant. He spent much of his time trying to talk with Louis, but he still had plenty of time to walk in the woods with Brutus, draw in his sketchbook, or talk with Marguerite or Koohsia. He found that he liked their company, and they were helpful in bringing Louis back to reality.

Since discovering the missing heads, he had been spending several hours each day talking with Koohsia and Louis. They could communicate tolerably in a mixture of English and French, though it was always easier when Marguerite helped with the more challenging phrases. Louis was coming more into himself. He remembered much of his former life and recalled bits and pieces of the voyage up the Maumee, but he still recalled only fragments of the night of the murders.

There was nothing unusual about Stone's trip as far as Philbrook could tell. They had stopped at the regular camping places and done some trading among the Ottawa when they passed through their villages. Louis recalled that Stone had not wanted to linger among the Ottawa, as he thought his cargo would fetch higher prices at the Miami communities farther up the river. Marguerite confirmed that this was fairly typical, since the Ottawa visited Detroit more often on their own to trade for the things they needed.

Meanwhile Sergeant Graham and his men had little to do. Idleness brought with it an edge of restlessness, especially in the sergeant, who was accustomed to keeping busy.

"Are you making any progress with the lad, sir?" Sergeant Graham asked, approaching him in the afternoon of their fourth day at Auglaize. He was in shirtsleeves, as the weather was too warm for wool.

"Yes, Sergeant," said Philbrook. "Louis remembers a little more each day. This place stimulates his memory."

"Glad to hear it, sir."

Philbrook sensed that Graham had more to say.

"I'm sure you've thought of this, sir, but there is a good chance that the lad is feeding you a load of blatherskite. Maybe there is nothing wrong with his memory. Maybe he killed his friends and employer, and now he's stringing you along."

"That is a possibility, but I thought you suspected the Indians, Sergeant."

"I do, sir. They seem the most likely culprits to me, but I'm willing to keep an open mind. There is something about this Ouellette fellow I don't trust." The sergeant looked over to where Louis was sitting and talking with Koohsia. "How did he know where the heads were? The lad is half Indian. Maybe he met up with some Menomonie friends and joined them in the killings."

149

"Perhaps," Philbrook said. "But why? A rendezvous would require a good bit of planning. Either way, my gut tells me we have more to learn if we linger here a little while." It occurred to him that Captain Turnbull might not appreciate the delay, and he would have to account for his time. Indeed, they would have to return to Detroit soon, no matter what Louis or Koohsia said or did.

"Well, the men are enjoying their leisure," continued the sergeant looking toward the river where two of the soldiers were baiting fishing hooks. "The fishing's been good, but like my Ma used to say, 'idle hands are the Devil's workshop.' The men will find trouble if they are kept idle too long."

"Noted, Sergeant. Your mother was wise. I assure you, we will be heading back soon."

Graham was right about idleness. There had been a spat between the canoemen and the soldiers the night before—the sort of thing that would only get worse unless he kept the men busy. The incident almost had fatal consequences. Thomas Bellows saw Louis go into the woods in the middle of the night to attend to the call of nature and thought he was trying to escape. The soldier rashly discharged his musket at the terrified man before Philbrook woke and ordered him to stand down. Luckily, his ball missed. The *Canadiens* were upset by Bellows's recklessness, and angry words were exchanged before Philbrook was able to calm everyone down.

He was forced to speak forcefully to the men. "Ouellette is not to be treated as a prisoner, and you are not his keepers. This is not a battlefield, so no one is to discharge his weapon without a direct order from me. Is that understood?"

"Aye, sir," the men mumbled.

"And your guns have no reason to be loaded unless the sergeant or I order it so."

"Yes, sir."

The *Canadiens* were angry at Bellows, but they were appeased when they saw that Louis was alright and was not to be mistreated further.

Koohsia was pulling Philbrook in a different direction. The old man was concerned more with Louis's welfare than solving murders, so he resisted the idea of taking the canoemen back to Detroit. Philbrook counted on Koohsia to draw out Louis's memories, and that would stop happening if he put Louis under arrest and dragged him back to Detroit against his will. He resolved to try the gentle way first, as time was on his side. In the long run Koohsia could not stop him from taking Louis.

But it was time for some pressure. After the midday meal, Louis and Koohsia played a game they called "knucklebones" as they talked. They each had eight deer bones painted black on one side and yellow on the other. Philbrook did not entirely understand the rules, but they put the bones into a dish and shook them to see which colors came out on top.

He approached and sat down.

"Have you thought about what I asked you this morning, Louis?" The young man would now speak directly with others, though reluctantly, so Philbrook had been prodding him to remember the night of the murders.

"Yes, Ensign," he replied in a discouraged tone. "I'm afraid I cannot be more help to you. I remember voices and shouting that night. I remember being afraid. I know someone was here—someone not part of our party—but I cannot say who." Louis and Koohsia continued playing. Philbrook saw that Koohsia was interested, but choosing to stay quiet for now.

"French and English voices, but no Indians?" asked Philbrook.

"I don't recall hearing any Native voices," said Louis.

"Did you recognize any that you did hear?"

"I think Lucien was one. The English voice might have been Mr. Stone, but I'm not sure. It could have been a stranger. Most Englishmen sound alike to me."

They had gone over this before, but each time he asked Louis to repeat his account, new details emerged, but sometimes also contradictory ones.

"During your voyage with Mr. Stone, did your group encounter anyone or any other group that you argued with? Did Stone make any enemies that you saw?"

"I don't think so. I mean, lots of folks don't like having the English in this country, so not everyone is as friendly as they could be." Louis shook his dish of bones and looked to see how they came up.

"How about when you passed by the Cheney place? Any encounter there that you remember? An argument, perhaps?"

"Not that I remember."

"Did Stone cheat anyone that you saw?"

"Not brazenly. That made him better than lots of traders. I could be forgetting something though. I still have... gaps."

"But your mind is becoming more focused," said Philbrook. "I can hear it in your voice. Your statements are more assured, more confident."

Louis looked up at Philbrook, then back to his game. It seemed to Philbrook that Louis was frustrated that he could not recall more. "I remember more about my life before," said Louis. "About home, family, and some previous voyages. But the time with Mr. Stone—it's still a blur. Bits and pieces. I don't like to think about it, but I think I was sleepwalking again. I may have just heard things from a distance and come back here afterward. But whenever I recall that time, my heart starts to race, and I want to think about something else."

"You're saying you were sleepwalking before it happened—or during?" Philbrook asked.

"Yes, both, but I sometimes have trouble now distinguishing between dreams and wakefulness."

Philbrook wanted Louis to feel more urgency to remember, so he pushed harder. "Do you think that maybe the reason you can't remember is that you killed those men yourself? Perhaps you are avoiding facing up to your own misdeeds."

Louis looked up, and Philbrook thought he saw anger flash in his eyes. "You still think I did it? Of course you would." He shook his head and looked down for a moment, slumping his shoulders. "Someone else was here. I know that much. I was running from something—from someone."

"Maybe you ran from the horror of your own actions." Philbrook reflected that some men refuse to recognize evil in themselves even when it is readily apparent to others. Maybe Ouellette was choosing to be willfully blind to the darkness in his own soul. "How is it that you knew where to find the men's heads?"

"I don't know." Louis shook his head.

"Did you take them there?"

"No. I mean, I don't know. But I remember being there with them. I think I found them before."

Philbrook sympathized, but he worried that his sympathy could be misplaced. Was he too trusting? Graham had been right in one sense. He had to return Louis to Detroit, and once back at the fort, the matter would be out of his hands. Most would assume that this mentally damaged boatman was the guilty party and that the tomahawk they found belonged to him.

"You are asking us to believe that you slept through six violent murders?" Philbrook continued, his voice louder now. "That you alone were spared? Why? Because you were sleepwalking? Your story, at least the small part you remember, is a little far-fetched."

Louis looked to Koohsia for support, but the old man looked away. Philbrook noted the gentle rebuff.

"We need to leave this place tomorrow morning," Philbrook announced with more resolution than he felt. He did not know when he had come to that decision, but now suddenly he was resolved.

"We are going back to Detroit" he continued. "Koohsia, you and Mihkosita can come with us or go back home as you choose.

Your help has been invaluable, but my duty is clear in regards to Ouellette. He is subject to English laws, and now that he remembers some things, it is my duty to take him back to give his account of what happened here to the proper authorities."

Philbrook did not know how the old healer would react to this new assertiveness—whether he still considered Ouellette to be under his protection—but he had no choice. The old man did not have the power to stop him, but Philbrook had come to consider him an ally—a friend, and this felt like a betrayal.

"I understand," Koohsia said to Philbrook's relief. "Louis must go back to prove his innocence, and you must discover who did this. And it is my duty to come with you to speak on the boy's behalf."

THAT NIGHT, Philbrook sat by the riverside with Marguerite as she smoked her pipe. Every night, the interpreter would sit with her little clay pipe for half an hour before turning in, watching the sun descend toward the horizon. Lately Brutus and Philbrook had taken to joining her. He was becoming accustomed both to her and to the pungent smell of the tobacco smoke that often lingered about her head.

"What do you think, Marguerite? We have Ouellette now, but we really know little more than we did before. Perhaps Ouellette killed his companions. He seems to be the obvious choice. There is certainly something wrong with his mind. He could have gone into a rage, and now he either does not remember, or he is a very clever liar."

"It is one possibility. But you do not believe it, do you?"

Philbrook shook his head. "No, I don't." He wished he did. Everything would be easier for him if Ouellette was guilty. He could take him back to Detroit, present him to Captain Turnbull, and be done with it.

"Nor do I. What about Stone's chest wound? That was done with a spear not a tomahawk, but we found no spear. How could Louis have gotten rid of it?" Marguerite asked.

"I've considered that. He could have thrown it into the river or left it somewhere in the woods. The fact is, he is the only person still alive who we know for certain was here. And what else could have happened? Random travelers passing in the night decided to stop and commit some murders? Shawnee from the south or Ojibwa from up north traveling through unseen, committing this one massacre, leaving a tomahawk, then disappearing into thin air? How do we find such people if they even exist?" Philbrook stabbed at the ground with a sharp stick as he spoke. Brutus meanwhile rested his chin on Marguerite's knee and looked up at her with his large brown eyes.

"Louis is a gentle soul," said Marguerite.

Philbrook could not contradict her. It was true. Louis did not seem capable of such violence.

"But his mind is not right," he observed.

"It is out of balance to be sure." Marguerite looked up at the treetops for a moment, as if making a decision. "There is something I have not told you, Ensign," she said after a moment. She stroked Brutus's head, making the great dog squirm with pleasure. Philbrook waited for her to continue. "Several days before Mr. Kennedy and I left the Miami villages, back before we found the bodies, Kennedy and his friend Cole borrowed horses and went on a hunting trip. Just the two of them. Kennedy would often take little side trips like that while I handled the trading, so I thought nothing of it, but that was when these murders happened."

"What are you saying, Marguerite? That Kennedy and his assistant rode down from Kekionga and murdered these men? Why?"

"No, I'm not saying that, not really. But those prints that Mihkosita showed us—men coming here on horseback, one in English-style boots—that reminded me of them. Kennedy always wears boots and Cole has taken to moccasins. It is a long day's ride here from the villages on a good horse."

"But Mihkosita showed us four sets of prints," Philbrook said, while in the back of his mind he tried to process this new information.

"Yes, but he was not sure about them all being together. The other prints might have been ordinary travelers. Or maybe they met with someone else. I don't know."

"Do you think it was them?" Philbrook sensed that Marguerite did not—that she was putting forth the theory as a defense of Louis.

"No. Not at all. I'm just pointing out that it is possible," said Marguerite. "Other people besides Louis were in the area. There is no need to keep circling back to Louis."

"But what motive could Kennedy and Cole have to kill a fellow trader?"

"I don't know, Ensign. Competition maybe? Kennedy will get a better price for his furs now. Turnbull shutting down trade along the river will reduce the supply, which will boost up prices in New York."

"Murder certainly seems a drastic way to make a few extra shillings."

"People have been killed for less around here. And I'm not saying it is likely. I'm just giving you some facts. I think the only reason you suspect Louis is that we know that the poor boy was here when it happened." The interpreter seemed angry, or maybe just frustrated. "But that is too easy," she continued, "and I think you know it. Many among your English see this land as empty, but it is not. There are folks going about all sorts of business both on the river and by land. Kennedy and Cole are just two. We know Alexis Cuillerier passed through. The Cheney place is nearby, not to mention the Miami and Ottawa villages. Besides, what reason would Louis have to do such a thing?"

Philbrook shook his head. He needed more facts and fewer

guesses. "This matter just gets more confusing the more we learn. When we left Detroit, I was sure that this would prove a simple matter of disgruntled Indians blowing off steam. Now you have me entertaining ideas of rival English traders killing each other."

"And you shouldn't discount the Cheney gang entirely," said Marguerite. "There are rivalries among the French families. They are often obscured by the conflict between the French and English and Natives, but not all *Canadiens* get along. Maybe the canoe-men, not Stone, were the primary target."

"Possibly," Philbrook said, "but the way Stone was mutilated more than the others makes me think he was the one who inspired the violence."

"Or someone wanted it to look that way," she answered.

"What about the tomahawk?" Philbrook asked. "If Koohsia is correct that it is from the Cree or Ojibwa, do you think there is any chance that a war party from the north came through here and killed Stone's group?"

"I never thought it likely that Natives did this," said Marguerite. "Certainly not the Cree, they have no reason to come this far south. Ojibwa do sometimes, but not without being noticed by someone or leaving a trace. Just because the tomahawk looks to have been made by someone from up north does not mean that was who wielded it. Folks trade those sorts of items all the time. A Shawnee might have a tomahawk that came from the Ojibwa. Most of the Cheney boys have tomahawks. English soldiers often carry tomahawks when they are in the bush. It could even have belonged to one of the boatmen, or Stone, or anyone."

"Including Louis," he said.

Marguerite furrowed her brow. "Yes, I suppose."

Philbrook wondered if the interpreter was swayed too much by personal sympathies. He did not understand how she ruled out Natives so easily or why she was reluctant to suspect Louis. Of course she liked Louis. He did too. Louis had a vulnerability that made one want to protect him, but misplaced sympathy could be dangerous.

"So, we are back where we started," he said. "We have no idea who did this or why. But someone did. I cannot eliminate everyone. Without something more, suspicion will always fall back to the one person we know was closest when it all happened but cannot, or will not, tell us anything useful."

The sun was getting lower in the sky and would soon dip below the horizon.

Philbrook got to his feet. "Goodnight, Marguerite. Talking with you, as always, has been most helpful."

He began to walk away before noticing that Brutus had remained lying next to Marguerite with his head on her knee.

"Come on, Brutus. Time to go."

The dog looked fondly at Marguerite, then reluctantly got to his feet and followed.

Chapter 20

Marguerite Boyer

Marguerite was happy to see Detroit come into view at the end of their journey. The waterfront was busy, as the brig from Fort Erie had arrived recently. Sailors and soldiers were unloading army provisions and trade goods—taking them by small boat to the wharf, then loading them into donkey carts to transport them up the hill to the fort. Nearby, carpenters were framing a new sloop. Its ribs were all bent in place and the men were working on the sheathing. As they got close Marguerite could smell the freshly cut wood.

The last few weeks, with all this focus on violence and murder, had been less enjoyable than her more peaceful trips into the backcountry. She missed Daniel and hoped to spend the next few days with him. If she could see to getting all their boats and equipment stored away quickly, she could go home to relax and enjoy her family.

"Sergeant Graham, Marguerite, I'm going up to the office to report to Captain Turnbull. Why don't you two join me." Philbrook stepped out of the canoe onto Detroit's wharf and stretched his legs. "Koohsia, Ouellette, I'd like you to come as well."

159

Marguerite swore to herself at the delay, but she could not say no. The ensign was right to ask them with him to report to the captain. She looked to Papan, who anticipated her concerns. "I'll see to everything here until you're finished, Margot."

"Thank you, Joseph. Maybe you could take Mihkosita under your wing while we are gone? Show him around a bit."

They headed up the bank toward the fort. The guards at their post eyed Koohsia warily as they entered, but Philbrook vouched for him, and they let him pass.

They entered Turnbull's outer office to find his secretary in his usual place. "Is the captain in, Patterson?" asked Philbrook.

"G'day, Ensign. Welcome back. Just a minute." Patterson disappeared into the inner office and came back a moment later. "Please go right in."

"Philbrook!" boomed the captain. "It's about time. I'd started to think you'd gotten yourself killed. I can't tell you what a relief it is for me to know I won't be having to write any awkward letters to General Gage and your parents concerning your untimely death."

"It is a relief to me as well, sir," Philbrook answered.

Marguerite followed Philbrook into Turnbull's office. It was dark compared to outside, and her eyes took a moment to adjust.

The captain looked at the group accompanying him. "And you've brought company."

"Yes, sir. You know the sergeant and *Mam'selle* Boyer of course, and allow me to present Koohsia, elder of the Miami People of Kekionga."

"Very pleased to meet you Koohsia," said Turnbull, shaking the elder's hand. "I trust things are in order at Kekionga. Pacanne is well?" He paused to yell out the door, "Patterson, bring me the ceremonial pipe and some tobacco."

"And this is Louis Ouellette, formerly a canoeman for trader Ben Stone."

"Indeed?" Turnbull raised an eyebrow. "Well sit down, all of you." Patterson came in with the pipe and tobacco, which Turnbull proceeded to fill and light for the benefit of the Native guest. The small room quickly filled with smoke as he passed the pipe around. Marguerite was pleased that Koohsia was being treated with respect. Not every British officer would concern themselves with courtesy.

"Mr. Philbrook, tell me what you've found," said Turnbull, leaning back in his chair.

Philbrook recounted the journey and everything they had discovered. Marguerite thought his account was succinct and accurate. When he came to the end, he summed up, adding, "You see, Captain, it still remains something of a mystery. I thought you might like to speak with everyone yourself to decide how best to proceed."

"No, I'm not going to let you pawn off this business on me, Ensign. I've got enough to contend with these days without worrying about some traders who went off and got themselves killed."

"Yes, sir."

"I'll ask you a few questions, then rely on you to get more answers." Patterson came in with a tray of tea and set it down on the table. Turnbull gave him the pipe to take away and began to pour. "Ouellette, let's start with you: Did you kill Mr. Stone and your other companions?"

Louis straightened in his chair. "No, sir. I did not."

"Milk and sugar?"

"Um. Yes, sir. I mean one scoop of sugar please, sir."

"How do you know you didn't kill them? You claim not to remember everything."

"I just know that I could never do such a thing."

"And you, Koohsia?" asked Turnbull, holding up the teapot.

"Thank you, Captain." Koohsia smiled and looked eager. "With a little sugar, please."

"Do you know who did, Ouellette?" the captain continued. "Tell me the truth now. I know a lie when I hear one."

161

"I don't know," said Louis. "Just... some men attacked our camp in the middle of the night, and there was shouting."

"French and English, but no Native voices is what Ensign Philbrook said. You stick by that?"

"Yes, sir."

"Just so. Miss Boyer." He turned to her and smiled. "I recall you take a splash of milk, no sugar?"

"Thank you, sir." She was flattered he remembered how she took her tea. The captain often seemed brusque and distant, but he sometimes displayed unexpected courtesies.

Turning to Sergeant Graham the captain handed him a cup and continued. "Sergeant, I don't suppose you killed those men, did you?"

Graham scowled. "Sir? No, sir."

"I suppose you could have if you'd wanted to. You were at Pontiac's village at the time looking into the Cuillerier business. No great distance." Marguerite realized he was teasing his sergeant. She had witnessed over the past year that Turnbull's sense of humor often came at his subordinates' expense. They all knew that the idea Sergeant Graham had done such a thing was preposterous.

"Yes, sir, but I had no interest in Mr. Stone or his men." The sergeant ignored the captain's needling.

"Just so. We may be able to rule you out despite the blood-thirsty look you sometimes get in that eye of yours. Then who killed those men, in your opinion, Sergeant?"

"I think it was either this man here," answered Graham, pointing to Louis, "or a roving band of Indians. Maybe some rogue Shawnee up from the south. Or even some of Ouellette's people from among the Menomonie. And there is always the Cheney gang. We can't rule them entirely out, though this seems a bit beyond their scope. It may be whoever did this disappeared into the forest and will never be discovered."

"That is not really narrowing it down very much is it, Sergeant?"

"No, sir."

"Miss Boyer." The captain turned back to Marguerite. "What is your opinion?"

She appreciated being asked, though she doubted that her answer would be helpful. "I don't think it was Louis, sir, and I don't think the Miami or Ottawa people along the river know anything about it. Besides that, I don't know what to think. A Shawnee or Menomonie party would have attracted notice if they were in the area. It's all very puzzling."

"Ah, yes. You eliminate the most obvious conclusions, but what possibilities remain?"

"I can't say, sir," she said.

"That does us very little good. I asked Louis and the sergeant, so now I ask you, did you kill all those men?"

"Of course not."

"But you were just a few dozen miles away, or so you say. And you were the first on the scene."

"Joseph Papan and my men can vouch for my whereabouts, sir, and I for theirs." The captain's manner was beginning to irritate her, now that it was at her expense.

"Good. Now we are making progress. Either you are innocent, or you committed the murders with Papan and your men. Getting rid of the competition perhaps? Strikes me that you've got a good motive and ample opportunity." Marguerite began to flush in annoyance; if the captain was going to mock her, she would just as soon go home to her son and put this matter behind her.

The captain smiled. He looked over at Philbrook and winked. "Had you thought of that ensign? These are the sorts of hard questions you need to start asking people. Can't worry about putting anyone in a huff. Sometimes, getting someone worked up is the best way to get to the truth from them. It puts them off balance. Find out who could have done this and who might want to do it. Then ask them questions they don't like."

"Yes, sir."

The captain turned back to Marguerite. "Philbrook said that you cannot vouch for the whereabouts of Mr. Kennedy and his man... What was his name, Ensign?"

"Jabez Cole, sir."

"Just so. Mr. Cole. Can anyone vouch for the whereabouts of Mr. Kennedy and Mr. Cole at the time in question?"

"Just that they were within a day or so of the Miami village by horse, more or less," answered Marguerite.

"Aye. Which could include Auglaize if they made good time. And that scoundrel Cuillerier passed through the Ottawa villages shortly before the murder, so he was nearby as well. With horses, it seems. And there is the bloody Cheney gang." Turnbull shook his head. "It's tempting to believe they were responsible for this, the damned thieves. They relish being a thorn in my side. And who knows how many other *Canadiens* were traipsing about the back-country, willy-nilly, stirring up trouble without authorization. This matter is a bit more complicated than I thought it would be. Seems like a whole host of people were around the area and could have done this."

"Yes, sir." Philbrook nodded.

"Well, this has been an informative little discussion," announced Turnbull, standing up. "Ensign, I want you to come up with more. I'm not ready to give up discovering the truth just yet. With all due respect to the sergeant, I don't think we are dealing with an Indian uprising or plunder here. That's what I thought it was when I sent you off—I assumed it was some drunken plundering—but those sorts of things are never hard to figure out. Pontiac or Pacanne would have known something. I trust Koohsia's and Miss Boyer's judgment there. That tomahawk showing up was just a little too convenient, if you ask me, like someone trying to misdirect us. Give it here Sergeant. Let me take a closer look."

Graham handed the weapon to Turnbull, who gave it a brief look and held on to it.

"No," continued Turnbull. "I smell the work of someone with a score to settle—white men hoping to blame Indians. A small group of renegades like the Cheneys, maybe. Perhaps some *coureurs des bois* in liquor. Ask around locally, Ensign. Talk to whoever you can. Start with Mr. Kennedy and his friend. I think they are still staying at Mrs. Belanger's boarding house, though I think they plan on departing soon. Get a sense of who could have done this and why. There are only a few hundred white men in these parts, and you should be able to exclude most fairly quickly. Talk to everyone and smell out the lies. Start up a list of probable culprits. Understood?"

"Yes, sir."

"And, Ensign..."

"Yes, sir?"

"That Cheney bunch. I should have told you before you left to pay them some attention. I overlooked that the deaths happened so close to their place. Find out what rumors are out there among the *Canadiens*. Maybe get one of our local friends to ask around for you, about French feuds and such. Locals still tend to keep mum when British officers ask questions."

"I'll do that, sir."

"And no offense, Mr. Ouellette, but I don't think we can consider you cleared in this matter, despite Koohsia and Miss Boyer's good opinion. You are to consider yourself under Ensign Philbrook's charge. And Ensign, you can have Graham keep him in the gaol or find somewhere else for him, but Ouellette is your responsibility. Got it?"

"Yes, sir."

"Sergeant, escort Louis and Koohsia outside for a moment while I talk privately with Ensign Philbrook and Miss Boyer." When they were gone, Turnbull relaxed and leaned back in his chair. "I'm glad you arrived back when you did. I hope to see you both at the festivities tomorrow night."

"Festivities?" Philbrook asked.

"Just so. Recall the date, Mr. Philbrook." He reached back and tapped on the calendar that hung on the wall behind him. "June twentieth. Tomorrow is Midsummer's Eve, or Saint Jean Baptiste Day, as the *Canadiens* call it. There will be bonfires and gatherings all over. The soldiers will be roasting a few beasts out in front of the gates at dusk, and then the merchants are hosting a dance at Mr. Williams' home. All the officers will be expected to attend."

"I'd quite forgotten the date, sir." Marguerite realized that she had as well. She always enjoyed Saint Jean Baptiste Day celebrations.

"No surprise. I've heard your dour New England clergy discourage feast days, but the Church of England doesn't. And the *Canadiens* are all papists or pagans of course, so they like to make a big to-do."

"Indeed, sir. I believe I recall the good Reverend Williams calling Midsummer's Eve celebrations a papist abomination, but I have fond memories of the holiday from my time in England."

"Pretty much everyone around here celebrates, even the dourest bloody Scots. They're willing to put their Calvinist qualms aside for the duration of the festival. You have not been here long enough to discover this, but you'll find no shortage of social engagements at Detroit. We've got quite the little society. *Mademoiselle*, I trust we will be seeing you for barbecue and dancing?"

"Of course, Captain. I wouldn't miss it," said Marguerite.

"Splendid. I will see you then."

OUTSIDE THE OFFICERS' Building, they found the others waiting. "Graham, you heard the captain," said Philbrook. "I'm to ask difficult questions regardless of anyone's feelings. Could you tell me which soldiers accompanied you to Pontiac's village?"

"Young and Bellows, sir. I will get you my report of the trip. It should tell you everything you need to know."

"Excellent."

"And shall I escort Ouellette to the gaol, sir?" asked Graham. Marguerite hoped Philbrook would say no. She knew that the Detroit gaol was no more than a dark, filthy room with a bucket.

"No, I think not," said Philbrook. "Koohsia, would you mind keeping Louis company while you are here?"

"I will look after him at the Native encampment outside the gates. I plan to meet Mihkosita there soon," said Koohsia. Marguerite was relieved.

"Good. The sergeant will need to escort you both to the gate. Louis, I am trusting you not to leave the area until we get this sorted out. I'll come find you tomorrow."

"Yes, Ensign," said Louis.

Chapter 21

Phineas Philbrook

After the others had left, Philbrook asked Marguerite to introduce him again to her mother, who he wanted to ask about the activities of traders back when the murders took place. She led him to the eastern end of the fort and out a smaller gate that led to a dirt track, which followed the northern bank of the river past the wooden cottages of French *habitants*. The Boyer home and shop overlooked the river about a half mile from the fortified part of Detroit. A half dozen canoes were up on scaffolds next to the building.

Madame Boyer was working in the garden as they walked up. She was nothing like her daughter, observed Philbrook. Sally Boyer was short and plump, dressed in long skirts in the *Canadien* fashion, with a shawl over her shoulders and beaded moccasins on her feet. Her hands were dirty from her work.

"*Maman*, I'm back," called Marguerite as they got closer.

"Oh, Margot," Madam Boyer smiled at her daughter. "I dreamed you would be back today, and here you are. I must be getting the second sight."

"You remember Ensign Philbrook."

Madame Boyer looked Philbrook up and down. "Of cou... How are you finding our little community, Ensign?"

"Very interesting, ma'am. I learn more about it every day."

"And your murders? Did you find the culprit you were looking for? I'm hoping that the captain will open trade back up."

Before Philbrook had a chance to respond a high-pitched voice yelled out, "*Maman!*" and a little boy came running out of the building towards them.

"Daniel!" Marguerite picked the boy up and gave him a warm hug. "Daniel, I'd like you to meet Ensign Philbrook. He and I have been on a voyage together. Ensign, this is my son, Daniel."

A son? Philbrook was surprised. The notion that the interpreter was a mother had not crossed his mind. When he found his tongue, he said, "I'm pleased to meet you, Daniel." The boy smiled, then buried his face in Marguerite's shoulder. "He is a handsome boy," he said to Marguerite.

Marguerite stroked the boy's hair then returned to her mother's question. "Ensign Philbrook has come to seek your guidance on some matters, *Maman*. The murders are all still a mystery."

"Captain Turnbull has tasked me to come up with a list of possible culprits from among the French and British inhabitants— people who might have wished Stone and his men harm," Philbrook said. "I was hoping you could help me with that. I need a clearer picture of who could have been around Auglaize at the time. Business relationships, that sort of thing."

"Better come inside." Madame Boyer led them in the front door of the cottage which opened to a shop, packed from floor to ceiling with merchandise. They passed through it to a small side room that was set up as an office. Inside was surprisingly bright, with natural light from windows on three sides. A table against one wall held papers and a large ledger book. On the shelf above were several other identical ledgers with numbers on their spines. "Margot, why don't you put on some water for tea." Marguerite

nodded and went through a door in the back with Daniel at her
heels, chattering to her in French.

"Tell me, Ensign, what was the date when the murders
occurred?"

"It would have been the last week of March."

"At Auglaize?"

"Yes, ma'am." Madame Boyer sat at the table and directed
Philbrook to the chair next to her. She put on a pair of spectacles
and began to flip through the ledger, jotting down names on a
piece of paper. After several minutes, Marguerite brought in a
small tray with tea cups and set it in front of them before taking a
seat in the corner with Daniel on her lap.

"To get from here to Auglaize would take at least four days no
matter how you went, but likely longer," said Madame Boyer after
ten minutes had passed. "A good horse might be the fastest way or
a strong group of paddlers in a canoe in favorable conditions, but I
think we can assume that anyone who was here at the fort within a
few days of the murders could not have been at Auglaize to kill
anyone. This list is of traders and locals I can rule out for you." She
handed Philbrook a list of about fifty French and British names. "I
cannot account for everyone, of course, but I know of several
parties that went down toward Lake Erie around the time in question. Some have come in and gone back out again or gone down to
New York or Montreal. Here is a list of the British and French
traders I think were in the general area." She handed him another
paper with the names of nine traders on it. "Each had a crew along.
Mr. Jacobs might know of more."

She wrote some more. "And here is a list of Frenchmen who
spend most of their time in the backcountry to the south and west
of Lake Erie. You probably met some when you were at Kekionga
or along the river." This paper held more than a dozen names. He
saw that most were Cheneys or Langlades. "Then, of course there
will be men who were out hunting. Accounting for everyone is

maybe a bigger job than the captain thinks. You may have to spend weeks on it, especially accounting for folks who spend most of their time in the backcountry and don't come in to Detroit often."

"All I can do is begin talking to people and see what emerges," Philbrook said. "Your lists give me a starting point. I wonder though, do you know of anyone who might want to do this thing? So far, we have been unable to discover any motive for such violence."

"I would guess the Demon Rum is the likely culprit, Ensign. Men around here tend to do awful things when they are in liquor."

Philbrook thought she might be right, but if these murders were simply the result of intoxication, how was he to solve them?

"I wonder, do you happen to know if the Cheneys had any connection with the men killed? Any rivalries you know of?" He raised his cup of tea to his lips, but found still too hot to drink.

"I know there were a few spats between them and British crews on the river last year. Old rivalries die hard. But I'm not aware of any problems between them and the canoemen with Mr. Stone. I can't say it would be like them to resort to such violence. They are not bad people, but they like their independence and don't so much like the British."

"*Maman*," interjected Marguerite, "I told the ensign and the captain that Mr. Kennedy and Mr. Cole were off hunting at the time of the murders. Do you know if Mr. Kennedy had any reason to dislike Mr. Stone?"

"I don't know anything about that, but they knew each other from before they came here. War comrades, I think. Do you really suspect him? He was here yesterday asking about hiring canoes and canoemen for a trip up to Lake Huron. He asked if you were available to interpret, leaving the day after tomorrow. Should I worry about sending you out with him again?"

"No, *Maman*, I was safe with him before. We just can't rule him out yet."

"We? Have you joined Mr. Philbrook in his investigations, dear?"

Marguerite glanced at Philbrook. "No, *Maman*, but I would like him to solve this mystery. We can't have a murderer out there. It interferes with trade. As to Kennedy, the man says everything that passes through his mind, so I don't think he could keep a secret like this. Do you want me to ask Joseph to put together a crew for him?"

"Yes. I told Mr. Kennedy I'd send you or Antoine to interpret for him, depending on who got back to Detroit first. You don't mind going away again so soon?"

"No. I like keeping busy," she answered.

Philbrook found himself hoping that Marguerite would decline the new journey. He had gotten used to sharing his thoughts with her as he investigated. But Turnbull had only hired Marguerite for the voyage, so he should have no expectation of taking up her time any longer, now that they were back.

"And Amos Jacobs is going to go along for the ride," Madame Boyer told Marguerite. "He needs to get to Michilimackinac to take care of some personal business."

Marguerite made a sour face. "That awful man? Alright. I'll take care of the arrangements. We can leave in a couple of days."

Daniel scowled.

"No hurry, dear," said her mother. "You just got back. Why don't you put them off for a few days so you can enjoy tomorrow's *fêtes* and some family time?"

"Yes, *Maman*, stay longer," said Daniel, holding on to his mother's arm as if preventing her from escaping him.

"Maybe, but I'd like to fit in a couple of more voyages while the weather is still fine." She stroked her son's hair, but Daniel did not look reassured.

"You've plenty of time, dear," said Sally. "And I'm sure the handsome young ensign here will keep you up half the night tomorrow dancing. I've seen his sort before. Looks mild enough, but he's likely to sweep you off your feet if you don't watch out." Madame Boyer winked at Philbrook, who found himself feeling embarrassed.

"Madame, it seems you are an excellent judge of character." He smiled his best roguish grin.

～

PHILBROOK WENT BACK TO THE OFFICERS' Building to track down Lieutenant Christie and ask him about the soldiers' activities when the murders happened. He found the lieutenant behind the building, drinking a beer and throwing knives. His target was the lid of a barrel hung on the back wall. Philbrook noticed that the lieutenant was not very accurate, for there were several gouges in the wall around his target.

"Ramsay went down to New York around that time, as you know," said Christie between throws, "and Graham was visiting Pontiac's village with a couple of men. There was a firewood crew out in a bateau with Corporal McAdams, but I think they went to the north. The rest of the soldiers never strayed far from the fort during that time."

"Thank you, sir."

"You don't think it was the Indians then, eh, Philbrook?"

"That's the consensus, except for Graham, who still blames Indians. But the captain and the interpreter he sent with us don't think they would keep it secret if they were responsible."

"There is sense in that," said Christie. "No surprise that Graham would blame the Indians as a matter of course. He is no fan of them, ever since they took his fingers and eye. I'd look harder at the *Canadiens* if I were you. They are a violent bunch. That Cheney gang especially is quite a parcel of thieves." Christie handed one of his knives to Philbrook. "Here, take a throw."

Philbrook felt the well-balanced steel throwing knife in his hand. He imagined it had cost a pretty penny in England. He recalled practicing throwing blunt knives with friends in Portsmouth as a youth. He took it by the blade and gave it a toss toward the target. It stuck near the center.

"Quite the shot!" exclaimed Christie. "I did not know knife-throwing was one of your skills." The lieutenant did not look entirely pleased.

"Just a lucky shot, sir."

"Surely," said Christie.

Philbrook retrieved the knife from the target and handed it back. He reflected that the Lieutenant might not be the best of sports. If offered another throw, he resolved to miss.

"Now if I had been in your place," Christie returned to what he had been saying, "I would have slapped the Cheneys around a little to see what came of it, then arrested them and brought them back here, but I understand why you didn't. That sort of thing would cause an uproar with the locals if they turned out to be innocent."

"You mentioned that Graham lost his fingers and eye to Indians?" Philbrook said. He had wondered about the sergeant's disfigurement, but thought it impolite to ask Graham.

"He didn't tell you? I suppose he wouldn't. He was a captive for several months during the war. One of his captors ended up taking a liking to him and kept him as a slave for more than a year, but not before others took his eye and mutilated his hands one joint at a time. Then he got captured again during the Indian uprisings."

"Ghastly," Philbrook said. "He told me about being captured but nothing of torture."

"It's not something anyone likes to talk about. He learned to speak the Indian jargon pretty well during his first captivity, which makes him quite useful to us when we need to send a message out to one of the communities."

Philbrook nodded. "I know several boys at home who spent some time in captivity or came home not quite whole."

"True enough. Some end up strangely sympathetic to the

savages after their ordeal. Even Sergeant Graham. He loves them and he hates them in turn, but gets along with them remarkably well considering. But I think the missing fingers and eye stop him short whenever he starts to sympathize too much." Christie turned back to his target, aimed carefully, and threw. The knife bounced off the target and fell to the ground.

Chapter 22

Phineas Philbrook

P hilbrook decided it was a good time to talk to Sam Kennedy again and, if possible, his friend Jabez Cole. Marguerite had confirmed that they could be found at an inn operated by Madame Belanger, a *Canadien* widow. Her establishment was a favorite of British traders who chose not to rent permanent rooms but wanted a solid roof overhead when they came into town. She provided a reasonably clean bed upstairs and a hearty breakfast and dinner in her tavern downstairs. Beer, wine, and rum cost extra. Philbrook found the building in the northeastern part of the fort. A plump middle-aged woman was tidying up a small dining area, though it was not mealtime, so no customers were around.

"Madame Belanger?" Philbrook ventured.

"*Salut. C'est moi.* What can I do for you?" Madame Belanger looked up and smiled, but continued her work.

"I'm Ensign Philbrook. I was looking for Sam Kennedy. I wanted to talk to him about the trader Ben Stone."

"You are in the right place. He's out now, but I expect he will be back soon." Madame Belanger was lifting chairs onto the tables so that she could mop underneath. "I heard about that sad business with poor Monsieur Stone. He stayed here, you know, before going up the river. Nice for an Englishman."

"I'm looking into his death. Was there anything notable that you remember about him?"

"Not really." She paused her work for a moment and looked at him. "I think it may have been only his second voyage in these parts. I remember him mainly because before he left, he stayed up late drinking. Mr. Kennedy and his little friend were here too, along with Mr. Jacobs, the agent. They kept me up half the night and left a mess to be cleaned up."

"Well, men are apt to do that sometimes."

"You don't need to tell me," she returned to her mop as she spoke. "I run an inn, after all. And I don't really mind. They were old comrades and had many memories to share."

"What sort of memories?"

"From the war. They were Yankee provincials, I think. They seemed to have shared much suffering. Not that I snooped on their conversations. I'd never do that. But sometimes it is hard not to overhear. Americans talk so loudly when they drink."

Philbrook suspected that Madame Belanger loved to overhear. She was likely one of the most well-informed members of the Detroit community, but he maintained his silence on the matter.

The front door swung open and Samuel Kennedy bustled in followed by his companion Jabez Cole. Both were wet from a rain that had begun to fall. Philbrook thanked Madame Belanger and turned to Kennedy.

"Mr. Kennedy. I was hoping to speak with you," he said.

"Philbrook! Well met then. What news of the massacre? Did you find the warriors who ended Ben's days?"

"It may be that we are looking for a different sort of murderer. It seems doubtful now that Indians were responsible for what happened at Auglaize."

"Oh, I'm not so sure of that," said Kennedy. "I saw the scene with my own eyes after all. I know the work of savages when I see it."

Philbrook had no interest in arguing with Kennedy, as he sensed that he was not a man whose mind was open to changing.

"We found a witness to the killings," said Philbrook, "a young canoeman called Louis Ouellette. His memories were damaged in the affair, but they are slowly returning. I'm sure that he will be able to tell us exactly what happened in a matter of days. But in the meantime, do you have a little time to sit and talk? Perhaps if Madame Belanger would allow it, we could use one of her tables. I'm sure your views on a few matters would be a great help." Philbrook hoped the flattery was not too much.

"Certainly," said Kennedy. "And I could use a beer. Madame, how about a couple of beers over here?" Cole slipped quietly up the stairs as Madame Belanger went behind the counter and poured two mugs of beer.

"I've been trying to get a sense of Mr. Stone," Philbrook continued. "What kind of man was he? It has been mentioned that you knew him back when you were in the provincials."

"Yes indeed. He was in my company."

"You were an officer?"

"No, sir. I was the sergeant. We had officers of course, but they never seemed to be around when things were happening. In any case, Stone was a good lad, I suppose. There was very little by way of discipline among most of the provincials, though I tried my best. Stone, like many of the others, was fresh off a New Jersey farm. Like the rest of us, he'd signed up for a summer fighting the French. He was a good soldier. Smart, but he liked to test the limits, if you know what I mean."

"He was insubordinate?" asked Philbrook.

"Well, not exactly insubordinate, but he was full of questions. He always wanted to know why this and why that. I preferred men who would follow orders without a damned conversation."

Philbrook was aware that Kennedy was a man who preferred

talking to listening, so he resolved to get him talking and see where it led.

"Did you know him before the war?" he asked. "When I served in the provincials, most of the men in my company were from my hometown."

"I knew some of the company beforehand. We came together from a collection of small villages and towns in northern New Jersey. Stone was from a town several miles from mine. I'd encountered him before, but I wouldn't say I knew him."

"Did he challenge your authority? Did you have to disciple him ever?"

"No, nothing like that," said Kennedy. "He was a good lad, mostly, and he was smart. Also a bit of a smart-ass, if you know what I mean."

"So he annoyed you?"

"Yes. Sometimes," admitted Kennedy.

"Madame. Belanger mentioned that you spent an evening here with Ben Stone along with Amos Jacobs and your friend Jabez Cole. All four of you served together. Is that right?"

"Yes. Cole and I have stayed friends since the war, but I'd lost touch with Stone and Jacobs. It was nice to reconnect. Though I'm not sure what any of this has to do with Stone getting killed."

"Probably nothing," said Philbrook. "We've been entertaining the notion that the killers were British or French, not Native. I'm trying to come to an understanding of Mr. Stone's personal relationships."

"I'm happy to help, but you're wasting your time. He was killed by savages."

"Be that as it may, I was wondering if you had lost touch with Mr. Jacobs, as well."

"Pretty much, but he had been in touch with Stone." Kennedy took a sip of his beer. "I encountered Jacobs when I showed up here and discovered that he is Daniel Campbell's local agent. Campbell is a merchant down in Schenectady who supplies most of my cargo. But Jacobs and Stone had been corresponding. They planned to work together."

"When you had drinks with them before Stone left on his voyage what was your impression of him and Jacobs? Had they changed much since the war?"

"Stone, not so much. He seemed the same. But Jacobs, that's another story. He went with you to retrieve those packs, right? Surely you noticed that he is crocked most of the time. He's never without his flask."

Philbrook nodded. It was hard not to notice Jacobs's drinking.

"And he refills the flask several times a day. He didn't drink like that before. Sad really," said Kennedy. "I don't expect he will survive long without making some changes."

"And what about Jabez Cole?" asked Philbrook. "He seems your opposite in most ways, but you've stayed in touch and work together. I'm a little unclear how he fits in your business. Seems like more than an ordinary boatman, but not a clerk or a partner?"

"That's about right," said Kennedy, looking toward the stairs that Cole had gone up. "He acts as my assistant, not a clerk really, as he can't write or keep accounts, but I give him a share in return for some extra responsibilities. He is an excellent hunter and unusually handy in the woods, but he doesn't really have a head for business."

"That seems generous, giving him a share," said Philbrook. "Plenty of good hunters around these parts would work for a few shillings." Philbrook thought there was something odd about Kennedy and Cole's relationship, but was not sure it had anything to do with Auglaize.

"He earns his keep," Kennedy said quickly, then remained uncharacteristically quiet for a moment. Philbrook had decided not to pursue the matter further when Kennedy added, "Well, the fact is I owe him."

"You owe him money?"

"Oh no, nothing like that. I owe him because he saved my life."

"Sounds like there is a story there. I'd love to hear it." Philbrook was not sure if he was wasting his time asking about events that were long past, but he felt that he had to get to know the victim as well as the people who knew him.

"Might as well. The story will tell you a bit about the others you've been asking about as well." Kennedy took a sip of his beer. "Like I've said, in fifty-seven, Cole, Jacobs, Stone, and me were all in the Third Company of New Jersey's Second Regiment. Ended up at Fort William Henry at the wrong time."

Philbrook had heard about what happened at Fort William Henry in the summer of 1757. Everyone in the American colonies knew the brutal story. General Montcalm had come down from Montreal with his army of French regulars, *Canadien* militia, and northern Indians. Their plan was to march on Albany and the Hudson River Valley, but first they had to take Fort William Henry on Lake George. Montcalm besieged the fort, and the British commander, Lieutenant-Colonel Monro, sent word to his superiors that he was outmatched. If help did not come soon, he told them, he would be forced to surrender to Montcalm.

No help arrived.

Days later the remnants of Monro's army began to trickle south with tales of a massacre.

"You had an awful time of it I expect," Philbrook said.

"You mean this?" said Kennedy, pointing to the scar that ran from his hairline down to his chin. "I've got General Montcalm and his damned savages to thank for this. But I've got Jabez Cole to thank that my whole scalp wasn't taken that day."

Philbrook sipped his beer and silently waited for Kennedy to continue.

Kennedy composed himself as if he were taking himself back to that time. "Word had gone around that morning that we were abandoning the fort as part of an honorable surrender," he began. "Honors of War—that's what Montcalm promised if we withdrew, but his Indian allies had not been consulted. They had gone to war for glory, captives, and plunder—Montcalm had promised them that much, and they had traveled far from home. Some of their companions had been killed during the campaign, and their deaths were still raw. They weren't about to go home with nothing to show for their efforts."

Philbrook had heard much the same before, but never from someone who had been there.

"We were near the end of the column when they attacked," Kennedy recalled. "I told the boys to stay together, to form up in ranks and seek safety in numbers, but we had no powder or shot—that had been part of the terms of our surrender. So we were easy prey for the hellhounds. Cole was right by my side. I don't think he was more than fifteen years old at the time, and he seemed to think that staying close to his sergeant would keep him safe. Stone, Jacobs, and some others lingered nearby as well, with no notion of what to do. The damn officers were nowhere to be seen." He spat.

Philbrook sat back in his chair to allow Kennedy to tell his story uninterrupted.

"The beasts were everywhere. Soon, the whole company seemed to dissolve. Soldiers broke up into groups of two, three, or four and fled into the woods or got taken captive or cut down. It was then I got knocked on the head. I was out for just a few seconds before I came 'round—lying on my face in the mud with a man's knee pressing into my spine. One of the Western Indians, I think. He had his knife to my skull and his other hand had grabbed a fistful of my hair. The point of the knife had just started to dig in when I felt it suddenly slide haphazardly down my face giving me this instead of taking my scalp." Kennedy pointed to his scar. "The warrior rolled off me, dead. Blood spurting from his throat with the last few beats of his heart. And there was Cole with his hunting knife, covered in the fellow's blood. I could hardly see, with blood running into my eyes and my head pounding from the blow. Cole picked me up like a sack of onions and set off for the woods.

"That's where we found Amos Jacobs and Ben Stone, along

with Paul Adams, another young member of our company, huddled in a thicket of small trees, keeping out of the melee. They had no idea what to do, so I told them we had to flee south. We could stay off the main road until we were out of the thick of it, then keep on until we reached Fort Edward.

"I'm afraid I was a great hindrance to our small party thanks to the blow I took to my head. I'd walk for a few dozen yards, then my head would begin to pound and swim. My eyes would lose all focus, and I'd fall. That and I couldn't stop puking. Why a knock on the head should make a man empty his guts is a mystery to me, but I can assure you it did. I still get the occasional headache and dizzy spell from the hit I took that day, but in the immediate aftermath it was crippling.

"The men fashioned a sling from an old blanket to carry me. They'd pull the ends of the blanket over their shoulders, and I'd sit in the middle with my arms around their necks. For the rest of the day they took turns, two men carrying and two resting. Every so often we would hear the savages, so we would hide for a spell. It was terrifying.

"We made only five miles that day. When we first set off, we were surrounded by other fleeing soldiers, but they soon left us behind, so that the only ones we would meet were the injured and abandoned. Those who could not walk anymore would cry out for our help, but I was burden enough for our small group. We would hear the occasional shout or cry that let us know that at least some of the enemy was still in pursuit, picking off the slow or unwary. At the end of that first day we found a patch of bare ground to collapse and rest. When I awoke shortly after dawn, the others were gone. All except Jabez Cole, that is."

"Gone?" repeated Philbrook. He had seen men dishonor themselves out of fear before, yet it always surprised him. "They deserted you?"

"Yes, indeed," resumed Kennedy. "But I don't blame them really. None of us had eaten in more than a day, and we were all convinced that the devils would be pursuing us in force. I was deadweight, and frankly I was lucky they had taken me as far as they did. I told Jabez he should go on alone and report where he'd left me when he got to Fort Edward."

"Did he?"

"No, the damned fool. He said he was going to get us some breakfast and he'd be right back. He was gone for about an hour, and I started to think he had gotten some sense and run off like the others, but then he came back with water and a pouch full of greens and a small fish. We ate it all raw. I still don't know where the damned fish came from. I thought the meal would make us sick, but it turns out that Cole knows all the plants of the forest, including which ones are edible. Comes from growing up dirt poor in the Jersey pine barrens. His people were squatters who lived here and there just beyond the edges of the established settlements, so his upbringing was not what you'd call civilized.

"When we finished eating, we started off. For a time, I was able to walk, but then my head began to swim again and my legs folded under me. Jabez found two small trees that he cut down with his knife to fashion poles about ten feet long. He tied some sort of vines between them and used the old blanket to make a stretcher. He dragged me behind him in it for several miles. Eventually, when we were within a couple of miles of Fort Edward, some Connecticut soldiers out looking for stragglers found us and helped us to safety."

"Remarkable loyalty," said Philbrook. He was impressed by this account of Jabez Cole. The little man had previously seemed to him like something of a wastrel, but apparently, he was both brave and talented.

"Jabez knew exactly where we were the whole time," Kennedy continued, "so we took a direct route back even though we stayed off the main road for the most part. The man may not seem too bright—he hardly got any education as a kid—but in the woods, he knows what he's about. And it turned out Stone and the others got themselves captured soon after they left us. A pack of Ojibwa got them, killed Adams, and dragged the other two all the way to Montreal for ransom." Kennedy laughed. "So they paid for their decision to leave us." He shook his head. "I did not know that part until later. At first, when they did not show up at Fort Edward, I'd assumed they'd all been killed. It wasn't till a year went by that I finally heard what happened to them."

"You never served together again after that?" Philbrook asked.

"The provincials that survived that damned fiasco were discharged for the winter shortly after. Cole and I served three more summer campaigns together. Stone and Jacobs never enlisted again, as far as I know. I don't blame them after their unplanned jaunt to Canada."

"I'm surprised the four of you seemed on good terms when you got together here," said Philbrook. "You have every reason to resent them, considering how they left you. According to Madame Belanger you stayed up half the night together before Ben Stone set out up the Maumee." Philbrook wondered if this resentment could have become hate. Could they have hated Ben Stone enough to murder him all these years later for his selfishness back then?

"Well it's been ten years, and all those lads did was run from a hellish situation," said Kennedy, seemingly oblivious to the notion that Philbrook might suspect him of the man's murder. "I don't know if I would have hung around if one of them couldn't walk. And they paid for their decision. If they'd stayed with Jabez and me, they would have been better off, but they just saw him as a scrawny kid and me as a dead weight. That and Amos Jacobs is such a sorry excuse for a man these days there's no point in resenting him."

"That is a remarkable story, Mr. Kennedy. I'm not sure how it might help me, but I feel I know a bit more about Mr. Stone now, which should help." Philbrook paused. He was hesitant to let Kennedy know that any suspicion had fallen his way, but he needed to ask directly. "And one more thing. When you and Cole were up on the Maumee River at Kekionga, I'm told you went off for a few days to hunt."

"That's right. I'd hoped to see a buffalo in the wild, so we traveled west for a little over a day then back to Kekionga. No luck, I'm afraid."

"You did not go north toward Auglaize?"

"No. Of course not." Kennedy seemed to dismiss the question at first. Then Philbrook saw its implication slowly reflected in his face. "Oh, I see what you're thinking. But no, Ensign, neither Jabez nor I bore any lasting ill will against Ben Stone. We went nowhere near Auglaize until we returned with Marguerite and the canoemen days later."

Philbrook believed him—at least for now. Marguerite had said that Sam Kennedy was too talkative to keep big secrets, and, so far, he agreed. Could there be a side to Kennedy that he kept hidden? Philbrook thought it was possible, but not likely.

"Thank you for your help, Mr. Kennedy. Is there anyone you are aware of who might have wanted Stone dead? Any enemies from his past that you are aware of?"

"I think you are on a fool's errand looking at anyone but the Indians, Ensign. And, like I said, I've hardly seen him these past ten years."

"Thank you for talking with me. Please tell your friend, Cole, that I'd like to speak with him as well when he has a chance. I'd like to hear his observations from when you found the bodies."

"I'll do that, but Jabez isn't the most talkative fellow. Regardless, I'm sure the truth will come out sooner or later." Kennedy finished off the last of his beer, left his cup on the table, and departed up the stairs.

*

Chapter 23

Phineas Philbrook

With the exception of a few London gin shops after dark, Philbrook had never seen such wild revelry. The aroma of wood smoke and roasting meat hung in the air. The orange glow of several bonfires pierced the darkness. Hundreds of people gathered around the flames: talking, laughing, drinking. Children ran about without restraint. Dogs ran after. One cur ran furtively by with a hunk of dripping meat held greedily in his jaws to disappear under a nearby building. Philbrook was glad he had left Brutus in the officers' kennel, where he would stay out of trouble for the night.

Music came from several directions. One fire, in the center of Rue St. Anne, was the arena of the soldiers, led mainly by the Irish and German Catholics among them. A few glum-looking redcoats soberly manned the stockade, but most had an eye only for celebration. The Scots and New Englanders watched the proceedings with Calvinist suspicion at first but soon put aside their misgivings and joined in. Around the fire, some soldiers were showing their fancy footwork to the sound of fiddles and whistles. None appeared overly sober.

Outside the gates there was another bonfire, this one lit and tended by local *habitants*, joined by representatives of the surrounding nations who looked on in fascination. The scene was much the same: dancing, drink, music. There was great sport being made jumping over the bonfire, a Saint Jean Baptiste Day tradition of particular interest to the younger men. Some jumped safely over the edge, where the flames were not so high, but the more daring jumped right through the strongest blaze to cheers and applause.

The celebration had been going on for several hours now, since well before sunset. Cooks had been turning pigs and steers over coals since a little after noon, and they now sizzled and dripped. While festivities were widespread, the locals seemed to be having the most fun, likely because there were more women among them, not to mention the children running about. Revelers wandered between different gatherings, and many a soldier found a nice local girl to try to impress.

Philbrook saw most of his erstwhile companions from his recent voyage enjoying themselves. Joseph Papan and the other canoemen were at the fire outside the gates. Several of them jumped the bonfire when prompted. Koohsia and Mihkosita were also there, quietly watching with Louis. Among the soldiers within, his self-appointed orderly Billy Smyth, none too sober, could be seen dancing a jig whenever he was given the least hint of encouragement. Sergeant Graham was on duty, so he stood off to the side watching the scene with Privates Young and Bellows. Sergeant Ramsay was nearby, wearing his habitual scowl. There was a rather pretty younger woman with him, holding the hands of two young children—a girl who looked to be about two years old and a boy of about three. They both looked disturbingly like miniature versions of the sergeant.

"Who is the young woman with Sergeant Ramsay?" Philbrook asked Lieutenant Christie, who watched the scene with him, drinking a glass of shrub.

"Why, that's his wife, improbable as it may seem. Marie is her name."

"Indeed?" Philbrook was surprised to see such an attractive young woman with the craggy middle-aged sergeant.

"He found her down in Niagara, the daughter of a French soldier who went back to France. I don't think she wanted to live with her mother's people—Seneca, I think. And her father was not inclined to take her or her mother back to his family in France. Our good sergeant is much besotted with her and their children."

"I can see why," said Philbrook.

"We will be expected at Mrs. Williams's soiree soon," said Christie. "I know she is eager to introduce you around what passes for society in this town."

They walked down Rue St. Anne and then north onto a side street. They came to the large two-story house of Thomas Williams, the scion of an Albany mercantile family. Williams moved to Detroit shortly after the end of Pontiac's uprising to manage the Detroit end of the family business. Soon after he married the daughter of a local *Canadien* family. The young couple were now the center of Detroit society. Philbrook heard music—a more genteel variety than the fiddles of the soldiers' celebrations—from behind the house.

"They will have set up around back in the garden to enjoy the summer night," said Christie as he led Philbrook around the side of the house.

There was a wooden porch in back, overlooking an enclosed patio and garden. Four musicians were playing a familiar tune while several officers and local merchants and their wives sipped punch and chatted amiably. Though the sun had just set, the garden was lit up with tin lanterns and candles. Christie led him to a long table that held pewter and tin cups, assorted glassware, and a punchbowl. He helped himself.

"Take care with the punch, Philbrook. Williams always mixes it stronger than it tastes." Christie handed him a cup. "He does not think his parties are successful unless a few guests have to be carried home."

At the far end of the garden, a bonfire burned, though it was more sedate than those he had seen outside. Several women were dressed proudly in what he knew was the height of London or Paris fashion a year past. Lieutenant Christie led him up to a remarkably pretty young brunette with a pale complexion in a tasteful light blue gown.

"Mrs. Williams, allow me to present Ensign Phineas Philbrook, the latest addition to our humble garrison. Ensign, Mrs. Williams, our hostess."

"Thank you for your gracious invitation, ma'am." Philbrook bowed. "Your garden amazes me. It is the loveliest place I've seen since leaving London many months ago."

"Why thank you, Monsieur Philbrook." Theresa Williams looked pleased with the compliment. "We do our best to bring a little culture to our community. But shame on you for taking so long to appear at one of our gatherings." She spoke excellent English with a charming French accent. "It must be several weeks since you first arrived."

"I'm afraid my time has not been my own. The captain sent me off on a journey within a short time of my arrival, and we just returned yesterday."

"I suppose I can find it in my heart to forgive you then, sir." Mrs. Williams smiled then looked to the lieutenant. "Now, be off with you, Lieutenant Christie. I am taking Ensign Philbrook under my wing to introduce him to some ladies who are longing to meet him at last." She took his arm and began to lead him around the garden. What followed seemed like an endless stream of introductions. When he emptied his first glass of punch, a servant took it from him and promptly replaced it with another. Mrs. Williams continued her introductions.

Philbrook had of course met all of the officers and several of the merchants before, but few of their wives. He knew what was required of him, and he made suitable small talk with each in turn as Mrs. Williams led him around. He found it interesting that several British merchants had found wives among the French-speaking population, and these families now formed an emerging bilingual society.

Mrs. Williams introduced him to an assortment of young women, mostly the unmarried daughters of French merchants. "And I have taken the liberty of arranging you several dance partners for later, Ensign. A presumption, I know, but I am determined that you make the rounds. We get so few new gentlemen in Detroit."

Philbrook knew this latter part to be untrue but also knew that his role for the moment was to go along with whatever his hostess asked of him. He generally did not like fashionable parties. Polite banter did not come easily to him, and unfamiliar people tended to make him uncomfortable. But Theresa Williams liked to talk, meaning that Philbrook could get by with smiles and short observations while she steered the conversation. He found that the punch was relaxing him. Alcohol always had a way of making social settings more tolerable.

Mrs. Williams led him up to a tall woman in a pale green dress. "I understand you've met Mademoiselle Boyer?" said Mrs. Williams.

Philbrook was surprised to realize it was Marguerite in front of him, dressed not in her soiled wilderness garb but in a simple yet fashionable dress. She was like a different person. Her hair, rather than haphazardly braided down her back, was neatly pinned up about her head. She seemed even to have combed it. She had a singularly scrubbed look about her, much in contrast to the unbathed look Philbrook had become accustomed to.

"Miss Boyer, you look lovely."

"Thank you, Ensign." He was not sure, but he imagined he saw her blush. "Theresa, can I take Mr. Philbrook off your hands for a moment?"

"Of course, Marguerite." Mrs. Williams gave Philbrook a knowing look as she withdrew. "I need to instruct the musicians for the first dance, so I'm happy to leave Ensign Philbrook in your capable hands."

"You'd best be on your guard, Ensign." Marguerite rolled her eyes as Mrs. Williams departed. "Theresa is determined to see every young man and woman in Detroit well married. I have been a great disappointment to her for several years now." She took a large gulp of her punch which tinged her upper lip red.

Philbrook was at a loss for words. Marguerite was not the sort he expected to meet at a soirée. Of course, he knew she would be here since Captain Turnbull had mentioned as much, but foolishly, it had never occurred to him that she would be transformed. Together, they watched as Mrs. Williams went off to instruct her guests to move out to the edge of the garden, turning the patio into a dance floor. She found her husband, and the two of them set an example for their guests as the musicians began to play a minuet.

"Don't worry, Philbrook." Marguerite smiled. "I am not going to make you dance with me. I just wanted to ask you about your progress."

"*Au contraire, Mademoiselle*, we cannot let down our host." Philbrook was emboldened by the punch. "Shall we?" he held out his arm. Marguerite laughed and took it with a callused hand.

"It would be my pleasure."

Philbrook was indeed happy to dance. While he did not consider himself a graceful man, he flattered himself that he could move with sufficient poise when it was required. He had spent over a year living in his uncle's household in London, where dancing was all the rage. He became the default partner for his three female cousins whenever they were invited to a ball. It was much preferable to him than polite conversation. He was surprised to find that Marguerite danced easily. This strange woman perhaps had more sides to her than what he had seen on their journey.

After the first minuet with Marguerite and another couple, Philbrook moved on to a different young lady presented to him by

Mrs. Williams, a Mademoiselle Langlade, who seemed nervous. Then came a Mademoiselle Denys, a short young woman who seemed very intent on being admired. She was followed by a perpetually amused Mademoiselle LaCorne and then another slim young woman whose name he forgot as soon as he heard it. After the first formal dances, the musicians moved on to country dances. The environment did not really lend itself to conversation, but he was happy to twirl around and hold on to the gloved hands of Detroit's eligible young ladies. None made much of an impression, though they were all pretty and well-mannered. He knew that some men would be charmed, and perhaps he would be too if his mind were not preoccupied.

Between dances, he and Marguerite often found each other again. They made easy conversation and drank punch liberally. His experiences with well-bred young women tended to entail strained conversation that either quickly dwindled when he ran out of his store of wit or silence on his part as the young lady rambled on about matters he cared nothing about. But he and Marguerite spoke naturally. They talked of Detroit, its people, how it had changed in Marguerite's lifetime. She asked him more about New England, about his time in London, and about his ocean voyages. Perhaps it was the effect of the punch, but he found myself more at ease with her than he had been during their recent trip. When they were in the backcountry, he had always felt like her ignorant student receiving lessons, while here they were on more equal footing. He returned to her frequently with requests to dance—a cotillion and several country reels. In between they sipped their drinks and chatted together in the garden.

"Did you find Mr. Kennedy today?" asked Marguerite during one pause in the music. "*Maman* wants me to accompany him to Michilimackinac, so I was counting on you to tell me if you think he is a murderer."

"I did find him, yes. He had an interesting story to tell about his past with Cole, Jacobs, and Stone." He recounted the main points of Kennedy's story.

"So he had reason to dislike Stone, hate him even," observed Marguerite.

"Yes, but well short of a motive to kill him in the manner he was killed. I thought about what you said about him being too talkative to keep a secret, and I think I agree unless more evidence were to come to light against him."

"Mr. Kennedy has his flaws, to be sure," said Marguerite, "but I never saw him as a shrewd man. I think he is very much what he appears to be—a man of supreme confidence and moderate ability."

He laughed. "I think you are a good judge of character, Marguerite."

As they talked, Philbrook's thoughts often returned to his recent discovery that Marguerite had a son. He was curious but not sure how to broach the subject. In his world, the situation as it appeared would be considered scandalous, though he had no wish to insult her.

"You never mentioned Daniel during our journey," he said at last. "He seems a healthy boy."

She looked him in the face. He realized she was looking for him to give away his thoughts, maybe his disapproval, so he maintained a passive, mildly inquisitive expression. He was not by nature a judgmental man and did not want to appear so. But he was a curious man.

"He's a good boy."

"How old is he?"

"He turns eight in September."

His curiosity got the better of his manners and judgment. "Is his father..."

"Daniel's father was killed at Niagara during the war," she said quickly. "We planned to marry when he came home."

He was a little taken aback at her bluntness. He knew of

similar situations from home, but those children were often given plausible histories to avoid the stain of illegitimacy. He was unsure what to say but did not want Marguerite to interpret his silence as disapproval.

"Will he be a fur trader when he grows up?" he asked.

She smiled and appeared to relax. "He wants to. He idolizes his uncles, and he has started to pester me to allow him to join me or one of them on a trip into the backcountry. But I hope to put him off for a few more years yet. He is still of an age where he is prone to getting in the way."

He sipped his punch. Lieutenant Christie had not been lying when he warned of its potency. A warm feeling spread through his stomach, and he felt a growing enthusiasm. He was not alone, and an impartial observer would have noticed that the quality of the dancing among the guests was declining in direct proportion to the confidence and joy of the dancers. Marguerite too seemed to have thrown off many of her inhibitions.

Soon, a young *Canadien* clerk proposed that he show everyone how *Canadiens* jumped the bonfire on Saint Jean Baptiste Day. He took off his jacket and, with a running start, leaped over the fire and through the flames to great applause, bowing deeply after his success. Most of the *Canadien* men under the age of forty followed soon after. Then, to everyone's delight Marguerite hitched up her skirts, revealing that she wore her customary moccasins, and ran for the fire and jumped, her skirts fanned the flames in a way that the men in their stockings and britches had not. Behind her, the fire leaped even higher than before. Philbrook had a moment of panic as he imagined her skirts catching fire. She landed safely then gestured to him with a grin that implied a dare.

He was not one to decline a challenge. He stepped forward, doffed an imaginary cap to the assembled partygoers with a flourish, and ran for the bonfire. The pulse of excitement rushed through his veins. He felt the hot wind rush up around him as he held his breath, closed his eyes, and burst through the flames. He felt like he could fly. Then as his right foot touched the ground, he realized that he had forgotten that he was wearing dress shoes with a smooth sole and flimsy heel rather than his sturdy boots. His front foot flew out from under him, and he crashed down on the back of his shoulder, tumbled, then skidded to a halt at the feet of Detroit society.

Chapter 24

Louis Ouellette

Louis was in a dark forest. He knew the spot. Their camp was not far off. There were sounds all around. Not the normal nighttime sounds, but sounds of struggle. Muffled cries of rage and distress. Angry voices. He stumbled through the woods toward the camp. Dark shapes gathered near the remains of the fire. Unfamiliar men. They did not see him. He hid. Mr. Stone had been struck down. Violent men kicked, stabbed, and cut at the lifeless body between them, the motions of their bodies displaying the hatred in their hearts.

He circled around toward his own bedroll. A figure stooped over a limp body on the ground. It was sawing with a large hunting knife to slice through the sinews of a man's neck. He finished with one, then moved on to another. The figure looked up, turning toward Louis. In the light of the full moon, Louis saw his fellow canoeman—the one known as Pero. He saw the gruesome burns that distorted a face now covered in blood. His mouth opened to emit a grunt, and drool fell from his lower lip. Hate was in his eyes.

Louis ran, but Pero came after him. He tripped and fell to the ground. A dark shape loomed above him.

LOUIS AWOKE. His heart was racing. For a few moments, he was confused, before wakefulness took back over. He was in a wigwam on the outskirts of Detroit. Outside the gates. Koohsia and Mihkosita lay sleeping nearby. He recalled his dream, but it was quickly fading from his mind as his heart and breathing slowed. He tried to hold on to the images, to grasp the ethereal wisps of the dream world before they fled his waking mind.

Memories detached themselves from the dream. They were confusing and disturbing. Some memories resembled the dream, but others differed. The more he thought, the more the memories asserted themselves. In life, Pero had frightened him. The only canoeman in Stone's employ, besides himself, who had not grown up in Detroit, he tried to be sympathetic. But Pero's scars were hard to look at. The missing tongue—the burns on his face. It was not fair, he knew. The man had suffered much. It was not his fault that his burns had left him so scarred that he triggered fear and loathing. His tongueless mouth sometimes produced inhuman sounds. Louis had tried hard to see past these outward horrors, as had the other men. But still, Pero had revolted him. Was his mind making Pero's ugly face stand in for the evil deeds at Auglaize? Pero was dead. The canoeman had been a victim like the others. He had not sawed men's heads from their bodies. It had been done to him. Louis knew this was true.

HE FELL BACK TO SLEEP, into dreams. He knew he was dreaming, but only with the warped awareness of slumber, a state in which one can think oneself awake and know oneself to be dreaming without any sense of contradiction. He was running. Running through the woods. He'd had this dream before. It was the moment he discovered his companions, but now they were not skull and bone and sinew. They had eyes and ears, lips and flesh. The necks seeped fresh blood. Louis stopped and stared. He saw the gruesome yet familiar faces of Baptiste, Pierre, Lucien, Bartolomi, and Mr. Stone. But then another face stared back at him. A face that was not supposed to be there.

Louis woke with a start. A memory had fallen into place. A dark curtain had fallen away, revealing what he had always known. It made no sense to him, but he knew it was important. He should tell the British ensign right away. Koohsia and Mihkosita slept soundly nearby, but dawn was starting to glow on the eastern horizon. He heard the call of an owl in the distance. He would let them sleep a little while longer. Meanwhile, he would go wake the ensign and tell him what he finally knew.

Chapter 25

Phineas Philbrook

Ensign Philbrook awoke in his room in the Officers' Building and had a moment of peace before he realized that he still wore his waistcoat and breeches and was lying on top of the blankets. His mouth was dry, and everything had a bit of a charred smell. Looking out the window, he saw it was at least an hour after sunrise. Fragments of the night before came streaming back. He groaned, rolled over, and saw his uniform jacket draped over his only chair. It was covered in dirt and ash, a bit singed, and the shoulder was ripped. It looked like the jacket of an artillery officer who had been through a battle.

His body felt as if it had been through a battle as well. His right knee and left shoulder felt stiff and bruised. His head throbbed.

He heard footsteps coming up the stairs and approaching his door. Knocking. "Ensign Philbrook?" It was Patterson's voice.

"Yes?"

"Captain Turnbull would like to see you right away."

The summons filled him with dread. Shame. His mind ran through the events of the previous night.

How much of that rum punch had he drunk?

How impaired had his judgment been?

Had he disgraced himself? Of course he had, but how badly?

He remembered his fall. Would Turnbull reprimand him? Take disciplinary action?

No, he had just fallen. It was all part of the celebration. Innocent fun. It's not like he came up with the idea of jumping the fire himself. It was the local custom. Everyone was doing it. After he had fallen, the other party-goers had helped him up and brushed him off. They had laughed at him, but all in fun.

"I will be down shortly, Patterson," he called through the door. He tried to pull himself together. He splashed water on his face from the basin on his trunk, changed into his spare stockings, breeches, and jacket, and went out the door.

"Sir, you wanted to see me," he said tentatively as he entered the captain's office. Sergeants Graham and Ramsay were there, and all three men had sober expressions on their faces.

"Philbrook, yes. Come in. Wait. No, on second thought, we'll come out. Ramsay, you lead the way." The men stepped out into bright morning sun that blinded Philbrook for a moment. Sergeant Ramsay turned toward the main gate.

"It seems there was some unpleasantness last night," said Turnbull.

"I'm sorry, sir. I think I may not have realized how strong the punch was."

"Punch? What are you talking about, Philbrook?"

"I just... You were saying, sir?"

"Ah, yes. You were in rare form last night, but I don't concern myself with the antics of junior officers at parties. No, no, quite the contrary. Your acrobatics were the highlight of my evening, even if they did not bring honor to the regiment."

Philbrook was relieved—but still felt a bit nauseous.

Turnbull chuckled to himself. "Ha. Quite a sight you were. A great jump it was, if you'd managed to stick the landing. No, no, this has nothing to do with that. It seems there has been another murder."

"No. Who?"

"We are just going to establish that. One of the soldiers stumbled on the body not long ago and reported it to Sergeant Ramsay. He thinks he knows who it is, but we need confirmation."

They went out the gates and turned toward the Native encampment a few hundred yards away. In the ditch, by the side of the path ahead, two soldiers stood guard over something. As they neared, Philbrook saw that it was a body, face down.

"Okay, lads," said Ramsay to the soldiers, "roll him over and show the captain now." The soldiers reached down and turned the body over onto its back. There, looking vacantly up into the sky, Philbrook saw the lifeless face of Louis Ouellette. His throat slit halfway through.

Chapter 26

Phineas Philbrook

The death of Louis Ouellette upended Philbrook's thinking. He had counted on his returning memories to eventually provide some breakthrough in the case. And he had begun to like the strange young man. Was his death linked to the massacre at Auglaize? The two sergeants, Graham and Ramsay, were inclined to think the murder had nothing to do with the previous incident. They chalked it up to a drunken altercation in the night, but Philbrook was not so sure.

"Sad to say this sort of thing happens around here more than anyone likes to admit," Captain Turnbull said, as they watched four soldiers lift the body and slide it into a donkey cart. "Ouellette likely got into a fight with someone he shouldn't have. It's been my experience that Saint John Baptiste Day generally ends with at least one death."

"If so, it is an unfortunate coincidence," Philbrook said. "Louis was our best lead, and he was remembering more every day. He did not seem a brawler to me."

"He certainly wasn't a good one, judging from the results," said Graham. Ramsay laughed. Philbrook suppressed the urge to lash out at both sergeants for making light of the poor boy's death.

"See what you can discover, Philbrook," said Turnbull as they walked back to the fort, "but keep the Auglaize matter your top priority."

"I can't help but feel it may be related, sir. Louis was the sole survivor of the massacre after all. Maybe someone was looking to resolve unfinished business."

"Well, there's a sinister thought," said the captain. "But don't let your imagination turn this into some great conspiracy. Drunken fights are more common than anything else around these parts, and as you are well aware, there was plenty of drinking going on last night."

"Indeed, sir."

Philbrook had Sergeant Graham accompany him as he went looking for Koohsia and Mihkosita. He found them in the Native encampment, where they were enjoying tea and bowls of stew outside a wigwam. As soon as he approached, Koohsia looked into his eyes and frowned. "What sad news have you come to tell us, Ensign?"

Philbrook came right to the point. "Louis Ouellette is dead."

Both Miami men stared back at him, speechless. Philbrook felt like he wanted to throw up.

"Dead," Mihkosita finally said. "That can't be. He was with us all night."

"His body was found between here and the fort," said Graham. "His throat was cut open. When did you last see him?"

Philbrook thought Graham was being too blunt. The sergeant had not liked Louis—he had made no secret of that—but Philbrook knew that Koohsia and Mihkosita had cared about the young canoeman.

Koohsia briefly mumbled something in his own language that Philbrook did not understand. Ignoring Graham, he looked at Philbrook. "We were together all night. We went to see the bonfires, visited with some relations, then retired here for the night."

"Could he have snuck out again after you fell asleep?" asked Philbrook.

Koohsia shook his head. "I'm an old man, Ensign. I wake frequently during the night. Louis was here with us until shortly before sunrise. When I woke an hour later and saw him gone, I thought maybe he had gone out for a morning walk."

That was not something Philbrook was expecting. He had assumed that Louis had been killed during late-night revelries when so many men were full of alcohol and excitement. A murder at dawn seemed like an entirely different affair.

"Did he get into any arguments last night? Did you encounter anyone who may have blamed him for the murders at Auglaize?"

Mihkosita and Koohsia looked at one another and shook their heads. "No, nothing like that," said Koohsia.

"How about this morning?" asked Graham. "Did you see anyone out and about, acting strangely?"

"I saw a couple of British traders heading down to the wharf not long after sunrise," said Mihkosita. "Is that usual? I do not know."

"Just someone getting an early start, I suspect," said Philbrook. "How do you know they were British? What did they look like?"

"They dressed and walked like British traders," said Mihkosita. "One was big, with a scar on his face. The other was little and unwashed."

"Sounds like Sam Kennedy and his friend Cole," said Graham, though Philbrook had already surmised as much. "They went out the gate first thing this morning.

"I'd appreciate it if you'd ask around in the Native encampment about this, Koohsia," said Philbrook. "He was killed not far from here, so someone may have seen something."

"Don't worry, Ensign," said Koohsia. "I will find whoever did this." The shaman's face was flushed, and Philbrook noticed a vein in his temple throbbing.

Mihkosita nodded his head in assent.

"WHAT DO YOU THINK, SERGEANT?" Philbrook asked as they walked back to the fort. "You and your men were on duty last night. Did you see anything that might point us in the right direction? The gate was closed until sunup, was it not?"

"Just the usual shenanigans, sir. Drunks stumbling around late. Men finding their way home looking like sorry fellows. We opened the gate early for a few soldiers who had passed out while visiting the Native encampments and needed to get back to the garrison. Mr. Kennedy and his associate were up much of the night. I think they skipped the festivities, as they didn't look worse for wear this morning. Just as well, as I've heard that Cole can be a mean drunk. They went down to the wharf early on, saying they needed to see to their cargo."

"Does that seem strange to you?"

"Not really. Some men like to get up early, especially traders, who need to beat the wind."

Philbrook did not know what to think. He thought he had ruled out Kennedy, but here the trader was in the vicinity of another murder. Perhaps there was a side to him that he did not see. And then there was Cole. He had meant to interview Kennedy's sidekick yesterday but never got the chance. Cole was certainly capable of killing a man, judging from Kennedy's account of having his life saved. He reflected that the few times when Kennedy had seemed to dissemble was when he spoke of Cole. Did the little man have some hold over Kennedy? Perhaps he should go talk with Marguerite again. Maybe it was not a good idea for her to go out into the backcountry with those two quite yet. And he needed to talk with Jabez Cole before another day passed.

PHILBROOK WENT to find Marguerite at her mother's house. He dreaded telling her what had happened, for he knew she would be upset by Louis's death. When he approached, he saw Madame Boyer outside, tending to her small garden. Daniel was playing with a wooden toy nearby.

"Ensign." She smiled when she saw him. "I trust you've recovered from last night's revelries."

"Yes, ma'am." He wondered how long it would take him to live down his initiation to fire jumping. "I was looking for Marguerite."

"Oh? She left with Mr. Kennedy and Mr. Cole this morning. They were in a great rush to leave first thing." Madame Boyer shook head and scowled, not trying to hide her disapproval. She was pulling weeds from around a row of young corn plants. "Cole got this idea that some bad weather is going to set in, so they wanted to be on their way."

This came as a surprise. When they spoke last night Marguerite seemed determined to wait a few days before heading out on another voyage. But it explained why Kennedy and Cole were out early.

"I thought Marguerite planned on waiting a day or two," he said.

"She did, but they found her late last night and convinced her to leave with them at sunup. Marguerite and the canoemen were not pleased, believe me. Most were still a bit drunk from last night when they left. And Mr. Jacobs—he was a sight to behold. I had promised to make room for him, and he had packed his things already, so I couldn't see him left behind. I sent some men to rouse him, and they had to carry him to the canoes, all but senseless, and drop him in."

"So all the people I need to speak with have suddenly departed." Philbrook spoke aloud, but mainly to himself.

"Is there something wrong, Ensign?" asked Madame Boyer, standing up and wiping her dirty hands on her apron. "What did you need to speak with Marguerite about?"

He told her about Louis's death, keeping his voice low so that Daniel could not overhear.

Madame Boyer looked grave. "Oh dear."

"Kennedy and Cole were seen nearby around the time it happened, so I'd hoped to talk with them in case they saw anything."

"Do you think they had anything to do with it?" she asked.

"I doubt it. I talked with Kennedy yesterday and surmised that there was little chance he was responsible for the murders at Auglaize. But it is a little unsettling that so soon after dismissing my suspicions, they are once again found nearby when a murder occurs. I have questions I'd like to ask them both. For instance, who else was up and about early this morning."

"That does not sit well with me. I had reservations about sending Margot out again so soon, but she was free to make her own decisions. I'd never forgive myself if something happened to her. They've only been gone a few hours, so a fast canoe might be able to catch up to them. If I didn't have Daniel, I'd go with you." She looked over at the child. "But I can provide a couple of canoes and paddlers."

"I'd need the captain's permission to go after them." Philbrook thought for a moment. He was unsure of himself but could not ignore that his investigation had shifted back to Kennedy and Cole twice in as many days. Was he over-reacting?

"I can accompany you to the captain's office," Madame Boyer said. Philbrook could see worry in her eyes. He hoped he was not upsetting her for no reason.

"Would you mind?" he said. "If he authorizes me to go after them, then I'd like to try."

MADAM BOYER LEFT Daniel with a neighbor, and they went off

to find Captain Turnbull. They discovered him in his office fretting over correspondence.

"Ensign. Madame Boyer. How can I help you?" He pushed the papers he'd been looking at aside. He seemed appreciative of the interruption. Philbrook suspected that the captain hated paperwork and relished opportunities to put it off.

They recounted the new information. "You see, Captain," Philbrook said, "I have nothing but questions at this point. I'd planned to talk with Cole today, but their departure this morning caught me off guard. In light of Louis getting killed, I have more questions for both of them. I'm also a little concerned for Marguerite's welfare. Last night I assured her that I considered Kennedy cleared of any suspicion."

"It sounds like a wild goose chase," said Turnbull, shaking his head. "Chances are Kennedy has nothing to do with any of this."

"But they must have seen something this morning," said Philbrook. "They were seen nearby within minutes of Louis getting attacked."

Madame Boyer was absently looking around Turnbull's office, when her eyes fixed on the tomahawk found at the murder scene. "Mr. Philbrook," she asked quietly, "you told me earlier that you found a tomahawk at Auglaize. Was it this one?" She picked it up.

"Yes."

"I recognize it." She turned it around in her hands, looking at it from every angle. "My son Antoine got it up north of Lake Superior from a Cree hunter."

"This tomahawk? It belonged to Antoine?" Captain Turnbull seemed suddenly more interested. "But hasn't he been up north since before this business started?"

"Yes, he has," replied Madam Boyer. "But when he was here early in the spring, he traded it to Mr. Kennedy's little friend, Jabez Cole."

Turnbull and Philbrook looked at each other. "This is looking much less like a wild goose chase now, sir," Philbrook said.

"Kennedy and Cole were, or could have been, nearby when all the murders happened, and now we know a tomahawk belonging to Cole was left at the scene with blood on it. I would not call that conclusive, but it's the best lead we've seen so far."

"I'm inclined to agree," admitted Turnbull.

Philbrook had been replaying yesterday's conversation with Kennedy in his mind, and he recalled something he said that may have been reckless. At first, he was too ashamed to admit to it, but he thought best to fess up.

"And Captain, just yesterday, I foolishly told Mr. Kennedy that I was counting on Louis' memory to return to reveal what happened at Auglaize."

"So?" the captain wasn't making the connection.

"So, I told him that Louis was a threat to the murderers. It was stupid of me to reveal that."

"I see," said the captain. "You're saying that if Kennedy was responsible for Auglaize, then you provided him with a strong motive to kill the canoeman."

"Yes, sir."

"Madame Boyer," said the captain, "can you supply a couple of fast canoes and a few paddlers?"

"Yes, Captain."

"Make it happen, Ensign. Take Sergeant Graham, Sergeant Ramsay, and some soldiers. Detain Kennedy and Cole and bring them back. Treat them well, unless they resist. We'll sort things out back here. Understood?"

"Yes, sir."

Chapter 27

Marguerite Boyer

Marguerite saw the frustration in Kennedy's demeanor. The wind had not been his friend these past weeks. She realized that Kennedy was a man who liked to be in control, so when he found himself confounded by forces of nature or unexpected events, he became anxious, and the anxiety got him talking nonsense. Their party had gotten up the Detroit River and most of the way across Lake St. Clair quickly. The trader had insisted that the men paddle until dark the first day, so they covered more distance than expected.

The next morning, a cold north wind with rain had set in, preventing further progress. Marguerite was a little annoyed by the great rush to get out of Detroit and up the river. She had not been in top form after the festivities—and after the punch—so the day had gone by in a fog as the effects gradually wore off. Granted, Cole was right that bad weather was on its way, but bad weather was always coming sooner or later. Now they had to sit it out anyway, just without the comforts of town or the company of her son, who she now missed. The enforced idleness, even if it was only a day, could be grating even on the most placid of temperaments.

"To tell you the truth, Marguerite, this is likely my last trip in these parts," Kennedy announced over breakfast. "Once I go down to New York this fall, I will not be coming back this way."

They were at a well-used campsite, protected from the wind by the surrounding forest, and from the rain by a canvas tarp that they had strung over the cooking fire. The men had gathered a good supply of firewood, and Marguerite had made a pot of porridge and heated water for tea.

"The sight of those bodies back on the Maumee has gotten under my skin," Kennedy continued. "It brought to the surface too many ugly memories. I think I'll be going back to New Jersey, where I have kin. Little village of Mendham, where I grew up. With this year's profits I'll have enough to set up a shop on Main Street, maybe peddle goods between New York City and the smaller towns of northern New Jersey. Margins are smaller, but at least I won't have to deal with hostile bands of Indians."

"You know what is best for you, Mr. Kennedy," she told him. She tried to be polite, while not encouraging him to talk more.

"Yes, I do. Indeed, I do. I think I could make a go of it. A little country shop is just the thing for me. Farmers, they like to come in, buy their monthly or weekly items, gossip a bit, learn what is going on among their neighbors. Yes, now small-town life can be slow for someone like me, used to being out in the wide world and venturing far afield, but I'd still travel when I needed to. I think I'd like that."

"I imagine such work would suit you."

"Now, I'm not sure what I'd do with Jabez. His dour continence is sure to scare off customers. I don't know if you've noticed, but the man does not have the same skills with people that I do. Now me, I can enter any room full of strangers and make fast friends of them all in short order. I'm like that, you know. I'm friendly. I can chat anyone up. But Jabez, you get him inside of four walls, and he will retreat to a corner and lurk. Yes indeed, the man is a lurker. It's off-putting to some. Don't know why I put up with him."

Marguerite took a burning stick from the fire and used it to light her pipe.

"No reason you should if you don't want to," she observed. "He is a grown man. He can take care of himself, can't he?"

Kennedy looked as if he had not considered that. "Yes, yes, of course. The two of us have just gotten accustomed to one another in the past few years. When I go somewhere, he goes too. Suppose I could send him off hunting or gathering mushrooms—or maybe ginseng. I hear there is a growing market for ginseng in the eastern ports. They collect it in the Pennsylvania hills. It's sent from New York or Philadelphia to London, then all the way to China, where they use it for God knows what. The Orientals believe it's some sort of medicine, I've heard. I bet Jabez would be good at finding the stuff in the wild." Kennedy nodded to himself in satisfaction with his plan.

Mr. Jacobs approached, looking discontented. "When's this wind going to die, Marguerite? I can't be sitting here too long. I've got business to attend to in Michilimackinac."

"Nothing Marguerite can do about it, Amos," interrupted Kennedy. "You know that as well as I do."

"We should have gone farther when the weather was fair." He looked up at the gray sky, as if expecting the clouds to break up. "If we'd kept going yesterday evening when it was calm, we could have made Huron before this north wind hit."

"That's easy to say when you spent the whole morning sleeping in the bottom of the canoe, Mr. Jacobs," Marguerite said, trying not to let her irritation show. "The men need their rest as well, and had we pushed on, we would be sitting just the same a few miles further north."

Jacobs was jittery. She suspected this was because he had not yet had a morning drink. Had he failed to lay in a sufficient supply of rum? She felt no pity for the clerk if he had. She'd never really liked him, even when sober, and was glad that her family seldom dealt with him. It would be best if he ran out of his chosen poison, but his mutterings and complaints were burdensome to listen to.

THAT NIGHT, Marguerite dreamed she was an old woman. Her hair was gray. Her ankles were swollen. Her back was crooked and hunched. She sat in a rocker on the front porch of *Maman's* home in Detroit overlooking the river. Philbrook's dog Brutus lay nearby. There were children all around. They were her grandchildren, she thought, though she did not know any of their names. When did she get all these grandchildren? They could not be Daniel's. He was still just a boy. Funny she could not recall their names.

They played, running around the yard, sometimes coming over and giving her or Brutus a hug. How trusting children could be. Brutus must be old by now. Too old for a dog, really. Out on the river, there were many boats. Some canoes. More bateaux. They went up and down the river like it was a great highway. A sloop and a schooner were anchored out in the deeper water, and boats went back and forth between them and the wharf. An unfamiliar flag flew over the fort.

One minute Marguerite dreamed she was alone on the porch, and the next she looked over and Sergeant Graham was there rocking in his own chair. He was old, but not old. She wasn't sure.

"Margot wake up," he said.

"Wake up yourself. I'm not asleep," she said in her dream.

"Don't be alarmed, but you need to get up."

There were shouts. Sergeant Ramsay and his soldiers were attacking the children. She heard his Scottish bellow issuing commands. "Don't move ye son of a whore or I'll run ye through," he shouted at one little boy.

No way to speak to little children, she thought.

"What is the meaning of this?" someone shouted. "Let me go."

Was that Kennedy? What was Kennedy doing in her dream? It was bad enough to see him in real life.

Brutus was barking now.

"Margot, wake up, it's Graham. Everything is alright. We are here for Kennedy and Cole." She finally shook off the lingering sleep, realizing that she was in her tent, and Sergeant Graham was at the entrance, leaning over her. "Don't be frightened. Everything will be fine," he said.

"What are you doing here?" she mumbled, utterly confused. Was she still dreaming? She heard more yelling outside. Mr. Kennedy and Sergeant Ramsay were shouting at each other.

Then she heard Ensign Philbrook's voice rise above the turmoil. "Have you got the other one? Who has Cole? Where's Cole?"

"Run off, sir, the slippery eel. Couldn't hold on to him," replied one of the soldiers.

Then she heard Joseph. "What is going on here?"

"Have your boatmen stay where they are, Mr. Papan," Philbrook ordered. "Graham, have you found Miss Boyer? Bring her out here, please."

"Right away," Graham yelled. Then, in a lower voice, he said, "Marguerite, we are here to arrest Kennedy and Cole. Come out and reassure your men."

"Why are you...?" she began before the shocking reason came into her mind. She looked around for her shawl.

She could still hear Philbrook talking with a soldier. "How could he have slipped off? We had this place surrounded."

"Can't say, sir. We had him one minute, then he scurried away into the trees. We went right after him, but he just vanished. But we found this one hiding in the woods when we went after the other."

"Get your dirty hands off me, soldier!" Jacobs shouted. "Will somebody please explain to me what is going on? Why have you assaulted me?"

"Billy, you can let that one go," ordered Philbrook. "Mr. Jacobs, I apologize for the inconvenience, but we are here to collect Mr. Kennedy and Mr. Cole so that we can take them back to Detroit to answer some questions."

"What questions?" sputtered Kennedy. "What the hell is the meaning of this? I've got a pass. I'm on my way to Michilimackinac, and you've no right to stop me."

"I have every right, Mr. Kennedy. I hold a commission from the king, and I am following Captain Turnbull's orders, which is sufficient authority in this case. You can play innocent all you like, but the evidence against you is damning. I'm detaining you for questioning in the matter of the murder of Ben Stone and his men. If you have any objections, you can take them up with Captain Turnbull when we get back to Detroit."

"You're mad," Kennedy exclaimed. Then there was a scuffle, a thud, and Kennedy went silent.

"That was perhaps a bit rougher than necessary, Sergeant Ramsay."

"Sorry, sir. Thought he'd wriggle free like the other one."

Marguerite emerged, her shawl wrapped around her shoulders against the damp predawn air. The sun had not yet risen, but the eastern horizon had begun to glow. Kennedy lay unconscious on the ground at the feet of Sergeant Ramsay. Two soldiers were tying his limp arms behind his back. A half dozen other soldiers crowded the campsite. She heard Brutus bark and saw him tied to a tree near the water, looking like he very much wanted to come to greet her. There were canoemen who were not part of her party. Among them, she saw Mihkosita and Koohsia. Her men were standing off to the side with Joseph, looking bemused by these unexpected early morning shenanigans. Several had pulled out their clay pipes and were busy creating small clouds of smoke about their heads. The scene was almost as strange as the dream she had just been woken from. Could she still be dreaming?

Philbrook looked over. "I am relieved to see you are safe, Marguerite."

"Why wouldn't I be safe, Ensign? Would you mind telling me what is going on? Why arrest Mr. Kennedy?"

"I will explain in a moment." Philbrook turned to Joseph and the canoemen. "You men can relax. Sorry to disturb your sleep. You are free to go about your business as long as it does not entail assisting Mr. Kennedy or Mr. Cole. Papan can you give me your word that neither you nor your men will interfere with my business here?"

"*Oui, bien sûr*, Ensign."

"Ensign," interrupted Sergeant Ramsay, "the men can't find any sign of Cole. I'm afraid he's run off."

"Have your men remain where they are, Sergeant. They are not to move until I say so. Graham, ask Mihkosita and Koohsia to come up."

The two Miami men heard him and stepped forward.

"Would Mihkosita try to locate Mr. Cole's trail?" asked Philbrook. The two men nodded then disappeared into the woods.

"Are you going to tell me what prompted you to arrest Mr. Kennedy, Ensign?" Marguerite was becoming impatient for an explanation.

Philbrook turned his attention fully to her and lowered his voice. "I'm afraid I have disturbing news, Marguerite."

"Did something happen to Daniel or *Maman*?" She blurted out her greatest fears.

"No. They are both well." She felt a moment of relief before he continued. "But Louis Ouellette was murdered shortly before you left Detroit."

"Oh." Marguerite felt like she'd been punched.

"His throat was slit, and Mr. Kennedy and Mr. Cole were seen nearby when it happened."

She thought of Louis. He was such a gentle soul.

"And you think they did it?" She was not sure she could fathom the idea.

"I think it is likely. Another bit of damning evidence was discovered by your mother," Philbrook spoke softly as if to temper the ugliness of what he described. "She recognized that tomahawk we found. Your brother got it up north, then he traded it to Jabez Cole. Seems little doubt now that these two are who we have been looking for all along. And the fact that Cole has fled from us does not help his case."

She looked down at the unconscious form of Sam Kennedy drooling slightly into the dirt. Quiet for once. Could he really be a murderer? She could easily believe it about Cole, but Kennedy, for all his faults, did not seem like an evil man. There was no time to ask more questions though, for Philbrook was in a hurry to be away.

A HALF AN HOUR LATER, the sun was above the horizon, and Mihkosita reported to Philbrook near the center of the camp. Koohsia was with him, but the elder let the younger man do the talking. "Your soldiers have obscured every track within fifty feet, but Koohsia and I circled around and found what we think is your man's trail. It leads west. If you want to catch him, we need to get after him now."

Philbrook turned to Sergeant Ramsay. "Which of our men are best in the forest, Sergeant?"

"Billy Smyth knows his way around the woods, sir."

"Can he track a man through these woods, do you think?"

"Not sure about that, sir. Not like an Indian."

"What do you think, Graham?"

"I think if we want to go after Cole, we'll want a small party. Billy knows what he's about, but Mihkosita is a better tracker, I'd think. I'd like to take Privates Young and Bellows. Those two can move fast through the forest."

"How about it, Mihkosita? Can you track our man?"

"Yes, Ensign, I can follow his trail." There was no sign of self-doubt in his manner. "But we will need to move quickly. Not too many men."

"I can join you," said Koohsia.

"Thank you. I'd like us to be on our way soon," said Philbrook. "Sergeant Ramsay, you will take charge of our prisoner. Take him directly back to Detroit and deliver him to Captain Turnbull. Leave one canoe cached here, so we will have some way to get back. I will lead the chase on foot. Private Smyth, Mihkosita, and Sergeant Graham will come with me. Understood?"

"Aye, sir. I'll tell Smyth."

Marguerite noticed that Philbrook spoke with confidence and authority, qualities she had not noticed in him when she first met him.

"Young and Bellows, sir?" said Graham.

"I want to keep our party small, like Mihkosita said. They can go with Sergeant Ramsay." Graham looked ready to object, but held back.

Philbrook turned to Koohsia. "I thank you for your offer to join us, but this chase may be a task for younger men." The old man scowled but did not argue.

"Marguerite," she heard the groggy voice of Kennedy as he regained consciousness. "Marguerite, you need to help me." He was still in his nightshirt and looked haggard and confused. A large purple lump had appeared on his forehead.

"And why should I help you?" she asked.

"This is all a mistake, Marguerite. I'm sure to have this foolish business resolved in short order, but if you return with my goods to Detroit, I will be ruined. If you continue on to Michilimackinac and sell my cargo for a fair price, we can settle when you get back.

Anything you can't sell to the Indians, unload on the local traders for as much as you can get."

Marguerite was both surprised and impressed that Kennedy was thinking of his finances at a time like this. She did not know what to believe. She trusted Philbrook's good intentions, but her gut told her that Kennedy was not a killer. If it was proved to her that he killed Louis, she would never forgive him, but for the moment she sympathized with his position.

"Very well, Mr. Kennedy," she said, "but my mother may want a larger percentage if I'm to do all your trading for you."

"No worries, Marguerite," agreed Kennedy. "Name your price as long as it is reasonable. My lawyer in Schenectady will wring any losses I suffer out of Captain Turnbull and Ensign Philbrook for unlawfully interfering in my livelihood. I'll work it out with Madame Boyer."

Ten minutes later, the four men were ready to go. They had fashioned light packs with bedrolls and some provisions for their journey. Each had a musket over one shoulder and a tomahawk or knife on his belt, except Philbrook, who had twin flintlock pistols and his sword. They were prepared to travel fast and light.

"We will be off without delay. Sergeant Ramsay, give the men some rest, then head back. Tell the captain we hope to find Cole shortly. If all goes well, we should get back to Detroit soon after you."

"Aye, sir, and watch out," said Ramsay. "Cole is a slippery one, liable to try to jump you if you get close."

"I thank you for your advice, Sergeant."

Philbrook turned to Marguerite, "I wish we had time to explain fully, but we need to be off."

Marguerite wanted to ask him all sorts of questions. She wanted him to take the time to convince her that Kennedy and Cole were indeed guilty of the murders at Auglaize and of Louis, but she knew that time was short.

"Safe travels," was all she said.

The men followed Mihkosita into the forest as Brutus trailed behind.

BY MIDDAY, the soldiers, too, were gone, taking an outraged Sam Kennedy with them. Marguerite was left with Joseph, her boatmen, and Jacobs, who had maintained a strangely shocked look since the morning. Koohsia too remained. Since Philbrook and Mihkosita had gone off, the old man had appeared deep in thought. Then, when Sergeant Ramsay was about to embark, he approached Marguerite and announced that he had decided to stay with her.

"I've not been to Michilimackinac in some time," he said absently. "I'd think maybe I'd like to join you, if I might." She could think of no objection, though it seemed strange that he would want to journey even farther from his home for no apparent reason.

The breeze had diminished considerably from the previous day, though it was still out of the north. Marguerite could see no reason to linger any longer.

"Well, Joseph, time to go?"

"*Oui*, Margot. We might as well be on our way. The men are antsy to be out of this place, and some wind in their faces might be just the thing for them."

"*C'est bon.*"

Chapter 28

Phineas Philbrook

P hilbrook worried that his legs would give out and his knees buckle under him if he did not stop and rest a bit, but he was determined not to let it show. A dull ache radiated up from his ankles to his thighs with each stride. For several hours now the chase had been relentless. They were not moving fast, trotting really, with periods of walking, but they kept at it hour after hour.

Mihkosita was a young man, who spent much of his time in the forest tracking game, so he was not surprised that the lad surpassed him when it came to endurance, but little Billy Smyth and Graham, too, seemed to outstrip him. Philbrook had always though Smyth an underfed little man, but his spindly legs seemed never to tire. At the very least he thought he would do better than Graham, who was ten years his senior and walked with a limp, but he too seemed fresh, while Philbrook was on the verge of collapse. Brutus, of course, pranced along happily, exploring the forest with his nose, as if this was all a wonderful game.

Perhaps it was time to rethink the boots. They did an excellent job protecting his feet and legs, and the sturdy heel could be an advantage in some conditions, but for a long run like this, he envied the lighter moccasins of Mihkosita and Smyth. His legs and feet were clammy and soaked in sweat, and he felt more than one blister forming.

Since the morning, Cole's trail had led them west, though as the afternoon progressed, it bent southward. How Mihkosita followed it, Philbrook could not say. Occasionally, they would pause, but within seconds, either Mihkosita or Billy would find a sign, and they would set off once again. Philbrook began to think his decision to join the chase himself was misguided. So far, he had contributed little to the effort. Maybe he should have stayed to get some answers out of Kennedy and let Sergeant Graham take charge of the pursuit of Cole. An interrogation would certainly be easier than this endless journey. But no, this was something he needed to do himself. He would not respect himself if he delegated too much to Graham, and Captain Turnbull could interrogate Kennedy more effectively back in Detroit.

The woods here were more open and the land drier than down along the Maumee. Philbrook occasionally saw well-used footpaths. Sometimes, Mihkosita would lead them along one of these established trails for a mile or two before veering off through the woods again. They passed through stands of white pine and a mixed forest of oaks, maples, and beech. They skirted dense swamps. This was an old forest, not heavily cut like the woods back home in New Hampshire. Some of the trees had reached massive size.

Up ahead, Mihkosita stopped, looking confused. He stood near the base of a large oak tree with branches that stretched out high above them forming a thick canopy. He motioned back to the others to stay where they were while he signaled that Billy should circle with him to pick up the trail.

"You were right. Smyth seems to know a good bit about tracking," Philbrook gasped to Graham as he caught his breath. "Where did he learn?"

"Billy's an old poacher. At least he was back in England before he got caught by a game warden. The magistrate made him decide between Newgate and the infantry. It wasn't much of a choice. That was back during the war, when the army needed all the warm bodies they could get. Poachers make some of the best soldiers if you ask me."

"I'm glad that you recommended bringing him along."

He watched Mihkosita and Billy conferring up ahead. Billy was pointing up at the tree canopy and over at a rocky ridge to their left. Mihkosita shook his head and said something in apparent disagreement. In response, Billy scrambled up the hill to the ridge. He disappeared from view for a minute or two, then came back to the edge and called to the others to climb up. When they got to him, they found him squatting, taking a long drink from his canteen.

"He's a tricky devil," observed Billy. "Trail starts up again right here. In my younger days I used to escape the warden sometimes by climbing a tree and jumping branch to branch like a squirrel." The soldier grinned, revealing several black or missing teeth. "See how he got up here using the trees so as not to leave any track up the ridge? Pretty quick thinking for a man on the run."

Philbrook saw that someone with the skills and nerves of an acrobat might indeed have climbed the tree where they first lost the trail, crossed to a neighboring tree, and used its branches to get up to the ridge they were now on.

"Fooled you, Mihkosita, didn't he?" Billy gloated. "And I thought Indians were supposed to know how to track. Ha."

Mihkosita looked slightly abashed. "I've been thinking like a hunter," he conceded. "But I see you know more what it is like to be hunted."

"The game warden only caught me that once," Billy boasted, "but that's only 'cause he got lucky, and I had a bit of a gripe that day."

"We have another hour before it gets too dark to find the trail, so we should go," advised Mihkosita. "We won't catch up today, but maybe in the morning."

Their pathway led due south now, suggesting that Cole was making his way back toward Detroit.

"By dusk, there will be little use trying to follow a trail," observed Graham. "If Cole is smart, he will keep moving through the night, and we will never hope to catch up. But if he stops to rest, then maybe we'll get him."

They spent that night in the open, dining on some dried meat and cornmeal mixed into an unappealing paste. The night was warm, so Philbrook simply lay his jacket on the ground to keep away the cold that seeped up from the earth. He pulled off his boots and lay down next to Brutus. It seemed like he had hardly closed his eyes when Billy roused him.

"Mihkosita wants to set off, sir. He hopes to catch the fellow napping, as he can't be far ahead of us."

"Very well, Smyth." He moved like an old man as he stood. Every muscle in his legs and lower back had stiffened overnight. It was just before dawn, and the stars had faded. He pulled on his boots, which rubbed against raw blisters, put on his coat, relieved himself against a nearby tree, and joined the others who had similarly accomplished an abbreviated morning routine.

Mihkosita's hope of catching their quarry sleeping proved in vain. More than an hour into the day they came upon a spot where even Philbrook could see that a man had spent a few hours. There was an imprint of a body in the ground cover and the remains of a hastily gathered and consumed meal.

"Looks like he gathered on the run," said Mihkosita. "This one knows what to eat in the forest when better things aren't around."

"Kennedy told me that Cole is unusually skilled in the forest," said Philbrook. "Not like your average trader or bateauman, so we should not underestimate him."

"He looks to be circling back toward Detroit," Graham said. "I wonder if we are wasting our time chasing after him. There are not that many places he can go, and if he returns to Detroit, he will surely be apprehended before too long."

"But he may be able to cause some mischief before he's caught," offered Philbrook. "I wouldn't be surprised if he tried to break Kennedy out of the gaol. Those two are unusually committed to one another. Kennedy is like a father or older brother to him."

"Indeed," Graham said.

The day proceeded much like the one before. They moved continuously, stopping only to refill canteens at the occasional creek and hastily consume some food. Philbrook felt his muscles loosen up with use, and the pain of his blisters began to numb. He noticed that Graham had a bit of a lopsided gait today—more than his usual limp—which made him feel better about his own aches and pains. Perhaps youth had its advantages after all. They did not move as fast as the previous day. Their breaks got longer, and their pace diminished. He reassured himself that the same was likely true of Cole.

As dusk approached, Mihkosita began to look discouraged. "We do not seem to be gaining on him at all. Unless he stops, I'm not sure we will be able to catch up. Maybe if I was alone..."

"Let's continue until dark," Philbrook said. "At this point, whether we stop or lose the trail in the shadows makes little difference. In the morning we head back to the canoe."

In another two hours, the sun had fully set, but a near-full moon gave Mihkosita and Billy enough light to make out what they thought must be the trail. But after another hour the moon too had sunk low enough that its light no longer penetrated through to the forest floor.

Philbrook announced what they were already thinking, "I really think this has become a fruitless journey at this point. If we've been moving faster than Cole, we should certainly have caught him by now."

"Yes, sir. That seems about right," responded Billy.

They set up camp with a general feeling of discouragement.

Not that there was much to set up, just coats to be lain on the ground and meager provision to prepare.

"No matter how good Cole is in the forest, he can't survive on his own for long," commented Graham as they sat smoking their pipes." Now if he were a Frenchman, it would be different. He'd have folks in the backcountry he could turn to, who would help him out. Same if he were a Native. But an English-speaking man from the coastal colonies would be pretty hard up to find an ally in the bush around here. His only option besides Detroit is heading for the Pennsylvania frontier where folks are unlikely to know anything of him. If Captain Turnbull puts the word out among the Natives and Frenchmen and offers a decent reward, he's likely to be apprehended in a matter of weeks."

"Let's hope so," Philbrook sighed.

"Do you smell that?" asked Billy suddenly. He was standing a bit apart from the others. "I thought for a second I smelled smoke."

"Probably just our pipes, Smyth," said Graham.

"No, Sergeant, that was wood smoke, not tobacco. Hickory, I think."

Mihkosita stood and walked over to where Billy sniffed at the air. He and Billy began slowly circling and sniffing at the light breeze. Philbrook was reminded of the hunting dogs he had seen in England. Brutus meanwhile, despite his nasal proficiency, was oblivious.

"He's right," announced Mihkosita. "There is a campfire not far. The smoke is getting trapped in this valley. If we head more-or-less uphill, we should find it."

Philbrook nodded to the others and they collected their things and walked slowly and quietly up the gentle rise. He looped a rope onto Brutus's collar to keep him from running ahead. After a few minutes he too could smell the smoke. It was unmistakably a campfire. Mihkosita motioned for all to stop.

"It's right up there," he whispered.

"Okay. Let's not let him slip away," Philbrook said. "We need to circle around and move in slowly."

"What if it's not him?" asked Graham. "Could be a party of Natives who would not take kindly to us barging into their camp after dark."

"We'll need to risk it," said Philbrook. "Mihkosita, go around the opposite side and try to get in as close as you can. Billy, you go partway around to the left, and Sergeant, you go right. I'll approach from this side. Wait for everyone to get into position, then we'll move in slowly. If he sees us before we are ready, give a holler, and we'll all go in fast. We want to take him alive. If it's someone else, and they spot you, just raise your hands in peace and let me deal with explanations. Got it?"

All silently showed their assent and moved off. After waiting for the others to get in position, Philbrook began to move slowly and quietly forward. His heart pounded in his chest, and he tried hard to control his breathing. He was painfully aware of the noise his boots made and the probability that Brutus would do something to give away their presence, but soon, he saw the orange glow of a dying campfire ahead. He continued the approach, eyes fixed on the rising smoke. He saw a blanket covering a solitary figure on the ground. With more coordination than he could have hoped for, he saw Mihkosita, Billy, and Graham approaching out of the shadows from their respective directions. They all came within fifty feet before he signaled for them to stop.

"You there! Get up," Philbrook commanded. "Show yourself."

The blanket did not move, but he heard a rustling behind him. Brutus pulled at his leash. Something hard pressed into his lower back, followed by the cold kiss of a blade at his neck.

Chapter 29

Marguerite Boyer

It was a clear evening after a long day of travel. Lake Huron had been calm when they got to it, and they had been able to make good time paddling north along its shore. The men had eaten and were relaxing now, sprawled out here and there with their tired backs leaning up against packs or tree trunks. They puffed away at their clay pipes with satisfaction. Some talked about recent events. Several had opinions about Kennedy and Cole. Most of them thought that the two men were guilty, but they offered up varied ideas about their motives.

Marguerite wondered how Philbrook and Graham were doing. Had they caught up to Cole? She hoped so, but she was still confused by their unexpected arrival and quick departure. Oddly enough, she found she missed Sam Kennedy a little. Mostly because, with him gone, Amos Jacobs talked to her more. This evening he had approached, uninvited, and initiated an unwelcome conversation.

"We were lucky getting delayed, eh, Marguerite?" said Jacobs. "It gave the soldiers a chance to catch up and take those scoundrels away."

"That is one way to look at it," said Marguerite. She hoped to discourage him by being as dull as possible.

"I should have suspected those two. They always resented Ben and me. They had this idea we abandoned them all those years ago, but that couldn't be further from the truth. It was them that hurt our chances of escape. That's right. If we hadn't had to carry Sam, we'd have fled to safety the first day. He caused Ben, Paul, and me great hardship, and in Paul's case, death."

"It's no concern of mine, Mr. Jacobs." She had little interest in British war stories. They always painted her people as the villains.

"It was all the fault of the French anyway. They think of themselves as civilized, but they have no honor, I tell you." The foolish clerk rambled on no matter how little she responded to him. She suspected he had found his way into Kennedy's rum kegs. She wished *Maman* had not agreed to give him passage to Michilimackinac. If it were solely up to her, she would refuse to travel with a man who could not control his urge for liquor.

In his inebriation he had apparently forgotten that she was half French herself, but his mind was back in an earlier time. "Montcalm, ha! He and his so-called officers pretending to be civilized men, but they were worse than the savages." He took another sip. "At least savages are what they are, don't pretend to have any morals. Your average Frenchman, though, is all puff and flattery on the outside, but a bloodthirsty hellhound within."

Marguerite remained silent. Jacobs was an ugly little man with a stale smell. Like so many of his kind, he did not realize when he was being a fool.

"You know what they did to the women, Marguerite? Do you? Some seem to think it was just soldiers that got massacred. Men, like in a proper battle. But it wasn't. There were camp followers too, families, you know. Little children. People forget that soldiers have families. They attacked them all with tremendous brutality." He looked at her with entreating eyes.

"It was not war. It was butchery," he continued, when she did not respond. "Babies thrown to the ground. Women cut open. Men running for their lives. Then the desperate scramble through the forest. Sam got himself knocked on the head, then expected to be carried. Dead weight is what he was. Pure dead weight to slow the rest of us down. Put us in risk. But Jabez insisted. You know how hard it is to carry a man through the woods? Especially a man as big as Sam Kennedy? Now Ben, he was sensible. He wanted to leave Sam behind from the start. But Jabez and Paul convinced him to help for a while. We never would have gotten captured if it weren't for Sam. We could have gotten to Fort Edward that day. He was not our responsibility. It was every man for himself, you know."

She locked eyes with Joseph Papan, who was nearby talking with Koohsia. She glanced at Jacobs then rolled her eyes. Papan got the message, and he and Koohsia came over and joined her.

Koohsia seemed genuinely interested in what the clerk was saying. "Is the ensign correct, Mr. Jacobs?" he asked. "Do you think Mr. Kennedy and Mr. Cole killed the other trader because of what happened back then after the fort fell?"

"Must have," Jacobs murmured.

"But why would they have killed all those canoemen?" asked Koohsia. "They had nothing to do with it." Marguerite had been thinking the same thing.

Jacobs shrugged. "They were in the way, I guess."

"It seems like things turned out well for those two," Koohsia puzzled aloud. "What would they want revenge for? Maybe I do not always understand British ways, but it was you who suffered."

"That's just what I was saying." Jacobs turned toward Koohsia. "We suffered sure enough. Getting marched off to Montreal. It was a horror." It was clear to Marguerite that Jacobs wanted sympathy more than anything else. But she was not sure why Koohsia was encouraging him.

"And who captured you?" asked Koohsia.

"Ojibwa. Saginaw Ojibwa. A few of their people had been

231

killed while coming down from Canada, and they were out for revenge."

"Can you blame them?" said Koohsia. "General Montcalm promised them a fight—a chance for honor, maybe some souvenirs. They traveled a long way from home to make war, leaving their families behind. Then, the general let the enemy walk away just when they came within grasp. Warriors can't simply go home with nothing to show for their troubles."

Jabobs looked at Koohsia through bleary eyes. "There are rules. I guess an Indian wouldn't know about such things, but civilized war has rules." Marguerite wanted to slap Jacobs for his rudeness. She wondered how a man could spend months in the *pays d'en haut* and still not understand the people who lived in it.

"We have rules, too," Koohsia explained, "but they differ from yours. When the enemy kills one of us, we kill one of them or take a captive to replace our dead. We go to war to earn renown and honor, or to control important hunting grounds, not to burn down forts or do the bidding of some far-away king."

"*Général* Montcalm did not understand his own allies at *Lac du St. Sacrement*." Papan added. "He broke promises to his friends when he made new promises to his enemies."

"And how would you know that?" Jacobs sneered. "I was there, and what I saw was senseless savagery."

"Koohsia and I were both there," Papan said. Marguerite admired his restraint. Jacobs's incivility did not warrant courtesy.

Jacobs raised his eyebrows, then shrugged. "I guess it should not come as a surprise. It's a small world."

"Many of us joined the *Canadien* militia and went down to fight the British. You don't have to look hard to find men in Detroit who fought," said Papan. "We wanted to keep this land for France and our Native allies."

"I suppose you would," said Jacobs. "I guess I found that out a while back when I ran into Lucien and the others in Detroit."

"Lucien Tremblay?" asked Papan. "Yes, he was at *Lac du St. Sacrement*. But how did you know that?"

Jacobs crossed his arms. "Well, let's say our paths crossed."

"Crossed how?" pressed Koohsia.

Marguerite, too, was curious. She thought about Lucien Tremblay, one of the canoemen killed at Auglaize. Yes, he had been in the militia. So too, she realized, had three of the other dead canoemen: both Beaulieu brothers and Barthelemy Bruno. They had all gone down to fight the British. The bond they formed then was why they so often worked together as boatmen later on. She wasn't sure about Pero, as he had not lived in Detroit before the war, and Louis was too young. But it piqued her interest that Jacobs seemed to be aware of Lucien's past.

"How had your paths crossed before?" Marguerite repeated Koohsia's question when Jacobs seemed reluctant to answer.

"Well, it appears I have your attention now, Miss Margot." Jacobs smiled unpleasantly. He took a sip from his tin pannikin. "Would you like to hear the story about how I met Lucien and several others once upon a time near Lake George, or *Lac du St. Sacrement* as your bunch calls it?"

"Yes, please tell us, Mr. Jacobs." Marguerite was not sure why, but she sensed that the story might be relevant to more recent events.

"You've all heard about what happened outside Fort William Henry in fifty-seven. You've heard I was there with Ben, Sam, and Jabez. I guess Philbrook heard it from Sam's big mouth, and the story, or some form of it, has trickled from the ensign to you. Of course, Sam Kennedy paints himself as the aggrieved party, he and his precious Jabez. The real story was a little different—a little more complicated."

Jacobs paused. "Now, I'm not saying Sam did not feel abandoned, because he and Jabez must have felt pretty sore at us to do what they did to Ben, but what I'm saying is that they have no right to see themselves as victims of any treachery." He looked up.

"Go on, Mr. Jacobs. Tell us your version," said Koohsia.

"Where to begin? It was all going to shit outside the fort, you see." He looked at the others, searching for understanding, then continued. "Kennedy started hollering at us all, but few paid him any mind. Except his dog Cole, that is. That's what we called Jabez Cole back then, 'Kennedy's dog,' for the way he licked the boots of our overbearing sergeant—always seeking his approval and attention. Well, Sam's shouting just brought more of the goddamn warriors down on us. We couldn't fight back, as we had no real weapons, so there was no reason to stand about yelling like fools. The Indians, they were mostly harassing the officers still because officers had things worth taking. They knew that provincials like us would have naught to plunder, and they were more interested in plunder than in killing. So me, Ben, and Paul, Paul Adams that is, we high-tailed it into the woods and hid."

"Tell us about this man, Paul Adams, Mr. Jacobs," said Koohsia. "I've heard you mentioned him before." Marguerite was puzzled by Koohsia's interested.

"Paul was my friend," said Jacobs. "My best friend. I'd known him since I was a boy. My whole life, really. We joined up together, looking for an adventure, hoping to see a part of the world other than northern New Jersey." Jacobs got a distracted look in his eyes, then looked at the ground as he spoke. "He may be the reason I'm here now. We used to talk about going west after the war ended. Paul had this idea we could become Indian traders, and then sometimes he would talk about pushing even further west to explore new territory. He had this Latin term he liked to use: *terra incognita*. Those were his favorite words."

"What do they mean?" asked Koohsia.

"'Unknown land.' His favorite *terra incognita* was the Straits of Anian. He had this dream of discovering it. He said that if we went northwest of Lake Superior we would come to Lac Ouinipegon, and not far beyond that we would find the straits, which we could take west to the South Sea. He said we would make great riches establishing a new trade route to China."

Marguerite saw excitement in Jacobs's face as he spoke. She recalled that Philbrook, too, had admitted to a passion for westward exploration. She had encountered men with this drive to make discoveries many times since she was a girl, but no good ever came from it.

"And this Paul Adams did not survive the war?" asked Koohsia.

"No... No, he didn't. I'll get to that. Hold tight and I'll get to that part." Jacobs looked distraught for a moment, then took a sip from his drink, which seemed to relax him.

"Anyway, as I was saying, all hell broke loose outside the fort, so some of us hid. Then Sam and Jabez stumble over to us, both all covered in blood, Sam's blood, and the blood of some warrior that Jabez had killed. Sam was making too much noise for us to keep hiding, so we went along with Jabez when he asked us to help carry him out." Jacobs shook his head. "Now you've got to understand that the sergeant was never much of a favorite to most of us. Ben, in particular, could not stand him. Kennedy was a bully, always trying to humiliate the young lads in our company, but he was still one of us, so we helped him at first. You'd think he would be grateful, but not at all. He kept ordering us about like he was a goddamned major general, without a word of thanks. By nightfall, me, Paul, and Ben were fed up. So, we left. We had every right to look out for ourselves."

Jacobs had been steadily sipping his rum this whole time. The alcohol had loosened his tongue, Marguerite observed, and he was in the mood to talk. Sometimes, he seemed to be talking more to himself than to the others.

"We slipped off when we saw that Sam and Jabez were asleep. We went south, moving faster now that we had cast off the dead weight." He looked slightly abashed but continued on. "Now, none of us were really what you'd call woodsmen at the time, so we found our share of thickets, thorns, and swampland to thrash through. It wasn't long before a party of Saginaw Ojibwa found our trail. They caught up to us around mid-morning. We didn't stand a chance, being outnumbered and unarmed. We might have made a desperate fight of it, but then one of them spoke up in broken English with a French accent and said if we surrendered, we would be taken captive, not killed. Well, that was Lucien Tremblay." Jacobs looked to Papan and Marguerite. "So that's how I know about him being in the *Canadien* militia."

Jacobs resumed his tale when no one spoke. "Bruno was there too. I guess they have friends or relatives among the Saginaw and were traveling with them. To us they did not look all that different from the Ojibwa, but at least we could talk to them. It helped that Ben spoke French because neither Trembley's nor Bruno's English was very good back then. They spoke the Indian language, too, and they told us that they convinced the Indians to take us north to Montreal as hostages instead of taking our scalps as trophies. We appreciated that at the time."

Marguerite was struck by the fact that Ben Stone had known two of the canoemen killed with him at Auglaize ten years before becoming a trader. Could that be a coincidence?

"Is that why Ben Stone hired them as canoemen," she asked, "because he remembered them from the war?"

"That's right, Marguerite. Once I told Ben that they were available, he was eager to work with them. Ben always liked those boys. Neither of us blamed them for taking us captive. That's the way war works. Better captive than dead. And they treated us pretty well along the way. They looked out for us. But that is not the whole story. There is much more to it than that. Let me top off my pannikin, and I will continue—now that I have sparked your interest." Jacobs got up and went to filled his cup from a small keg by his things. He was quite drunk by now and staggered a bit, but he managed not to spill a drop.

"The Indians insisted we run all that day," he resumed, when he came back. The drink did not seem to affect his tongue, though his eyes were glassy. He seemed to enjoy holding court to an audience that showed interest in his tale. "I'm not quite sure how we managed it. We followed the western shore of Lake George to the north. The party that captured us was five Ojibwas plus Tremblay and Bruno, but the next day, we met up with another party of warriors. They had captives as well: four lobster-backs, one of them a young British officer. That's when we first met the Beaulieu brothers. Like Tremblay and Bruno, they were traveling with their Ojibwa friends. There was a French lieutenant with them too, not a *Canadien*, but a real Frenchman from France."

"Wait," interrupted Marguerite. "Baptiste and Pierre Beaulieu were there too? You're saying four of the men killed with Ben Stone met him back then?"

"Yes, that's right."

Marguerite looked to Koohsia and Joseph, whose expressions told her that they too thought this was too much of a coincidence.

"It was a brutal journey north," Jacobs continued. "Not a moment passed when we didn't think we were about to be killed. The warriors would threaten to knock us on the head if we fell behind, or worse, they would list the parts of our bodies that they intended to cut off or burn."

"It is important to keep captives frightened," observed Koohsia, nodding his head. "It helps them cooperate."

Jacobs did not seem to hear him. "The French officer would sometimes intercede, especially when they threatened the British officer, but we realized that his authority was limited. He could try to persuade the Ojibwa, but he could not order them to do anything they did not want to do. A couple of them had lost friends in the campaign and wanted to exact revenge, but others were more interested in selling us at a profit. We knew if we didn't keep up, we would not live.

"There were seven of us captives now, and we all handled our captivity differently. Ben thought it best that we cooperate, because that is what the *Canadiens* told him. Paul and I followed his lead. The British officer was pretty cooperative and seemed to trust in the protection of the French lieutenant, but one of the lobsters, a redcoat corporal, well, he resisted. Sometimes, he refused to walk, or he spat out the food he was given. I recall several times I became convinced that he would be dispatched for his insolence. But they let him live. Maybe they admired his bravery, but I think they simply thought he would fetch a higher ransom than the rest of us because of his rank.

"After a couple of days, we came to a place along the western shore of Lake Champlain where they had canoes cached. They had us paddle in turns. Those of us who were not paddling at any given time had their arms tied. Well, after the first full day of this, the redcoat corporal told us in whispers that we must try to escape. The other lobster-backs were loyal to their corporal and agreed, but the three of us provincials saw an escape attempt as too dangerous. The *Canadiens* told Ben that we were headed to Montreal, and as long as we kept up, kept quiet, and made no trouble, we would be ransomed when we got there. Maybe it would take months—or even a year—but we would eventually get home. Ben believed them. It helped that he was a reader, and he had read all the narratives about folks being taken away to Canada from New England and later redeemed. He told us about Mary Rowlandson and John Williams and some other old-time settlers who'd survived similar ordeals."

"He was right," said Papan. Koohsia nodded in agreement. "If you were going to be killed, they would have dispatched you straight away. They wanted you alive."

"The corporal thought we would be taken back to the Ojibwa villages and tortured to death," continued Jacobs, "or held captive until the end of the war, and he was pretty persuasive. The British officer with us seemed to defer to him. He was just a boy really—the officer—a young lieutenant from a good English family but with little experience. The corporal had more real authority. When we had the chance to whisper to each other, the corporal would try to lay out his plans to overpower our captors, take the canoes, and head south, but then Ben would poke holes in his plans. We were a good way up Lake Champlain by now, and none of us was as proficient as an Indian or a *Canadien* at handling the canoes. Ben argued that if we attempted escape, we would be hunted down and killed.

"The corporal would have none of it. 'Tis our duty to try to escape,' he'd insist. The other redcoats would nod in agreement. He had a way of inspiring trust and seemed to hold sway over them. But me, Paul, and Ben were not won over. I think the English officer agreed with us, but he was too young and weak to contradict his corporal. Moreover, the French officer kept him close and largely preventing him from conferring with the rest of us.

"Then the next afternoon, the corporal spread the word that we were going that night. He refused to hear any more objections. We were past Crown Point by this time. He revealed that he had a small blade hidden in one of his gaiters. That night he would cut his bindings and free the rest of us. We would kill any Indian or *Canadien* who tried to stop us. Ben called it insanity, but he seemed to be resigned to going along.

"We got to a camping place late that afternoon, earlier than usual, but our captors were not behaving as normal. They were arguing among themselves in their Indian jargon, and the *Canadiens* seemed to be trying to convince them to calm down while the French lieutenant tried to reconcile the two groups. The warriors who had been the most hostile toward us seemed to be getting the better of their argument with the *Canadiens*. One of them, I knew, had lost a brother not long before in a skirmish with a group of British Rangers and wanted revenge, though the others had been keeping his anger in check so far. Then, they seemed to come to some sort of agreement, and the Ojibwa and the *Canadiens* began to divide their belongings.

"Lucien, Barthelemy, and the Beaulieu brothers came over and bid Ben and I to get in one of the canoes. We did what we were told, asking them what was going on. We were splitting up, they said. They were taking us to Montreal while the Ojibwa had decided to go west toward Niagara and the lakes. They wanted to hunt, they said, and they knew that the game would become scarce closer to Montreal.

"I asked them about the others. They told us that Paul Adams and the lobsters were going with the Ojibwa. Paul began to plead with Lucien, asking him and the other *Canadiens* to take him to Montreal as well. Lucien told us that they had been negotiating with the Indians all day, but only Ben and I could go with them. We would be safe they promised, but they could make no promises about the others. The Ojibwa would not relinquish them no matter what they offered in return."

"So, you split up?" asked Papan.

"Yes. And Ben was right. We were ransomed once we got to Canada. As soon as we contacted friends at home, and they figured out how to send the required sum, we boarded a sloop heading to France. From there, we crossed to England, and in six months we were back in New York. We walked home from there to give our families a nice surprise."

"And what happened to the others?" asked Marguerite.

"We ran into the English lieutenant in Montreal several weeks after we split up. Turns out the French officer ransomed him for a hefty sum and escorted him north to Montreal with a few Ojibwa friends."

"And the others? The redcoats and your friend Paul?" asked Koohsia.

Jacobs looked down at the ground and took a sip from his cup. "I can't say for sure. Dead, I expect. I never heard a word about their fate."

Marguerite was suspicious. "Did you not think it strange, Mr. Jacobs, when you heard of these murders at Auglaize, that Ben Stone and several of the canoemen killed with him had this shared history? Why didn't you mention this to Captain Turnbull or Ensign Philbrook?"

"Ancient history, ma'am. And I did not consider it any of my business." Jacobs gulped down the last of his rum. "Enough talk for one night. I am going to sleep." With that he lurched up and went off to his bedroll.

Marguerite filled her pipe, and Papan and Koohsia followed her lead. After a moment of reflection, she spoke. "Koohsia, you mentioned something that has been puzzling me. If Mr. Kennedy and Cole acted out of hatred of Ben Stone and a desire for revenge for being left behind, as Ensign Philbrook seems to believe, why did they kill our *Canadien* friends? Kennedy and Cole had no history with those canoemen, but, according to Jacobs's story, it seems that Mr. Jacobs and Ben Stone did."

"I've noticed that Ensign Philbrook assumed from the start that Mr. Stone was the primary target of this massacre, and the local victims were just in the wrong place at the wrong time," observed Papan. "I suppose it is possible that our friends were simply in the way, but that does not sit right with me."

"No. And another thing. Why would they go to so much trouble to find Stone at Auglaize, where the others would be present?" Marguerite said. "It seems like there were easier ways to get revenge on him."

"I think they did it in the backcountry because they wanted to blame Indians," said Papan. "And we both saw Kennedy blaming the Potawatomie every chance he got."

Koohsia spoke up. "So why have they not killed Mr. Jacobs? If Cole and Kennedy wanted revenge for being abandoned, wouldn't they want revenge on both men, Jacobs and Stone? Maybe I don't understand how the British resolve such things."

"No, I think you understand well enough," agreed Papan. "It would be the easiest thing in the world to murder Mr. Jacobs. They could have simply drowned him in the river, and everyone would think he had fallen in drunk."

"Don't tempt me, Joseph." Marguerite laughed. "No matter how much Jacobs likes to talk, I don't think he was telling us everything he knows."

"No, I think maybe not," agreed Koohsia.

"And Ensign Philbrook's suspicions may be mistaken," said Marguerite.

"Yes, Margot," said Papan. "He may well be chasing the proverbial goose."

Chapter 30

Phineas Philbrook

"I'd be obliged if you would all put down your weapons," said a voice inches behind Philbrook's right ear. He felt the knife at his throat and recognized the voice of Jabez Cole. He supposed he should be afraid, but more than anything he felt foolish for walking right into Cole's trap.

"Cole, don't be a damned fool," said Graham.

"I try not to be, Sergeant. Perhaps you and the ensign could do the same. Then you can tell me why you attacked our camp and why you've been chasing me." As he spoke, Cole took Philbrook's twin pistols and slid his sword from its scabbard. He stuffed the pistols in his belt and sheathed his knife, keeping the sword handy. Philbrook thought about putting up a fight, but realized that his position was weak. He would have to try to talk some sense into the little man until there was an opportunity to resist.

"You know perfectly well why we are here, Mr. Cole," Philbrook said, feigning more authority than he felt at that moment. "If you surrender now, you have my word that you will be sent down to Montreal for a fair trial."

"How kind. And what would I be tried for, if it is not too much to ask?"

"You can play dumb if you'd like, Mr. Cole. You are to be tried for the murders of Ben Stone and his men, as well as the murder of Louis Ouellette."

"Ah, interesting," said Cole. "I don't even know who Louis Ouellette is. Or was. But considering your collective wisdom led you to chase me through the woods for the past two days, after who knows how long investigating this business, I hope you understand if I don't take much stock in your promises. A trial directed by idiots before a jury of fools is hardly what I need."

Philbrook found it remarkable that Cole was insulting him as well as holding him helpless. He always thought Sam Kennedy's sidekick was witless. How had he let such a man get the better of them?

Billy began to inch back toward the woods.

"Private Smyth," ordered Cole. "Take one more step and I will slice your ensign's throat clean through. Have you ever seen how far the blood spurts when a healthy man's throat is slit? It might even reach you over there." Cole snorted strangely in what may have been meant as laughter. "Then I really will be guilty of murder." He snorted again and grunted.

"We seem to be at an impasse, Cole," Philbrook said, trying his best to sound confident. "You can slice my throat, it is true, but I assure you, one of my men will dispatch you soon after. Either that or Brutus will tear you apart."

"I'm aware of that, Ensign. But a farce of a trial would be a death sentence to me as well, so I've little to lose. You, on the other hand, have everything to lose. That is if you value your life."

Philbrook realized that he was correct.

"Let me tell you how things are going to be," Cole continued. "First, everyone will drop their weapons where they are and take a seat by the fire."

Everyone stood still.

"Do it now!" Cole shouted.

"Go ahead," Philbrook said. Best to humor Cole for now.

Smyth, Graham, and finally, a reluctant Mihkosita dropped their weapons, approached the fire, and sat down.

"Throw a few sticks on the fire, Sergeant," ordered Cole as he inched forward, keeping behind Philbrook with weapons at the ready. He directed Philbrook to sit on the ground while he stood behind. The sky was glowing orange through the trees to the west. It would be dark soon.

"Sergeant, come take the dog's leash and secure it to that tree over there." Cole indicated an oak tree about twenty feet away. Graham did as he was asked. Brutus was never happy to be tied, but he did not yet understand that Cole was a threat, so he went along. "Now go tie Smyth's wrists behind his back."

Graham did as he was asked, though Philbrook could see that cooperating with Cole filled the sergeant with rage. So far, Graham appeared to be suppressing his anger, but Philbrook worried he might try something foolish that would get his own throat slit. He thought about Sam Kennedy's story of how Cole killed the warrior outside Fort William Henry. The man was certainly capable of anything when he felt threatened. Philbrook pictured the Indian bleeding out back then, then imagined his own blood soaking the ground at his feet. He did not want to die like that.

"Now tie the Indian, if you please," ordered Cole. "I suppose I will have to get to you later, Sergeant. Alright, Ensign, what made you believe that I killed Ben and his men?" Cole made a threatening motion with the sword. "And if anyone tries anything while I am hearing this, I will open your neck. Then, I will shoot Sergeant Graham in the face. I should dispatch the others fairly easily after that if they try to get free of their ropes." Cole snorted.

Philbrook cleared his throat and began to explain the evidence he had uncovered, which led to his conclusion that Cole and Kennedy had killed Stone and his men. As he spoke, he wondered if he sounded foolish. Had he jumped to conclusions? He had not yet been certain when they set out from Detroit. At that point, he had just wanted to ask questions in the wake of Louis Ouellette's murder. But when they caught up and Cole ran, he had become certain of their guilt. Was he wrong?

When he finished, Cole grunted.

"Congratulations, Ensign. I commend you on your vivid imagination. On your ability to leap to conclusions based on fragments of so-called evidence." Philbrook was taken aback by having his intelligence mocked by someone he had thought a simpleton. "The notion that Sam and I could have ridden to Auglaize from Kekionga, murdered those men, then ridden back in the time allotted is a farce. How would we have known where to find them? No, you have fabricated an elaborate scenario based on shadowy impressions. Moreover, Sam and I encountered several Miami hunting parties while we were out who could tell you, if you asked them, that we went nowhere near Auglaize."

"I know you do not think much of me," continued Cole. "Not many people do. Most find me off-putting because I lack the genteel graces. I choose not to speak when speech is not necessary, so people fancy me dumb. Even Sam has little respect for my intelligence and thinks me just a skilled hunter and tolerable companion. But I assure you I notice things. I'll remind you that I was at Auglaize when those bodies were discovered, and the scene was yet fresh. Don't you think I saw the tomahawk and recognized it? Don't you think I saw the tracks in the woods? I examined the wounds on those men's bodies, and unlike Sam and the French girl, I remained calm. That has always been a skill of mine, you see, to remain calm when others are losing their heads."

Philbrook considered what Cole said. He was reluctant to admit that much of it made sense. But why had Cole run? Why did he now threaten him? Was that the behavior of an innocent man? An innocent man would have explained things back at Marguerite's campsite.

Cole stepped back but kept the sword handy. Philbrook considered turning on him, but, before he'd decided, he felt the tip of the sword flicking at his right ear.

"Believe me, Ensign, I won't hesitate to cut you if you try anything. Think what you like of me, but while it has taken you weeks to come up with faulty assumptions, I know some interesting things that you failed to discover."

"Like what?" Philbrook demanded, slowly turning to face the ugly little man.

"Well, for starters, there's the canoeman, Pero, the burnt one, who you all took to be one of the corpses."

"What of him?" Philbrook's fears and doubts were being supplanted by irritation.

"He isn't dead," said Cole.

"What do you mean not dead? You saw his body."

"No, Ensign. I saw a headless body wearing Pero's clothes."

"Why do you say that?"

"You were probably told that Pero had no tongue and that his face was badly burned," Cole explained. "War injuries due to a cannon exploding during the defense of Quebec. At least that was the story."

"Indeed, I was told that."

"But the body we found had no head. By the time you discovered the heads, I imagine enough flesh had rotted away to make recognition impossible."

"Yes," Philbrook said. "Your point?"

"If you want to hide a corpse's identity, removing the head can be a most effective method," observed Cole. "Had you even thought of that, Ensign?"

Philbrook admitted that he had not.

"Even if you only wanted to hide the identity of one, all the heads would have to go. It would be too obvious to remove the head of just one. It would call attention. No, no. They all had to be treated the same. It never figured that the heads were taken otherwise. To Sam, it was evidence that Indians were responsible, but I know better."

"Perhaps," Philbrook said. He was wary, but he had to admit that Cole made sense. It was an obvious explanation for the decapitation, but it had eluded him.

"Marguerite and Papan identified him and the others by the clothes they wore," continued Cole. "Of course they assumed that the one wearing Pero's clothes was Pero. Why wouldn't they? But I looked more closely at the bodies. The others would not have known this, but Pero also had his lobcock burned and his balls ripped off back when he lost his tongue."

The image took Philbrook aback. "How would you know that?" he asked.

Cole stepped over, took a burning stick from the edge of the fire, and used it to light his pipe, keeping one eye on Philbrook the whole time. "Let's just say I saw him once." He smiled unpleasantly between puffs. "Not a sight to be forgotten by a man, I assure you. It was no secret—ask around among the canoemen in Detroit. Naturally neither Marguerite nor Papan bothered looking closely at the body. I did."

"Why would you do that?" Philbrook asked. "Did you look down the breeches of the other dead men as well?"

"No, Ensign. I took a second look at the body dressed in Pero's clothes after I noticed a distinctive set of footprints. You see, there were several sets of tracks around that campsite when we first stumbled upon the massacre. There were the prints from Stone's boots and the moccasins of his men. Then there were others that came in on top of these, all but one wearing moccasins."

"Go on," Philbrook said, becoming interested.

"You see, Pero walked with a limp, so his prints were very distinctive," explained Cole. "One foot always made a deeper impression than the other."

Billy and Mihkosita nodded at this. Mihkosita spoke up. "Yes, I noticed those tracks. They were faint by the time I was there. But they could not have belonged to one of the murdered men. Some of them were more recent and were made after the killings."

"Exactly," said Cole. "Keep in mind that I was there well before any of you, and the prints were yet fresh. The others with us at the time knew nothing of reading tracks, so I did not show them to anyone, but as soon as I saw them, I knew they came from Pero's lopsided gait."

"How did you know that?" Philbrook asked.

"Our party had been a few days behind Stone's group ever since leaving Detroit. We often camped for the night at places they had recently been. The track was distinctive, so not hard to link with the burnt cripple. After I saw them, I checked the body that was supposed to be Pero and saw that it did not share his mutilations."

"So, are you saying that Pero killed the others and dressed up a corpse in his clothing?"

"Yes indeed, Ensign. That seems to be part of the story, at least."

"Whose corpse?"

"An excellent question. I don't know the answer, but there were others there as well. Three or four other men came to Auglaize that night. Their tracks were all over and, with the exception of Pero's, distinct from the murdered men."

"And you said nothing of your observations this whole time?" Philbrook regretted that he had not found the time to talk with Cole back in Detroit. But a normal man would not have kept this information to himself.

"No one asked me, and it was not my business, at least it wasn't until you began to threaten me and Sam."

"Well, I'm asking you now. What else do you know?"

"I know that the tomahawk you found did not belong to Indians," said Cole. "It once belonged to me."

"We discovered that, as I told you," Philbrook said.

"But what you did not learn was that I traded it away soon after I acquired it."

"Traded it? Traded it to whom?"

"To Amos Jacobs. Last I knew, the weapon belonged to that worthless remnant of a man."

Chapter 31

Phineas Philbrook

P hilbrook paced back and forth next to the campfire, angry with himself. What had he done? Had they raced all the way north to apprehend the wrong men? Had he foolishly left Marguerite in the hands of the true killer? His suspicion of Cole increased after leaving Detroit—up until the man began to speak. But now...

"Why should I trust you, Cole?" He turned toward the unpleasant man. Cole had loaded Philbrook's pistols and now sat with his back to a tree, guarding his captives. The sun had set, but the moon was bright. "How do I know that anything you tell me is the truth?"

Cole eyed Philbrook, his face reflecting the moonlight and the glow of the dying campfire. "You don't, Ensign. In general, you know very little." Cole gave a perverse grin. There was something in Cole that Philbrook found repellent. So much so that he wanted him to be guilty.

"I don't like that we left Marguerite with Jacobs," Graham spoke up. "If there is a chance that Cole tells the truth..."

"I know. I know. Damn." Philbrook stamped his foot, which only served to make him feel childish.

"Why don't you tend to the fire again, Sergeant," instructed Cole. Graham grabbed some sticks and branches from a pile and threw them onto the glowing embers. Soon flames began to rise, reflecting their flickering light onto nearby trees. Billy and Mihkosita watched Cole and Philbrook helplessly, their arms bound behind them.

"Well, what is your plan, Cole?" Philbrook asked. He hoped to talk some sense into him. "You've got our weapons, so we are no threat to you any longer. You may have outwitted us for now, but you've nowhere to go. Surrender to us. I promise, you'll be well treated. We will tell your story to Captain Turnbull. If you and Kennedy are truly innocent, it will come out. Don't you want to clear your name?"

"Think about it, Cole," added Graham. "If what you say is true, we can get to the bottom of it. Pero will be found if he is still alive. A man like that is sure to attract notice."

"And it's not as if Jacobs could stand up to an interrogation," said Philbrook. "He's weak. We can simply take his rum away until we get the truth out of him."

"Sorry," replied Cole. "That is not going to happen. I don't trust a parcel of redcoats to care about the truth, and I've no interest in being confined to the goddamn gaol starving on rotting food while they try. No, the army is just as likely to hang Sam and me along with Amos just to consider themselves finished with the matter."

"The army can't execute a civilian," Philbrook explained, "not in peacetime. If Turnbull thinks you guilty, you'll be sent down to Montreal for a proper trial."

"Sent in chains you mean. Shackled in the bilge water of a leaking bateau for weeks with my skin rubbed raw. I'm sure you can understand, Mr. Philbrook, that is not a journey that tempts me at all. I think my chances of reaching Montreal in good health would be slim."

"Your information leaves us with plenty of unanswered questions and hardly exonerates you and Kennedy," Philbrook vented. "Maybe Pero and Jacobs were your accomplices."

"If you are still trying to convince me to throw myself on your mercy, Ensign, you are doing a horrible job of it."

Philbrook ignored his sarcasm. Even if Cole was not guilty of murder, Philbrook considered him a thoroughly unpleasant person. Or perhaps he just resented the man for besting him. Back in Detroit, he had not made talking with Cole a priority, and now he was paying the price. He had lost the opportunity to make an ally of him. Now Cole felt threatened.

"You leave us with too many questions still," said Philbrook, trying to reason with him. "What was Pero's connection to Jacobs? Or Stone, for that matter? Where is he now? Whose body was left in his place? We need to go get Jacobs and return with both of you to Detroit. We can then answer our questions with everyone concerned in the same room."

"You're not going to change my mind, Ensign. Those are all legitimate questions, but it's your job to answer them, not mine. I don't care to risk my liberty to satisfy your curiosity."

"Well, you can't hold us here forever, Jabez," observed Graham.

"No, you're right in that." Cole got up and circled the four men, pistols in hand. Billy and Mihkosita kept their eyes on him. "But I think I have a solution," Cole murmured as he passed behind Graham. Without warning, he smashed the butt of a pistol against the back of the sergeant's skull. Graham slumped forward, unconscious.

"Damn you!" Philbrook shouted, lurching forward.

"Hold it there, Ensign, if you want to live."

Philbrook stopped where he was. "Why did you do that? Graham didn't threaten you."

"Think for a moment, Ensign. If that is not asking too much of you. I need to get away from here, and despite your vivid imagination, I am no killer. I can't leave you all tied up when I go because you'd starve to death before anyone came along. And I can't release you, as you outnumber me. No, I need one of you unconscious for an hour or two. Graham will wake with a nasty headache and untie the rest of you when I'm far away from here. Now be a good lad and let me bind you so I can be off tonight. I'll even tell you how to get your weapons back in the morning."

Philbrook thought on this for a moment. His priority now was to get back to the canoe and go find Marguerite and Amos Jacobs. He would have preferred to take Cole into custody first, but that was no longer a realistic option.

"Not a bad plan if you ask me, sir," said Billy Smyth. "Sergeant Graham has a thick skull, and he looks to be breathing normal. He'll wake in no time and let us loose."

"Very well, Mr. Cole." To submit to Cole went against Philbrook's nature, but he had to be realistic. He turned and brought his arms behind his back.

"I'm glad you've seen sense," said Cole as he bound Philbrook and seated him back-to-back with the other men, positioned so that the warmth of the fire reached them, as the nighttime air was beginning to chill. "I'm going to go back the way we came for about a half mile, and I'll leave your weapons where you can find them. Do you remember that large boulder with the flat top? That's where they will be. I'm not saying which way I'm going after that. Best not try to follow me, for you won't catch up. If by any chance you do, I won't be so forgiving a second time. You understand me, Ensign?"

"Yes, Cole, perfectly."

"Good. And good luck finding the killers." With that, Cole trotted off into the darkness, laughing.

Graham lay there insensible while the rest of them waited for him to revive. Brutus whimpered. When Cole was gone, Philbrook realized how exhausted he was from the chase. He wanted to stay awake, but his eyes quickly began to droop. Sleep overwhelmed him.

~

PHILBROOK DREAMED ABOUT MARGUERITE. They were back in Detroit at the party. She was wearing her dress, and they were dancing a cotillion with three other couples—two officers and a merchant and their wives. Hands were held. Partners were exchanged and turned. All was manners and grace—as fine as London could offer.

Now Koohsia joined them with Madame Boyer as his partner. Madame Boyer was a remarkably graceful woman. Funny, Philbrook had not noticed that before. Now Sam Kennedy was there with Cole as his partner. The bonfire burned brightly. They moved faster. The music broke out of its more formal patterns and sped up into a country dance. They moved in elaborate circles, ducking under arms, turning, spinning. They moved even faster around the fire, with each of the four couples taking turns jumping through the flames.

As Philbrook jumped the fire, he looked down into the embers and saw skulls among them. He did not know how, but he knew that these were the skulls of Ben Stone and his men. Their jaws were open in a silent scream and their eye sockets were filled with fire. Then Philbrook noticed that one skull looked back at him with pain and betrayal. He knew somehow that it was all that remained of Louis Ouellette, the young man he had failed to protect as he should have.

~

MIHKOSITA WAS the first to wake as the rays of the morning sun reached them. "Ensign, Billy," he called to the others as he shook the ropes that bound them together.

Philbrook heard him, roused, and looked around in a fog until he recalled the situation. It had been a cold night and his body was stiff and sore. His clothes were slightly damp from the morning dew. "Sergeant Graham, wake up," he yelled to the figure still sprawled out in the leaves snoring.

The sergeant opened his bleary eyes, looking around like a man who had recently been knocked on the head. "What? What happened?"

Philbrook filled him in as Graham touched the lump on the back of his head, then moved to untie the others. "I guess we should be glad he did not do us in," said Graham.

"How kind of him. Remind me to thank him when we next meet," grumbled Billy.

The men stretched and rubbed their arms, which had lost all feeling from the ropes. Philbrook freed Brutus. After making a meal from what provisions they still had, they headed back the way they had come. Philbrook was embarrassed by the ease with which Cole had rendered them impotent. He wanted to find Marguerite as soon as possible, to make sure she was safe. Then he wanted to interrogate Amos Jacobs.

"If we backtrack, we should find our weapons," said Philbrook, "if Cole did as he said he would do. Then we should head back to the canoe as fast as we can."

"And where do we go from there?" asked Graham.

"Let me think on that until we get there," Philbrook said. He could go back to Detroit first to get help, but that would risk Captain Turnbull interfering. He was inclined to go after Jacobs directly.

"Do you believe Cole was telling the truth?" asked Graham as they walked through the woods. Mihkosita and Billy were ahead finding the trail.

"I don't know, but Mihkosita supports the part about Pero's prints, and the fact that he did not slit our throats when he had us at his mercy gives him some credibility."

"There's that," said Graham.

"Tell me, Sergeant," Philbrook said, "could Jacobs have gotten to Auglaize to murder those men? I mean, as a logistical matter, could he have gotten there on his own and not been missed? I'd assumed he was in Detroit the whole time." If he was going to go after Jacobs, he wanted to be sure that it would not be another case of mistaken suspicion.

"I suppose he could have ridden. Jacobs isn't bad on a horse. Three or four days. Maybe two if he really pushed."

"The tracks that Mihkosita found suggest horsemen," said Philbrook. "But would Jacobs have had time? Surely his absence would have been noted."

"I can't be sure," said Graham.

"I believe Mr. Jacobs was off on a bender then," called back Billy. "Least that's what we assumed, sir. I'm sure you are aware that Jacobs is a drunk. He has a way of disappearing for a few days then showing back up looking like a dead rat. Some of the men have a running bet going on how long before he passes out and never wakes up."

Philbrook had seen enough of the world not to be shocked by casual cruelty.

"So, it is possible," said Graham. "But it's hard to picture Jacobs showing such energy."

Philbrook too had difficulty imaging Jacobs killing anyone. He seemed too pathetic in a way. But he had owned the tomahawk found at the scene. If he had not taken it there himself, he would at least know who else might have.

THE FOLLOWING DAY, they arrived back at their cached canoe. Philbrook was surprised to see Privates Young and Bellows waiting there. The soldiers jumped up as they came out of the woods.

"Sir. Good to see you, sir," Young said to Philbrook. "We've been worried. Did you catch him?" They looked around for Cole.

"No. He got away," said Philbrook.

"No worry, men," said Graham. "We'll catch him eventually—or find his body."

"The captain got worried for your safety," said Bellows. "He sent us up to offer what help we could. It's just the two of us in a small canoe."

The presence of Bellows and Young with a second canoe solidified Philbrook's plan to head north to Michilimackinac to find Jacobs and Marguerite. But first he asked the privates what had transpired in Detroit with Kennedy. Had Kennedy confessed anything?

"No, sir. Kennedy maintains his innocence. All indignation and righteousness, he is. He threatens lawsuits, that sort of thing. Traders are like that. Litigious, that's what Captain Turnbull calls them."

"I'm glad you are here," said Philbrook. "We are going to go north to Michilimackinac, and the extra canoe will be useful."

"I wonder, sir," said Graham. "Jacobs will be coming back through Detroit after he finishes his business in Michilimackinac anyway. Is it a good use of our time to go chasing after him?"

Philbrook appreciated the sergeant's advice most of the time, but his mind was made up, so the second-guessing was not welcome.

"I think so, Sergeant. If he has killed before, then no one is safe in his company. I will not feel at peace until he is in our custody."

"But Captain Turnbull's orders—" Graham began.

"Let me worry about the captain's orders, Sergeant Graham," The sergeant was crossing into insubordinate territory, and he did not have the patience to debate him. He did not mean to be rude, but the responsibility was his, and he was hungry.

"We will have a good meal, then start north directly. Understood?"

"Yes, sir," said Graham.

THAT AFTERNOON, they paddled north on a placid lake under a bright blue sky. Graham, Young, and Bellows manned one canoe, while Smyth, Mihkosita, and Philbrook took the other. Philbrook was finally getting the chance to paddle. The motion stretched his shoulder muscles pleasantly, and he removed his boots and gave his blistered feet a chance to heal.

"Tell me about Michilimackinac, Sergeant Graham. Is it like Detroit?"

"It's much smaller, sir. It is not so much of a permanent community as a seasonal meeting place. Fewer farms. Besides the army garrison, it's a mere sand bank with a trading post. There are a few Ojibwa and Ottawa villages a day or two travel away, and their people come in to trade."

Graham, too, was paddling, but with the old wounds to his hands, he was fairly ineffective. Privates Bellows and Young took up the slack.

"Why not more farming?" asked Philbrook.

"There's some gardening and livestock, but the soil is poor, not like around Detroit. And the season is shorter. They need to bring most of their provisions up from Detroit to get through the winter. In the outlying areas, the Indians harvest wild rice in the fall, and they tap maple trees and boil it down to sugar in the early spring. They trade their bounty at the fort."

"I've heard it is well positioned for trade further afield," said Philbrook.

"True," said Graham. "It sits at the strait that joins Lake Huron and Lake Michigan. It's a natural meeting place. The canoe brigades come up from Montreal via the Ottawa River route, and most of the traders, bound for the Mississippi country or the Northwest, use it as a base."

"I see. Do you know what business Mr. Jacobs could have there?"

"Damned if I know. I assumed it was some side trading. I would not be surprised if we come upon them on their return journey. If Marguerite finds an easy way to unload Kennedy's goods, she will have no reason to linger."

As it was, they did not see Marguerite before arriving at Michilimackinac. The canoes traveled along the low-lying shoreline for several days. Occasionally, they passed the canoes and bateaux of traders making their way south. Several mentioned seeing Marguerite's party a few days ahead. None mentioned any signs of problems. The last of the traders they saw confirmed that Marguerite, Jacobs, and Papan were in Michilimackinac looking to sell Kennedy's goods.

Fort Michilimackinac eventually came into view. The square wooden stockade, made of logs on end, sat near the sandy shore, almost at a level with the lake. It was much smaller than Detroit, barely 200 yards across at its widest point. An abundance of trade canoes and several temporary Native encampments lay outside the gates, but there were few fields, farms, or pretty *habitant* cottages.

"Private Smyth, Mihkosita, I should go call on the commander. Would you two try to locate Marguerite and Jacobs? Take Brutus with you."

"Certainly, sir."

"Sergeant Graham, I assume you know your way around here?" Philbrook asked.

"Yes, sir."

"Then let's go."

Chapter 32

Marguerite Boyer

Most of their work in Michilimackinac was done, and Marguerite was thinking about Daniel. He had been upset when she left. He had cried and told her he hated her, as she went out the door. It was just an eight-year-old's temper tantrum, but it hurt her just the same. He had done this before—yelled and screamed like the world was ending when she left him—and each time, when she returned, everything was fine. It would be this time as well, she reassured herself.

She was glad she had *Maman* to care for him. Daniel loved his *grand-mère*. When he grew older, he would cherish the time he got to spend with her. She would be home soon, and this time she would stay longer. Before she knew it, he would be old enough to join her on her travels. Then, he would grow into a man, leading his own brigade of canoes one day.

Michilimackinac was bustling. Every day traders and canoes arrived. Some had come up from Montreal with packs full of trade goods that had come off of ships from Europe that spring. Others, like her, were up from Detroit. But the most interesting groups came from the west and north. Traders were venturing further afield every year. Some went to the headwaters of the Mississippi

261

River where they encountered other traders who had come all the way up the river from New Orleans. They traded with Natives who spoke languages entirely different from the ones she knew. Others were back from Lake Superior which was surrounded by the rich fur grounds of the Ojibwa and Cree Nations. She had met one trader who, with his men, had been all the way to Dauphin Lake, west of Lake Winnipeg. They had left their winter camp to return as soon as the ice allowed and traveled weeks to get back here. She heard stories from them of vast grasslands and huge herds of buffaloes that they hunted to keep themselves fed through the cold winter. She would like to see that land someday.

She had also been thinking of Louis. The way Philbrook had told her of his death had been so blunt, she could hardly process that it was real. She had come to feel for Louis in a way similar to how she felt for Daniel—she had wanted to take care of him, because he seemed not to be able to take care of himself. Philbrook had seemed sure that Kennedy and Cole were responsible for his death, but she had trouble putting it all together. She had spoken with Koohsia about the sequence of events the morning she left Detroit. Louis would have been killed within an hour of her departure, but Kennedy and Cole had not been acting like men who had just slit someone's throat. Not that she knew how such men behaved, but she assumed that when a man committed murder, it would show in his face for a long time.

The men had been working hard since they had left, and she had decided to reward them with a day of rest. They would be returning soon, and she wanted them to be fully recovered from the trip up. Most of them were lounging at their campsite outside the stockade. Some of the men napped. Other played games or socialized with the canoemen from other groups, especially those who had wintered in the West or Northwest—they had the best stories. She knew that a few of her men were considering engaging with traders who wanted winterers for the coming season. If that was what they wanted, she could not object. It would not be hard to find replacements for the trip back to Detroit.

She and Joseph had just finished repacking gear for their return journey and had sat to enjoy their pipes.

"Margot, there are a few things I don't understand." Joseph took a puff, a serious expression on his face. "Why would Mr. Jacobs need to get to L'Arbre Croche? I've never known him to do any backcountry trading."

"I didn't think it my place to ask, Joseph. I just told him we would be here until Friday if he wants to go back to Detroit with us." Marguerite had been surprised when Jacobs told her that he had hired a horse and planned to ride to the Ottawa village on Lake Michigan, but he was a free man and his choices were none of her concern. Still, she couldn't help but wonder.

"He said not to worry if he does not make it back in time. We can leave without him," she added, "and I will not mind if we do."

"I can't help but think that something is not right with that man." Joseph shook his head. "Besides the obvious, I mean. That story he told about the being taken captive with Stone. How can it be a coincidence?"

"You mean that it involved so many of the men killed at Auglaize?" She had been thinking the same thing.

"*Exactement.*"

"I don't know, Joseph. Let Philbrook and Turnbull figure it out. I'm ready to wash my hands of the whole affair." She knew this was not true. Her mind would not be settled until these questions were resolved.

"And I don't understand Koohsia's behavior either, Margot. First, he decides to come north with us instead of going back home, then he walks off into the bush before we get here. Why wouldn't he tell us where he planned to go?"

"You know some of these old Native elders, Joseph. It's hard to know what they are thinking. Maybe it is something to do with his religion, and he fears telling us about it would spoil things with his spirits."

"Maybe. I've heard some consider it bad medicine to speak aloud of such things."

Marguerite was more puzzled by Koohsia's behavior than she let on. The morning after Jacobs had told his story, the old man had gathered his things together and told her that he was going to wander about on his own for a bit.

"You are far from your own country here, Koohsia," she said. "Are you sure you feel safe traveling alone?"

"Do not worry about me, Marguerite. I've taken care of myself for many years, and my dreams have shown me that I have many days ahead of me."

"I hope you do," she answered. "But where are you going?"

"Maybe I will tell you the next time I see you." And with that, Koohsia shook Marguerite's hand and trotted away down a forest path. That had been days earlier, and she wondered if she would ever see Koohsia again.

At least their business had gone well. Soon after they arrived in Michilimackinac, Marguerite found a French trader, just in from the Mississippi River via La Baye, who was eager to renew his supplies and head back to the Nadouessioux country. He had taken most of Kennedy's cargo off her hands in exchange for a mixture of furs and promissory notes drawn on a reputable Montreal firm. She still had a few items left to dispose of, but she was reassured that she would be able to pay the crew and help Mr. Kennedy avoid bankruptcy in the immediate future.

"Is that Philbrook's orderly and Mihkosita?" asked Joseph, looking toward the river. She saw the familiar form of Billy Smyth ambling toward them followed by Mihkosita. Their eyes met, and Smyth gave a little wave. Two other redcoats followed behind, but no sign of Philbrook. His absence caused an unexpected rush of worry in Marguerite.

"Marguerite, Joseph, glad to see you both well," Mihkosita greeted them.

Marguerite stood up. "What are you doing here Mihkosita? Is Philbrook with you? Did you find Cole?" She looked from one to the other.

"Ensign Philbrook went with Sergeant Graham to see the Commandant, ma'am," said Smyth. "He should find us shortly. Young, how about you go to the office and tell the ensign and sergeant where to find us."

Private Young nodded and went off, followed by Bellows.

Philbrook and Sergeant Graham showed up a few moments later. Marguerite was struck by the difference in the ensign. She supposed that the change had been gradual over the past weeks, but it hit her now, all of a sudden. His uniform was faded and worn, and he looked more comfortable in it than he had a few weeks before. His face and his hands were tanned and firm from being outside all the time. And he seemed to walk with a more erect posture than the green young ensign she had first met at Detroit.

"Mam'selle Boyer, Monsieur Papan, good to see you both again. I don't suppose I could get a cup of tea from you? We all ran out a few days back." It was a hot day, so Philbrook took off his coat. He sank down and took a seat with his back to a log, placed for that purpose near the fire, and placed his folded coat behind his back as a pillow. He stretched his slim legs out before him, crossing his ankles.

"Certainly, you are all welcome to what I have," Marguerite said. "Make yourself comfortable." She put the kettle on the fire.

"Is Jacobs still with you?" he asked.

"No," she said. "He went off to L'Arbre Croche on horseback. I don't really know why he went or when he is coming back."

"L'Arbre Croche? That's strange," said Graham. "Alone? What business could Jacobs possibly have there?" The sergeant took a seat next to Philbrook.

265

"That's what I was wondering," said Joseph.

"What about Cole?" asked Marguerite. "Did you find him?"

Philbrook looked at his feet. "We did indeed, though it did not go exactly as planned. He told us some interesting things."

"We heard some remarkable stories from Mr. Jacob's as well," Marguerite said. "About his past with Mr. Stone. I think you'll be interested."

"It seems we have all learned a thing or two since we last saw each other. It is about time we got caught up. Marguerite, Joseph, why don't you begin."

Papan and Marguerite recounted the story that Jacobs had told them, and Philbrook, in turn, told them about Jabez Cole's claims. When they were done, they sat and thought for a moment. Then Philbrook said, "I have some thoughts, but I'd rather hear from the rest of you first."

"Cole was not lying when he said he looked more closely at the scene of the murders than the rest of us," offered Marguerite. "The idea that the one dressed in Pero's clothing was not Pero did not occur to me. I saw Cole examining the bodies and walking around, looking at tracks. At the time, Joseph and I did not expect the killings to remain a mystery, so I suppose we were not as observant as we might have been."

"And he is right that Pero had been mutilated in his privates," added Joseph. "Those who voyaged with him saw his body now and again, and I've heard talk of repulsive scarring, but I did not look so closely at the body we found."

"What else do you know of Pero, Papan?" asked Philbrook. "I understand he was not local?"

"No. He showed up a few months back—maybe half a year," said Joseph. "Folks say he was from Quebec City. He wasn't easy to look at, I can tell you that. I take it you've heard that he had repulsive burn scars on his head and face, and he'd lost his tongue, so he could not speak. Battle injuries. I never traveled with him, but Jacobs gave him work. He kept to himself mostly when in town.

Are you thinking that he might be the answer to all of this? If he truly isn't dead, well, maybe he just got up and killed the rest and then ran off. He might have stolen Jacobs' tomahawk before they left. Nothing complicated there."

"Except the matter of the body left in his place," Marguerite observed. She realized from what Philbrook had told them that one of the bodies they had buried at Auglaize had belonged to someone who was not supposed to be there.

"I hadn't thought of that. A passing stranger, maybe?" offered Joseph.

"I have an idea but no real evidence at this point," said Philbrook. "I've entertained the notion that Pero killed the others with accomplices who met him there, and that he betrayed one of those accomplices."

Philbrook was describing a plan—perhaps a conspiracy. The thought frightened Marguerite for its coldness, but the unidentified body left little doubt. She understood rage or a moment of violent passion, but there was something far worse about preplanned murder.

"Marguerite, why do you think Koohsia joined you and then left?" Graham said, changing the subject. "When we went after Cole, I assumed Koohsia would return home."

"I don't know. He said he wanted to come north with us, then a couple of days later, he said he was leaving."

"I think I know," said Mihkosita quietly. "Koohsia took personally the death of Louis. He considered himself Louis's protector, and he takes very seriously his obligation to protect the weak and needy. It is part of the path given to him by his dreams. If he thinks he has learned something, he will try to make things right in his own way, and he will not give up."

"Does Koohsia know something that we do not, Mihkosita?" asked Philbrook. "About Pero, perhaps?"

"I do not know, but we talked as we first traveled north from Detroit. He did not understand why you thought Mr. Kennedy and Mr. Cole had sufficient reason to kill Mr. Stone and the *Canadiens* with him. He saw that the two men might be angry at Stone for his actions years ago but not angry enough to kill him. Killing the *Canadiens* too would have been senseless, well beyond any proper call for vengeance."

Marguerite looked at Philbrook, wondering if he would be defensive about having his theory about Kennedy and Cole dismissed. It appeared, though, that his encounter with Cole in the forest had already caused him to reevaluate.

"And he left after hearing Jacobs's story," Philbrook mused. "Did that story implicate anyone else?"

"What the story told us," Marguerite said, "was that Stone, the Beaulieu brothers, Lucien, and Bartolomi had a shared history we did not know about. Going back close to ten years—to the fall of Fort William Henry."

"But as far as we know, neither Kennedy nor Cole had any prior connection with the canoemen as Stone did." Philbrook frowned. "They were not taken captive like Jacobs and Stone, so they did not meet the *Canadiens* back then. That complicates things. It further undermines my former premise."

"Yes. Kennedy and Cole made it home, and Jacobs and Stone made it to Montreal without injury and were redeemed," said Joseph. "They were all lucky really. Luckier than all the men killed. It seems to me that Koohsia was right. None of them had much reason to be resentful, at least not enough to murder."

"Except..." began Marguerite.

Sergeant Graham cleared his throat. "Excuse me, sir, I'm not sure I understand. The war is over and done many years now. So what if Mr. Stone knew his canoemen before? There's lots of folks around that I knew back then. Same for most everyone around here. The Upper Country is full of war veterans."

"You've got a point, Sergeant," said Philbrook. "Billy, you, too, were at Fort William Henry when it fell, right?"

"Aye, sir," answered Billy, who had been quietly listening to the conversation. "I run into folks all the time who I knew back then, both in and out of uniform."

"And Young, Bellows, and I served in the war together," said Graham. "We were stationed in Albany when Montcalm took Fort William Henry, but we knew lots of the folks killed and taken there. These coincidences you are pointing toward are quite commonplace, sir. You really wonder who has a reason to want revenge? Pretty much all the Indians around here who feel abandoned by their French allies and are now bullied by the British, that's who. They suffer great disrespect from us and grow discontented with the *Canadiens* who help us. I've said it before, sir, but this looks like a few warriors blowing off steam and fed up with the British and the French alike."

"Thank you, Sergeant," said Philbrook. "I take your point."

"The past is past," continued Graham, "but murder is all about immediacy. About rage here and now. Maybe they offended or cheated some folks on their way up the river, perhaps an Ottawa hunting party or the Cheney gang. Stands to reason that revenge would be taken out on the whole crew right on the spot. And maybe they kept it quiet out of fear of Pontiac."

"You may be right," said Philbrook.

"And another thought, sir," said Graham. "What if this Pero fellow and Louis Ouellette acted together? The other canoemen were all long-time friends, but Louis and Pero were outsiders. I know some of you had come to trust Louis, but it is certain that he was there. What if those two had an argument with the others that got out of hand, then later the two of them had a falling out? Pero would have then had ample motive to silence Louis back at Detroit."

"An interesting thought," said Philbrook.

"But we know of nothing that connects Pero and Louis besides this voyage," Marguerite said. She reflected that the sergeant's views were unusually rigid. They did not change when new information came to them. "Let's not forget about Mr. Jacobs and his tomahawk."

"Or the body left in Pero's place." Philbrook ran his fingers through his hair. "We have lots of possibilities to think about and new information to digest. I can't help but think that Jacobs is an important piece of this puzzle. I propose that tomorrow morning we leave here to track him down and get some answers, starting with what his tomahawk was doing at the scene and ending with the question of who Pero is and why he is not lying in the ground with the others at Auglaize."

Marguerite had no reason to accompany Philbrook to *L'Arbre Croche*. It was not her business anymore. Nonetheless she found herself speaking up. "I'd like to come with you, Ensign."

He looked at her with a smile. "Of course, Marguerite. I could not imagine going without you. We will need both your interpreting skills and your ability to confirm what he said to you the other night in case he tries to change the story."

"Joseph can stay here to tend to our trade, so you will need to make room for me in one of your canoes," she said.

"That can be arranged. We should not be more than a few days. Once we find Jacobs, either he tells us something useful or he doesn't. Then we'll come right back here."

"Do you plan on detaining him, sir?" asked Sergeant Graham.

"That is an excellent question, Sergeant. It depends on what he tells us."

SEVERAL NIGHTS LATER, on Lake Michigan two canoes approached a small rocky point near the mouth of Little Traverse Bay. Marguerite paddled with Mihkosita and Philbrook while the soldiers manned the other canoe. They were only two or three miles from L'Arbre Croche when they pulled up to shore just past the point, where a bay with a pebble beach made landing easy.

Marguerite had advised that they did not want to enter the village late in the day when they had not been invited. That would be rude. They made camp, where their presence would be noted, so they could approach the village in the morning.

For two days, they had been coasting the shoreline of Lake Michigan. They'd seen the occasional small village, but not stopped anywhere. Summer was now well underway. The weather had been sunny and calm, and the days were long, allowing them to cover distance quickly. Marguerite tried to put all the pieces together in her mind as they paddled, but she found that each new fact seemed to come with two new questions. And she mourned for Louis. She had been thinking a great deal about the boy since learning of his murder. She supposed he was a man, but she could not help but think of him as a boy. She was certain that Louis was an innocent in all this—someone caught up in evils that had nothing to do with him. These scars and loose ends from a war that ended six years before were not his concern. He had been little more than a child when the fighting ceased. He was just a charming—if somewhat eccentric—young man trying to make his way.

She and Philbrook agreed that whoever killed Louis wished to silence him. His fragile memory had been returning, so someone, maybe Pero or someone else out there, was worried that inconvenient memories might come back. Or maybe Louis's killer did not know what the boy knew but did not want to risk finding out. Either way, it was a sad shame. A waste of a good young life.

"I think Louis's murder may confirm a few things for us, Marguerite," Philbrook said one afternoon in the canoe. "We can dispense with the idea that Louis killed his companions at Auglaize. Whoever killed Louis must have done it to silence him. That points us toward Detroit people, or someone who comes and goes from Detroit, and those who had knowledge of our investigation either directly or indirectly."

"Like Kennedy or Cole or Jacobs?" Marguerite said.

"Exactly, or this Pero fellow or friends of his."

"That's still a lot of people," she said. "The one thing about Pero is that, if he is still alive, he can hardly walk about without folks noticing him. Wouldn't we know if he had returned to Detroit? If Cole is right that Pero is not dead, he must be hiding out somewhere."

"Or he has allies," said Philbrook. "Maybe he only goes out at night when he can keep his face in shadows. I feel our evidence thus far points to Pero acting with accomplices, maybe Mr. Jacobs among them. I find it interesting that Jacobs hired Pero several times while none of the other merchants ever did."

"It's possible, sir," suggested Sergeant Graham, "that Pero had allies among the renegade *Canadiens* living along the river. They could be hiding him. This is just a thought, but families like the Cheneys are pretty tight-knit. One could easily have come to Detroit to take care of loose ends when they heard we found Ouellette. Maybe there was some French feud that got settled at Auglaize, and Stone was just in the wrong bloody place at the wrong bloody time."

"An interesting idea, Sergeant."

"But I still think it's a mistake to rule out the notion that Louis was killed in a drunken fracas that had nothing to do with your investigations, sir," continued Graham. "I had an officer once, an educated English fellow who considered himself something of a philosopher. He used to talk of what he called Ockham's razor whenever we were trying to figure things out. He said it meant that the simplest answer to a problem is usually the right one. If we follow that, then the men at Auglaize were killed by a roving band of Indians or renegades, and poor Ouellette was killed by some drunk in a fit of anger. Nothing complicated or unusual there."

AFTER THEIR EVENING MEAL, as Marguerite and the men smoked pipes and prepared for sleep, two figures approached from the east along the sandy shore. Marguerite could see that they were Ottawa men from the village. She and the others all stood, and Philbrook motioned to Graham and the soldiers to make room by the fire.

"Marguerite, would you ask them if they would like to join us?" he said. She called an invitation to the two, who came over but did not sit.

When one of the men spoke, Philbrook recognized his own name amidst the unfamiliar words.

"They are asking for you and Mihkosita," said Marguerite. "They want you to go with them."

"Who told you to look for us?" he asked them. "We told no one we were coming this way."

The men responded that they were simply messengers from elders in the village.

Philbrook was cautious. "What do you think, Marguerite?" he asked.

"I think it would be rude not to accept the invitation, but it seems strange. How could they know your name?"

Philbrook shrugged then turned to the two men. "Give us a minute to break camp and we can all come with you momentarily."

"The others are welcome to join you in the village tomorrow," one replied, "but for now, only you and Mihkosita must come."

Philbrook thought for a moment, then asked, "Mihkosita? Are you with me?"

"Of course, Ensign. I will gladly join you. I cannot interpret as well as Marguerite, but I will do my best."

"Splendid. Then let's go. Billy, keep an eye on Brutus for me and keep him from following after us."

"With pleasure, sir."

With that, Philbrook and Mihkosita followed the two men down the shoreline toward the village. Billy kept a hold on Brutus's collar as the dog whined softly at Philbrook's receding figure.

Chapter 33

Koohsia

When he was traveling on his own, Koohsia usually looked for turkeys. They were slow and easy to kill, and they provided enough meat for a filling dinner with enough left over for a morning meal. He was eying some now. A small flock of a dozen were pecking at the ground, absorbed in their search for seeds and insects. He picked out a hen that looked about right and notched an arrow on his bow. As he drew it back, several of the birds lifted their heads, sensing something. Fear spread through the flock, and they all took flight with a pounding of wings, taking refuge in the lower branches of a nearby tree.

The old hunter at first thought that he had spooked them, even though he had been very quiet in his approach, but then he saw someone else moving through the woods. A solitary man crept carefully toward the flock. Koohsia assumed he was a Native, but as he came closer, he thought maybe no. He was a little man in a dirty tricorn hat. There was something foreign in his walk. Not like a Native at all, but still graceful and cautious.

Koohsia knew how to blend in with the surrounding forest when he needed to. He crouched on one knee, silent and motionless, with an arrow still on his bow. The stranger was no more than fifty feet away now, his attention fixed on the birds in the branches. He planned to take one. He had a fowling piece slung over his shoulder, but the man reached instead for his bow. An arrow was usually a better tool for hunting small game, as one blast from the gun would spook nearby animals, while a bow could be used a second time if the first arrow missed its mark.

He realized that he had seen this little man before. He was the companion of the trader Sam Kennedy. He must have eluded Ensign Philbrook and Mihkosita. He watched Cole string his bow, place his arrow, and draw it back to take aim at a hen. His back was turned now as he inched closer to the birds. A competitive impulse took hold of Koohsia, and he raised his own bow and let fly his arrow. It was a long shot, but he knew in his heart he would make it. The arrow whistled past Cole and embedded itself into the body of the hen. The bird fell to the ground, weakly flapping its wings a few more times before it lay still.

Cole swung around, lowering his bow. Meanwhile Koohsia had quickly notched another arrow, and if necessary, he had his knife handy in his belt. Cole saw his mistake, but too late, so he dropped his bow and squatted down. "Nice shot," he said in English, but thinking that Koohsia would not understand, he switched to French. "*Joli coup.*"

"*Kway,*" said Koohsia in his own language.

Cole returned the standard greeting. "*Kway.*"

Koohsia walked over to the turkey, knelt down, and gave it thanks. Then, he drew out his arrow and began to pluck the bird. "*Je parle un peu le francais,*" he said, "and a little English."

"*Moi Aussi.*"

He continued in a simple mix of French, English, and Native words. "You are the one who Ensign Philbrook suspects of killing the men at Auglaize."

"Yes." Cole nodded. "But I didn't."

Koohsia did not know why, but he believed him.

"Why did you run?" he asked.

"Men attacked our camp in the night without explanation. They presented a threat, so I escaped. I don't trust Redcoat soldiers."

He understood. When someone ambushes you as you sleep, it is a natural impulse to either flee or fight. And he did not trust most Redcoats either, though he had come to like Ensign Philbrook. He asked Cole where he was going now.

Cole seated himself on the ground and made himself comfortable. He looked Koohsia in the eye. "The soldiers took my friend Sam prisoner. I'd like to prove him innocent of the things they accuse him of. I don't trust the soldiers to find the truth on their own."

"And you do that by hunting turkeys?" prodded Koohsia. He had finished cleaning the bird and was preparing a small fire to roast it.

Cole told Koohsia he was heading to the village of the Saginaw Ojibwa. He said that he believed that the boatman Pero was alive and his body replaced by that of another man.

"Back in Detroit I began to ask around about Pero." Cole told him. "Most of the *Canadiens* told me the same story—that he was from Quebec and had been injured by an exploding cannon defending one of the forts from the British. But then I met some Ojibwa from up north who told me a different story. Either that or a story of another man with surprisingly similar mutilations. I expect the Saginaw will have some answers."

"Then we are on similar errands," said Koohsia as he used his knife to cut the turkey into pieces. "Why don't you cut a couple of green skewers while I kindle a fire? Then I'll share my meat with you."

The two men spent the hour that followed roasting pieces of the bird over a small fire, filling their empty bellies, and sharing what they knew of the murders. Koohsia retold what he remembered of Jacobs's captivity story.

"So you see, I have my own reason to visit the Saginaw. There are men among them who may know the fate of the other prisoners. When I ask myself who had a reason to seek vengeance on Stone and the *Canadiens* at Auglaize, my mind keeps returning to the men taken west by the Saginaw. I think if I discover who they were, maybe I will find some answers."

Cole was interested. "So, Amos and Ben hired the Frenchmen who took them captive. That is news to me. I never learned much about their experiences after they left us."

"I must ask you one more thing," said Koohsia. "You know that my friend Louis Ouellette was murdered in Detroit the morning you and Kennedy left town?"

Cole nodded. "Yes, Mr. Philbrook told me when they caught up with me."

Koohsia looked up quickly. "They caught you?"

"They did not catch me. They merely caught up. I was able to disarm the four of them."

Koohsia's face darkened. "Did you harm them?" Koohsia was willing to work with this man to find answers in the Saginaw village, but not if he had harmed Mihkosita or Ensign Philbrook.

"No. Relax, friend. The sergeant likely woke with a headache, but they should be fine."

"And Mihkosita?"

"Fine when I left him."

"That is good, for I would not want to have to kill you. But as I was saying, Louis was killed before you left Detroit. Is that something maybe you know about?"

"No."

"For I do not really care who killed those men at Auglaize. I did not know them, so they are not my concern. But Louis was under my protection, and I will see his death avenged one way or another."

"I understand you. I don't really care who killed them either, but I would like to see Sam released from the gaol."

Chapter 34

Marguerite Boyer

Marguerite woke to the sound of footsteps on pebbles and rolled over to see Mihkosita and Philbrook returning to camp and Brutus galloping over to greet them. She had consoled the dog for much of the previous night by allowing him to lie next to her and gently nuzzle her as she tried to sleep. He was certainly a different sort of bedfellow than she had experienced before. Hairy and somewhat slobbery but warm and affectionate. The sun was up but had yet to top the trees to the northeast. The morning was still cool and a little damp. Graham and the soldiers were already up, and she could smell the smoke from their cooking fire.

"Did you find Jacobs?" she called out.

"He's in the village," Philbrook answered as Brutus pranced around him with his tongue hanging out.

"And what did he say?"

"We did not talk with him."

"No?" Marguerite was puzzled. "Why not? What was your summons all about?"

"A full explanation will have to wait until later, Marguerite. Suffice it to say, we did not enter the village but rather spoke with some elders outside of it. They had some important information to share." Philbrook turned to Graham. "Is there tea?"

"Come on over, sir. We made plenty."

She looked to Mihkosita, who shrugged, then followed to get some tea. She was puzzled that neither man seemed to want to give her a simple answer to her questions.

Marguerite went a short way into the wood to relieve herself, then down to the edge of the lake to wash up and rinse off the dried dog saliva. As she stood by the water, she looked west. On the horizon she saw the tops of a few clouds, but above her head, it was clear and blue.

"I don't understand. Why didn't you go into the village?" she asked when she got back to the men by the cooking fire.

"It is a complicated matter," Philbrook told everyone. "I need to ask you to be patient for a while longer. Mihkosita and I learned that Jacobs is indeed in L'Arbre Croche, though the villagers are not pleased he is there. Some elders wanted to talk of their concerns about him." He turned to Mihkosita. "Show them what we got."

Mihkosita reached into his bag and produced a cloth containing a leathery grey-brown slab of flesh.

"Fresh beaver tail. A gift," Philbrook said. "Let's cook some up as I tell you the plan."

"Yes, sir," said Billy Smyth, grabbing the frying pan and eagerly reaching for the tail.

Philbrook cleared his throat. "It should not come as a surprise to you that the people here have little use for Mr. Jacobs. They're not sure why he is hanging about, and his presence disturbs them. They want him gone. But they do not want soldiers in their village, so they promise to deliver him to us shortly."

Marguerite was aware that Native communities sometimes came to dislike the traders who came into their villages. She had heard of traders who were either evicted or killed by their unhappy trading partners.

"How did they know we were here, sir?" Sergeant Graham asked what Marguerite too was thinking. "And how did they know to ask for you and Mihkosita?"

"It seems we have been observed coming down the shore. Some Ottawa hunters saw us and recognized the two of us. Anyway, Jacobs should be here in a few hours. The elders I spoke with promised to bring him to us unharmed as long as we take him and go."

Marguerite thought it strange that anyone would recognize Mihkosita and Philbrook around here. She suspected that Philbrook was hiding something, but she could not imagine what.

Smyth finished roasting the beaver tail, and Marguerite could smell it as he sliced through the scaly skin to reveal the fat and meat inside. The soldiers had made some bannock in the pan earlier, so Smyth spread the soft, fatty meat onto pieces of bannock and passed it around as they talked. She ate her portion greedily. Being out in the backcountry always made her hungry, and the fat of a beaver's tail made a satisfying breakfast.

"Did you find out what business he is on?" asked Marguerite, as a bit of grease dripped down her chin.

"Not entirely. It seems he was looking to meet someone about some business." Philbrook yawned. "We will learn more as soon as they bring Mr. Jacobs out to us. In the meantime, friends, I'd like to get some rest. Mihkosita and I have had a long night with no sleep. I've learned that the Natives around here are loathe to get quickly to any point. The rest of you, please stay close. I want everyone available to deal with Jacobs when he gets here, in case he is uncooperative. Wake me when our visitors arrive."

With that, he grabbed his bedroll and went off to nap in the shade of a nearby oak tree. Mihkosita too found himself a shady spot to shut his eyes and doze off.

The rest of them looked around for something to occupy the time. After the soldiers polished off the rest of the bannock and beaver tail, they pulled out some playing cards and began a game of whist. Graham and Marguerite went for a walk down the shore. They were both puzzled by Philbrook's vagueness.

"I can't help but suspect that something is in the air that the ensign does not want us privy to," observed Graham. "They were gone all night, after all. There must have been much more talked about than what he just told us."

"True," Marguerite said, "but I can't think what. He is staying tight-lipped, but I'm sure he has his reasons."

"Has he shared any with you?"

"Nothing that he hasn't shared with you as well."

Marguerite was confused by all this, but she decided that she trusted both Philbrook and Mihkosita. They seemingly had a secret, but they must also have a plan. For now, it would remain a mystery to her.

It was mid-afternoon before they saw any sign of Jacobs. A single bark canoe approached from the village, paddled by the same two young Ottawa men who had visited the night before. They pulled in close to shore, stepped out into knee-deep water, then reached into the bottom of their canoe to lift out the writhing figure of Amos Jacobs. He was bound and had a gag in his mouth. The men carried him roughly to shore and dumped him unceremoniously onto the ground. He looked puffy and exhausted. Marguerite was confused by such treatment, though she could sympathize with the impulse to put a gag in Jacobs's mouth. Jacobs had only been in the area a few days. How could he have created such ill-will so quickly?

Philbrook had been awake for some time, but had remained tight-lipped. She went with him to greet the Ottawa visitors, but they had little interest in conversation. One simply said, "I've been told to tell you that if he comes back to our village, he will be knocked on the head." With that, they got back into their canoe and paddled back the way they had come.

"Ah, Mr. Jacobs. Thank you for joining us," Philbrook said, pulling the gag from the agent's mouth. "Seems like you've worn out your welcome with the locals. Lucky for you, we are in the neighborhood to take you to safety. I'm fairly certain they would have dispatched you had we not arrived when we did."

Jacobs squirmed. "Untie me. I insist. Why am I being treated this way?"

"We will untie you," said Philbrook, "but let me assure you that if you try to run away before you answer my questions, you will be shot. Sergeant Graham, untie Mr. Jacobs and bring him up to the fire. Take my pistol in case he is difficult. You can work the mechanism despite the damage to your hands, I trust?"

Marguerite saw confusion in Jacobs's eyes. She didn't blame him, for she did not understand why Philbrook wanted him guarded. Had he, perhaps, discovered proof that Jacobs was the killer they sought?

"Please make sure he does not go anywhere or take a drink of anything intoxicating. For his own welfare, of course." Philbrook turned to Young, Bellows, and Smyth. "You men, keep your muskets handy in case we get any unwelcome visitors. And everyone, please come gather around the fire where we can listen to Mr. Jacobs explain himself."

The fire still smoldered, even though the cooking was done. It was surrounded by a circle of logs that served as benches, so it provided a comfortable place for them all to sit.

Graham undid Jacobs's bindings as the agent continued to complain. "What's going on here? Why have I been accosted? I demand..."

"You'll demand nothing. Just sit down and shut up," said Graham, pushing Jacobs down onto a log and pointing Philbrook's pistol in his face. "You understand me?" He glared at the clerk, who cowered under the sergeant's gaze.

"It's quite alright, Sergeant," said Philbrook. "Mr. Jacobs can speak all he wants. We detain him strictly for his own well-being. Indeed, I look forward to hearing what he has to say."

Jacobs sat mute, looking around him in confusion.

"No? Not in the mood to talk, Mr. Jacobs?" he continued. "Well, we will see. All of you come over and sit. We are going to try to figure this business out."

The eight of them sat. Brutus lay down at Marguerite's feet. Philbrook walked slowly behind the circled group and addressed everyone with an air of command that Marguerite had seldom seen in him.

"Now Mr. Jacobs, I do not know what you have been up to out this way. Certainly nothing usual to your business interests. And you've managed to upset the locals to an astonishing degree. They see you as a man with uniquely bad medicine, likely to bring ill fortune to their community. Do you have any explanation as to why you are here?"

"I'm a free man," said Jacobs. "I don't need to explain myself to you. Besides, the Indians are just superstitious, that's all."

"Well, actually, you do have to explain yourself to me. You may have gathered that since we last saw you, certain facts have come to light that reflect poorly on you. First of all, Mr. Cole has informed us that the tomahawk found at the scene of the murders was, in fact, yours. Do you have any explanation for that?"

Jacobs looked around the assembled group. "I... I don't know anything about that. What tomahawk?"

"The tomahawk acquired by Marguerite's brother up north and traded to Jabez Cole. Mr. Cole then traded it to you. Do you deny this?"

"You found it at Auglaize? How do you know it is the same one? Anyway, I don't know anything about that. I... I haven't seen it in weeks." Marguerite thought Jacobs looked genuinely confused.

"But you acknowledge that you bought it from Mr. Cole?"

"Yes, yes, that was months ago. I don't know what happened to it after that. It disappeared shortly after I got it." Jacobs eyes darted from one person to another, as if searching for sympathy.

"It seems that you dropped it at Auglaize while murdering Ben Stone and his men." Philbrook fixed Jacobs in his gaze. Marguerite had never seen him look so severe. One of the reasons she liked Philbrook was that he never seemed to make a show of his own authority, but he was doing that now. He was trying his best to intimidate Jacobs—and succeeding.

"I... I did not," Jacobs stammered. "I was in Detroit when that happened. If... if it was mine, then someone must have stolen it from me."

"Really? Or perhaps you gave it to Pero?"

"P-Pero? What are you talking about?"

"Yes, Pero. Let's talk about Pero. You seemed to have a special relationship with him. Do you care to explain?"

"Special? I don't know what you mean. He... he was a canoe-man. He was just someone who worked for me."

"It seems strange that this man came to Detroit a few months back, supposedly unknown to you, with a face that most seemed to find disturbing, yet you repeatedly hired him as a canoeman though there appears to be no shortage of more qualified and better liked men in the local community."

"I engage lots of canoemen, Ensign. It's part of my duties. Or at least it was."

Philbrook had his hands behind his back as he walked around the outside of the circle. He stopped directly behind Jacobs, which seemed to make the clerk nervous.

"Yes, yes, I'm sure you do, but according to Monsieur Papan and Mam'selle Boyer, this fellow worked exclusively for you. From what I've heard he was not exactly someone who an employer would normally gravitate to. Certainly, no one else saw fit to hire him."

"Oh, I wouldn't say that. Pero did his job well enough. He was frightful to look at, but that did not matter. I try to look past such trivial things." Jacobs looked around the assembled faces, as if looking for sympathy. "Now if I'm to be interrogated like this, perhaps a small dram would settle my..."

"Tell me, Mr. Jacobs," Philbrook continued, "how was it you put together the group of paddlers that went with Mr. Stone?"

"They... they were all available, that's all. Not much more to it than that. Some of the men liked working together."

"But you and Mr. Stone had a history with the men you chose for this voyage, all except for Pero and Louis Ouellette," said Philbrook. "You told as much to Mam'selle Boyer and Monsieur Papan the other night. Indeed, can you explain to me how it was you failed to mention earlier that five of the men killed at Auglaize had a rather singular history with you?"

"It was just a coincidence. I don't know what Marguerite told you." He looked over at her as if she had betrayed a confidence. "Those folks liked working together. Ben and I owed them for getting us through our captivity safely, so I gave them work when I could. I don't see what the past has to do with anything."

"And what about Pero?"

"What of him?"

"Did you have a history with him as well? Did you owe him?"

"I... I don't know what you're getting at, Ensign." Philbrook had moved around to face Jacobs, but the clerk had trouble meeting the ensign's gaze. Marguerite saw sweat beginning to bead on his brow.

"It's a simple question, really. Did you have a history with this fellow Pero similar to the history you had with the others?"

"N-no. Not before he arrived in town—in Detroit I mean."

"Are you aware, Mr. Jacobs, that Pero is alive?"

"I... No... what do you mean? I was told he was killed at Auglaize with the rest." Marguerite sensed that he was lying.

"It seems now that he was not," said Philbrook. "As I believe you are aware, the body thought to be his at Auglaize was, in fact, some other man dressed in his clothes. Before you continue lying, let me tell you that I spoke with some people from L'Arbre Croche last night who confirmed that a man answering to Pero's rather singular description has been seen in the area and that it was generally believed that you met with him."

Jacobs looked at his feet, then up at Philbrook. "Those are just rumors, Ensign. Indians lie about everything." Marguerite saw fear in Jacobs. She did not know what he was hiding, but he was certainly hiding something. Moreover, he was afraid that Philbrook knew what it was.

"Yes, yes, Mr. Jacobs, rumors and lies," said Philbrook. "Let me tell you some other rumors. Among the Ojibwa and Ottawa around here it is believed that Mr. Pero is not who people in Detroit think he is. They say he is no *Canadien* from Quebec. Rather, he was a New England soldier captured at Fort William Henry in 1757 by Saginaw Ojibwa and tortured quite brutally. Does this ring any bells, Mr. Jacobs?"

Philbrook now had everyone's close attention, but Jacobs just stared at his feet, saying nothing. Marguerite finally realized where Philbrook's interrogation was going. She looked over at Graham, but his face was expressionless.

"Marguerite told me the story of your captivity that you shared with her the other night. Tell me Mr. Jacobs, what ever happened to your friend Paul Adams?"

Chapter 35

Marguerite Boyer

More pieces fell in place in for Marguerite. She had heard Paul Adams mentioned several times, but she had never thought twice about him. He was just some provincial soldier who had died years earlier. But the idea that he was Pero made sense. She looked around and saw that the others were rivetted on Philbrook's exchange with Jacobs. Their eyes were all on Jacobs now, waiting for him to respond. She too waited to see what Jacobs would say.

Jacobs looked at his feet. "Paul died," he said.

"Did he, Mr. Jacobs?" Philbrook crossed his arms. "How do you know that? Did you hear how it happened? Do you know who killed him?"

"The Ojibwa warriors who took him away must have killed him. They went west, and he never came back." Jacobs spoke like a child, stubbornly refusing to admit a mistake.

"I see," said Philbrook. "That does seem likely. You and Mr. Stone were very fortunate in your captivity, it seems, if one can be fortunate in these things—being taken to Montreal and redeemed as you were. Same with the Regular officer with you. But Mr. Adams and the redcoat soldiers were not so lucky, were they?"

"No," said Jacobs, glancing furtively around.

"Did you ever hear what happened to them? Did any of them survive? Assuming that is, that you disbelieve what I was recently told about Pero."

"I... I don't know," Jacobs sputtered. "I mean, it's likely they were held as slaves, if not tortured or killed. I've told you. I don't know."

"They must have had a rough time of it even if they survived. I do not envy them. If half of what they say about Indian torture is true, then I do not envy them one bit. Maybe it's best if they were killed outright."

Philbrook continued to walk around the circle but did not speak again for close to a minute. No one else spoke up either, as they waited to see what would come next. A gentle wind had risen since they'd been sitting there, which caused a rustling in the tree-tops. Philbrook was toying with Jacobs now. That much was obvious. Marguerite was curious to see what would come out when he finally broke down.

"Mr. Jacobs," Philbrook finally resumed, "what do you suppose they thought about you and Mr. Stone? I mean your friend Paul and the others. Do you ever wonder what they thought about you as they were marched west expecting to be held captive, tortured, or killed, while you were on your way to being redeemed?"

"I... I don't know. How could I know? Why would they think of me? It had nothing to do with me. At least not after they left us."

"Nothing?" Philbrook questioned. "But you got away, Mr. Jacobs. You survived without a scratch, while, I imagine, if any of the others lived, they were left with scars. Deep scars."

Jacobs stared back at Philbrook. "It was not my f-fault."

Marguerite did not think that Jacobs believed his own words. She realized that he was a man who harbored a great deal of self-loathing. Perhaps that explained his addiction to drink.

"Scars," Philbrook repeated. "Indeed, I've heard that one of the Ojibwa's favorite means of torture is fire. Have you heard that, Mr. Jacobs?" Everyone stared at the clerk, but remained silent. "Have you ever been badly burned?" Philbrook continued. "The pain is excruciating. I accidentally spilled boiling water on my feet once as a child. I screamed all night. To this day, it is the worst pain I've ever felt, and I still have scars from it." He paused. "Come now, Pero's scars were caused by burns, were they not, Mr. Jacobs?"

He did not reply, but he began to weep quietly, looking at the ground.

The silence became uncomfortable. There was the sound of a raven's caw in the woods. Mihkosita cocked his head. Marguerite caught Mihkosita's eye, but he quickly looked away.

"I'm done beating around the bush." Philbrook finally broke the silence. "Tell me truthfully now, Mr. Jacobs. Pero is Paul Adams—or at least he was. Correct?" The others looked as if they had already figured this out, but no one broke the silence that followed. It was Jacobs who needed to admit the truth.

After a long pause, he nodded his head and sobbed. "I... I thought he was dead. I thought they'd killed him, but then Paul... Pero confronted me in Detroit. Horrible. They... they let him go free in the end. But Paul, he couldn't face going home, not the way he looked," Jacobs glanced furtively up at the others. "And he couldn't speak anymore, but he understood French well enough, so it was easy for him to pass for a mute *Canadien*."

"So you kept his secret?" Philbrook sounded sympathetic. "You tried to help him by giving him work?"

Jacobs nodded.

"That was kind of you," said Philbrook. "But Paul, or rather, Pero, was angry. Unspeakably angry. Angry with the *Canadiens* who gave him up to the Ojibwa, angry with you, but especially angry with Ben Stone."

"I don't know about that."

"Not long ago," Philbrook continued, "Koohsia told me something that has stuck with me ever since. He spoke about all the men around here with scars from the violence of their wartime experiences. Paul Adams was such a man. The scars on his soul were even more severe than those on his body, weren't they?"

Jacobs shook his head. "No."

He was having trouble admitting to himself that his friend had become something grotesque," thought Marguerite, not just physically, but inside as well.

"Why was his anger directed at Stone, Mr. Jacobs?" asked Philbrook. "Stone didn't torture him. The *Canadiens* did not torture him, even if they let it happen. Why wasn't his anger directed at the Ojibwa who mutilated him? Did he tell you?"

"N-no. He... I don't know... I didn't know."

"He was angry enough to kill. After years of waiting. He must have said something to you, his childhood friend."

"He... he never did." Jacobs's temper flared. "He couldn't speak, goddamn it."

"But you must have communicated somehow. He could read and write, I assume."

"Yes, of course, he sometimes wrote me notes when no one else was around to see."

"When did he first tell you, or write to you, that he planned to kill Ben Stone?"

Jacobs looked up, his mouth hanging open. "He couldn't have. It was someone else. Paul would never murder someone."

"Maybe not the Paul you knew as a young man, Mr. Jacobs, but Pero would. Pero hacked the heads off of corpses. Pero walked away from the scene, leaving another body in his place. What's more, I think you helped him do it."

"No."

"You did. How else do you explain that he is still alive, that he survived the attack, that you are here to meet him? Mr. Jacobs, you are an accomplice to murder. Unless you give us some better explanation for your peculiar behavior, I am certain you will hang."

Jacobs looked up and surveyed the group around him. "Hang? I... I didn't have anything to do with what happened at Auglaize, besides organizing the voyage. I swear. I liked all those men. I was not there." He directed his appeal toward Marguerite. "I thought Paul was one of those killed. I... I didn't know. I swear I was not there. The first I knew he had survived was a note I got in Detroit. I was not even sure it was really from him. I thought it might be a cruel hoax. It said to meet him here. We were going to go west. We always talked about going west together, when we were boys, discovering a way to the South Sea." Jacobs put his face in his hands and sobbed. Marguerite felt sorry for him. He was pathetic and weak, but she had trouble seeing him as a killer.

"You put together the group, Mr. Jacobs," Philbrook resumed. "You arranged it so that they were all there to be killed. Your tomahawk was found at the scene. Do you really expect me to believe you are the least bit innocent in all this?"

"I don't care what you believe."

"Did Pero ask you to put those particular men together for that voyage?"

"Yes. But..."

"Did they know who Pero was? Did Stone recognize him? The others?"

Jacobs shook his head. "Paul said he was ashamed. He... He did not want anyone else knowing who he once was. Pity made him angry. The *Canadiens*, they only knew him for a short time as Paul. And Ben, well, once he said there was something familiar about Pero, but he didn't put it together. Paul, he... he was always a happy, cheerful man. Before that is. He was always smiling and laughing, telling stories about explorers that he had read about, like La Salle and Hennepin. Pero... Pero was... is different. When he smiles with that awful scarred face of his..." Jacobs shuttered.

"Do you really not understand that Pero killed those men?" asked Philbrook. "He arranged everything with you. Your claims of ignorance are hard to believe."

"I thought he was killed. At... at first. I thought he was killed along with the rest. I assumed it was Indians. Then, when I heard from him, I figured he had escaped."

"Escaped? From whom? From Indians?"

"From whoever killed the others."

"But you say you don't know who killed the others?"

"I'm not sure. And I don't care." Jacobs remained very still, looking at the ground before him.

"Really? I think you care. I think you care very much. And you have some ideas, don't you? Some ideas besides Indians. You surely realize by now that Pero killed those men. Moreover, you must know that he did not act alone. There were others, and even if you were not there yourself, I think you know who they were."

"I don't know. Truly." Marguerite did not know whether or not to believe this.

"You knew about the backgrounds of these men, Mr. Jacobs. And you kept it all secret from us. You knew Pero wanted them together for this voyage. He wanted this to be a reunion. A sick, twisted reunion befitting his mutilated body and scarred soul. When you heard of the murders, you must have had ideas."

"No," insisted Jacobs.

Marguerite sensed that something was stopping Jacobs from admitting the truth to Philbrook, but she could not imagine what.

"Well, the fact is Pero committed these murders, but not alone," said Philbrook. "We know from the tracks that others were there. Put it together for us, Mr. Jacobs. Who else, if not you? Who else wanted those men punished? Who else wanted revenge on Ben Stone and the *Canadiens* you arranged to go with him on that voyage?"

"I don't know. I wasn't there. This... this has nothing to do with me. How could I know?"

"Because you have always known far more about this business than you've let on."

Marguerite saw Philbrook's anger well up, but he pushed it

down so that he could draw Jacobs out. Meanwhile, Jacobs folded into himself with his head down, as if he was trying to shut out the world around him.

"Tell me, Mr. Jacobs," continued Philbrook. "When you told Marguerite about your captivity, did you happen to mention the names of the soldiers held with you—the redcoats taken west along with Pero? Those men would have shared Paul Adams's trials. And they would share his anger."

Jacobs was shaking and sobbing, but he seemed unable to speak any more.

Philbrook lifted his gaze from the distraught clerk and continued walking around the assembled group.

"Sergeant Graham," Philbrook spoke at last, "perhaps you could take up the story."

Chapter 36

Marguerite Boyer

Sergeant Graham raised his pistol so that it pointed directly at Philbrook. The normally open expression on his face hardened into a vacant stare. At his signal, Privates Young and Bellows stood up and leveled their muskets at the others.

"I think you can stop your games now, Ensign," he growled.

"What is this?" exclaimed Marguerite, jumping up. She had been slowly putting the pieces together, as she listened to Jacobs, but she had not been prepared for this. Graham could not have had anything to do with murder. Could he?

"You can sit right back down again, Marguerite." Graham waved the pistol in her direction.

"It's alright. Everyone just relax," said Philbrook.

She sat, looking around at the others. Billy Smyth looked as confused as she felt. Jacobs continued staring at his feet, shaking. Mihkosita's face gave away nothing.

"Yes, listen to the boy. Everyone stay put," ordered Graham. "Young, Bellows, keep everyone covered." Graham stood and motioned for Philbrook to sit in the spot he had vacated. "I congratulate you on putting it together, Ensign. You are not as stupid or naive as I first thought. But it was only a matter of time after Jacobs here blabbed of those times that someone started asking about the redcoats with him. So, yes, Ensign, it was us—Young, Bellows, and me."

"But you were not posted at Fort William Henry, then," said Marguerite. Something in her could not accept the sergeant's confession.

"That's right, Marguerite, we weren't. We were stationed at Albany, as I've said, but we were sent north with a dispatch just before the fall of the fort, and the three of us were taken by a scouting party." He turned back to Philbrook. "How did you figure us out?"

"In time, Sergeant," said Philbrook, "but first, tell us about your captivity. What happened that made you hate Ben Stone and his men so much?"

"Stone, that bloody coward. The world is better off without him."

"How so, Sergeant?" asked Philbrook. "It seems to me that he and Jacobs were simply lucky while the rest of you were not." If Philbrook was disturbed by the two soldiers with muskets pointed at him, he did not show it. His curiosity seemed to outweigh any fear.

"Lucky? Luck had nothing to do with it. Betrayal and cowardice, more like it. I'm sure Amos told his tale well enough, but I expect he left out the way Stone groveled and sniveled to his French friends, trying to gain their bloody sympathy to the detriment of the rest of us." Graham's face was composed, but his remaining eye darted from person to person with a cold fury. "Do you realize that many of the men captured at that time escaped in the first couple of days?" He turned to Billy Smyth. "Smyth, how many men trickled in to Fort Edward in the days after the massacre having escaped Indian captors? How many?"

"I can't tell you an exact number," replied Billy, "but there were about two score."

"There was Lieutenant Knaggs of the 35th Regiment with

three men, and Sergeant Williams of the Connecticut provincials with five. I could go on. When the captives had a goddamn leader, they often got away in the confusion of the flight to Canada."

Graham stood up straight. Marguerite saw no guilt or shame in his demeanor—just overwhelming pride.

"I could have done the same. I could have gotten us all home within a bloody week with brave men like Young and Bellows here at my side." He motioned to the men. "Instead we were saddled with sniveling Ben Stone, trying to make nice with the enemy. It sickened me."

"You could have left him behind, Sergeant, if you thought he would hinder your escape," observed Philbrook.

"Aye, I might've, had I gotten the chance before the savages split us up. I made a plan and shared it with the others. I even told them about the folding knife I'd kept hidden. We could've been on our way that night. If Stone had refused to join us, he could have stayed behind, and I'd have wished him all the best in his continued captivity. But no. He had other plans."

"What do you mean?"

"Why, he betrayed us, that's what I bloody mean. Aye, and this one here was happy to go along with him." He pointed at Jacobs with the pistol. "I'd have killed him, too, with pleasure. But Adams wouldn't agree to that part."

"I'm not sure I understand you, Sergeant," said Philbrook.

"Well then, *sir*, I'll spell it out for you. I told everyone my plan to make off, and Ben blabbed it to his French friends to curry favor. As a reward they took him and Jacobs away to be redeemed, while Adams and the three of us faced unimaginable suffering."

"Stone gave you up?" said Marguerite.

"Aye."

"Is that true, Jacobs?" she asked.

"I... I never knew." Jacobs hung his head. "I thought it was strange the way things happened. One day, we were all on our way to Montreal, and the next, Paul and the lobsters were taken off to the West. I chalked it up to the Indians changing their minds."

"Oh, they changed their goddamn minds, alright," Graham fumed, "because of Stone's cowardice. They taunted us with it. They told us later about how their French friends came to them and revealed the deal. Tremblay and Bruno had promised Stone they would take the three provincials safely to Montreal in exchange for information about any escape plan. When the Indians heard of it, they thought it stank of cowardice and wanted to kill Stone for it. Tremblay and Bruno offered them Adams instead."

Marguerite had always found Graham's confidence appealing. She saw him as someone who could take charge, whatever the situation. But, in this case, he seemed to have been in over his head. He certainly believed that he could have escaped, and time had solidified that belief, but his chances had been remote. She did not blame Stone for doubting him. Cooperating until they reached Montreal was the only sensible thing to do.

"What about the lieutenant?" asked Philbrook.

"The French officer took him and left when he saw how things were going. He was of little use anyway. You know how officers stick together even when they're supposed to be enemies. The French officer paid a pretty penny for him, too.

"Is that when you lost your fingers and eye and Adams was disfigured?" asked Philbrook.

"Aye. The first day it was my turn," said Graham. "They surrounded me, kicked me, and hit me with their war clubs. Not hard enough to kill me or knock me out, because they did not want me dead. But hard enough to crack some ribs and leave my whole body in pain. Then they interrogated me about my plan, which, of course, I denied. Each time I denied it, they took a sharp shell to a finger joint and sliced right through."

"Sergeant Graham stood up to it," added Young. "He didn't give them the satisfaction of crying out." Marguerite was struck by how the two soldiers idolized Graham.

"Be that as it may," continued Graham, holding up his mutilated hands, "they took them, one joint at a time. They left me just
three fingers, two thumbs, and a few stubs. Then, one of the more
enthusiastic fellows pressed his thumb in my eye socket and
gouged it out. Thankfully, he left me the other." That eye looked at
them all defiantly.

"I got off easy compared to Adams," continued Graham. "I
could still see, and once my hands healed, I could still hold most
things. But Adams—something broke in him once we left the
others. He started to live in a constant state of panic. He whined
and he cried. During the days, he kept falling down, and at night
he murmured and wept, called out in his sleep. That sealed his fate.
You have to realize that the Ojibwa had lost a couple of men in a
skirmish before the siege, and some of them wanted to take their
grief out on us. We were tolerated only as long as we cooperated.
Then Adams became a nuisance. The ones who had protected
him, withdrew their protection and gave him over to the ones with
grief and hate in their hearts. They began working on him three
days after we left the others."

Graham paused a moment. "Have you ever seen a man get his
tongue cut out, Ensign?"

"I can't say that I have."

"Well, it ain't a pretty sight. Aye, the tongue, it's a great deal
bigger than you'd think. They got right back into his mouth with a
thin copper blade and ripped out the whole thing by the roots. It
was disgusting." Graham spat. "He screamed. An odd, strangled
kind of scream. Blood poured down the front of this weskit. Then
they stripped him and the burning began. He shrieked as they
worked on him, a little at a time. They used hot embers at first.
Then they loaded up a musket with powder but no shot and
blasted burning powder at his naked skin."

Marguerite felt ill.

"Finally, they heated up a knife 'til it was red-hot and used that
to make a mockery of his manhood. I'm quite sure he would have

299

rather bloody died at that moment and for many months after. And his pathetic cries continued after they'd stopped the burning. Then, they left him to suffer, assuming that he was not far from death. For hours, he writhed and called out for his mother until Bellows finally knocked him on the head."

"I didn't hold back," said Bellows. "I hit him hard, thinking if I killed him, I'd be doing him a favor. He was out for hours, and when he woke, the pain from his burns had subsided."

"How did he survive?" asked Marguerite softly. She felt a mixture of sympathy and disgust.

"Hate," answered Graham. "Shear unadulterated hate if you ask me. It's like when they burned his flesh, the fire reached down and burned into his goddamn soul. Turned it into a charred bitter thing, but as tough as a year-old chunk of salt pork. You might think that his hate would be directed at the men who tortured him, but no. It was all focused on the man whose cowardice brought it about. His good friend, Ben Stone."

"And we carried him," added Bellows. "I think our captors were a little surprised the next morning when they found he was still alive, but by that point, their passions had cooled. They wanted to leave him behind to die on his own, but John and I made him a litter and brought him along. And the Native women helped—once we met up with the larger group near Niagara that included women. They kept the corruption away from his wounds with their poultices."

"Where did they take you?" asked Philbrook.

"West," said Graham. "Back home to Saginaw Bay. Once we got close, they split us up, used us as slaves. They kept talking of killing me, but I guess they just got used to having me around to do their bidding. And I got them to like me. I know how to make friends when needed." Graham smiled. "Once I'd picked up enough of their lingo to talk back and forth with them, I began to feel safe."

"And you remained with the Ojibwa for the rest of the war?" asked Marguerite.

"We lived with them for three years, seeing each other now and again. We lived as they did. I made friends with many of them, even if they are savages. Hell, most British soldiers are bloody savages, too, in their own way. Indian ways start making sense once you get used to them. I came to like living among them and all but forgot about any other life after a while."

Marguerite had heard much the same of others who had gone through captivity. It was hard not to sympathize with people once you've lived with them.

"And what about Adams?" asked Philbrook.

"Adams, the poor wretch. I heard he spent months convalescing in an Ojibwa village but miraculously pulled through. He ended up with a band up on Lake Superior. Once he recovered, the Indians began to hold a certain reverence for him. Saw him as a bloody shaman of sorts the way he'd survived. That and his sheer ugliness was interpreted as powerful medicine. And he is quite mad. Indians have a certain respect for a lunatic."

"He lost his senses?"

"Are you surprised? I thought it obvious that the man is mad. He had started to lose his senses even before the torture. Then the poor fool suffered in a few hours more pain than a man should be expected to endure in a goddamn lifetime. Either way, Natives from all around here held him in awe. They would go to him when sick or injured for healing. He lived comfortably enough with the offerings they brought him. Seems he came to understand the Indian languages, but with no tongue of his own, he never could communicate with anything other than rude signs. Somehow, he found a wife among his healers, and the two of them began to travel freely all around the villages north of Superior."

"Did you encounter him during this time?" asked Philbrook.

"No. I just heard things here and there. Word was that he and his wife went north, traveled from village to village, getting into Cree lands. I learned from a Menomonie hunter that he'd gone west from there to the Shining Mountains. Even when they went into strange communities, the people would take one look at him and see strong medicine. I lost all word of him before the British took over, so I figured he'd died."

"But he came back," said Philbrook.

"That he did. He was the last of us to reunite in Detroit. Bellows, Young, and I found each other when the British convinced the Ojibwa to return their captives—at least those willing to go back. Then the *Canadiens*—I mean Tremblay, Bruno, and the Beaulieu brothers—we encountered them soon after we came to Detroit, but they didn't remember us. They never did put two and two together. No bloody reason they should. We all looked and acted differently back then, and it had only been a few days we were together—days that meant much more to us than they had to them.

"Anyway, when Jacobs showed up as a clerk a few years later, after Pontiac's uprising, I saw that he and those *Canadiens* were all bloody friendly now. Those men had caused me to be tortured. They were the reason I see with only one eye and struggle to do simple things with my hands. And now they were friends. That's when the anger started coming back. The way they curried favor. The way Jacobs gave them work. It goddamn sickened me. But I never thought to do anything about it. Just stuck in my craw, that's all."

Marguerite saw the depth of Graham's anger. He tried to make it sound reasonable, but she saw that the anger consumed him.

"The fighting was over, Graham," whimpered Jacobs. "They did their duty, just like you and I tried to do. It was the Ojibwa that tortured you, not Ben or the *Canadiens*."

"You're a damned fool, Amos, and a coward." He pointed the pistol at him. "The French and their brutal allies attacked unarmed men after their surrender, yet you thank them for it like a whipped dog."

Jacobs looked back down at his feet.

"Well, as I was saying, I gave Jacobs here a piece of my mind about the way he'd abandoned us. Showed him these and thanked him for it." Graham held up his mutilated hands with defiance shining in his eye. "But then I let the anger pass. I let the past stay where it belonged."

"But that was before Ben Stone showed up," prompted Philbrook.

"Aye."

"And Pero? When did he make himself known?"

"Funny thing was, Adams, or Pero as he was now called, showed up shortly after Stone did. It was like he sensed his prey from whatever dank hole he had been hiding in. He came to me one night. I knew who he was immediately, though he had healed quite a bit since I'd last seen him. He handed me a note. It had just one word written on it, but one was enough."

"And what word was that?" asked Marguerite.

Graham looked up at her and smiled his old charming smile. "Why the one word that gets right to the bloody point, Marguerite. 'REVENGE.'"

Chapter 37

Marguerite Boyer

It all seemed rather senseless to Marguerite. These men had held on to their hate and anger even when it brought them nothing but more suffering. Why not let scars heal? Why pick at scabs? She preferred to look to the future. She filed her pipe and lit it from one of the remaining embers from the fire. She hoped that Philbrook had a plan. If he did not, they were in a dangerous situation, but she saw that his curiosity was not yet fully satisfied.

"And what about you, Mr. Jacobs?" Philbrook asked. "When did Pero first make himself known to you?"

"It... It was less than a year ago, not long after Ben showed up." Jacobs looked submissively to Graham, and the sergeant nodded for him to continue.

"I came back to my room one evening and there was this... this horror lurking in the shadows. I thought it was the Devil come out of the underworld to fetch me. I ran, as fast as I could, out into the night. Once my heart calmed down, I went to Mons. Lavigne's tavern and tried to sort my thoughts. I decided it had been a hallucination—the effects of too much drink. At least, that is what I told myself. I have no memory of going back to my room that night, but when I woke there in the morning, I was alone.

"But... but then the next night, I went to my room, and there he was again. This time, I didn't run but grabbed my dirk and told him to go back to Hell. He laughed. An ugly, choking kind of laugh that sent drool dribbling down his chin. I stood there confused, disgusted... and he just laughed more. He took a charred stick from my hearth, pointed at himself, and, with the blackened end, began to scratch letters on my table. I looked down and saw his name written there: 'PAUL.'"

"And you believed him?" asked Philbrook.

"I don't know. I was too shocked. There was nothing familiar about the awful scarred figure. At least not at first. He rose and pulled an envelope and a notebook from his waistcoat, placed them on my table with his mutilated hand, and brushed past me out the door. I don't know how long I stood there, a mixture of thoughts flying through my head. But in time, I cautiously picked up the envelope, opened it, and read."

"And what did it say?" asked Marguerite.

"It said... It was a shock to me. The memories it stirred. The horror of it all... I... I have it still." Jacobs reached into his coat and pulled out a small vellum-bound notebook. He opened the cover, exposing a sheet of weathered paper folded into quarters. He returned the book to his pocket and unfolded the letter. For a moment it looked as if he was going to read it, but then he shook his head and handed the papers to Philbrook. "You read it."

Philbrook looked over the letter briefly, cleared his throat, then began to read aloud:

DEAR AMOS,

A part of me had hoped that you would recognize me, old friend. But it does not surprise me that you did not. I hardly recognize myself these days. The boy named Paul, who I used to be, has receded far into the past, like a fading dream. Yes, there once was a Paul Adams: a young striver. No more. Now I am Pero: a nightmare. Is there some connection between the two any longer? I do not rightly know.

You thought me dead, I'm sure. When the warriors dragged me away from you that day so long ago, I thought myself dead. For clearly that was the intention of my captors. To punish me as a way of assuaging their own pain—their own losses suffered in war. They intended to cause me unspeakable pain and suffering, and then leave me slowly to die. But I fooled them. My body fooled them. It fooled me. For death did not come as easily as pain. Perhaps it never will.

Pero has done things that Paul only dreamed of. Remember the maps Paul used to show you? That I used to show you? Remember my excitement when I told you of Lac du Bois and the River Ouinipigon? Remember? We were to go there, to places I had only seen on poorly drawn maps, created by men who never left their libraries. We were to find the mythic River of the West and take it to the Straits of Anian and the South Sea. What great travelers you and I were going to be! Explorers! Discoverers!

Well, let me tell you now, I have been there. I found no river flowing west, so I went further still, up broad rivers that meander through endless grasslands. And then I came to mountains. Not like any mountains you have ever seen. No, not like the Blue Hills of New Jersey nor the Catskills of New York. These are massive peaks perpetually covered in snow. I spent many months near these mountains, venturing into them to explore on a horse I bought from the people of the grasslands, the Assiniboine. With crude sign language and the help of my wife, a Cree woman, I conversed with people who live in these mountains and had been across them. They spoke to me of routes they use to pass through, and they spoke of a great river that flows down the opposite slope into a great water. They say that it ebbs and flows and no one can see across its vast expanse. The South Sea no doubt! This great continent is vast, but I now know how far away that elusive goal lies. More importantly, I know how to get there.

There is more. During all my travels I wrote almost daily in my journal, which I now give to you. It tells of places unknown to any mapmaker. Terra Incognita, *that's what I used to tell you it was called. Well it is no longer unknown to me. I want to return, and this time I want you to come with me. Together we will discover the River of the West, the Straits of Anian, and the South Sea, like we always spoke of.*

But first I must take care of some personal matters, my friend, and I need your help.

PHILBROOK LOOKED UP AT JACOBS. "This journal he refers to. Is that the book in your pocket now?"

"Yes... yes, it is. It's just like he says. It is a journal of amazing travels in the Northwest."

Marguerite saw that Philbrook was drawn toward the book. She knew from their conversations together that he was fascinated by Western exploration. Pero had done things that Philbrook longed to do. He wanted to climb those mountains. He wanted to paddle down that river flowing west. For a moment she thought that he was going to reach out, grab the notebook, and forget everything else that had brought them here.

Instead, Philbrook looked down at the letter in his hands and continued reading:

I AM PAUL NO LONGER. I have no wish to resume my former life. It is a thing not possible to me. I have instead adopted the name Pero. Since I cannot talk, I pass for a Canadien. *I've been a* coureur de bois. *I've worked as a boatman. I've traveled all around. I need to work for a while as a canoeman here in Detroit. Don't tell anyone you know me. Don't tell anyone who I really am. If things work out as I plan, in a few months I will be able to make one final journey to the West. I will find the Straits of Anian, and I will set my eyes on*

307

the South Sea. If you do this for me, I will take you with me when I go.

That is if you still share such dreams.

PHILBROOK LOWERED THE PAPER. "You did as he asked?"

"Yes."

"He did not mention his plans for revenge?"

"No. Never," insisted Jacobs.

"You didn't think it strange, this desire to work for you?"

"Of course. Of course it was strange. It was awful. It... He was frightening. But I had to do as he asked me. I had no choice. And besides, he was really just asking for work. That he did not wish anyone to know his true identity seemed natural to me. I thought him ashamed, and rightfully so, for he had become a horror to look upon."

"In your mind, you were helping out a troubled old friend," offered Marguerite. She understood Jacobs's impulse to help.

"Ex... exactly." He looked over at her with gratitude. "And then I began to read his journal. It was a wonder. I had almost forgotten the conversations we used to have of discovering a passage across the continent. Maybe the Straits of Anian, or maybe a great River of the West. But his journal awakened all those childhood dreams. It was possible. With Pero as a guide, it was all really possible."

"To reach the Western Sea..." Philbrook began, then stopped. Marguerite saw that he was distracted by the topic of Pero's travels, but then he refocused on his attention on Jacobs. "But you had misgivings," he said.

"Of course. There was something wrong with him. He was different. Not just the obvious, I mean. I knew he had been through many trials, but there was something off in his mind. Something broken. He kept asking about Tremblay, Bruno, and the Beaulieu brothers. He wanted to work with them, but he insisted that I not tell them who he really was."

"Did you think he was insane," asked Philbrook, "or, perhaps, dangerous?"

"All I knew was that he frightened me, and it was best to accommodate him. I did what he told me to do, even if part of me realized that things were not right."

"But he was indebted to you," said Marguerite. "You gave him work and kept his secrets for him. You did not owe him more than that."

"But don't you see?" Jacobs pleaded. "He had suffered— suffered instead of me. I passed through my captivity. I was redeemed, but he remained. He would always be trapped inside that ugly godforsaken body. A captive to its scarred horror. I would always owe him for the simple fact that I survived... that I was whole, while he was broken."

"His fate was not your doing," said Marguerite. She sympathized with the broken man, though he disgusted her.

"No reason you should understand, but it was how I thought of it. But Paul's imbalance just grew, especially when he brought up Ben. He trembled when he told me that I must set up an expedition where he, Tremblay, Bruno, and the Beaulieu brothers would serve as boatmen for Ben. He wanted me to come too. 'Why don't you tell Ben who you really are?' I asked him. 'He will be happy that you are alive.' He just said I mustn't. I asked him why he wanted to be with those men—when none knew his real identity—and he just shrugged and called it his little reunion."

"So, you did as he asked," said Philbrook.

"I did not feel like I had a choice. Except, in the final days, I decided not to go myself. I sent Louis Ouellette in my place. It did not make sense for me to go up the Maumee when all my duties were in Detroit."

"Did you ever talk to Pero about Graham and the other soldiers?" asked Philbrook. "You must have known that they would recognize him despite the mutilations. They had seen it done after all."

"He would not speak of them with me."

"So," said Philbrook, turning back to Sergeant Graham, who all this time had sat patiently listening—pistol in hand. "We know how the victims all came to be where they were. Jacobs here arranged it for Pero. But I still have some unanswered questions. I take it that you carried out the murders, Sergeant, along with Privates Graham and Young, and, of course, Pero, who met you there." Graham nodded, so Philbrook continued. "But whose was the body that was left in Pero's place? That question still bothers me."

Graham stared back and grinned. Not the friendly smile that he had always shown until now, but a vacant grin that exposed an empty pit usually kept hidden. "Yes. I'm rather proud of myself for that subterfuge," he said. "Take a guess, Ensign. You seem to know everything else."

"Proud? You are proud of yourself?" Marguerite blurted. "How could you be proud of anything that you've done?"

She should have held her tongue, but she was taken aback by this glimpse into Graham's true nature. She had thought him charming, but the charm she had enjoyed until now was just a facade. She realized that Graham was not someone who had feelings like other men. There was something deeply wrong inside of him, but he was very skilled at hiding it. He had manipulated her from the start, with his smiles and subtle flirtation. And he had manipulated Philbrook. He had seen his weaknesses, his insecurities, his need for approval, his thirst for knowledge. Graham had given his ensign what he most wanted, the illusion of respect. But had all been a performance.

Philbrook looked to Marguerite, as if to reassure her. He was still acting like he was in control, but it looked to her like Graham held all the cards.

Philbrook addressed Graham. "Alright, allow me to advance a theory. You and your men needed a reason to be sent south to the Maumee River. Once there, you needed horses to get up to

Auglaize quickly. And you needed an extra body when the time came. You came up with a clever plan to take care of everything. Now this is largely conjecture, but I think the body was that of Alexis Cuillerier."

"Very good, Ensign." Graham smiled again and clapped his scarred hands together. "But please enlighten me. How did Cuillerier become involved?"

"I suspect you helped him escape from the gaol in Detroit, knowing that Captain Turnbull would send you to Pontiac's village looking for him. I'm not sure what you could have offered Cuillerier as an explanation, but whatever it was, it worked. You arranged some pretext to meet up with the escaped prisoner after he passed through Pontiac's village. You stashed your boat and switched to horses that Cullerier had acquired from some locals. You rode to Auglaize with him, pretending to still be aiding him in his escape, but instead you killed him along with the others, leaving his headless body in Pero's place."

"Very impressive, Ensign. Aye, that's about it," said Graham. "Cuillerier's family offered me a tidy bribe to assist in his escape. Rather funny, really; they unwittingly paid me to dispatch their loved one. As far as they are concerned, Alexis is living happily in the Wabash country by now. But that child murderer deserved to die. He knew what we were up to, and he volunteered to take part in our vengeance even though it had nothing to do with him. I did everyone a favor getting rid of him. The others deserved death just as much for what they'd done. I don't feel a bit of remorse."

Marguerite wondered if remorse was something Graham was even capable of. "Yes, I see. Revenge," she said. "You justify it all to yourself as revenge for Stone's cowardice and the atrocities of war. Maybe Stone was a coward. Maybe he betrayed you, but what about Louis? What did he do?"

A dark look passed across Graham's face. "The boy was not my responsibility. Jacobs condemned him when he sent him with us. No innocents were supposed to be there."

"You can't pin that on me, Graham," Jacobs whined. "I had no part in your evil deeds."

"If you'd done exactly as Pero asked, exactly as you had promised, the boy would be alive," said Graham.

"You murdered him in cold blood," said Philbrook.

"It was self-preservation."

Mihkosita broke his silence. "Tell me how Louis died."

Graham looked to Mihkosita and smiled. He seemed to take pleasure in the young man's sorrow. "If you must know, Bellows and Young held him down while I cut his throat. We ran into him, quite by chance, early in the morning, and he told us he was looking for Philbrook. He said he remembered seeing Pero taking part in the killings. He knew that Pero was alive and Cuillerier was dead. Unfortunately for him, we couldn't let those facts get out."

"It was not your first attempt, was it?" said Marguerite. "The shots that Bellows fired at Louis up at Auglaize was a deliberate attempt on Louis's life rather than a misunderstanding."

"It would have saved us a great deal of trouble if I'd had better aim," admitted Bellows.

"And I imagine," said Philbrook, "that if I had allowed you to take Louis to the gaol in Detroit, you would have found a way to dispatch him without raising too many questions."

"Aye, Ensign, that would have made things bloody easier as well. I had plenty of opportunities to kill him, but few that I'd be able to frame as self-defense."

"You attempt to justify your deeds as worthy vengeance," said Mihkosita, "but in killing Louis Ouellette, you reveal your cowardice. When avenging his friends and family, a brave man lets the world see justice done."

"Think what you like," said Graham. "I'll take no lessons in morality from a savage."

Mihkosita stared back at the sergeant with contempt. Marguerite worried he might do something rash, but he remained seated.

"I gather you took it for granted that the deaths would all be pinned on Indians, and you planted the tomahawk to point in that direction," resumed Philbrook.

"Aye. I assumed that Captain Turnbull would send me to investigate the deaths. He always sends me on those kinds of missions, since most of his officers are too lazy to leave the fort for such matters. I could easily have pinned it all on some roving band of southern Indians passing through the area. I had not taken into account that he would use the investigation as a way to break in his newest ensign."

"I'm not sorry to have ruined your plan, Sergeant. "Now I'm afraid I'll have to ask the three of you to surrender your firearms and return to Detroit in my custody." Philbrook looked from face to face. They all quickly took stock of who held weapons and who did not, seeing that Graham and his men had the clear advantage. Marguerite wondered if the ensign had lost his mind.

"Really? I'm not sure you understand the situation here, Ensign," said Graham.

"How so, Sergeant? You are my subordinate, and I gave you an order."

"You fool. Your investigation is over, and I don't think you will be seeing Detroit again. The three of us enjoy our lives and have no desire to see them change. That makes the rest of you, and the things you have learned, something of an inconvenience." Graham's expression was cold. "Your deaths will not be hard to account for. We will tell Captain Turnbull that you discovered that Mihkosita was responsible for the murders at Auglaize. When you confronted him, Mihkosita lashed out and managed to kill Marguerite and you before the three of us put him down. I expect that the captain will thank me. He trusts me, you see." For a brief moment he adopted the charming smile of the knowledgeable and obedient sergeant, but the next instant the expression dissolved.

"I had hoped that you would voluntarily place yourself in my custody, Sergeant," said Philbrook. "Once again, I am ordering you to do so." Everyone looked at the ensign as if he were deluded. The soldiers clearly had the upper hand.

"Smyth," ordered Graham crispy, "push your musket over here. And you, Ensign, give me your other pistol." Billy looked nervously to Philbrook, who shook his head.

"I think Private Smyth will hold on to his gun for now, and I my pistol."

Graham nodded to Bellows, who pointed his musket at Billy's face.

Just then, something whistled past, and an arrow buried itself in Bellows's throat. The force of the blow took his head backward and his body followed. He landed senseless on his back with a dull expression, looking up at the sky as blood pumped from his neck.

All turned at once to see Jabez Cole step from behind a nearby clump of trees with a bow, followed closely by Koohsia, painted for war.

Chapter 38

Koohsia

K oohsia thought that Cole had acted rashly. Their quarry was outnumbered and mostly defenseless, so they should have gotten closer before giving up the element of surprise. They tried to make up for the miscalculation by running to close the distance between them and the others as quickly as possible, though it was a good fifty yards. Up ahead, they saw Graham use both hands to point a pistol at the ensign's face and pull the trigger. It snapped in the pan.

Despite Cole's hasty shot, their plan was working. Mihkosita and Philbrook had said they would take the morning to quietly make sure the bad soldiers held weapons that gave them a false sense of security but would not function. Koohsia had given Philbrook the idea to lend Graham his own pistol, the powder replaced with a fine sand. The soldier they called Billy—the one who was not one of the killers—was the only one who was supposed to have a working musket, though he was not appraised of this fact.

As Koohsia and Cole ran toward the others, John Young pointed his musket at Mihkosita and pulled the trigger, but it did not fire either. Young took it by the barrel and swung, but

Mihkosita deflected the blow with his war club. Koohsia was reminded of years earlier when he had taught young Mihkosita how to defend himself in such a way. The boy had learned his lessons well. It helped that he had naturally quick reflexes. He would be a great war chief like his father had been someday.

The sergeant yelled something to Young, then both men fled, sprinting toward the woods on the other side of the clearing. Fear gave them a burst of energy that caught the others by surprise. If Cole had not loosed his arrow prematurely, they would have been much closer and able to stop the flight, but as it was, Cole and Koohsia had too much distance to cover. They ran after Graham and Young. Cole notched another arrow and let it fly, but it flew harmlessly over his target's head.

Koohsia heard Philbrook shout to the others, "After them!"

The ensign turned and handed Marguerite his remaining pistol and pointed to Jacobs. The rest started after the fleeing soldiers. Mihkosita lead the way, war club in hand, as he was the only one, besides Philbrook, prepared for the day's events. Smyth followed, looking confused. Koohsia and Cole strove to catch up.

Philbrook looked briefly to Jacobs and Marguerite, then trailed after the others. Billy Smyth sent a musket ball after the two fleeing soldiers, but it passed over their heads. He fell back as he tried to reload on the run. Koohsia and Cole tried to angle in front of the fleeing men to cut them off from the trees, but they were too far ahead.

Such was the nature of the hunt, thought Koohsia. At the realization of danger all prey gets a burst of energy to help them flee. The fear was a powerful medicine that made legs fly over the earth, barely touching the ground. Even the fastest hunter could not keep up with this temporary speed. Severe wounds would not slow such prey down. Graham and Young had that medicine now, but Koohsia knew it would not last long. They were like the deer with an arrow in its thigh. A good hunter would follow doggedly until the last burst of life faded and the prey slowed.

He saw Smyth falling behind, but Philbrook was catching up, and Mihkosita was ahead. They followed. When they reached the trees, they heard the men crashing through the thick forest ahead. It would be a deadly chase.

KOOHSIA AND JABEZ COLE had developed a strange sort of partnership over the past several days. After meeting in the forest near the Saginaw village, Koohsia suggested they combine their efforts. He told the strange little man that they should start their investigations with the Ojibwa war chief known as Le Canard, a leader of the Saginaw warriors who went down to fight the British when the French called on their Native allies. Le Canard would know the identities of the men who had captured Stone, Jacobs, and the others. He would also know about the redcoat soldiers taken captive, and he would know about Pero, if he had indeed lived among the Ojibwa.

When they found Le Canard at his village, the old war chief immediately understood what Koohsia wanted to know. Yes, he remembered the man who so stubbornly refused to die. He told them a story about a cowardly New England soldier who had betrayed his fellows and another who had endured torture that was meant to have killed him. The mutilated captive had gone on to be a trusted healer.

Then Le Canard told them about the three redcoats who became captives. One had been roughly treated at first but withstood it bravely and was accepted into the village. All three had lived among them for a time and learned the Anishinaabe language before they were returned to the British at the end of hostilities. This was the information that Koohsia was looking for, and he immediately knew who the three were and what they had done. He did not fault them for killing Ben Stone. It had been their right to avenge themselves upon the man who had betrayed them. But they had inflicted new injuries on the innocent. Louis Ouellette had been under his protection, and his death needed to be put right.

Koohsia was not surprised to hear that Sergeant Graham was a killer. He had never trusted him as the ensign and Marguerite did. The man had a hollow charm and a false smile that allowed him to ingratiate himself with people. It made him well-liked, but Koohsia seldom trusted superficial charm. Such outward graces too often hid a dead or crippled soul.

Once he figured out the truth, he wanted to hunt down Graham and his soldiers and inflict justice for Louis. But Cole objected. He needed proof to exonerate Sam Kennedy, so he had urged him to look for Ensign Philbrook. Koohsia found British law tedious, but he consented. He had come to respect the ugly little man of few words. When they finally found and talked with Philbrook last night, the young ensign understood that Sergeant Graham had exploited his trust, but he resolved to draw out confessions. Graham and his two men could not be slowly tortured and killed, as they deserved, argued Philbrook. Instead, he would trick them into confessions that would hold up in a British court-martial. The shaman consented to the ensign's plan because he knew the tall sergeant would never surrender peacefully. He would fight, and he would die. Koohsia preferred it that way.

Chapter 39

Phineas Philbrook

Graham and Young had a lead, but not an insurmountable one. Things had not gone exactly as Philbrook had planned, but close enough. He heard the confession he sought, in front of witnesses, leaving no doubt as to the sergeant's guilt as well as the guilt of Young and Bellows. But he had left open a small window of escape, through which Graham had jumped. He would have preferred it if the culprits had surrendered.

All morning, he had imagined a best-case scenario in which Graham gave up to him peacefully after the sergeant realized he had been exposed. Philbrook would return to Detroit with the three killers in custody to face proper justice. Pero would have to be hunted down later of course, if that was even possible. With no doubt concerning their guilt, the three soldiers would be sent down to Montreal for courts-martial and then executed as they deserved.

But, of course, in the back of his mind, he knew that Hugh Graham was not the kind of man to surrender. Just as in his captivity, he would not submit, and there would be violence. Philbrook was prepared for such an outcome, but he felt it his duty to attempt a more orderly resolution.

Judging from the sound, Mihkosita was still hurtling through the woods not far ahead of him. The forest was thick with small trees and brush in some places, while in others it opened up with mature, widely spaced trees. The ground was littered with stones and fallen branches, which made running difficult. The others had fallen back. He heard shouts and saw fleeting images of a commotion ahead. When he caught up, Mihkosita was lying on the ground, dazed but conscious, with a nasty-looking gash on his head. Philbrook considered stopping to help him but realized that there was little he could do. The others would be up soon and could tend to him.

He rushed on, emerging from a thick patch of spruce. A redcoat disappeared behind a large oak ahead.

He was gaining.

Then something hit him from the side. Graham. Philbrook fell hard with the sergeant on top of him. Graham smacked Philbrook's head into the ground, then struck down on his left ear with an elbow. As he went to do it again, Koohsia and Cole arrived. Koohsia had his wooden club raised above his head and Cole wielded a long knife.

Graham scrambled away fast enough to avoid their clutches, leaving Philbrook to regain his senses. Cole leaped over him and continued after the fleeing soldiers.

Koohsia bent over him for a moment, panted, "Come," then resumed his chase.

He was dazed and bloodied but still able to rise and run after them. He heard a ruckus ahead. Shouts.

Between the trees, he saw Cole struggling with John Young. They had dropped their weapons and were resorting to bare hands. Cole tore at Young's eyes with his fingernails as Young gripped Cole's throat. The soldier seemed to be getting the better of the smaller man. Then Koohsia was there, emitting a triumphant cry as he brought the smooth ball of his wooden war club down onto the soldier's head. There was a spray of blood. Young dropped senseless to the ground with a noticeable dent in his skull. Koohsia raised his arms to the sky and emitted a victorious howl.

Philbrook was shocked by the brutality. He would never get used to the sight of men doing violence to one another, but he counted himself lucky to have Jabez Cole and Koohsia on his side.

The men gasped for breath. They were spattered with their own and Young's blood. Cole had inflamed scratches around his neck. Young's body gave a few final twitches, then went still. Philbrook looked around and listened, but Sergeant Graham was nowhere to be seen. There was no sign of which direction he had gone.

When the others arrived, Mihkosita had a torn strip of cloth around his head. Blood was seeping through, but the boy was on his feet and seemed alert. He looked down at Young's inert body, giving it a disdainful kick. He gave Koohsia a quick nod.

Billy Smyth was red-faced and panting. He looked with distaste at Young's body on the ground. "Did you need to keep us all in the dark like that, sir?" he said. "Or was I the only one here kept out of the loop?"

"Sorry, Smyth, when Mr. Cole and Koohsia put the pieces together for me and Mihkosita last night, we decided it was best not to inform you or Marguerite lest someone give something away inadvertently."

"So Cole is on our side now, sir?" asked Billy, eying the little man skeptically.

"Yes, Private."

"We should be after Graham," said Cole, with bloodlust still in his eyes. "We outnumber him now."

"I thought best to regroup," said Philbrook. "Besides, it is a matter of tracking him now, so I needed my best trackers to catch up."

They found Graham's trail easily enough, but it ended at a river flowing back toward the lake.

"Well, sir," said Smyth. "We'll need to follow both banks in both directions to find where he got out. The only way to do that with any speed is to split up."

"No, we need to stay together," said Philbrook. "Graham is a dangerous man, and we can't go after him in ones and twos, lest we find ourselves killed in ones and twos."

They walked upstream together, looking for a sign of where the sergeant left the river. They saw nothing, and after the better part of an hour Philbrook was beginning to despair. "I think we should turn around and try the other way."

"Maybe our best course is to head back to the canoes," said Mihkosita. "Graham has nowhere else to go."

Then, they heard a long, desperate howl coming from the direction of the lake.

Brutus.

Chapter 40

Marguerite Boyer

Marguerite waited with Philbrook's pistol in one hand and Brutus's collar in the other.

"You don't need to keep pointing that pistol at me, Marguerite," said Jacobs. "I would hate for it to go off by accident, and I've no desire to escape. I've done nothing wrong. I had no idea Paul and the sergeant planned to murder Ben and his crew. I never would have gone along with that."

Brutus wanted to run into the woods to find the others, but she held him back.

"I'll point it as I please, Mr. Jacobs." She was disgusted with the pathetic man. "You've hardly earned anyone's trust."

"As you wish, but please be careful." He looked over at the corpse lying a short distance away. "It seems Private Bellows is starting to collect flies."

He was right. She had thrown a blanket over the soldier, but she could not bring herself to pull the arrow from his neck. The shaft held up the cloth and created a space inside where flies could congregate.

She worried about the men. With the exception perhaps of Koohsia, none of them seemed much of a match for Sergeant Graham and Private Young in a fight. There was a brutality to the soldiers, especially Graham, that would give them an advantage over the others. She saw Graham for who he really was now, behind the handsome smile. He had always been so appealing to her with his good sense and confidence, his subtle flirting, but when he had spoken this morning, his true self had pierced the veneer. The man she thought she knew did not exist. In his place stood a soulless creature she hardly recognized.

At least the culprits were outnumbered. She hoped that Mihkosita was not risking himself recklessly. He was still so young and so eager to prove himself a warrior. Why did young men feel like they had to prove themselves so much? Much of the time their attempts were self-defeating.

A farting sound came from under Bellows's blanket, and Jacobs laughed unpleasantly. Marguerite had been around enough recently dead bodies that she was not surprised at the sounds they made.

Brutus's ears pricked up, and he looked to the woods. Following his gaze, Marguerite saw a figure emerging from the trees. She registered the red coat and thought for a moment that it was Philbrook. But no, it was Graham. His clothes were torn, dirty, and wet. He was breathing heavily, and he had scratches on his face. Could he have overcome all the others? Brutus tore out of her grip and pranced over. The dog had no idea that Graham was a threat, so he circled excitedly around the man, seeking attention, as if this was all some sort of game.

"You stay back, Sergeant Graham," she shouted, "or I'll put a ball through your chest."

"You can't hit me from this far away, Marguerite. You've got to be within spitting distance of a man to get him with a ball from a flintlock pistol." He spread out his arms with his palms facing forward, as if providing a target.

"A good reason for you not to come any closer, Sergeant."

"I think I will, Marguerite. I doubt you know how to use that thing." Graham continued to walk toward her, grinning. "Amos, slide the smaller canoe into the water for me and grab the paddles," he ordered. "We're going on a trip."

Jacobs did as he was told. Of course he did, she thought. Such a weak man. Graham was about twenty feet from her, and she judged that she could hit him now if she fired. What the sergeant did not know was that she was actually rather good with firearms. Her father had taught her to shoot at an early age, first with a simple fowling piece and later with a variety of weapons. She continued to hunt and target-shoot with her brothers after their father died.

"I would not get any closer, Sergeant." She focused on her voice. She did not want it to quaver or pitch too high, though the sinister man frightened her.

Graham ignored her appeals. As he got closer, she chose a spot about a dozen feet in front of her and decided that if Graham reached it, she would aim at the center of his chest and fire as her father had instructed her to do if her life or safety was ever threatened.

She was calm. She was ready.

She had killed all variety of animals before, but never a person. It would not be like killing a deer at all. She thought about Louis Ouellette, and it gave her resolve. Her mind ticked down. Three more steps, two, one. She raised and steadied the pistol and began to squeeze the trigger.

Then Brutus decided to join the game. He jumped up and grabbed Marguerite's wrist in his mouth. Marguerite's arm was jerked down and the pistol fired into the ground. Brutus yelped and jumped back, surprised and frightened by the explosion. Graham rushed the remaining distance to her and knocked her off her feet. She fell. He loomed over and hit her hard in the face with the callused palm of his mutilated hand.

Everything went dark.

SHE AWOKE minutes later with a splitting headache and Brutus lying protectively on top of her. She reached up and felt her nose, which she found was now the size of a small potato. Blood had poured out of it while she was unconscious, but the flow had largely subsided, leaving her with a red stain down her front. Graham and Jacobs were loading one of the canoes. The other one, she saw, had a large hole kicked in the bottom of it. Graham did not want to be pursued.

"Time to go, Marguerite. We're taking you with us as a bit of insurance." Graham held one of the muskets to which he had affixed a bayonet, and the pistol was in his belt. Presumably, he had equipped the firearms with fresh powder. He came over and prodded her. Brutus growled. Graham kicked the dog in the ribs, and it yelped and shied away. For such a large dog, he certainly was not very fierce.

"You sit in front where I can see you," Graham ordered, thrusting a paddle into her hands. She knelt in the bow of the canoe as instructed. It went against everything in her nature to comply with this man's instructions, but until she came up with a better plan, that was all she could do.

"You go there," Graham said to Jacobs, pointing to the middle of the canoe. Graham got in the back and pushed off. He could hold the paddle with his mutilated hands, but not very well. As they set out onto the lake, Marguerite could feel by the motion of the canoe that he could barely steer. The best he could do was brace his paddle against the gunwale and use it as a rudder. She and Jacobs, however, could propel the canoe forward well enough, and they soon left the shore behind. They paddled northwest toward the main part of the lake and away from the village, angling farther from land as they did. Behind her, Marguerite could hear Brutus bark and whimper.

Then, as they got farther away, he let out a desperate howl.

Chapter 41

Phineas Philbrook

Philbrook and Mihkosita were the first to emerge from the forest. Brutus rushed over to them, then he ran back to the shore frantic and whimpering. They saw the canoe in the distance, at least a half mile away already and getting farther every second. Then they saw the broken canoe left on the rocky beach.

Philbrook swore under his breath. He cursed himself for letting Graham out of his grip and for putting Marguerite in danger. "We need to get after them," he said.

"We can find another canoe in the village," suggested Mihkosita.

"They'll be out of sight by the time we get it." The others were all there now. If they did not act immediately, they would soon run out of options. "Cole and I will run along shore and try to keep them in sight," Philbrook decided. "The rest of you go find a boat and follow after us as fast as you can."

Three ran toward the village, and Cole and Philbrook went the other way, following Brutus, who had run ahead, keeping his eyes on Marguerite's receding figure and letting out the occasional howl of distress.

Moving along the shore was not always simple. There were

stretches of open shoreline where they could run, but sometimes, the forest came right down to the water, impeding their progress. There were small streams to cross and rocks, roots, and boulders to scramble over. They could still see the canoe receding in the distance, but it would be out of sight before too much longer.

Philbrook tried to reassure himself that Graham could really do nothing but follow the shoreline to the west and north unless he risked the exposed crossing at the mouth of the bay. He might try to cross almost twenty miles to some large islands out in Lake Michigan, but Philbrook doubted he would take such a risk. The sergeant knew the danger of paddling too far from land where a change in the weather could result in death.

He hoped Mihkosita and the others would be back with a canoe before long. With five strong paddlers, they could catch up quickly as long as they knew which way to go. But time was running out. A point of land soon obscured their vision of the fleeing canoe. Brutus howled louder and outpaced the two men.

Soon, Philbrook could not see the dog either, but he could still hear his pathetic cries.

Chapter 42

Marguerite Boyer

Marguerite could hear Brutus howl. She hoped he was alright after the cruel kick Graham had given him. Every time she turned to look, Graham threatened her, so she kept her eyes pointing forward, but she knew the dog was following along shore. She hoped the men could hear Brutus too. That is if they were still alive. For all she knew, Graham had killed them all in the forest, but his destruction of the other canoe told her that he feared pursuit. That gave her hope that they still lived. The punch and Graham's threats had left her stunned, and her broken nose throbbed and felt like it had grown to several times its normal size. She was angry at herself for letting Brutus grab her wrist—for not seeing it coming. That foolish dog never left her alone for long.

After close to half an hour of paddling, her mind began to clear, and she realized that she could not count on anyone to rescue her. If she continued to follow Graham's orders, he might eventually let her go, but he might just as soon kill her. Why should he release her? She thought about what he had said about killing them all so that his secret would not come out. If he had killed the men already, then she and Jacobs were the only ones left who knew the truth. If that was the case, she was as good as dead.

She had to fight.

Sergeant Graham's death or capture was the only way to end the threat he posed. If only she had shot him when she had the chance. Marguerite found that she hated Graham all the more because of how she had liked him before. What a fool she had been to admire a man who could kill Louis Ouellette the way he had. He might have a handsome face, but he had no soul.

A plan began to take shape in her mind. To resist was dangerous, but doing nothing was not an option. She needed to get the canoe closer to land. She angled her paddle to pry the bow a bit to the right with each stroke. Just a little, so that it would not be too obvious. The sergeant's steering was already erratic, so he did not notice. She wanted to get within a mile of the shore. There was a wooded peninsula coming up ahead where they would pass closest to land. That was where she would act.

"It is getting too hot," she said as she put down her paddle, removed her shawl, and loosened her outer skirt. At the same time, she slipped off her moccasins.

"Get that paddle moving," threatened Graham.

Marguerite picked the paddle back up and gave some extra hard strokes to placate the sergeant. She eyed the spot up ahead where she would make her move. There was a stand of white pines leaning out over the water and a rocky shoreline. It came closer. The end of the little peninsula was now no more than a mile across the water. They were as near as they would come—near enough to swim. She stood up without warning, lifted her foot onto the right gunwale, and drove it down with all her weight as she jumped. The canoe overturned behind her, as she'd intended. She hit the water, and the cold knocked the breath out of her for a moment when she submerged, but she had prepared herself for the shock. She slipped out of the outer clothing that might slow her down.

She heard Jacobs and Graham curse as she kicked hard and pulled toward the shore and out of their reach. She dared not look back. She did not know if either man could swim, though she thought it unlikely. Few men ever learned, but if they could, she wanted to make sure that she swam faster.

After the first few seconds Jacobs's shouts stopped, but Graham's continued. He was staying with the overturned canoe. She flipped over onto her back for a moment so she could look back as she kicked with her feet, and she saw him clinging to the bottom of the craft. His hands did not have a good purchase, and his heavy woolen coat and waistcoat weighed him down, but he was managing to keep his head above water as he tried to remove his jacket. Jacobs was nowhere to be seen. She felt some pity for poor Jacobs, but not for long. He may not have been evil. He may not have killed anyone outright. But he was a weak and selfish man who seemed happy to cooperate with murderers.

The water was cold. Much colder than the air. While summer was well underway, it had been a cool spring, and the big lakes take a long time to warm up, even when the surrounding air is hot. Marguerite was a good swimmer, but she knew that if she did not swim her best, the frigid water would claim her before she reached dry land. The distance would take her over half an hour if she kept up her pace. She had swum that distance before but never in water this cold. She cleared her mind and took stroke after stroke, kicking hard as she was taught. She was finding it difficult to regulate her breathing. Graham's blow to her face had left her without the ability to breathe through her nose, so she gasped for air through her mouth, trying to keep from swallowing water.

After a mere five minutes, she felt herself growing weaker from the cold. She looked up and saw that she had made it less than a quarter of the way so far. She was beginning to worry that she could not make it, but she kept her head down and persevered. The chill of the water seeped into her, making her shiver. She was having difficulty expanding her lungs. The chop this far out on the lake made it hard to get up any momentum. The tops of waves slapped at her face. Another five minutes and she was feeling stiff, then drowsy. She knew her pace was declining, but she was still less than halfway. At least the throbbing in her nose had subsided. The cold water must be helping with the swelling.

She closed her eyes and continued as best she could. She must focus on the swimming, not on the distance or her chances of survival. Stroke, breathe, stroke, breathe. That's all she should worry about.

She recalled learning to swim as a small child. Her mother had encouraged it. The two of them would go down to Lake St. Clair or find a private spot along the river, and her mother would give her lessons. Not many of the other boys and girls she knew were encouraged to swim. Their parents thought it would make them sick to submerge in cold water, but her mother thought differently. She said that anyone who was going to spend time in boats should know how to swim. She had given Marguerite challenges to accomplish. Increasing distances. Longer times treading water. Swimming deeper down to the bottom of the rivers or lakes to gather pebbles. Holding her breath. She became adept at all these skills and enjoyed any time she could spend in the water. She imagined that she was engaged in one of her mother's challenges now.

"Just swim to shore, Margot. It isn't far, and you are strong."

She misjudged the crest of a wave, and she breathed in just as it slapped at her face. She inhaled some water. Not too much, but enough to make her cough. She managed to expel the water, but the effort made her breathless. She needed rest, so she flipped over onto her back and kicked while looking at the sky. This gave her arms some rest, but her speed diminished, and she began to feel sleepy. She realized that her chance of making it the remainder of the way was slim. Maybe she should just give up. It would feel so nice to stop and float for a while, looking up into scattered white clouds surrounded by blue. To float and drift into a peaceful sleep as the remaining warmth left her.

Then she thought of Daniel. Growing up without a father had been difficult enough for him. It would be harder still to have no mother. But *Maman* was always there, ready to take care of him, and his uncles gave him guidance when a man's perspective was needed. Marceau and Antoine would take him voyaging when he grew a little older. They would make sure that he chose the right paths in life. Daniel would always have kin he could turn to. She could die knowing that Daniel would be alright.

No. No, she couldn't. She could not give up. She swam. She would go on as long as her body had any strength to propel her. She did not hear Graham yelling anymore. She looked back, but she could not see the canoe. She hoped he was dead. She hoped the cold water had pulled him down. There were creatures deep down who would be attracted to his evil. At least, that was what some of her people believed. Some Anishinaabe cousins had told her of Mishipeshu, the great wildcat with horns, scales, and feathers who lived in the deepest parts of the lakes. Maybe Mishipeshu would tear Graham apart or pull him down into the icy depths to consume. He deserved it for what he did to Louis.

She thought she heard Brutus barking again. Such a ridiculous dog, but she was sorry she was not going to see him again. She was sorry that she was not going to see home again either. Daniel, her mother, her brothers, even Ensign Philbrook. Philbrook was a nice man, she realized. Surprising, really, that she should find a British officer so enjoyable to be with. She would like to see him again, but that did not seem likely. The warmth of dry land was just too far away. The urge to sleep was growing stronger.

She closed her eyes as she swam. She thought of home and pretended that she was swimming across the Detroit River, as her mother had challenged her to do when she was only ten years old. She pictured her mother right there the whole time like she used to be, paddling beside her in her small canoe, keeping her safe, ready to throw her the wooden block they used as a buoy if she needed rest. Her mind was on the verge of dreams. She couldn't fall asleep. Sleep seemed soft and comfortable. Inevitable. Warm. If only she had something buoyant to hold on to. She had to stay awake. But her eyes just couldn't stay open. Her arms and legs were turning heavy and needed rest.

There was an abrupt wet snorting near her face. She thought for an instant that Mishipeshu had come for her. Then her arms felt fur, sodden but warm. She opened her eyes, and the huge black panting face of Brutus was inches from her nose. His great pink tongue came out and licked the water off her face. She felt the heat of his breath and his tongue. She had never appreciated his slobber so much. So warm. She reached out and wrapped her arms around the huge beast's neck and pressed her chest against his long back. She imagined his heat passing into her. Brutus was gasping, a mixture of spittle and lake water spraying from his huge mouth with every breath, but he was determined, and he floated. He turned and swam for shore.

Marguerite closed her eyes and hung on.

Chapter 43

Marguerite Boyer

Marguerite awoke feeling cold and weak. She looked around at the interior of a bark wigwam and decided she was in L'Arbre Croche, but she had no memory of how she had gotten there. A fire burned hot, but the heat reflected off her skin, leaving her insides chilled. Brutus lay next to her, dry now, looking at her lovingly.

A stooped figure appeared at the door. Koohsia came in and knelt next to her. "Marguerite. I am happy to see your eyes open." He took a kettle off the fire and poured some of its contents into a cup. "Drink this."

"I thought I was going to drown." Her voice came out as a croak. She sipped the weak brew, and she could feel the warmth passing into her.

"You did drown, Marguerite. I had to take the water out and put air and life back into you. My grandfather taught me the method many years ago, but this was the first time I got to try it." He smiled in satisfaction with himself. She had seen such a thing once when they dragged a child out of the Detroit River after he fell off a sloop's deck. He was not breathing, so everyone thought he was gone until someone picked him up by his feet and water came pouring out, along with his breakfast, and he started to breathe again.

She reached out and stroked Brutus's back. His whole body wagged in pleasure. "I guess this one was worth having along after all."

"He is a faithful beast. He would have drowned too if we had not come up in the canoe when we did. The distance was too much for him. He saved you though. You would have sunk to the bottom long before we got to you without him. Ensign Philbrook was putting himself in great danger, attempting to swim out to you as well. Thankfully, we got there before he managed to drown himself."

Marguerite stroked the dog's fur again, and his long tongue flopped out as he panted. He looked happy.

"I'm glad. How long was I asleep?"

"Just two days."

"Two whole days!" She did not think it possible to sleep so long.

"You had a close call. We came paddling after you as fast as we could. We saw Ensign Philbrook's red coat lying on the ground near shore and Cole pointing. Then we spotted the ensign swimming just a hundred feet out. He directed us further; then we saw you and the dog. At first you were clutching his back, but as we approached, you slid off. Brutus turned around and took your arm in his mouth."

Marguerite touched her upper arm and felt a tender bruise.

"He could not have gotten you to shore like that, but he kept you from going to the bottom until we came up and hauled you into our canoe. You were cold like a corpse. We took you to shore as soon as I got the water out. We thought maybe you were too far gone, but I stripped the wet things off you and wrapped you up in my dry blanket. I had Mihkosita and Philbrook get on each side and press their warmth into you while Jabez started a fire."

Marguerite's face flushed as she realized for the first time that she was naked under the blankets.

"You had no warmth, Margot, it had to be done. You are not bashful like a British lady, are you?"

"No, I guess not," she said, still not looking happy. "Were all of you there?"

"Oh, yes. Mr. Philbrook and Mr. Cole chased Brutus down the shore after you while the rest of us went to fetch a canoe from the village. Some of the local people followed us. They were curious because we came running into the village shouting for a canoe and not waiting for permission. We were able to get you back here while some others went out to get the overturned canoe."

"Everyone is alright? I thought maybe that Graham had hurt you. Or worse."

"We are all quite well, Marguerite. Mihkosita got a knock on the head, but the experience will make him a better warrior. I killed the soldier they called Young. It gave me some relief after what they did to Louis."

"What about the sergeant?" asked Marguerite.

"Gone. Him and the other one, too. We saw no bodies. They must have sunk. Or a serpent got them. Too bad. I would have liked to kill the British sergeant slowly for what he did to Louis."

"Me too," said Marguerite before realizing that of course she probably had. Did she feel remorse? No, not really. Maybe she would later, but right now his death was a relief. Jacobs was perhaps another matter. He had been more weak than evil, but he chose his own path.

During the next several days, Marguerite remained chilled and tired. When the sun came out, she would bask in its heat with Brutus, but the rest of the time, she stayed by the wigwam's fire sipping warm tea. Brutus seldom left her side. Her broken nose throbbed and felt huge on her face, but it was slowly healing. She could breathe through it a little more each day.

The others came to see her. Mihkosita showed her the gash on his head. He was a little proud of it and glad that it would leave a permanent scar—a memento to his adventure.

Philbrook came in to talk. He sat near Brutus gently scratching him behind his ears. "I was wondering, Marguerite," he asked, "if I will ever get my dog back?"

"I'm not sure I have any say, Ensign."

"No, I suppose not," he said. "Brutus's affection for you knows no bounds."

"Yes," said Marguerite, smiling at the dog, who looked pleased by the attention.

"And what is the plan now, Mr. Philbrook?" she asked with a smile. "Are we to go chasing after this Pero character. Follow him into the wilderness to bring him to justice? I feel like I've done nothing but traipse about the backcountry with you since you arrived in the *pays d'en haut*."

"I know what you mean. As we've waited for you to recuperate, I've asked around. It is thought by the locals that Pero has gone west, but we have nothing more to go on other than rumors. I think the captain would want me to return to report to him. And Mihkosita and Koohsia want to return to Kekionga as soon as they feel assured you are recovered. I've spread the word that a reward will be given for information about Pero or for anyone who brings him in to Detroit or Michilimackinac, but I am not hopeful he will be apprehended. From what Jacobs told us, it seems he plans to go west again. All the way to China, maybe." Philbrook looked wistful.

"Yes, and why do I have the feeling that you'd like to follow him? Or use his journal to explore on your own. You share his curiosity about *terra incognita,* don't you?"

"Perhaps, Marguerite. But the book is lost. Jacobs surely had it on him when he perished. Someday, I would like to travel west, but I will have to wait and see what the future holds."

Chapter 44

Koohsia

Koohsia and Mihkosita sat, looking out over the water of the big lake. They had a fire left over from roasting their dinner. It gave them some warmth against the late evening chill and filled the air with the scent of burning pine. Koohsia reached into his bag and pulled out a small vellum-bound book. Mihkosita resisted the urge to immediately ask about it but instead waited politely for Koohsia to begin at his own pace.

"I found this near Private Bellows when we went back to bury his body. I have been wondering what to do with it."

"Is it the book Mr. Jacobs told of? The one that recounted the travels of his friend?" asked Mihkosita.

"Yes." Koohsia gazed at one side, then the other. "I think so." He opened it and flipped through the many pages of handwriting and drawings. "Did you see the ensign's eyes when he looked on this, Mihkosita?"

"Yes. He wanted it very much."

"Philbrook is not a man who ordinarily wants to take and possess what belongs to others, but when he looked on this book his soul was consumed by cravings."

"They spoke of *terra incognita*," said Mihkosita. "Pero and Mr. Jacobs wanted to go there."

"Yes, and Ensign Philbrook shares that desire." Koohsia looked again at the pages. "Many English do. I cannot read the words in this book, but I can read what was in the ensign's heart when he looked at it. His face bore the look of a man who lusts after something he cannot have, or maybe should not have."

"I saw but did not know what to make of it. Will you give it to him, since he wants it so much?"

"A good question. I am an old man, Mihkosita. When I was a child, there was more of this *terra incognita,* as the English call it. But now, each year, we find them pushing into new places. They are a curious people, these English. Restless. Impatient. And Philbrook, he is a seeker. I admire seekers, but the desire for new things, new knowledge, can become a curse if not held in check. The ensign is not a bad man, but his curiosity about *terra incognita* is the sort of hunger that should not always be fed."

"I'm not sure about this idea of unknown land," said Mihkosita. "All land is both known and unknown. There is always more to discover, even in familiar places. I found a place near Kekionga not long past, where the sweetest water bubbles up from the ground. I did not have to go far to discover it. I only had to look more closely than I had before."

"True. You are wise beyond your years, Mihkosita. But the English love their maps. They are never happy where they are but always want to go somewhere new and possess it as well. They always want to know what is over the next hill, to search for more people to buy their blankets and kettles."

"I like their blankets."

"So do I. They provide much comfort. But those blankets come at a price more costly than the furs we exchange them for."

Koohsia turned over the book, looking at it as if for answers. He opened it again and looked at the pages inside full of symbols he could not read. "I sometimes wish I could understand writing. I imagine there is great wisdom to be found in it."

"But the man who wrote those things was not right with the world."

"No, he was not. Perhaps the knowledge of *terra incognita* found here is best kept unknown for now." Koohsia tossed the book down onto the hot coals of the fire. Black smoke curled up around its edges as it began to burn.

Afterword

This is a work of fiction, but like all historical fiction, it blends our knowledge of a real past with speculation and imagination. The setting is as accurate as could be managed. In the 1760s Detroit and the Upper Country surrounding it was a land where cultures clashed, cooperated, and compromised. Algonquian, Iroquoian, French, and British individuals interacted on a daily basis. They traded with each other. They married and had children together. They fought, and sometimes they murdered one another.

If one looks at a map in a text book one might see this region depicted after 1763 as part of the British Empire, but as Captain Turnbull acknowledges early in the novel, everything outside the gates of the handful of British forts was still contested ground.

While all of the characters in the novel are used fictionally, some are based on real historical figures, either well-known or relatively obscure. Pontiac, the war chief of the Ottawa after whom Pontiac's War is named, was perhaps the most famous. There was also an historical Pacanne, who was the hereditary leader of the Miami.

Captain George Turnbull was a real officer in the British Army who commanded at Detroit around this time. He later became a

Loyalist officer in the American Revolution. The sentiments he expresses in the novel are based on letters he wrote to his superior, General Thomas Gage, which are held at the Clements Library at the University of Michigan.

There was also an historical Alexis Cuillerier who was accused of drowning a little girl named Betty Fisher in the Miami River at Pontiac's behest, as described in the novel. Cuillerier was indeed jailed for murder in Detroit. Pontiac appealed to Captain Turnbull to release him, but Turnbull declined. The historical Alexis Cuillerier escaped from jail and fled, but, as far as we know, he did not end up beheaded at Auglaize.

The historical background of the Seven Years War and the Indian rebellion generally known as Pontiac's War is presented as accurately as possible. The fall of Fort William Henry in 1757 was a real event, so I have placed my characters there, much as James Fenimore Cooper did in *The Last of the Mohicans*. Similarly Sergeant Graham's description of the capture of Fort Miami during Pontiac's War follows historical sources. There was a real Ensign Holmes who was lured out of the fort by his mistress much as the fictional Graham describes.

Marguerite's mother, Sally Boyer was inspired by a real woman. Sarah (Sally) Ainse was a merchant/trader in the Upper Country, who leveraged a multicultural background into a career in trade. The connection between the historical Ainse and my Sally Boyer is quite loose. Ainse had not yet established herself at Detroit by 1767, and her family did not resemble the one in the novel. But Ainse's life shows that a woman with a mixed ethnic background could succeed as a merchant/trader in this era for the same reasons that the fictional Sally and Marguerite Boyer do.

I have used several real names for characters who are mentioned in passing, but everything they do in the novel is fiction. Daniel Campbell was an actual merchant in Schenectady who supplied fur traders. Thomas Williams was an important trader in Detroit who married a francophone Detroit woman and probably hosted a party or two. Other characters possess family names common around Detroit in the 1760s, including Boyer, Cheney, Bourassa, Ouellette, Beaulieu, Tremblay, Bruno, Belanger, Langade, La Corne, and others. And there were probably dozens of Sergeants Ramsay and Graham in the British Army of the time.

Phineas Philbrook, Marguerite Boyer, Koohsia, Mihkosita, Joseph Papan, Billy Smyth, Ben Stone, Sam Kennedy, Amos Jacobs, Pero, Jabez Cole, Sergeant Hugh Graham, and all the other soldiers and boatmen who appear are fictional, based solely on the sorts of people who inhabited the Upper Country in 1766.

And lastly, Brutus is a creation of the author's imagination. Any resemblance to a real dog is entirely coincidental.

Printed in Dunstable, United Kingdom